ONE

DARK

KISS

Also by Rebecca Zanetti

ONE
DARK
KISS

REBECCA
ZANETTI

KENSINGTON
PUBLISHING CORP.

kensingtonbooks.com

KENSINGTON BOOKS are published by:

Kensington Publishing Corp.
900 Third Avenue
New York, NY 10022

kensingtonbooks.com

For Elizabeth May.
Our first story together marks
the beginning of something truly
special. Thank you for believing in
this dark journey and for bringing
your insight and passion to every
page. Here's to many more stories
yet to be written.

GRIMM BARGAINS:
TALES OF POWER AND DARK DEALS

Ancient cultures first used crystals in rituals, medicine, and adornment. The smartest of these people quickly learned that gems hold a vibrating energy that can be captured and exchanged with human beings. This exchange grants health and clear thinking, which in ancient times, when a cold could kill, quickly led to power and wealth.

As the world turned away from natural medicine and philosophy, four powerful families continued exploring their connection to certain stones. They began to hide their ability to exchange energy and thus exploited this extra health and strength to become leaders throughout the centuries without fear of pandemics, most diseases, and non-lethal injuries.

In the modern age, these families are no longer kings and queens, but modern moguls, true billionaires who have learned how to utilize the energy of crystals in business systems. Today, with social media and AI infiltrating every aspect of our lives, these four families have created social media companies by harnessing and using the power from these precious stones.

Now, not only do the families control social media companies, but they run mafia-like organizations where members obey their every command. In the social media world, the more follower interactions, the more the stone powering the system draws. The families with their companies have jockeyed for position, and currently, as of the writing of this book, here is the ranking when it comes to number of followers and financial assets:

1. *MALICE MEDIA*, powered by the energy harnessed from garnets, is a next-generation platform that uses neural interface technology to share thoughts, emotions, and experiences directly. It offers glimpses into a user's mental and emotional state. Thorn Beathach charges and exchanges energy with the garnets. Its call to action is: MINDMELD NOW.

2. *AQUARIUS SOCIAL,* powered by the energy harnessed from aquamarines, is an emotional intelligence platform that uses AI to analyze a user's emotional state. There are real-time updates of connections where people can share emotions over long distances. Alana Beaumont charges and exchanges energy with the aquamarines, and she's trying to teach her cousin, Scarlett Winter, to do the same. The call to action is: EMOTE NOW.

3. *HOLOGRID HUB*, powered by the energy harnessed from amethysts, is a 3D holographic social media platform where people can share experiences together at any location, including Mars or the Moon or Ancient Rome. Hendrix Sokolov and Alexei Sokolov charge the amethysts. The call to action is: PROJECT NOW.

4. *TIMEGEM MOMENTS*, powered by the energy harnessed by citrines and/or diamonds, uses advanced

temporal technology to record, save, and replay moments in real time, so people share memories with each other. Sylveria Rendale can charge diamonds, and Ella Rendale can charge citrines. Its call to action is: CAPTURE NOW.

5. There have been hints of a fifth social media company making moves, but nobody knows if this is just a rumor or if there is a new player on the board.

ONE

DARK

KISS

ONE
Rosalie

Alone, I cross my legs beneath the intimidating metal table secured to the floor, feeling as out of place as a raven in a nursery rhyme. The heat clunks and whispers from a grate in the ceiling but fails to warm the interview room, and when the door finally opens, the heavy frame scrapes against the grimy cement floor.

My spine naturally straightens, and my chin lifts as my client stalks inside, his hands cuffed to a chain secured around his narrow waist. He doesn't shuffle. Or walk. Or saunter.

No. This man . . . stalks.

His gaze rakes me, and I mean, *rakes* me. Black eyes—deep and dark—glint with more than one threat of violence in their depths. He kicks back the lone metal chair opposite me and sits in one fluid motion. The scent of motor oil in fresh rain, something all male, wafts toward me.

I swallow.

The guard, a burly man with gray hair, stares at me, concern in his eyes.

"Please remove his cuffs," I say, my focus not leaving my client.

My client. I don't practice criminal law. Never have and don't want to.

The guard hesitates. "Miss, I—"

"I appreciate it." I make my voice as authoritative as possible, considering I'm about to crap my pants. Or rather, my best navy-blue pencil skirt bought on clearance at the Women's Center Thrift Store. I don't live there, but I'm happy to shop there. Rich people give away good items.

In a jangle of metal, the guard hitches toward us, releases the cuffs, and turns on his scuffed boot toward the door. "Want me to stay inside?"

"No, thank you." I wait until he shrugs, exits, and shuts the door. "Mr. Sokolov? I'm Rosalie Mooncrest, your new attorney from Cage and Lion."

"What happened to my old attorney?" His voice is the rasp of a blade on a sharpening stone.

I clear my throat and focus only on his eyes and not the tattoo of a panther prowling across the side of his neck, amethyst eyes glittering. "Mr. Molasses died in a car accident a month ago." Molasses was a partner in the firm, and he represented Alexei in the criminal trial that had led to a guilty verdict. "I take it he wasn't in touch with you often?"

"No." Alexei leans back and finishes removing the cuffs from his wrists to slap onto the table. "You're responsible for my being brought to the minimum-security section of this prison?"

Actually, my firm has juice and a named partner had made this happen. "Yes, and it's temporary. You're back to your normal cell block after this meeting."

His chin lifts. "So this plush locale for our conference is for you, princess? The prestigious law firm doesn't want you dirtied by the bowels of this place?"

Probably true. "I'm here to help you, Mr. Sokolov."

His eyes glitter sharper than the panther's on his neck. "Don't call me that name again."

I frown. "Sokolov?"

"Yes. It's Alexei. No mister."

Fair enough. I can't help but study him. Unruly black hair, unfathomable dark eyes, golden-brown skin, and bone structure chipped out of a mountain with a finely sharpened tool. Brutally rugged, the angles of his face reveal a primal strength that's ominously beautiful. The deadliest predators in life usually are.

Awareness filters through me. I don't like it.

Worse yet, he's studying me right back, as if he has Superman's x-ray vision and no problem using it. He lingers inappropriately on my breasts beneath my crisp white blouse before sliding to my face, his gaze a rough scrape I can feel. "You fuck your way through law school?"

My mouth drops open for the smallest of seconds. "Are you insane?"

"Insanity is relative. It depends on who has who locked in what cage," he drawls.

Did he just quote Ray Bradbury? "You might want to remember that I'm here to help you."

"Hence my question. Not that I'm judging. If you want to do the entire parole board to get me out, then don't hold back. If that isn't your plan, then I'd like to know that you understand the law."

It's official. Alexei Sokolov is an asshole. "Listen, Mr. Sokolov—"

"That name. You don't want me to tell you again." His threat is softly spoken.

A shiver tries to take me, so I shift my weight, hiding my reaction. I stare him directly in the eyes, as one does with any bully. "Why? What are you going to do?" I jerk my head toward the door, where no doubt the guard awaits on the other side.

Alexei leans toward me and metal clangs. "Peaflower? I can have you over this table, your skirt hiked up, and spank your ass raw before the dumbass guard can find his keys, much less gather the backup he'd need to get you free. You won't sit for a week. Maybe two." His gaze warms. "Now that's a very pretty blush."

"That's my planning a murder expression," I retort instantly, my cheeks flaming hot.

His lip curls for the briefest of moments in almost a smile. "Women who look like you don't usually have a brain."

My eyebrows shoot up so quickly it's a shock a migraine doesn't follow. He did not just say that. "You are one backassward son of a bitch," I blurt out, completely forgetting any sense of professionalism.

That smile tries to take hold and almost makes it. Not quite, though. "Fuck, you're a contradiction." He flattens a hand on the table. A large, tattooed, dangerous looking hand. "As a rule, a beautiful woman is a terrible disappointment."

Now he's quoting freakin Carl Jung? "You must've had a lot of time to read here in prison . . . the last seven years."

"I have." A hardness invades his eyes. "You any good at your job?"

The most inappropriate humor takes me, and I look

around the room. "Does it matter? I don't see a plenitude of counselors in here trying to help you."

"Big word. Plenitude. I would've gone with cornucopia. Has a better sound to it."

I need to regain control of this situation. "Listen, Mr.—"

He stiffens and I stop. Cold.

We look at each other, and I swear, the room itself has a heartbeat that rebounds around us. I don't want to back down. But also, I know in every cell of my being, he isn't issuing idle threats. A man like him never bluffs.

Surprisingly, triumph that I refrain from using his last name doesn't light his eyes. Instead, contemplation and approval?

I *really* don't like that.

My legs tremble like I've run ten miles, and my lungs are failing to catch up. I suppose anybody would feel like this if trapped with a hell beast in a small cage. There's more than fear to my reaction. Adrenaline has that effect on people. That must be it. I reach into my briefcase and retrieve several pieces of paper. "If you want me as your attorney, you need to sign this retainer agreement so I can file a Notice of Appearance with the court."

"And if I don't?"

I place the papers on the cold table. "Then have a nice life." I meet his stare evenly.

"My funds are low. I don't suppose you'll take cigarettes or sex in trade?"

Is that amusement in his eyes? That had better not be amusement. I examine his broad shoulders and, no doubt, impressive chest beneath the orange jumpsuit. How can he look sexy in orange? Plus, the man hasn't been with a woman in seven years—he'd be on fire. A little part of me, one I'll never admit to, considers the offer just for the, no doubt, multiple and wild orgasms. "I don't smoke and you're not my type. But no worries. My firm is taking your case pro bono until we unbind your trust fund."

He latches onto the wrong part of the statement. "What's your type?"

I inhale through my nose, trying to keep a handle on my temper.

"Don't tell me," he continues, his gaze probing deep. "Three-piece suit, Armani, luxury vehicles?"

"Actually, that's my best friend's type," I drawl. Well, if you add in guns, the Irish mafia, and a frightening willingness to kill.

Alexei scratches the whiskers across his cut jaw. "Right. When was the last time you were with an actual man? You know, somebody who doesn't ask for guidance every step of the way?"

That fact that I don't remember is not one I'll share. My thighs heat, and my temper sparks. "Was this approach charming seven years ago?"

"Not really. Though I didn't need to be charming back then."

True. He was the heir to one of the four most powerful social media companies in the world before he went to prison. Apparently, his family had deserted him immediately. "You might want to give it a try now."

His eyes warm to dark embers, rendering me temporarily speechless. "You don't think I can charm the panties off you?"

"All right. You need to dial it down." I hold out a hand and press down on imaginary air. "A lot."

Heat swells from him. Somehow. "Dial what down?"

"You," I hiss. "All of this. The obnoxious, rudely sexist, prowling panther routine. Use your brain, if you have one. It's our first meeting, and you're driving me crazy. You want me on your side."

"I'd rather have you under me."

I shut my eyes and slam both index fingers to the corners, pressing in. This is unbelievable.

"Getting a headache? I know a remedy for that."

I make the sound of a strangled cat.

His laugh is warm. Rich. Deep.

Jolting, I open my eyes. The laugh doesn't fit with the criminal vibe. It's enthralling.

He stops.

I miss the sound immediately. Maybe I need a vacation.

Using one finger, he draws the paper across the table. "Pen."

I fumble in my briefcase for a blue pen and hand it over.

He signs the retainer quickly and shoves it back at me. "What's the plan?"

The switch in topics gives me whiplash. Even so, I step on firm ground again. "The prosecuting attorney in your case was just arrested for blackmail, peddling influence, and extortion . . . along with the judge, his co-conspirator, who presided over your trial and sentenced you."

His expression doesn't alter. "You can secure my freedom?

That's my plan, but I don't want to raise his hopes. "I don't know. My best guess is that I can secure you a new trial."

"Will I be free for the duration?"

"I'll make a motion to the court the second I leave here but can't guarantee the outcome." I tilt my head. "Your family's influence would be helpful."

His chin lowers in an intimidating move. "I don't have a family. Don't mention them again."

I blink. "One more comment."

"Go ahead."

"I'm sorry about your brother's death." His younger brother, rather his half brother, was killed a month ago, possibly by my friend's boyfriend, if one could call Thorn Beathach a boyfriend.

Alexei just stares at me.

I feel like a puzzle being solved. "There's a chance his death was part of some sort of social media turf war against Thorn Beathach, who owns Malice Media." Alexei's family owns a rival social media platform, and from what I understand, it's war between them all.

"So?"

This is a mite awkward. "Thorn is currently dating my best friend, so if there's a conflict of interest, I want you to know about it." Not that anybody would ever catch Thorn, if he had killed Alexei's brother after the man had injured Alana. I'm still not sure he was the killer, anyway.

"Are you finished mentioning my family?" Alexei's tone strongly suggests that I am.

"Yes," I whisper.

He cocks his head. "How many criminal trials have you won?"

"None," I say instantly. It's crucial to be honest with clients. "I haven't lost any, either."

His head tips up and he watches me from half-closed lids. "You're in charge of the pro bono arm of the firm?"

"No."

"Why you, then?"

It's a fair question as well as a smart one. "I've never lost in a civil trial, so the partners assigned me your case, even though this is a criminal procedure."

"Why?"

"Because I'm good and they want you free." I shrug. "This is positive exposure for the firm." Which is what my boss, Jaqueline Lion, told me when assigning me to the docket. "We have several verdicts being overturned because of the judge's corruption, and yours came up, being the most high profile. Losing your case harmed the firm seven years ago."

His nostrils flare. "The firm? The loss hurt *the firm*?"

"Yes." Damn, he's intimidating. Do I want him free to roam the streets? "This is a chance to fix the damage caused."

"And promote you to partner?" he guesses.

My life is none of his business. "I'm good at my job, Alexei." Yeah, I don't use his last name. "You can go with outside counsel. I'll rip up your retainer agreement if you want."

"I want you."

I hear the double entendre and ignore it. "Then it's my way and you'll follow my directives."

Now he smiles. Full on, straight teeth, shocking dimple in his right cheek.

Everything inside me short circuits and flashes electricity into places sparks don't belong.

He taps his fingers on the table. "I signed the agreement, and this means you work for me. Correct?"

"Yes." But I call the shots.

He moves so suddenly to plant his hand over mine, that I freeze. "You need to learn now that I'm in charge of every situation. Do you understand?"

I try to free myself and fail. His large palm is warm,

heavy, and scarred over my skin, with the hard metal table beneath it a shockingly cold contrast. My lungs stutter and hot air fills them. "Whatever game you're playing, stop it right now."

His hand easily covers mine, and his fingers keep me trapped in sizzling heat. "I don't play games, Peaflower. Learn that now."

"Peaflower?" I choke out, leaving my hand beneath his because I have no choice.

"Your eyes," he murmurs. "The blue dissolves into violet like the Butterfly Pea flower. A man could find solace from everlasting torment just staring into those velvety depths."

I have no words for him. Are there words? Scarred, barely uncuffed, and intense, he just whispered the most romantic words imaginable. And he's a killer. Just because the judge was corrupt doesn't mean Alexei hadn't committed cold-blooded murder. Two things can be true at once. "We need to keep this professional, if you want me to help you."

He releases me and stands. "Guard," he calls out.

My hand feels chilled and lonely.

Keys jangle on the other side of the door.

"Rosalie, this is your out. If you tear up the retainer, I'll find another lawyer. If you stay, if you decide to represent me, there's no quitting. You're in this for the duration. Tell me you get me." Fire burns in his eyes now.

I stand, even though my knees are knocking together. "I'm doing my job."

"Just so we understand each other."

The door opens, and the same guard from before moves inside, pauses, and visibly finds his balls before securing the cuffs on Alexei, who watches me the entire time. He allows the guard to lead him to the door.

Once there, he looks over his shoulder. "I hope you stick with me in this. Also, you might want to conduct a background check on Miles Molasses from your firm. He was a co-conspirator to the judge and prosecutor." His teeth flash. "How convenient that he just died in an accident. Right?"

TWO

❋ Rosalie

Some bean counter from the accounting firm two floors above mine chews peanut brittle on the way up in the elevator, and the sound cuts through me like a sharpened blade. I cast him a couple of looks over my shoulder, but he munches contentedly away, his gaze on the different numbers lighting up above the door. What a jackass. I try to concentrate on the soft elevator music, but the melody is no match for his teeth.

The door opens and I leap out, barely keeping myself from running as I hustle onto the seventh floor of the Cage and Lion Law Firm. It's rare I forget to keep my earphones with me just in case assholes chew or sniff near me. Most people have never heard of my condition of misophonia, and that sucks.

I nod to the receptionist and continue beyond her and several offices to my own little spot of prestige. I don't understand why Cage and Lion has the top two floors, eleven and twelve, the seventh floor, and the second floor as their law firm. It makes much more sense to have all of the floors together, but maybe the rent is cheaper on the lower levels.

My small office has light, rose-colored walls and a wide window that looks out over Silicon Valley. The bookshelves are oak and my desk glass. It's one I chose when I accepted the job, and I like it quite a bit. The decorations are subtle with crystal-framed pictures of my grandfather and me when I was a child, a picture of me and my two besties when we graduated from a stiff and isolated boarding school, and one of my seven renters in the Victorian home I inherited from an aunt I never met. The people in my life who matter.

There's also a stunning and ornate silver mirror on the side wall, between bookshelves. I found the piece at a garage sale after I passed the bar exam, and sometimes when I look at myself in it, I feel strong. I'm sure it's the way the light reflects in it, but I'll take all the help I can get.

I cross around to sit in my white leather chair and then look up as a body fills the doorway. "Joseph." I stand to my heels again. We very briefly dated, and I still regret those two weeks. Oh, he's handsome and smart, but he was looking for either a quick fling or a society lady to make looking good on his arm her entire profession. I fit neither of those categories, and we parted amicably. Well, after he told me I was the perfect lawyer because of how cold I am. I didn't so much like that, even if the words held truth. Most men bore me for a reason I have never nailed down. Including Joseph Cage.

"Sit down, Rosalie," Joseph Cage says, his smile charming and his black hair with just a hint of gray at his temples smoothed back from his tan face. "How did it go at the prison?"

"It was interesting." I sit and cross my legs, tempted to reach for the one remaining red apple from the bowl on the corner of my desk. "I'm not sure allowing Alexei Sokolov out into the world is doing anybody a bit of good." Just saying his name catches my breath in my throat, and I mask the feeling with a cough.

Cage leans against my door frame dressed in black slacks, a white button-down shirt, and a green tie. His office is, of course, on the top floor, but he does spend time with the associates and paralegals on my floor more than his partner, Jaqueline Lion, does. A couple of the other associates and I have joked that Cage and Lion probably changed their surnames before they created a law firm to obtain the cool sounding name. The running agreement is that their names were actually Smith and Patterson.

"When we lost Sokolov's case, it was a blow to the entire firm," Cage says. "We should have won that one."

I straighten, my ears perking. "You think Alexei was innocent?"

"No." Cage shakes his head, his blue eyes earnest. "I do not believe that man was innocent. Yet, there was enough reasonable doubt that we should have won the case."

I move my heavy silver paperweight to the side. "Do you think somebody paid off the judge?"

Cage shrugs. "Dunno. I believe the investigators are still combing through the many charges against the judge, but so far, nothing about Alexei's case has come up. At least we have cause to overturn the verdict just based on the allegations of impropriety."

I need to make another motion to be kept in the loop on that one. "I made the motion to the court earlier, and the clerk said they're expediting those matters. We could even hear tomorrow, without a hearing." My brief had been thorough and above attack. "Do you think Alexei's stepmother or stepbrother would've bribed the judge?"

"Maybe. I know Hendrix and I sure as hell wouldn't mess with him."

I see Hendrix Sokolov at various events during my time as a lawyer, and he seems both handsome and freezing cold to me. If people are snakes, he's a Golden Lancehead Viper with its beautiful golden-yellow skin. I studied reptiles and animals in school but figured spending my time with exotic animals as an adult wouldn't lead to financial security, so I turned to law. Clearing my throat, I force myself to focus. "Alexei said something about Miles Molasses and his death not being an accident."

Cage's eyebrows rise. "Seriously?"

I shrug. "He could have been blowing smoke, but I think it's something we should investigate. Instinct tells me that Alexei doesn't randomly make statements."

"I'll look into it," Cage says. "For now, we've acquired the trial transcripts, the courtroom videos, and all of the evidence used to convict Alexei seven years ago." He nods his head toward a stack of what looks like compact discs on the corner of my desk.

"Thanks." I now know exactly what my night will include. "Do you remember the case very well?"

Cage shakes his head. "No. I was involved with a pretty serious RICO case at that time, and Miles Molasses was our best litigator. It was a shock when we lost the case, to be honest, although the Sokolovs had stopped paying us."

"They had?" I look up. The Sokolovs own one of the most powerful social media companies in the world and have more money than I can imagine. "What's the story there?"

Cage shoves his hands in his pockets. "If I recall, Alexei's mother died when he was young, and his father remarried Lillian Sokolov. She then had two sons, Hendrix . . . and what was the other one's name?"

"Cal," I say softly. "His name was Cal."

"Oh, yeah. The guy who was murdered last month." Cage nods. "I forgot about that crime. Did they find who butchered him?"

I keep my placid smile in place. "I don't know." I have a sneaky suspicion that Thorn Beathach killed Cal Sokolov, but I can't prove it, and I would never ask Alana, his fiancée, who also happens to be one of my best friends.

"I'm sure the family has investigators on it," Cage notes, admiring himself in my ornate mirror. "But it's my understanding they'll be of no help in this case. They disowned Alexei even before he was convicted of murder."

"I see," I murmur.

Cage straightens. "Although now that Cal is dead, maybe Hendrix will want another brother to help at the helm."

Not based on the way Alexei had objected to his last name. "I'll need to speak with the family."

"I agree, and I'll go with you if you like."

"Thank you, but I can handle this case."

His gaze warms. "Of course. Also, look on the bright side. If you do get a new trial and we get him off, you'll probably score an office on the 11th floor."

I meet his gaze evenly. "I'm aiming for the 12th."

He chuckles. "I know. We all know." With that, he turns and disappears from my doorway.

My ambition has never been a secret, but I'm sure they don't understand the reasons behind it. It's not only money I crave. It's security. A stack of unpaid bills sits over to the right of my computer to remind me. My student loans are due, as is payment for the mortgage I took out on my home after inheriting it outright. But there had been no other alternative. Not really. I look at the pearl and silver letter opener that had been a present from Alana when I graduated law school, now sitting innocuously on the bills, ready to shred them open and stress me out.

My attention is drawn to the evidence from Alexei's trial.

Idly, I grasp the top disc, noting it was filmed the night of the murder, and shove it in the disc bank attached to my computer. I had secured the attachment from the basement earlier in the week. These days, a USB would be used. A lot has changed in seven years. I'll go through all of the discs later, but I'm just curious for a hint of what they might show.

The video appears of Alexei from at least seven years ago. He's smiling with his arm around the neck of another man at a bar, who's laughing and spitting up what looks like beer. Women cling to Alexei's arms, and a stunning blond futilely tries to remove the choke hold, snorting with giggles.

I open a file folder and scan notes and annotated pictures to see that Alexei and his friend Garik Petrov owned the Amethyst Pony. What a stupid name for a bar. The guy being choked is Garik. He's around Alexei's age but wears a tattered T-shirt and has forgone a haircut for an immeasurable amount of time. He seems rough, like he should be the bouncer and not co-owner.

I watch them laugh and joke and goof off on the screen. Alexei looks different. Younger definitely, but more free with fewer tattoos. The panther on his neck must've been inked while in prison.

When he looks at the camera, obviously knowing he's being videoed, there's still an edge in his eyes. The same one I saw today. He's dressed in an expensive-looking white shirt with embroidered dragons on each breast, and it's unbuttoned to his navel. His slacks are black and perfectly creased. He was slimmer back then, in good shape but not nearly as hard cut as he is now. On the video, he releases the other guy, and they move past several women trying to grab them, to reach a stage.

Both pick up guitars.

I lean forward, curious. They play a hard rock song and Alexei sings. His voice is smooth and sexy, even with a hint of devilment in it. He smiles as he croons about lost love and murderous dragons. It's impressive. The man can sing. At least he could. Today in the prison, his voice had been darker, deeper, raw, and more scratched like he'd screamed for years.

As I watch, women throw panties and bras onto the stage. He grabs several pairs and laughs, tossing them in the air and catching one. He stops singing, holding white lace panties up. "It looks like we have a winner tonight, and they're still warm. Who just pulled these off for me?"

A woman shrieks happily from the audience and runs forward, climbing onto the stage wearing a sheer white dress, sans the undies. She's a young brunette, hopefully at least eighteen. Pink flushes her face, and her nipples are hard beneath the barely there material. She hops up and down, her hands clutching at one of his arms.

"I guess you won, darlin'." He leans over and kisses her, one hand sweeping down to grab her ass, the epitome of a spoiled rich boy accepting a gift. "Free drinks for the entire month."

She squeals and presses closer to him.

I note that his business partner has his lips pressed tightly together. So Garik didn't like his buddy giving away booze.

Alexei cuts him a quick look. "I'll cover it."

Garik's face relaxes.

The brunette leans up and whispers something into Alexei's ear.

He grins and shakes his head, looking over the crowd to the bar. "I'm afraid not tonight, sweet thing. I have plans."

I zoom in to study a woman sitting on a bar stool turned to face the stage, her legs crossed with a slit up the sparkling red material that reveals her well-toned thigh. It's Blythe Fairfax, and her platinum blonde hair is cut with sharp edges across her shoulders, which are bare except for thin spaghetti straps holding up the elegant and sexy dress. Her lips, painted in matching scarlet, and her eyes, adorned with heavy makeup, complete the look. Her smile looks possessive.

At the time of the recording, Alexei had to be in his early twenties, and she was at least in her late thirties, maybe early forties. There's no doubt she's beautiful, yet I find it odd that she was so public with their affair. They hadn't seemed to hide it from anybody. I scratch a note on a sticky pad to dive deeper into her deceased husband. Anybody partying at the Amethyst Pony that night would've clearly seen that the two were involved.

Another figure catches my eye, and I scan the video

and zero in on a man at the far end of the bar, surprised to see Hendrix Sokolov standing with a beer in front of him, watching the interplay. Even ten years ago he was handsome, with blonde hair swept back from his face and intense blue eyes. He's not smiling and seems to be on alert. They didn't get along to the point that the family failed to support Alexei during and after the trial.

So what was Hendrix doing at his half brother's bar that night?

THREE

Alexei

I slip out of my hiding place in the vast laundry room and strike with the shank, instantly stabbing into Anton Lebetev's neck from the side. I slide away and allow the blood to spurt on the overlarge washing machine—away from me. Kicking him in the back of his knees, I take him down flat. His hands claw the rough cement before his body convulses several times. Blood glides gracefully away from him to pool near the drain.

Death has its own whisper.

Two seconds ago, he was the most powerful member of the Russian Bratva in this prison, and he tried to kill me several times.

He failed.

I did not.

His second in command already has agreed to follow me, should I regain control of not only Hologrid Hub but the local Russian mafia. I plan to do both.

I toss the homemade shank into a bucket of bleach I have waiting and then turn, walking nonchalantly out of the laundry facility and down to the cafeteria, my way blissfully unguarded. Oddly enough, the cameras are experiencing a momentary glitch as well.

My allies in this place have a long reach.

Just in time to line up and return to my cell, I keep my gaze ahead of me, my arms loose, and my senses on full guard.

An alarm blares, and we're ordered into our cells immediately, the doors clanging shut nearly in unison. Apparently, Lebetev's body has been found. We remain in lockdown for nearly an hour, but no trace of the killer will be found.

I doubt very much that anybody cares enough about Lebetev to truly investigate his death.

Near lunchtime, I find myself leaning against the wall in my six by eight cell, with my roommate sitting on the top bunk. Urbano Reyes is one of the most dangerous men in north block, and we became uneasy allies my first day when a member of the local Russian Bratva, no longer following me, had made a move to slice my jugular. Reyes had jumped in to help me. I hold no illusions that he did it out of friendship or kindness, because the leader of the Twenty-One Purple gang wouldn't know kindness if it bit him on his tatted ass.

"It sounds like you succeeded," he notes.

I give a short nod. "Yes." He made the kill possible, and for that, I owe him another favor.

"You really think you're getting out?"

"That's what the guards told me. Apparently, my lawyer got my conviction overturned," I say, my body relaxed but my gaze missing nothing. We have a deal, but I still won't be surprised if he tries to kill me before I get out. Many people want me dead, and money talks.

A smile widens his already round face. "I ain't going to kill you." Prison tats cover his head down his neck and along both arms, confirming a life of danger and crime.

"Don't think you are," I reply easily, still waiting for him to make a move. Ending my time in prison by murdering him will cause issues for me, but I'm ready, just in case.

"We have a deal," he says quietly.

I nod. We do have a deal. When I arrived at the prison, he offered protection from my former followers in the form of his gang, and many of his members fill the desolate cages in every direction. Of course, nothing is free. He knows I'm wealthy. At least outside of these walls I am—once I unfreeze my funds. Inside, my financial resources are dry.

The only person who has deposited money into my account has been Garik, my ex-business partner. No family, no girlfriends, no friends at all, had tried to ease the life of prison. I never forget a debt, and I'll make sure Garik is set for life. I have it on good authority that these last seven years, he's been trying to prove me innocent and find who set me up, but he's reached nothing but dead ends.

Our partnership was an uneasy one, but in the end, he's proven to be a friend, unlike Urbano. His interest in me has been mercurial from the beginning. Once he told me that a rich guy like me wouldn't stay in prison long—that somebody would get me out. He was wrong. Seven years is a long time, but he was correct that it looks like I'm going free.

For now anyway, until I'm convicted again since, apparently, I now get a new trial. I have no intention of letting that happen, no matter what I have to do.

"So you got yourself a new lawyer?" he asks.

I shrug, unwilling to discuss the beauty of the woman. "The old one died."

"Huh? No shit." His smile widens again.

Yeah, I owe him for that one as well. "His death was ruled an accident."

Urbano's eyes glitter. "You remember my code?"

"I do." He'll send me a coded list once I'm on the outside. A list of people I've agreed to kill for him—for his gang. A deal is a deal. I've now agreed to five kills, and that's what he'll get from me. I appreciate that he's too paranoid to give me the names now—I've learned caution from him.

"And don't forget the money." He still looks casual sitting on the too-thin mattress. He's a beefy guy, slightly claustrophobic, and needs to be on the top bunk. He and his followers kept me from being killed. Oh, I can fight, and I know the exits of every room as well as any object that can be used as a weapon, but prison is prison, and in here I'm greatly outnumbered. At least I was until I made the deal with Satan.

It wasn't my first time, and it won't be my last. The key, I've learned, is to become more dangerous than the devil.

Footsteps sound outside our cell, and then a voice barks for us to get against the wall. Reyes jumps down, his heavy feet hitting hard, and then goes to the wall. I turn around, but I keep every sense in tune to him, just to make sure.

Before I know it, the door opens, the guard comes in, and I'm handcuffed with ankle chains as well.

"Have fun at R and R," Reyes mutters. "I'll be in touch."

"I know," I answer, shuffling from the cell. "I'll fulfill my part of the bargain, and then we're done." I've played my part for seven years and accepted protection from his gang in exchange for promises to be fulfilled once I'm free. He doesn't know me. Doesn't know I've already killed for him while within these walls. For myself, actually. A couple of his lieutenants had accepted contracts to end me, so they died. Their bloody deaths had been blamed on a rival gang, and Reyes has had no clue of the killer sleeping in the bunk beneath his.

My time in prison has unleashed the real me. The one that had lurked beneath wealth, duty, and the pursuit of power as a rich kid in a bad family.

The guards take me to Receiving and Release where they double-check who I am about ten times with pictures and my prison files, then I have to sign multiple documents. I don't read them because I don't care. I'm getting out of here.

Finally, we move into another room, and a guard named Donnelly, who's a badass ex-Marine with no problem going hand to hand with murderers, hands me a bag. "Someone sent you clothes."

I frown, not expecting to receive dress-outs. "Who?"

"What the fuck do I know?" Donnelly says. "Go change."

"Huh." I quickly change into a pair of definitely used black slacks, a white button-down shirt that scratches my skin, and brown loafers three sizes too small. Whoever sent the clothes doesn't know me.

Then the discharge officer delivers to me the twenty bucks cash that had been in my possession when I was arrested, as well as the two hundred dollars they give to every prisoner before being released. Other than that, I have nothing. Many prisoners have boxes of legal work or books, but I've given away everything I had to Reyes, and I learned a long time ago not to write down anything important. I've made good use of sketch books during my time, but I destroyed the drawings after doodling, not wanting to give insight to my enemies. I've found that drawing relaxes me.

I climb into a minibus, still in handcuffs and chains, waiting for the other shoe to drop. There's no way I'm actually getting out. The pretty lawyer whose image tortured me all night, forcing me to awaken sweaty and hornier than a lonely teenager, wouldn't succeed.

We drive out of the front gates of the prison, park, and Donnelly removes my chains. I stretch out of the van.

He nods. "I'm sure I'll see you again."

I face him directly. He's been fair but tough on everybody, and frankly, I figure in this world that he's a decent guy.

"No, you won't," I say honestly, meaning it. "For the record, Salisbury is making a move on Libertine this week. Contract." Salisbury is an asshole, but more importantly, Libertine is my mole in North block. He's with the Russian mob, is seriously crazy, and enjoys the candy he can buy each week with the money I slip into his account. Normally, I wouldn't snitch on anybody because I don't give a shit, but I need Libertine in place for now and not dead.

Donnelly stiffens, nods, and climbs back into the van.

I look around and note a champagne-colored SUV up ahead. The door opens and Rosalie Mooncrest steps out, today dressed in a light-yellow skirt and jacket set, her long legs leading down to sensible blue kitten heels. I like that they're blue. My dick hardens to rock and reminds me that I haven't fucked a woman in seven long years. That one has legs that could wrap around a man and hold tight.

Then that mouth. Lush, red, perfect. I wonder how good she is with it.

I lope toward her, noticing her swallowing and looking around. It was one thing to have a guard outside of the door, quite another to face me directly, and I'm surprised she is here standing unprotected. I don't want to like her and fully plan on using her like I do everybody else. "What are you doing here?"

She shrugs. "I figure you don't have anybody to pick you up."

It is a kindness, and one I don't recognize. What does she want from me? I definitely know what I want from her, and I'm more than amenable to an exchange. I glance at the vehicle. It's tough-looking and yet sleek. "What is this?"

"It's a Volkswagen ID.4," she murmurs. "Electric."

"Huh." I've heard about electric vehicles, but this is the first one I've seen up close. I glance at her, once again drawn by the violet hue of her eyes. Would they change to a deeper blue in the throes of orgasm? Is she a screamer? Does she like to be tied up? Held down? "You must be doing all right. These are expensive, correct?"

She shakes her head, and little apple earrings dangle from her delicate ears. "No. The government forced car manufacturers to create a bunch of electric vehicles, even though we don't have the electrical grid for it, so you can get a great deal on a lease." She pats the car as if she's proud of the beauty, and I note her slim fingers. I'd bet my entire fortune her skin is soft. "In fact, with a four-year lease, the cost is minimal."

So the girl is careful with money. This makes sense. Her clothes are fitting and elegant, but definitely not high-end. I don't know anything about her, and this sense of curiosity is new. I figure the better I know her, the easier it'll be to get her into bed. Or bent over a table. Right now, I don't very much care where. I move toward the driver's side door.

She holds up a hand, as if that will stop me. "You're not driving my car."

"If there's a car, I drive it," I say, curious how she'll react.

"No. You don't even have a license right now. Do you honestly want to get a ticket when you're barely on probation?"

That's a point, it's a good one, plus it's her car. I weigh my options and then decide to give in this time. My license probably is expired. "Fine."

I walk around and enter the passenger side. The leather interior smells like expensive indulgence. I look up through the sunroof. The sky is so wide and blue, and I take a moment just to breathe as I roll down the window. The sense of freedom has yet to hit me, but the familiar anger boiling in my gut keeps me stable.

She settles herself in the driver's side and fastens her seatbelt before turning those unreal eyes on me. "Seatbelt."

"No."

"It's the law." She presses her lips together, making me want to kiss her and force them open. What does she taste like? Sunshine and heaven? Strawberries that match her lips? "Put on your seatbelt," she repeats, reminding me of my tenth-grade English teacher. I wanted to fuck her, too. The attraction had been mutual, and I learned quite a bit from Ms. Lemon. "Now, please," Rosalie says briskly.

I've been shackled enough in this life. "I said no."

"Fine." She starts the vehicle. "If we get in a car accident and you go through the windshield, it's your own damn fault."

The woman sounds like she might hit a concrete barrier just to prove her point. Amusement ticks through me, shocking me. I haven't smiled genuinely in seven years—maybe longer. Now isn't the time to start. "Fair enough."

She pulls out on to the quiet road. "So where to?"

That's the question, isn't it? I don't have anywhere to go.

FOUR
Rosalie

Alexei overpowers the car in a way I should have expected and yet failed to do so. The panther tattoo on his neck is apropos. He stretches like that deadly predator, his legs long, his gaze on the world outside of the vehicle.

We drive for miles until he frowns and kicks off the brown shoes.

I wince. "I'm sorry. I had to guess at the size."

"You were about three inches off," he says, not looking my way or sounding concerned.

I borrowed them from one of the tenants in my Victorian house, and Wally has the biggest feet. "I do need to return them to a friend."

Alexei turns suddenly, his gaze piercing. "You took these from another man?"

I clear my throat as a wave of tension rolls across the vehicle. "I didn't borrow them from a woman."

He doesn't smile. "Whose shoes are these, Peaflower?" His tone is hard and demanding with an unnerving edge.

The hair rises on the back of my neck, and I watch him

carefully from the corner of my eye. We're now flanked on both sides by a dark forest with sturdy pine trees blowing in the wind. "I think you should just say thank you."

He looks down at the other clothing. I borrowed the shirt from Percy and the pants from Felix. Neither fit very well. "Whose clothes am I wearing?"

Why is he sounding so demanding? "Friends of mine." I press my lips together. I don't discuss my tenants, or rather my family, especially with a recently released convict who has a good chance of returning to prison after the next trial.

"I don't like asking questions twice." His voice grinds to a low rumble.

I cut him a look and then stare back at the long road in front of us. "Then you should stop asking."

He glances outside again. "Stop the car."

"What?"

He reaches for his door handle. "Stop."

I jerk the wheel and pull off of the road next to a series of bushes, my heart thundering. "What are you doing?"

He opens his door and steps out, shutting it quietly behind him. The atmosphere inside the vehicle calms almost instantly. As I watch, he strides in the borrowed socks toward an imposing and scarred pine tree and reaches out to plant his large hand on the bark.

Something stirs in me. I release my seatbelt and step out of the car, walking around to the front, watching him. "Are you all right?" I gentle my voice.

The wind increases in force, and he lifts his head, shutting his eyes. The breeze tosses his thick hair over his forehead, and his nostrils flare when he breathes in deep.

I look around, seeing nature and freedom.

He remains in that position and lets the wind batter at him.

I shiver and rub my hands down my arms.

"Rosalie, do you understand that a pine tree like this can release between forty-five and sixty pounds of oxygen every year?" He remains still as he asks the question.

My heart stutters. No, I didn't know that. "So all oxygen comes from trees?"

His lips twitch, but he doesn't smile, and his eyelids remain closed. "No, trees generate around twenty-eight percent of the Earth's oxygen production. Between fifty and seventy percent comes from phytoplankton."

I'm not following the discussion. "Phytoplankton?"

"Yes, marine plants."

He must've read up quite a bit in prison. I imagine he had plenty of time the last seven years. "Alexei?"

He opens his eyes and watches his broad hand slide down the rough bark of the tree. "You know where they don't have trees or phytoplankton?"

"In prison?" I guess.

"Real oxygen smells different."

I take a big whiff and basically smell pine and the possibility of an oncoming storm. "It's going to rain," I say, wanting to give him warning.

He tilts his head back and looks up to the tops of the trees and the darkening skies. "Real rain," he murmurs. "I haven't felt that in way too long."

The day is darkening, and my knees are starting to knock together. "Alexei, it's cold out here. How about we get in the car with the heater and watch the storm?" I feel for him. I can't imagine not being able to touch a tree or feel the wind in my face for years.

Remaining by the tree, he bends down to look at a scar with dried pitch sealing it shut. "Somebody ran into this little one," he murmurs.

As a tree, it's pretty large, but I don't argue. A couple of raindrops plop on the metal of my car. I sigh and look up. Then several more drops.

He glances sideways, his gaze drifting upward to meet mine, his eyes pools of unfathomable darkness. "Do you believe in fate?"

For some undefinable reason, butterflies wing through my abdomen. "I've never given it much thought." As he stands, looking at home against the dark forest, those butterflies flap harder. "Do you?"

"Most definitely." He leaves the shelter provided by the trees and stands at the front of my car, allowing rain to start falling on his head and shoulders. In the light storm, accepting the downpour, his eyelids now shut and his face turned to the clouds, there's something primal about him. I can't quite put my finger on it, but this hint of vulnerability somehow makes him seem even more dangerous.

His eyes open suddenly, and those dark orbs focus on me. "I don't like wearing another man's clothes," he rumbles.

I blink at the change in subject. "I don't blame you, but it's all I could get."

He lifts a hand. "I'm not complaining. I just would like to know whose clothes they are."

"Why?" I challenge.

He shrugs as more raindrops land on his forehead and slide down the hard angles of his face. "Let's chalk it up to curiosity for now."

I think that's probably a good idea. "Fine. I have some

elderly boarders, and I borrowed clothing from all of them. None of them are your size."

He cocks his head. "Elderly boarders?"

"Yes." I smile automatically as I think with fondness about the seven men. "They pay rent and keep the house I inherited in good condition." Well, they try to keep it in good condition. Sometimes when they help, things get worse, but I choose not to share that with Alexei. Rain is soaking my hair and clothing, and I allow it, trying to feel what he does. How unimaginable to be kept cooped up inside a tiny cell, especially if you hadn't done anything wrong.

He studies me as intently as he did the tree. "Why did you pick me up today?"

I shift my weight uneasily. "I didn't want you to be alone your first minutes out." His family doesn't want him. It doesn't seem like he has friends. The idea of him trying to hitch a ride into town all by himself kept me awake most of the night. Oh, I argued with myself whether I should pick him up or not. But in the end, I went with my heart.

"I'm not used to kindness," he murmurs.

"I know." I can't even imagine what the last seven years in prison have been for a man like him, one who had all the wealth and freedom in the world, some that most of us can't even imagine, and then to have it stripped away.

He moves toward me slowly—like the lazy panther across his neck. "Kindness is a danger to you, Rosalie." He sounds as if he's giving me a warning, and I heed it.

"I understand."

He reaches out and smooths my wet hair away from my face to tuck behind my ear. I shiver, and it's not from cold this time. His callused fingers are warm, and the deliberate movement enticing.

"You are beautiful." His gaze drifts to my mouth.

I'm acutely aware of those hard muscles beneath those borrowed clothes, and for the briefest of moments, I'm tempted. Yes, I'm losing my mind. "You're good-looking and have that dangerous vibe going on. Plus, you've been locked up, possibly unfairly, and you come from one of the most powerful families in the world."

"Your point?"

Is he being dense on purpose?

"You will find plenty of women who will be happy to jump right into bed with you." My mind flashes back to the video of him in the bar, throwing panties in the air to choose a woman to sleep with or at least kiss, depending on who waited in the wings for him. "I'm just the first woman you've seen in too long."

His wide chest moves as he exhales. His gaze wanders down to my bare legs, up along my breasts, lingering long enough on my lips this time that they tingle. Then he meets my eyes, and his intense look is piercing. "You believe that, don't you?"

That he can find willing partners? Even if he wasn't a Sokolov, the hard angles of his face combine into something deadly alluring. Too dangerous to be handsome—his fierce features reveal the predator he doesn't bother to hide. He not only promises a wild time, he naturally hints that it'd be worth every terrifying second. "Sure. You won't be alone if you want company."

"No. That there's not something incredibly special about you." He sounds curious.

"Um." Where is he going with this?

The heat in his eyes has my knees weakening. "Not one inch of you is forgettable."

"Thank you," I breathe, feeling way too feminine. If I were a different woman, one who takes risk, I'd kiss him. Jump right into that temptation. But I need to win his case to rise to partner and gain some security, as well as money. "You're compelling, Alexei. It's that simple. I'm your lawyer, and we need to keep a professional relationship—especially if you want to stay out of prison. I'm sure the second you're back on a stage with a guitar that you'll have more, ah, interest than you want."

A shield draws down over his eyes. "I'm done with the stage. Probably not music, but I'm not sharing that any longer."

That's his decision. "Have you written songs in prison?"

"No." He steps away. "There's no music in prison."

While no emotion hints in his tone, a sadness wanders through me.

Thunder rolls deep and loud above us. We both automatically turn and get back inside the car. My hands not so steady, I pull away from the side of the road.

My phone buzzes.

Alexei looks beyond me to apparently read the navigation pane. "Who's Merlin?"

Damn it. "A friend."

"Huh." He reaches beyond me and loudly taps on the screen.

"Rosalie?" Merlin says, somehow sounding distracted even over the speaker. "That dumb plumber called again and is insisting on another payment. I'm telling you, we don't need him. We can fix the downstairs shower. Probably. I mean, maybe. I'll try later today."

Alexei leans back, watching me.

I clear my throat. "Let's talk about it later, okay? You're on speaker and I'm not alone."

"Oh my. Sorry, dear. See you at home." Merlin clicks off.

Alexei cocks his head. "Merlin is one of your boarders."

"Yes. He's a sweetheart." I watch Alexei out of the corner of my eye. I'm drawn to him, but I definitely don't know him. While I think he might've been unjustly convicted, there's no doubt he's dangerous.

A chill slithers down my spine. Have I just put Merlin and my other boarders, my created family, in danger?

FIVE

Alexei

Rain slashes up from the cracked cement sidewalk, dispersing the smell of old piss and decaying meat from several fast-food wrappers crumbled against the standalone building. I cast my gaze down both directions of the now vacant and quiet street in the bowels of San Jose. The area holds several boarded-up buildings as well as businesses with dingy windows, including a nail place, a minute convenience store, and a massage parlor that no doubt finishes with dubious and clap-enhanced happy endings.

My attention is caught by the tail end of Rosalie's SUV as she turns a far corner and quite happily deserts me. My groin hardens. Again. Her scent swirls around my head, licking through me. Something good and clean and sweet—way too sweet for an asshole like me.

I glance up at the damaged electric sign swinging drunkenly in the light storm. The words 'the' and 'pony' have died out, leaving only AMETHYST in faded purple letters. A buzzing echoes from the letters. If the sign falls on somebody, the damn thing will probably electrocute them.

Striding toward the peeling red metal door, I shove it open and step inside the darkened interior. Hard-gut whiskey scent instantly assails me, and my stomach cramps in need.

"We're fucking closed. Get out before you get shot," a rough male voice bellows from a room beyond the long wooden bar planted on the right side of the structure. A second later, Garik Petrov appears, dark hair ruffled, faded jeans ripped, and irritation cutting lines into the sides of his mouth. "Shit. Alexei."

"Yeah." On alert, I stalk closer to the bar, nodding at the bottles lined haphazardly on the cracked glass shelves mounted to the wall.

Garik tosses a box aside. "You don't want that crap." He moves toward the bar and reaches below it, his gaze intense and guarded. Like always. He was orphaned young and taken in by an uncle who was a low-level operative in the Bratva. The uncle was killed years ago, and I'm fairly certain Garik gutted the old man.

I tense and then force my shoulders to relax as Garik pulls out a bottle of Beluga Gold Line vodka. My mouth waters. It has been seven long years since I've tasted anything for pleasure instead of for simple sustenance. "The front door is unlocked."

He grabs two somewhat clean-looking shot glasses and fills them to the top. "Yeah. I'm waiting for a shipment of beer in about thirty minutes, and the delivery guy is too scared to go through the alley to the back door. Can't blame him. Last guy got his head smashed before being robbed."

Irritation clacks through me and I reach for the shot glass. "Did you make a statement with that?"

"Tried but haven't found the guy." Garik secures his own glass. "I don't have the resources you once shared."

Having the Russian mob at my back is quite handy. I planned to take control from my stepmother once I finished screwing around, and perhaps I should've cut that shit out long before. A mistake I'll never make again.

"Nazdorovie." He lifts his glass.

I clink with him. "Nazdorovie." Then I tip back the drink, and wild spice explodes down my throat to my gut. Heaven. Pure and simple. I place the glass on the bar, and he refills it. "Thank you." I mean for more than the drink, and he knows it.

"Of course." He takes his second shot. "You're my only friend in this world."

It's a true statement for us both. I was too young and stupid to realize my vulnerability in life, and the way he has deposited money into my commissary account every week—when he obviously doesn't have much—ensures I will be loyal to him until the day I die. He could've joined the mafia as a low-level thug and made some money, which he has not done. His lineage would make it impossible for him to rise far, but he still could've made a nice living—and hasn't tried. Which makes his dedication all the more powerful. "Who do we have?"

"We have at least eight men." He names them, and I mask any surprise. "Your brother has made mistakes. Namely with daughters."

So Hendrix still can't keep it in his pants. He should be smart enough to stay away from the daughters of his lieutenants, but apparently those sexual drives are too strong. Our father had the same problem. "I'm surprised nobody has taken him out."

Garik shrugs. "Hendrix has loyal guards and knows how to fight. It won't be easy for you to retake the helm."

I study Garik. The seven years took a toll, with two new scars on his neck, but he stands almost to my height, and his torso has remained muscled beneath his worn black T-shirt. His nose holds a bump as if it has been broken in my absence.

Life has never been kind to Garik, from what I can tell. I've never asked and had only known that his deceased father was a low-level Bratva drug mule and his mother a hooker who disappeared years ago. I initially opened the bar with him because he can sing and is strong enough to handle problems and toss them out on their asses if necessary. It was one of the many reckless and immature moves in my overly arrogant youth, entered into carelessly.

Yet here we stand. Both pissed off survivors.

"How would you like to be second in command?" I ask softly.

His chin lifts. "I'm not from a known family."

"You're my family." He's earned as much trust as I can give, which isn't all that much.

"I accept." He glances down at my old-man pants. "When would you like to meet your very few followers?"

I consider my options. "Tomorrow here after closing."

He nods. "I'll make the arrangements. For now, I live upstairs and have clothes you can borrow. You're welcome to stay. There's a sofa that kind of folds out into a bed."

"Thank you," I say, meaning it. "But I plan to stay with my lawyer." I mean that, too.

One of his dark eyebrows rises. "Rosalie?"

Her name on his lips nearly has me lunging for him, and I tamp down on emotion. "You know her?"

He shrugs, his gaze alert against danger again. Smart man. "No. She dropped by yesterday with the news that you'd be released this week. She wanted to make sure you had a place to stay."

I scan the dismal bar with its scattered tables, small dartboard area, and lone torn pool table. A small, raised dais sits in the far corner with a guitar leaning against the wall. "She came here?"

He grins. Slowly. "Yeah. Even sat on a bar stool without wiping it off first. Said she wasn't sure she'd be able to keep you on the outside but wanted you safe while she tried."

A thoughtful and sweet heart to go with that spectacular body. Sometimes the gods are kind. Yet, they've tossed her into my path, so perhaps not. "I see. I plan to go buy clothes with my measly two hundred dollars in a few moments, but I appreciate the offer. How are the finances here?"

"Not great. We're afloat but barely. The books are in order in the office, and they're all yours."

"I trust you." Words I wouldn't give to anybody else in this world—even those I'll soon rule. My contacts inside had kept me informed about the Russian organization, and not much has changed. Yet. "I've heard my half brother is dead." I take the second shot and my limbs relax.

Garik pours two more. "Yeah. I've asked around and nobody knows who did it."

Perhaps Thorn Beathach had done me a favor by ending Cal. The little shit had been a weak link in the future organization—and he liked to beat women. There's no love lost between my father's second family and me. My father had not chosen well with a second wife. "Has Hendrix been by?" I wonder about my other half brother.

"No. He doesn't visit this part of town," Garik says wryly. "But a few of his guys have dropped by and caused damage before. Just reminding me that he's in the world and knows I am as well."

I'm certain Hendrix is running the organization right now. Using the word Bratva has always seemed like overkill to me. When I take over, it'll be referred to as Organizatsya, or Organization.

Garik finishes his third shot. "What are the chances you'll be released for good?"

"I don't know." Yet I have no intention of ever going back. Which means time is limited to gain enough power to prevent that from happening. "Did you keep my go bag?"

"Yep." Garik crouches again and rustles in the back of a cupboard, pulling out a worn black leather bag and plunking it on the bar. The sound of a couple of amethyst gems clunking is obvious. They're small and not charged, yet a trill of power comes from them. "Here you go."

Besides the Beretta 92FS I managed to hide before being arrested, I placed passports and cash in the bag. Just enough to buy new clothing and not much else. "You never opened it?"

"Of course not."

I might have to knight the guy. "Thanks."

The outside door opens and we both turn. Instead of a beer delivery man, a tall blonde in a form-fitting red silk dress slinks through, her shiny black high heels clipping seductively on the dirty floor.

Blythe Fairfax. A woman I might've loved. She could be a murderer.

"Uh." Garik replaces the bottle beneath the bar. "I'm going for a walk." He crosses around and moves toward the door, nodding at her and keeping a wide berth as he exits.

I wait for a feeling to hit me. Any sensation. Nothing.

She glides across the worn linoleum and reaches me, her expensive perfume clogging my senses. "You're free."

I turn to face her more fully. While the years apart had been rough on Garik, she looks better than ever. Her blue eyes sparkle in her still unlined face, probably helped along with Botox and whatever other treatments have been invented lately. The dress clasps in a halter behind her neck, leaving her toned shoulders and arms bare.

She blinks at my lack of answer and looks up at my face. "Did you kill him?"

It's the first time she's actually asked the question. After my arrest, she cried a lot for the media, making herself into a victim instead of an adulterous thrill seeker. "I figure you did."

Her smile is catlike. "We both know that's not true."

Do we?

She runs a bright red nail down my arm. "These clothes don't suit you." Her color heightens and her perfect nostrils flare. Like a horny mare's would. "I've missed you. Even if you are homicidal."

I missed her for my first six months in prison while I tried not to be shanked in my sleep. In my youth, I thought myself in love with her.

An emotion I will never allow myself to feel again—if that had been real. I have my doubts. Either way, I'll never be unguarded and vulnerable to anybody again. The image of sweet Rosalie flashes through my mind, and my muscles tighten. I need to work that woman out of my system.

"That's the look I remember," Blythe purrs, stepping closer.

"The look isn't for you." I remain in place, unwilling to move away.

She laughs, the once twinkling tone sounding grating now. "Do you have a new lover named Bubba? I've heard the joint can change a man."

Her using the word 'joint' shows her absolute stupidity. So I step into her, forcing her to tilt her head back to see me. I hope that she actually does. "If I discover you set me up and sent me to hell for seven years, you'll beg for death long before I grant it." Adding one more name to the kill list coming my way will take minimal effort.

She blinks. Once and then again. Her flared nostrils widen—from arousal to fear instantly. Yet she masks the emotion. Somewhat. "You and I had the real thing. Our love was true and can be again." Going with her strengths, she moves in, her full breasts brushing my lower chest. She smells like money. "Even if you stabbed him to death. That's in the past." Her lids partially cover her eyes.

"You're in the past." Gripping her bare arms, I lift her and plant her ass on the bar.

Her eyes widen and meet mine, and a small smile curves her blood-red lips. Then, smoothness gained from, no doubt, many Pilates classes, she shifts, turns, and slides down on her belly while lifting her skirt up and showing her bare butt.

How many times had I taken her against that old bar? She likes it rough.

So do I.

"No," I say softly, tamping down on anger.

She pivots and stands so suddenly, her long blond hair flies in every direction. "No?" she repeats, her eyebrows rising faster than her shrill tone.

I step back, enjoying her confusion. Years ago, I would've fucked her until she begged to come. Had more times than I could count. We had both played at being something we weren't. Me, a playboy, music-playing rich kid. Her, an adventurous and trapped wealthy woman. We were both useless assholes.

Her skirt falls down to her thighs. "You've changed."

"Yes." I stare back evenly, letting her see the killer set loose inside me. There is no containing him. I don't want to hide him any longer. "You want to stay the hell away from me. And if you are the person who set me up, you should start running now." I'll find her but I have work to finish first.

She licks her lips, the movement nervous . . . and aroused. Her gaze runs over my body and flares with interest. She's not smart enough to see the killer inside me and thinks I'm playing like we used to do. "I know exactly how to make you happy."

True. Her mouth held more talent than an experienced call girl. I stare at her. How in the hell had I allowed her into my world years ago? Talk about my having no standards.

She smiles again. Reaches for me.

I lean around her and fetch my bag off the bar. "I'm done with whores." With that, I turn and stride toward the battered door.

"You'll regret this," she shrieks, her voice reaching the rafters and probably scaring the shit out of the spiders.

I pause and glance over my shoulder, watching her until she visibly shrinks. "I've given you the only warning you'll get." Then I push open the door and forge into the storm.

SIX

Rosalie

I smack my hand against my forehead several times as the rain beats down against my car when I execute a quick U-turn to return to the bar. I cannot believe I forgot to have Alexei sign the two affidavits I need to file with the motion to release his funds. He flustered me so much that I can barely think even now.

Thunder ripples above me, and in the distance, lightning strikes. I shiver and turn on a little bit of heat. The rain isn't unexpected this time of year, and yet the storm seems angry. Right now, the whole world feels furious.

I shake my head and then see Alexei walk out of the Amethyst up ahead. He even prowls like a panther, and I shove that thought into an abyss.

If he just signs these documents, I can get myself home. It's my turn to buy dinner for my boarders, and they get cranky if I'm late.

A brown car, dented and rusty, zooms out of the alley in front of me, headed straight toward Alexei. I gasp and stiffen. He sees the car, and his body braces. A black barrel emerges from the driver's side of the back door, and I scream, frantically trying to press my button to roll my window down.

"Alexei, run," I yell.

A pattering fills the air as Alexei ducks back into the bar. The man shooting continues to spray the bar's exterior as the car accelerates and quickly zips out of sight. I didn't see a license plate. I gasp, panting, shock buzzing through me.

I speed up and park near the curb before ducking out and running to shove open the door and almost fall inside the dim-lit bar. Twin barrels meet my startled gaze, one from a tall man behind the counter and one from Alexei. Upon seeing me, they both lower their weapons.

"Are you all right?" I sputter.

Alexei, red blooming over the left side of his chest, looks over at the man I recognize as Garik. "You okay?"

"I'm good," Garik says. "Are they gone?"

I nod numbly. "We should call the police."

Garik's eyebrows lift, and Alexei tucks his gun at the back of his waist.

"Were you shot?" I hurry toward him and gently pry the material away. The borrowed shirt is quickly turning crimson.

"I'm good," he says, looking at the back door. "She ran fast."

Garik lopes around the bar and moves toward us without ceremony, ripping Alexei's shirt over his head. I gulp. Blood now slides down his well-tattooed and scarred front to pool at his waistband. Garik prods his back, and Alexei growls. "Looks like a through and through. You're going to need stitches." He returns to the bar and throws a filthy bar rag towards Alexei, who snatches it out of the air with one hand.

I hold up a hand. "Don't put that against . . ." He covers his bleeding wound. I wince.

"Come on, lawyer," he says, his face pale beneath his bronze skin. "I need a ride."

I can't believe this.

He walks outside, looks both ways, and moves slowly around to duck into my passenger seat, holding his arm to his body. He's going to get blood all over my car. I shake my head, give one look to Garik, and follow Alexei outside, shutting the door behind me before glancing back at the bullet holes. They match many of the others in the buildings down the street.

What have I gotten myself into?

I get in the car, which is still running, and pull away from the curb. "I'll take you to Catholic General."

"No," he says. "Go left here."

I need to turn left anyway, so I do. "What do you mean no? Is there a hospital you prefer?"

"No, just follow my directions. I know how to heal this."

If he wants to bleed to death, I guess that's his problem. It would certainly fix my current schedule. I wonder if I still get credit for having secured his release if he dies. "Shouldn't we call the police?"

"No. There's nothing to tell them, and I don't want to be on their radar right now."

Not liking this, I follow his terse directions and end up a few miles away from town in a rundown area showing very little life. "This area's even worse than where your bar is located," I murmur.

"Take another left," he orders.

I'm really getting tired of his commands, but I do so, emerging onto a forlorn neighborhood of, most likely, abandoned homes. Five houses scatter down the street with boarded-up windows, broken down fences, and tall weeds.

"That one." He points to a decrepit white house at the end of the block.

I slowly pull into the weed-riddled driveway.

"Hold on." He pushes open the door and moves toward the one-car garage door to lift it, the muscles in his chest straining and the tendons in his neck bulging.

I can't imagine the pain he's in right now. I've never been shot.

Once he gets the door open, he motions me inside the dim space, looking even paler than before.

Unease filling me, I glance guiltily around and then pull inside. He quickly yanks the door down with his good arm, his jaw clenched. Silence descends now that we're out of the rain. I cautiously step out of my car. "What are we doing here?"

"This way." He walks up two wooden stairs and opens a door to the house.

I don't like this at all. "Um, I think I'll wait here."

"Don't make me carry you." The last is said through gritted teeth.

Oh, like he could carry me with a bullet wound. Yet, something tells me he probably can. I wish I had a weapon. I climb the two stairs, hoping they don't break, and step inside a dirty, yet uncluttered seventies-style kitchen with cracked linoleum on the counters and floor.

He immediately opens a door to his left and starts descending down more wooden slats of stairs, his gait losing its natural grace. "Come on."

"Is this where you leave all the bodies?" I gingerly pick my way down the stairs. Cool air washes over me.

His chuckle is dark. "You've never been safer, Peaflower."

Somehow, I'm not comforted by that fact. I follow him into a square-shaped basement with dirt on the floor and no windows. I shiver. This would be an ideal place to hide a body, actually.

He walks to the far concrete wall, plants his good hand right above his head, and waits.

I gulp, the hair on the back of my neck standing up. "Listen, I'm not sure what . . ."

A door slides open in front of him. He looks over his shoulder and flashes me a grin, one that warms me in inappropriate places.

"Come on, Rosalie," he says, his voice low with pain.

I have to admit, my curiosity has just sprung wide awake. I hurry across the dirt floor, my kitten heels sinking annoyingly, and follow him inside. We're in pitch darkness. The door closes behind me, and I try not to scream. I hear something fumbling, and then lights flick on down a long tunnel.

"Whoa," I say, and then my gaze catches on . . . "Is that a golf cart?"

He smiles. "Do you mind driving? I'm kind of dying here."

I like the idea of still being in control, because this is crazy. "Sure." I run around to sit on the driver's side of a pretty standard blue golf cart.

He sits next to me, his heat instantly warming me. "That way."

"There's only one way." I marvel at the can lights attached to concrete walls every five feet or so. "Where are we going?"

"Just drive."

I don't want to be curious or amused, but this is the most fun I've had in a long time. So I press the gas pedal, and the cart instantly zings off. "Don't you have to charge these things?"

He jolts. "Wait."

We both wince as a loud pop echoes, and I turn to see an electrical cord fly through the air and land hard. "Oops."

He scratches his head. "Yes. It's always plugged in."

I probably just broke it. But it's not my fault he didn't explain what's happening. I hit the gas again, entranced at our speed. We go several miles in a short amount of time, until we reach the end of the tunnel with an obvious door. I stop. "Where are we?"

"Hologrid Hub." He hitches painfully out of the golf cart.

I hop out and hurry around to look at his face. He's gone pale beneath his bronze skin, and he's partially bent over. "I told you we should go to a hospital."

"Right." He moves forward and flattens his hand against the top part of the door like he did before.

I squint my eyes and peer up. "Is that some sort of sensor?"

"Yes," he says. "It's a palm sensor that reads the fingerprints. My hand's the only one that will open it."

I don't want to be impressed, but I am. That's kind of cool.

The door slides open, and we walk into one of those fancy computer server rooms you see on TV. "Whoa," I say. Computer consoles with blinking lights line all four walls except for a doorway opposite us, whereas in the center on a big pedestal sits an amethyst, raw and natural, bigger than a basketball. The stone's cuts and valleys sparkle purple and slightly white in the dim light. The servers hum around us, so clean they reflect our images.

"Hold this." Alexei hands me his gun, his gaze locked on the crystal in the center of the room.

"What are you doing?"

He moves toward the amethyst as if unable to refuse its draw. Taking a deep breath, he places both hands on either side of the precious gem. "I'm healing myself."

I move to the side, watching as the crystal begins to glow a brighter purple. "Wow," I whisper.

As one of the four major social media companies in the world, Hologrid Hub runs on amethysts. The three other companies run on either garnets, citrines, diamonds, or aquamarines. I know this because my best friend, Alana, is the person who actually charges the crystals at Aquarius Social. I've never quite understood what that means, and not once has she mentioned she can receive healing energy from a stone.

Alexei throws back his head, and electricity arcs through the air. I blink. Alana has explained how the four families learned to harness the power from crystals back in the stone ages, which gives them better health and longevity. They've taken that gift and amassed wealth and power through the centuries.

As I watch, the hole in Alexei's shoulder begins to mend.

I stumble back. "Holy moly." Alana never said that the stones could actually mend wounds.

Alexei's eyes open and he looks at me, his gaze slumberous. "This is a secret."

Holy crap. Crystal energy really can heal. "It's sad that

most people don't know about crystals," I blurt out. Alana taught me that I have an affinity with angelite, but it would take centuries to exchange this much power with crystals. "It really is quite unfair your families didn't share this."

He gives me a pointed stare and steps away from the stone, which is now glowing a brighter purple.

The opposite door opens, and Hendrix Sokolov walks in. "Well, hello brother."

Alexei turns. They're about the same height, but Alexei is cut sharper with more obvious muscles. "How did you know I was here?" he drawls.

Hendrix lifts a shoulder. "Please, I have sensors in this place." He glances at the open doorway. "However, that's news. I guess I'll have that filled in."

Alexei's smile lacks humor. "This company's mine, brother. You going to give it up?"

Hendrick smiles. He's blonde with startling blue eyes and is quite handsome in a different way than Alexei. Where Alexei is dark, Hendrix is light. At least, he gives off that impression. "Not in a million years. I'll kill you first."

Alexei lifts his shoulder. "It's a date then. We'll go back the way we came." He grasps my arm and pulls me toward the tunnel.

Hendrix snorts. "Alexei? Is this really your play?"

Alexei pauses. "Yes. Why do you ask?"

"There are rumblings of a new player with a new platform. Something with even more advanced AI than the rest of us put together. Could be gossip. But the internet is humming. You know anything about that?"

"No." Alexei's jaw hardens. "That's a problem for another day." He propels me toward the back door.

Hendrix chuckles. "I would think that as a lawyer, Ms. Mooncrest, you wouldn't break and enter."

I stumble and then regain my balance, pulling Alexei to an abrupt stop. I'm surprised he allows me to do so. His brother recognized me through the surveillance equipment? "We've never met. How do you know my name?"

Hendrick winks. "The second you became Alexei's attorney, I had you investigated. I know more about you than he does."

"I doubt that," Alexei says, moving us both toward the exit again.

"We're not done, brother," Hendrix calls out.

Alexei looks over his shoulder. "You've got that right."

SEVEN
Rosalie

An hour after dropping a rather grumpy Alexei off at his bar, two heavy trays of tacos heat my arms as I lug them out of the small diner to my SUV. Thursday is taco night, and if I don't show up with extra hot sauce, Merlin will be cranky. Not that Merlin's default setting isn't cranky, because it is, which is just one more reason I adore him.

A black car turns and drives partially up on the curb next to me. Startled, I back away. In impossibly choreographed movements, the two doors open, and a man reaches for me. I shrink and kick, too startled to drop the trays. Within seconds I'm shoved inside a long town car.

The hulking badass slides in next to me and slams the door, and then we're driving away from safety.

I gape, fear tightening my limbs. I cannot believe how quickly that happened. Gulping, I look over at the man next to me. "Who are you?"

He doesn't answer. He's at least six-foot-five with buzz-cut dark hair and glacier-blue eyes. He has to weigh a good two hundred and eighty pounds, and it's all muscle. His face is an interesting configuration of dents and hollows, and his nose has been broken so many times the bridge is nearly flat. He has cauliflower ears, obviously from boxing.

Terror rips through me, and I try to see outside the windows, but they're tinted so dark that only blurred images fly by.

I scoot toward the other side, for some reason not losing the tacos. They're not hot enough to make a decent weapon, but if I smash him in the face with the tinfoil tray, he'll at least be blinded.

"Door's locked." His voice is as flat as his nose.

Across from me is a bench seat, and the partition between us and the driver is up.

"I don't think you know what you're doing," I say.

He looks straight ahead and doesn't answer. My kidnapper wears slacks and a black jacket with an obvious bulge in the side. I'm sure it's not his only weapon. It's a little embarrassing he kidnapped me without having to pull it.

The car fills with the aroma of fresh, spicy meat and melted cheese. His gaze flicks down to the two large platters. "Family meal?"

"Four of them," I mutter. "I don't suppose you'll let me go for a taco?"

I'm not entirely sure, but I think a hint of a smile twitches his lips. I surreptitiously reach to the side and try to open my door. Nothing happens.

"Told you, locked from the outside." He still stares straight ahead.

I calculate my chances of stealing his weapon. I don't

know how it's secured beneath that jacket, but a face full of tacos will at least give me a chance.

"No need," he mutters, not looking at me again.

I blink. "Excuse me?"

"Save the tacos. You're not in danger."

If that isn't a lie, I don't know what is. "Right. You kidnap people for fun."

He lifts one gargantuan shoulder. "Sometimes."

"Who are you?" I shift slightly toward him and get ready with the platters.

"Doesn't matter, and don't hit me with the tacos." His voice holds certain threat. "You won't get out of the car, so why take the chance?"

He's not wrong. Maybe my best move for an escape is when we stop, but anybody who knows anything knows that you never let a kidnapper take you to a second location. Unfortunately, considering the car is moving, I don't have much of an option.

"Is your door locked?" I ask.

"Of course."

I think he's lying. All right. New plan. I calculate the distance in the small interior of the vehicle. Getting between him and that door is going to be difficult, and the tacos are not hot enough to burn him right now.

The vehicle slows. I stiffen, and cold sweat breaks out on my brow. We roll to a stop. City sounds surround us, so we haven't reached some remote wooded area where they can bury my body. I try to take comfort from that thought.

I hear the driver's door open, and then shock of all shock, my door opens. I move to scramble out, but the hulk grabs my arm and yanks me toward him. Bruises instantly rise along my skin.

"Hey, take it easy." I shove him with the same elbow.

"I told you not to move."

I'm starting to really hate this guy. "No you didn't."

One female leg enters the car, a long foot trapped in a truly glorious Rene Caovilla sparkling pump. It's odd to find them in pumps and not sandals. A curvy body encased in a classy black Chanel dress then follows, before Lillian Sokolov takes her seat across from me. The dress is a little tight on her. I recognize designer labels because Alana wears them all the time. Sometimes I find one or two at the women's center, but it isn't often.

The door shuts again and the lock clicks loudly.

"What is happening?" I blurt out, glaring at Lillian.

Her lips tremble into a smile. "I'm so sorry about this."

I stare at the owner of one of the four powerful social media and AI companies in the world today. She also happens to be Alexei's stepmother. She has let her blondish hair slide into gray, and she appears boxier than she did before her youngest son died. Her shoulders hunch as she clasps her hands together.

"This is kidnapping," I say slowly, making sure she hears every word. "I don't care who you are or what you own, I will have you arrested."

She wipes her eyes with one hand, and as she moves, a gorgeous festoon necklace, which has to be from the Victorian period, sparkles across her upper chest. The amethyst and pearls decorating the filigree are stunning. In fact, the jewels sparkle at me just like Alexei's tattoo from the panther on his neck.

"I know, but I just have to talk to you." She swallows and wipes away mascara that has pooled on one cheek, crow's feet digging deep from her eyes. "I won't hurt you."

"It's still a kidnapping," I say boldly, trying to hide the relief that filters through me. "Do you want to explain?"

She sniffs toward my platter of tacos. "Is that what stinks?"

"It could be your bodyguard here." I jerk my head toward the guy to my right, although truth be told, he smells like a woodsy cologne. Kidnappers should stink. They should have their own specialized smell.

My thoughts zing to Alexei, and then I discount that idea. I quite like the way he smells. "What do you want, Lillian?"

"That's Mrs. Sokolov to you," she says, her chin up and wobbling just a little.

"Sorry, but the whole kidnapping thing negates any formality we might've had." I glare.

Her smile softens her face but doesn't reach her sad eyes. "I like you."

"I'm losing my temper." Anger shakes my voice. "Now tell me why you kidnapped me, before I call the police." It's a bluff, because my purse is still in my car. I usually forget it, and I have an account at the taco place, so I didn't need my wallet. I have no phone to use right now.

She stares at me for several moments, her gaze somber, and I try to stay strong. There's no doubt she's still grieving from the death of her son. Cal. Her sadness permeates the entire vehicle. Finally, she speaks again as the car winds to wherever we're going.

"Have you spoken with Alexei?" she asks.

"I'm his attorney," I say softly. "I believe you already know that fact."

"Yes, I do. What are his plans?"

I blink. "His plans?"

"Yes. Did he say anything about Hologrid Hub?"

I stare at her, having just learned that Hologrid Hub can heal wounds. I've always considered the platform to be a lot of fun. It uses a 3D holographic social media platform where people actually feel like they're in the same space together. I've enjoyed meeting friends in faraway, unreal places. The AI that Hologrid Hub utilizes can put a group on the moon for a short time with their friends—and apparently heal members of the Sokolov family. One member, anyway.

"He didn't say a word about Hologrid Hub," I mutter. "You have to know that anything he says to me is covered by attorney-client privilege." Although, truth be told, the guy hasn't said a thing. "I would assume, and again I'm assuming here," I say quietly, "that his main focus is proving himself innocent and not returning to prison."

"That's the wrong outcome here," she says, leaning slightly toward me and smelling of gardenias. "Hendrix is the rightful heir, and I can't see him be killed. I can't lose another son." Her voice breaks at the end.

I stiffen. "What do you mean?"

She sighs. "Please. Alexei will kill sweet Hendrix. Everybody knows that Alexei murdered David Fairfax. Alexei was brutally in love with Blythe, even though I'm sure he was one of many. She always kept a stable of young hunks to play with."

"Do you truly believe Alexei killed David?" I ask.

"Of course he killed David. Alexei had a terrible temper. I'm sure he still does. You might want to stay on your toes around him." Tears pool in her eyes. "You are quite beautiful, even beneath the frugal clothing."

The clothing is actually expensive, or at least it was

before I purchased it second hand. "I'm thinking you have a crush on me," I retort, trying to hold on to my mad and not feel sorry for her.

The mammoth man next to me shifts his weight, and I can't tell if it's out of amusement or irritation. "Please get to the point, Mrs. Sokolov." I use my best lawyer voice.

"This is just a warning so you can keep yourself and, hopefully, Hendrix safe," Lillian whispers.

I allow both of my eyebrows to slowly raise since I'm not going to show this woman fear, even though her bodyguard could probably snap my neck without taking a deep breath. "What kind of warning?"

"Alexei is dangerous, and worse yet, he's obsessive. If he becomes fixated on you, he'll kill everybody around you to isolate you, the same way he tried to do with Blythe."

"Are you saying there are more murders besides David Fairfax?"

She pales until even her lips look blue.

"There are plenty more murders. The best thing for everybody is to contain Alexei in prison, and that means safety for you and everybody you care about."

I study her. "He's your stepson. Last I heard, Hologrid Hub isn't in the lead of the four social media giants. Undoubtedly, Alexei has skills beneficial to your company."

She blinks once. "You shouldn't know about that."

Yet I do. How the social media servers run is a secret to most people, but I'm on the inside on this one. They run on crystals, and there's a reason the same families have been in power through the beginning of time. These people have an affinity with certain crystals that grant health and strength and power. This health helped them to avoid plagues during the early years and thus prosper. It's only recently that the four families learned how to take those crystals and use them to power their social media servers.

I wonder idly what would happen if Alexei and Hendrix both charge the crystal at the same time. "You might need Alexei."

Her face goes slack for the briefest of seconds. "We don't." Her gaze flicks away, and she presses her lips tightly together, showing deception and a healthy amount of fear.

So they do need Alexei.

I think idly about the death of Cal, Alexei's half brother and Lillian's son. Had he been the one to charge the amethyst crystals that power their servers? Has his death actually hurt Hologrid Hub? Lillian seems terrified of Alexei returning.

"You and Alexei don't like each other, do you?" I ask.

"He doesn't like any of us," she says, showing a hint of a southern accent.

I perk up instantly. This is new. I really don't know anything about her, except she married Alexei's father and became one of the most powerful women in the entire world. I'll need a background check on her. Perhaps Alexei going to prison was exactly what she had wanted. The result she seems to want right now.

"How's Hendrix doing?" I ask. "He's in charge of Hologrid Hub, isn't he?"

"Yes, and he's very dedicated to the company. There is no place for Alexei in the organization."

"Yet Hologrid Hub was started by his father," I say. "Don't you want the brothers to work together?"

Her eyes flare and the blue darkens. "They're not brothers."

"They're half brothers."

The car rolls to a stop.

"Remember what I said," Lillian says, looking much older than her years. "You need to see the danger in Alexei before it's too late. Also, it's hard to explain, but to look professional to our, um, organization, it will be better for him if he marries. He'll want to look stable and settled. Do not get caught up in his schemes."

Organization? Why would investors in Hologrid Hub care about his personal life?

As the bodyguard opens the door, Lillian leans forward to stare at my three-story, light-pink Victorian townhouse.

"Your home is charming," she says softly. "I know about your boarders, and I know how much you care about them. Alexei will take everything you love and destroy it, just so he can have you all to himself." She rubs her arms as if freezing in the warm car. "I believe you have two best friends, Alana Beaumont and Ella Rendale, as well."

I laugh. The idea of anybody getting to Alana Beaumont, now that she is with Thorn Beathach, is hilarious. "Alana is safe from any danger, don't worry. Thorn will never let anything happen to her." He owns the number one social media company while also running the Irish mob.

I don't even want to think what he will do to anybody who tries to hurt her now. I wonder if Lillian has any idea that Thorn possibly killed her youngest son. I doubt it. As for Ella, she can disappear on a moment's notice if needed. Her family owns TimeGem moments, one of the four powerful social media companies—although her stepmother has kicked her out of the family. For now.

The bodyguard steps out of the car and holds a hand to help me out. I have to take it, since I'm balancing the two platters. I look behind the vehicle, not surprised to see my SUV also parking by the curb. Another hulking bodyguard jumps out, tosses me the keys, and moves toward the other side of Lillian's car.

The guy next to me snatches the keys out of the air and then places them gently on my tin foil wrapped tacos. "Thank you for not throwing these in my face."

I blink. "I didn't see a reason to do that."

"You're smart." With those words, he gets back into the car.

Lillian leans over and looks at me, her expression somber. "Remember what I said. You're in more danger than you can imagine right now."

The door slams shut, and the car smoothly drives away. I shiver in the sudden cold and look up at my refuge. A window from the second floor opens, and Merlin pokes his gray head out. "It's about time. You're half an hour late with the tacos. We're starving."

EIGHT
Rosalie

After a mostly successful taco night topped off by a delicious apple pie I baked the night before, two of my boarders help me finish cleaning up the old-fashioned kitchen. I recently updated the counters into marble and the appliances into stainless steel, but the worn and uneven wooden floor is too costly to change for now.

Merlin finishes drying one of the plates. He's dressed in his usual fancy slacks and shirt. With his thick gray hair and eyebrows, he looks like a distinguished professor and not the retired computer hacker I know him to be. We've hacked more than one secure system in an effort to help people who need assistance with the pseudo-doing-good group I created with Alana and Ella. "I'm sorry Percy crunched his taco so much at dinner. We'll buy him new dentures."

"He was fine," I protest, having thought I hid my reaction.

"Huh," Felix says. "There are some new treatments out of the Misophonia Institute."

I nod. "I'm working through one of the trials now."

Most people have never heard of misophonia, which is a weird and extreme internal reaction to certain sounds, usually mouth or nose sounds. Sniffing sends me spiraling for my EarPods.

Felix finishes replacing the glasses into the cupboard and then turns to stare at me. "Good. We can try hypnotism again when you're finished with their sound protocols. Speaking of your overall health, are you taking those vitamin D supplements I prescribed for you?"

"Yes," I say. "I take one every day." I'm not entirely sure I need 5,000 milligrams of vitamin D every day, but my energy level has increased.

He crosses his arms, his bald head gleaming beneath the soft light. The lines on his face are well worn, and I still find it amusing he won't tell anybody his age. I guess him to be around eighty years old. Merlin has offered to hack into government systems and find out, but I figure if one of my boarders wants to keep a secret, they should. Felix worked as a doctor at a large hospital in Pennsylvania in his youth and then moved to a more rural area before he ended up with me, one of my renters who lack family.

I like to think that the seven of them have formed their own friendships, but I feel like they tolerate each other. At least they seem like a loyal group, and everyone needs friends.

For me, they're as sweet as they get. More importantly, they really try to pay their rent on time. I yawn and can't help it.

"You do look tired." Merlin nudges my shoulder. "Are you working too hard again?"

I refrain from telling them about my brief kidnapping. "Probably."

"Go get some sleep," Felix orders. "I'm your doctor. You have to do what I say." He is the closest thing to a doctor I have.

"All right, fine." Who am I to argue with a doctor who doesn't charge me a cent? Yeah, he's retired, and I have no idea how he still writes prescriptions. But he does come in handy. "I'll see y'all tomorrow." With that, I turn and head out of the spacious kitchen and up the interior stairs to the top level, which is all mine. My bedroom is in the turret, and I have my own bathroom and small office area as well as private exterior entrance. The place is my sanctuary and I love it.

A momentary pang of sadness hits me that I never met the great aunt who left this wonderful home to me, but I'm thankful for her every day. After my father died five years ago, I was adrift. I have the two best friends in the world, and either one of them would've taken me in, but my father's will had directed me to this home that had been granted to me years ago. I found boarders almost instantly and have been repairing the building since. I'm uncertain about the pink color outside, and yet it really does lend that Victorian look to the place.

Sighing, I shut the door at the top of the stairs and move into my sanctuary. Something's off. The air feels weird. I walk into my bedroom and pause at seeing Alexei Sokolov lounging in my one chair by the window near a fully stacked bookshelf. He's thumbing through the latest J.T. Geissinger romance.

"There's some good stuff in here," he says. "She can write."

Instant fire flashes through my body. Both anger and something else. A sensation I won't admit to, no matter what. He exudes sex, even sitting in the plush pink chair. "What are you doing in my room?" I've about had it with the Sokolov family today.

He shrugs. I look over near my vanity, which is an antique that I've lovingly restored, to see a small shopping bag. "I'm staying here," he says slowly.

I blink once and then again, my gaze wandering to the ornate silver mirror on the wall. The beautiful piece had been my grandmother's, and sometimes when I look at myself in it, I see a hint of her. My grandfather always said I favored her, so the thought warms me. Right now, I take strength from that idea. "You most certainly are not sleeping in my bedroom."

His gaze is so piercing, I feel it to the bottom of my spine. Maybe deeper. "I don't think you understand the danger you're in by representing me." He stands, crossing to me and gently taking my wrist to turn my arm. "Who bruised you?"

I glance down at the purplish marks. "Your stepmother's goon doesn't know his own strength." I tell him about my forced ride home.

Alexei's nostrils flare. "What is his name?"

"I don't know."

"Describe him."

Warning skitters through me. "He was actually kind of funny." At Alexei lowering his chin, I give the best description I can.

He nods. "Don't worry. He will never bother you again."

I gulp. It sounds like the guy will never bother *anybody* again. "I don't want him dead."

"Don't worry about it." Alexei leans down and kisses the bruises before releasing me.

Warmth encloses my heart, and I shrug the feeling away to put my hands on my hips. "Back to the matter at hand. All I have is the bed. There's no sofa, no air mattress, and my desk chair in the other room is not comfortable." He glances at the bed, which I have to admit is large. I like rolling around at night and spreading out.

"That's big enough for the two of us." His upper lip quirks. "Although I could do without the frilly red bedspread."

I like frills, and I like red, and I like all girly things. He does not fit in this room. The man exudes raw male sexuality, and I'm in no mood for it. At least intellectually. My nipples harden and my hoo haw wakes right up and does a shivery dance that energizes my clit. How does he do that? Must be pheromones. I've read about them. The horny-creating chemicals must roll right off him and zero in on any available vagina.

It's the only explanation for the sudden dampness between my thighs. Or the way my lungs are stuttering and holding onto oxygen I need for my brain.

I stare and am reminded of his overpowering height. Then I check out his clothes: faded jeans, plain black T-shirt, worn leather jacket, and motorcycle boots. "You found clothes that fit," I mutter, telling my clit and traitorous vagina to go back to sleep. Now.

He nods. "I had enough cash for one outfit but will need my funds released soon. The clothing is in the farthest bag. Please return that to whichever boarder you borrowed it from."

I look at him, naturally breathing him in. Male and something undefinable and dangerous. "What do you know about my boarders?"

"Not enough," he admits. "I'll know more soon, unless you want to tell me all about them."

"They're nice and retired elderly men who pay their rent the best they can," I say evenly. I tilt my chin, hoping my bra is hiding my erect nipples. I have to concentrate on the case and not his broad shoulders. Is he as hard and rough as he looks? "Why does your stepmother fear you?"

If my words throw him, he doesn't show it.

"She doesn't fear me. She hates me with every fiber of her being. Why?"

"I think she's terrified. Perhaps losing one son has made her realize what's important in life. But she does fear you."

While his eyes spark, his stance remains relaxed and his expression bland. "I'll take care of it," he says. "Like I said, neither she nor her employees will bother you again."

"I don't need you to take care of anything," I retort. "I want to know if it's possible that Hendrix set you up for David Fairfax's murder seven years ago." While I won't call Lillian as a character witness for Alexei, she could be questioned to point toward Hendrix's motive in the death and set-up of Alexei. Reasonable doubt is all I need.

"It's entirely possible," he admits. "The only reason he didn't try to kill us at Hologrid Hub is because you were armed with my gun, and he wasn't prepared. Which is another reason he shouldn't helm the organization. I'm always prepared."

I watch Alexei carefully like I would any predator. The entire atmosphere has swelled, heated, and changed from his presence. My skin electrifies, and I don't like it. My clit tries to argue, and I mentally order that bitch back to hibernation. I've never had a man in this room—and I usually date easy going and carefree men. Not intense possible murderers. "Is there any way to find peace with your brother?"

"I don't have a brother," Alexei returns. "Hendrix is anything but."

"I think he's probably charging the crystals at Hologrid Hub," I murmur, waiting for a reaction. I don't get one.

The man is a master at masking his thoughts and emotions. "Probably, but the crystal felt weak to me. Speaking of which, I'm surprised you didn't ask any questions when you dropped me back off at the bar."

I shake my head. The guy was half-asleep as if healing himself had taken a boatload of energy, and I didn't know what to ask. "I wasn't surprised. I know all about the use of the crystals in powering the servers." Sure, it's a lifelong deadly secret, but he has a right to understand my insight as his attorney.

His chin lifts very slightly. "I was not aware of your knowledge, which unfortunately puts you in danger. I suggest you don't advertise, to anybody but me, your comprehension about crystals and power. My guess is that yes, Hendrix is charging the crystals at the company. I think Cal was better at it, but there's no choice now, is there?"

"So you're better at interacting with the gems?" Not everybody in the lineages is able to charge the crystals.

"Yes." Alexei smiles, making my vagina perk up again. "I touch an amethyst, and the charge is immediate." The purple eyes on the panther dance across his skin.

I blink. That must've been a hallucination. The panther looks like he wants to take a bite out of me. Maybe two. My breasts tighten more as if trying to reach for him. I have totally and completely lost my mind—and any control of my body. I must get him out of here. "Since you have very little money, at least right now, I can help you find a hotel. I don't have an empty room here."

He glances at the bed again, and awareness ticks down my back. "Like I told you, I'm staying here." He runs one knuckle down my face.

I gulp, my feet frozen to the ground. Which doesn't make sense because my entire body has gone firestorm hot. "You can't sleep with your attorney." My voice shakes, and I concentrate on watching the panther watch me.

"I have no plans to sleep." His voice is low and dark, licking across my skin.

I shiver, and his answering half smile should piss me off. But there's so much intent in it that wings flutter through my abdomen . . . and lower. Much lower. I press my lips together, tight, to keep from whimpering. "Sex is off the table," I whisper.

"How about over the bed?"

Over the bed. Not *on* the bed. Not *in* the bed. But bent over the bed. My core screams a holy yes while I shake my head. "No."

He clasps my jaw between a roughened thumb and finger. "I know when a woman wants me, Rosalie." He says my name like he's tasting heaven.

I'm sure every woman within a two-mile radius wants this man, just from the pheromones zinging around. "You want my brain and not my body. Trust me."

"I'll possess both."

Who says that? Seriously. "You get neither." I look up, meeting his gaze evenly, instantly wishing I hadn't.

His eyes are black pools of intrigue and desire along with warning. "Your choice." He releases me and turns his back, pulling the T-shirt over his head. He flings it to the chair, revealing hard muscle and several scars down his strong back. Knife wounds, whip marks, and other scars I can't identify—including a fresh one on his shoulder. My vagina rolls over and moans. That fucking bitch. She needs to crave safety and not . . . this. Whatever this is.

I glance at the bed. "You are not staying here."

He turns, his hands already unzipping his jeans. "Then call your ancient boarders for help, and we'll get this over with now. I'll try not to harm them too badly, but I can't guarantee all seven will survive."

My knees tremble. There's too much trembling, shuddering, and vibrating throughout my entire body right now—with different feelings and emotions attached. He knows more about me and mine than I like.

He tosses the pants, leaving himself in black boxer briefs that are filled out. I mean seriously filled out. His gaze softens. Slightly. "I'm tired, Rosalie. It's been a long seven years, and the next couple of months aren't going to be any sort of picnic. Get your sweet ass in that bed, and I promise, this once, I won't touch you tonight. Won't even tempt you."

The man tempts me just by existing. "Fine." I'm too tired to fight him. But I'll cover myself with heavy vanilla scented lotion while preparing for bed. I'm sure that will mask his scent and send those pheromones fleeing. "You'll love my winter pajamas. I find them in the great-grandma aisle at the women's shelter."

NINE
Rosalie

Pleasure drowns me, and I moan, every nerve in my entire body shooting electricity. Colors and mysterious shapes flash in front of my eyes. I gasp, on fire. Somehow, I'm flying. The smell of motor oil battered by pelting rain fills my senses.

A sound awakens me, and my eyelids flip open even as another moan escapes from my chest. I jerk awake, gyrating against fingers playing with my clit. My pajama bottoms and panties are gone, and I'm bare to the cool air. "Oh God," I whisper, the blood rushing through my head so fast, my ears ring. I partially roll to face Alexei. The breath bursts out of my lungs, and I grab onto his biceps, digging my nails in. "What are you doing?" I gasp, my head spinning, my nipples sharpened to fine points beneath the thin camisole top.

"Playing." His eyes are liquid coal just lit with flames.

I gulp. Where's the sweatshirt I had worn to bed? "Stop."

"You don't want me to stop." To punctuate his point, he scrapes his calloused thumb across my clit.

I jolt, head to toe, pleasure ripping through my body. The wetness spilling from me, onto his hand, will embarrass me later. Not now. My traitorous body moves against him, seeking relief. I can't think. "You—you said you wouldn't touch me."

"Last night," he whispers, sliding another finger inside me. "And I didn't."

I'm strung tight like a bow about to break. This is wrong. I know it is. Yet my body doesn't care. Something bad has never felt this good. I should stop him. My hands drop from his body.

His chuckle licks along my skin, right before his tongue does the same, marking from my collarbone, up my neck, and over my chin. "You taste delicious. I want more." His fingers scissor inside me, slamming against a spot I'm just realizing actually exists. My eyes roll back, and I whimper, pleasure swamping me.

This isn't fair.

I can't think. Trying to force my brain to work, I note my nails digging into the sheet on one side of my gyrating body and the other into . . . his bare leg. The muscles are bunched beneath my hand, rough cut and strong. The length of his cock, even inside his boxers, is heated against the side of my hand. Oh God.

His mouth is against my ear. "You ever beg, Rosalie?"

"No," I hiss, heat flushing from my breasts to my face, no doubt warming his lips.

"That's gonna change." He murmurs something else, something I can't grasp. A low rumble in Russian that sounds like a vow. A dangerous one.

Helplessness, especially with a man, is something I've never felt. Never allowed myself to feel. A status that had more than one former boyfriend calling me cold and un-feeling. So much for that brand. Freeing my hand from his thigh, I clamp onto his arm, feeling the tendons shift as he works his magically dangerous fingers inside me. "Stop or I'll scream." My panting might negate the order some.

He bites into my earlobe.

I jolt, my body flushing cold and then hot. Toes to head. "That hurt," I whisper, trying to clamp my legs together.

"Good." He continues stroking me, his broad hand staying firmly in place.

I'm climbing the crest too fast and can't stop. No way can I let him win this. So I suck in air, and that unique and deadly smell of drilling rain into motor oil fills my senses. Sexy and primitive. I yank on his hand. "Stop," I hiss.

His fingers slide out of me, and my pussy tries to follow them. She has to get a fucking grip. Not on him. On reality.

Then, as if he's choreographed the move a million times, he shifts, slides one knee against my thigh, and shoves it to the side. Then he moves down me, faster than I can grasp, and his teeth sink into the top of my pubic area.

I squeal and freeze in place, slapping a hand over my mouth. The last thing in the world I want is for one of my boarders to run in here. My body trembles.

"You should've just let me play." His breath is an inferno against my abused and very bare skin. I swim a lot, so I pretty much wax everything. I'm regretting that right now. Well, kind of. "Now you're going to obey."

The word takes a second to penetrate. The moment it does, I shove against his shoulders with both legs.

He bites me again, this time a little lower. Pain and an electric pleasure zip up to my breasts.

I blink wildly, staring up at the ceiling.

"Spread your legs, Rosalie. Now, or I'm biting lower."

The words come from far away. Electricity uncoils inside me, deep. I press my lips together so tightly my jaw aches, but I won't beg.

His teeth latch onto my clit.

I yelp and spread both legs before he can bite, holding my breath.

"Good girl." A low hum of pleasure rumbles from his mouth as he sucks my clit into his mouth with just enough pressure to have me seeing stars. He slides two fingers, then three, into me, forcing my clit up into his mouth more.

I'm swollen in his heated mouth, my body strung tight, right on the edge. One tear leaks out of my eye. A tear of need or fury, I'm not sure. I know this is wrong. Also, I know I'm about to have the best orgasm of my life.

Then I'll have to kill him. There's no other option.

The thought cheers me finally.

He releases my clit and rests his chin on my cleft. "Why are you smiling?"

I lose the grin and look down at him. "I'm plotting your death," I pant.

One of his dark eyebrows rises. His fingers slide out of me.

This is good. I want him to stop. But I don't. Not at all. As I'm struggling to find a thought, he flips me onto my stomach and smacks my ass five times.

Hard.

Then he turns me back over and roughly shoves all three fingers inside me again.

I gasp and arch against him, an erotic pain burning through me from both sides. What just happened? He hit me hard enough that I'll wear his palm print for days. Even now, the burning cascades across my butt. My desire spirals even higher. The need is so great it hurts. Deep.

"Insolence and disrespect will be handled swiftly." His black eyes hold the fires of hell. I just know it.

Then he dips his head and sucks my clit into his mouth, lashing me with his tongue.

I make an embarrassing sound deep in my throat and throw my head back on my pillow, colors flashing behind my closed eyelids. So many sensations bombard me that I can't breathe. Don't care to try.

His mouth releases me. "Say please, Rosie."

Pride and a battered instinct for self-preservation battle with this unreal craving. Pride always wins with me. "Fuck you."

The hard smack he delivers to my clit has my body bucking. Pain . . . then pleasure. "Try again."

I can't take another one of those. I just can't. "Please."

"Good girl." He smacks me again for good measure, just to show he can.

I hate him.

He nips me with his lips and I jolt. His chuckle rumbles through me, and he licks my clit again, his tongue rough, forcing me back up again.

Even as I climb, I plot his murder. Gun? Knife? I want to throw him off a cliff. Yeah. That's the plan. We'll go hiking, perhaps to talk about the case, and I'll just shove him right over.

Then I forget all about committing a homicide, because those fingers and his way too hot and talented mouth find a rhythm that has me bucking against him.

Just as I'm about to explode, he pauses, releases me, and slaps my clit with the heel of his palm. Once and then again. The orgasm starts to take me, and his mouth sucks me in again, his tongue working me like a master.

I grab a pillow and shove it over my face, my body gyrating so hard the headboard protests. Molten lava pours through me, and I try to muffle my screams as the orgasm rips electricity through me with a fine edge of pleasure that can't be real. It's wild and dangerous, and it's owning me.

Then the waves hit, and I'm drowning in them, riding out the storm.

With a pathetic whimper I hope he doesn't hear, I come down, throwing the pillow off my face. I'm sweaty and trembling, and he's still between my legs. I fight the urge to slap his head, because I can't take another hit to my clit.

With a pleased murmur, he kisses my clit and then looks up. His gaze is raw and intent. All male. With a promise in there, or maybe a threat. "Say thank you, Rosalie."

I gulp. Not a bit of me wants to give in. Yet his teeth are right there, as is his hand. "Thank you," I say weakly.

He kisses my bare mound again and then stands.

Finally, I clap my thighs together and push away from the bed, standing on very shaky legs. "That will never happen again."

His smile lacks humor. "Watch yourself."

I take a step back. "I'm not joking. You do that again, even think of it, and I'll have you arrested." Yet the orgasm had been spectacular. The best. Ever. For sure.

He stands there just in boxers, his ripped and cut body proudly bearing scars. So many. His thick black hair has fallen over his forehead, and the angles in his face are sharper than any blade. His aroused and apparently huge cock is obvious in the boxers. "You liked it. I heard you scream."

"Did not." I lie.

His arm snakes out to tumble us back onto the bed, and he grips my chin with his thumb and forefinger as he partially covers me with his big body. "Say you liked it."

I blink and parts of me quiver. Yeah. Those parts. "No." I stare up at his burning black eyes. How am I back under him on the bed? Why hadn't I run to the damn bathroom?

"Say it."

My throat dries up. "No." My voice wobbles a little and softens as my heart rate kicks into a higher gear. Even my skin feels sensitized. I need to get away from him.

His gaze doesn't soften. Not a bit. "I'm not that guy, Peaflower."

I try and fail to swallow, trapped in place. "Wh-what guy?"

"The one who'll see your vulnerability and protect it." His finger scrapes roughly across my lips, and somehow, those black eyes darken even more. Deepen. "Give me an inch, and I'll swallow all of you." His voice is guttural. "Now say it."

Feminine instinct slides through me. "Fine. I liked it." When he doesn't even twitch, I sigh. "A little. Not a lot. Now get off me before I scream."

He ducks his head and scrapes his whiskers on my delicate cheek. "You'll be screaming soon enough. My name, that is." With one smooth motion, he releases me and rolls off the bed, landing gracefully on his feet. "Baby, I'm going to fuck you hard next time, and you'll feel me forever. I gave you the truth in the shitty prison, and you made your choice. Now you're mine, Rosalie. In every way that I want you."

My lungs stutter. The muscles across his bare back, covered in scars, shift easily as he prowls to reach for his shirt tossed carelessly over my pink velvet chair next to a bag showing the top of a sketchpad? "You bought a sketchpad?"

He squares his shoulders. "Yep. I like to draw."

That's intriguing. Shouldn't be but is.

Shaking myself out of it, I roll to the side and flee to my bathroom, shutting the door and locking it. Only when I lean back against the worn wood, my heart thundering, do I hear his soft chuckle from the other room.

The low tenor sounds sadistic.

TEN

Alexei

The fact that she thinks a locked door will keep her safe from me is adorable. Last night, I barely slept, unaccustomed to actual silence and a soft bed. Silence doesn't exist in prison. On the rare nights when nobody talked to themselves or yelled in maniacal fits, snores and sleepy grunts still filled the air. I'm used to remaining alert at all times and, apparently, it's going to take time to dream again.

Yet sleeping with a snuggling woman in my arms provided a peace I haven't experienced in way too long. Or perhaps, it's just my woman. I don't remember ever feeling peace like this.

For now, I choose not to examine why I didn't push things with her the night before. I could have. Shit, it's been years since I fucked a woman. But touching her this morning was all about her pleasure.

So much so that she tempts me to be somebody else. Not a killer. It can't happen, and I need to get myself under control before I draw her further into my world. We both need that control.

Last night I proved to both of us that I have it.

I dress in the cheap jeans and leave Rosalie's as quietly as I arrived, climbing down the exterior stairs and avoiding a prickly rosebush at the bottom. Once I retake my organization, I'll need to buy a couple of high-end suits like I used to wear. I even tried one on when buying the jeans. It felt wrong and not just because I lacked the funds to buy it. As if I was a panther trying on a deer skin. Now, in the jeans I bought, I still don't feel like myself. I do know that I'll never wear orange again.

Fuck. I don't know what or who I am or how I should feel. At the moment, the only connection I have with this world, on the outside, is Rosalie. Her scent fills my head, and the sounds of her moans are carried in my chest. Deep. She'll never make that sound for another man. While she remains unaware of that fact, it's absolute. She's my mirror image and doesn't know it. I was wild and had to learn control in prison, and she's way too controlled and needs to embrace her wild side.

I'm going to insist on it.

On the outside, taking back my birthright, I plan to create the very life I should've claimed when I was young and stupid. Carelessly unaware of the dangers around me. But this time, I know what woman I will have beneath me every night. My time with bar girls or bored older women is over.

I know what I want. Who I want.

And I will have her.

Garik is waiting down the street in a dented and rusting Ford truck, its engine running surprisingly smoothly. I slip inside and give him directions. He drives away silently with just one curious look at the pink Victorian home.

Years ago, he picked me up often at random women's homes, but this time is different.

"I'm keeping her."

A light rain begins to fall, and he flicks on the windshield wipers. "Your lawyer?"

"Yeah." It's crucial he know that.

"Okay." It's equally important that he makes the vow I need. Both his expression and his tone remain level. "I'll protect her with my life."

Good.

She's just the beginning. The soft and spirited foundation I plan to hone to retake the empire my father wanted me to run. It's not just birthright. Or revenge. The need, the desperate craving, to put my hands on the amethyst crystals that power Hologrid Hub at a regular interval and not just once, is a physical pain. I'm meant to charge those.

Every time somebody uses the platform or likes or shares, my crystals gain strength. As do I now that I'm connected to the large crystal again. In prison, I paid plenty for amethyst rocks to hide around my cell and made sure the purple ink of my tattoo held crushed-up particles of the purest one I could find. Having that extra protection helped me to stay alive. Even so, I felt the loss of that connection to a larger stone every second.

"Tell me about the meeting tonight." I watch the rain fall. It has been seven years since I felt the tears of the gods. By the look of the bulbous clouds, I'll feel plenty when we arrive at my storage unit.

"I have the eight planning to be at the bar. Three are solid, three are close, and two are unsure but unhappy with your brother."

There isn't a need to remind him that Hendrix is my half brother. "Who's the mole?"

"My guess? Uri Sorokin."

I nod. "He's one of the unsure ones?"

"No. He's solid. But I think he'll turn to you if he sees a good future."

That makes sense. Hendrix isn't going to give up the helm easily, even though I have a stronger connection to the stones than he does. Not once did he visit me in prison, not that I expected it. If he'd gone to prison, I certainly wouldn't have visited him.

His mother arranged for us to be enemies from his birth. "Tell me about Hendrix."

"Don't know much about him," Garik drawls, driving the decrepit truck fast and with ease. "We don't run in the same circles."

No shit. "You've kept an eye on him. What do you know?"

"According to page six of the social register, he's busy representing Hologrid Hub at every high-end function in town. Named one of the ten most eligible bachelors in Silicon Valley, he's still in mourning for his younger brother."

Right. Hendrix and Cal had hated each other. "What number is he?"

"One," Garik says. "Of course, now that you're out, you'll probably end up back on top again."

Like I care about that. Even back in the day, that part of my life amused me. Now it irritates me. "I'm not eligible."

"You're serious about that?"

"Da," I say, dropping into Russian because this matters. I don't believe in love and certainly have no intention of allowing any woman to dissuade me from my path. But there's something about Rosalie Mooncrest that calls to the darkest part of me. I have no clue if she's a decent lawyer and couldn't care less. She's soft and kind, and there's intelligence in her too-blue eyes. Even after one night sleeping next to her, I feel her beneath my skin. The life I'll build will be solid and true, and it'll need goodness in it for my children. I plan to have many to ensure the longevity of Hologrid Hub, and she's the one I want for this life. There's no need for me to question why.

Who cares? It is as it is. I'll have both my personal and professional lives in place, solid, and impenetrable.

Garik hands me his phone. "Here's the latest annual report and stock earnings of Hologrid Hub."

I hold the device and then press on the screen. My phone seven years ago certainly lacked several of these impressive abilities. "I need to update my phone."

"They cost more than a grand these days."

I also need to access my money. Sooner rather than later. I would've given much of it to Garik, if possible, but my greedy stepbrother had managed to have it frozen the second the jury had declared me guilty.

Somebody had gotten to the jurors, because the evidence against me had been full of reasonable doubt. Mostly. I shook myself out of the memories and read through the reports . . . on a screen. Hendrix has done a good job with the company. Not as good as I can do, because he doesn't have the connections with the amethyst servers that run through my blood faster than any electrical charge.

Hologrid Hub uses a next-gen platform so users can meet in holographic form and do whatever they want with one other. There's a sexual component to the platform that has not been explored enough, and I plan to change that. The more users to the platform, the more power to my amethysts, which leads to more power and strength, not to mention health, for me. I won't live forever, but I also won't be struck down by disease or deterioration too soon.

I finish reading as Garik takes another turn into the northern part of San Francisco and a rough looking storage facility with multiple pods, once painted white that now has rust scarring down each face. "Who killed Cal?"

Garik lifts one shoulder. "Not sure. Your younger half brother had a problem with women telling him no. Your stepmother had to settle several assault cases against him, and those that couldn't be settled . . ."

No doubt Hendrix or his enforcers had taken care of the problem. "Has Hendrix discovered the killer?" If so, surely he killed them.

"Hell if I know."

I thought through what Rosalie had said about Thorn Beathach possibly killing Cal. Beathach runs Malice Media, which is currently in the number one spot. It's a next generation platform that uses neural interface tech to share thoughts, emotions, and experiences directly. In other words, it translates neural data into shareable formats. His AI is more advanced than mine—for now. "What about Thorn Beathach?"

Garik nods. "Maybe. The gossip rags hinted at an arranged marriage between Cal and Alana Beaumont, and now she's living with Beathach. Word is out that if anybody touches her, they die and not quickly. She's under his protection."

Alana has always had protection. Her family owns

Aquarius Social, an emotion sharing based platform. They're currently in second place, and Thorn's company, Malice Media, in first. Are they going to combine their platforms? I don't see how, but it's something to consider.

I dig deep to see if I have a need to avenge Cal's death. Maybe. I hated him, but we shared blood.

However, I have more urgent matters to handle. Irritation cuts through me at my lack of a following. If I make a proclamation about Rosie's safety, it might plant a bull's-eye on her back. I need to consolidate power fast, and that means spilling blood. A lot of it. "You ready for this?"

"I've been ready since they took you away in chains." Garik pulls to a stop in front of the storage unit at the end. Rust scars the door in stripes reminiscent of a panther's claws. Dents punctuate the bottom, and if a storage unit could look lonely, it does. "I hope you have piles of cash in there. Jewels too. Maybe some silver?"

I open the door and step out into the rain. "If I had cash in here, you'd have cash."

A quick flash of emotion crosses his broad face before he masks it. "You need me to stay?"

"No. Thanks. See you tonight." I shut the door and turn toward the unit.

He drives off, leaving me in the quiet area with the rain. I lift my face and allow the liquid to slide down the planes of my face with a sense of freedom very few can understand. The wind whistles between the units; a forlorn sound that still beats any cacophony found within prison walls.

Alone. It's the first time since they shackled me that I really feel alone. There's no alone time in prison. Not really. The sense of desperation within those locked places makes its own sound.

I allow the rain to land on my mouth and tongue, tasting freedom.

And the hint of vengeance.

I don't know who ensured I languished behind bars, but I will find them. Then they'll wish for me to send them to prison.

I won't.

God, I won't. I gave up on God a long time ago, but if there's any such deity, even He will fail to protect those who betrayed me. Only someone close to me, a being with access to me, could've ensured I was found guilty. For them, I'll be the judge, jury, and fucking executioner.

I make the vow as the rain pummels down, drenching me. My T-shirt molds to my chest and my jeans to my legs. The boots I wear are leather and new with a rough edge.

Finally, I lean down and flick open a carefully hidden keypad before punching in my code. A lock releases. Grunting, I grasp the handle and lift the door, allowing natural light to illuminate the narrow space.

She's still here. My MV Agusta Brutale 1000 Serie Oro—black with a hint of red and so sleek she purrs like a genuine animal. Calling her a motorcycle is an insult I've never issued. She's a goddess on two wheels.

Moving to the rear of the structure, I find my weathered backpack with the two loaded guns in it. Good. I shove them both at the back of my waist and pull my jacket down to cover them. They'll need to be cleaned and oiled as soon as possible, but for now, having their weight against my skin grounds me. I left the older Beretta at Rosalie's home under her frilly bed.

I can't count the number of enemies coming for me right now, and that's not even considering the kill list from my old prison pal. His gang will be dangerous to me if he gives the order, at least until I have my men back in place. But I'd rather prevent a full-out war on the streets of Palo Alto. Plus, a deal is a deal.

I need to receive that list now to handle those kills before the authorities put a tail on me, which should happen any moment. Not that I couldn't ditch one, but even so, the clock is counting down quickly.

A crow cries in the distance, and I pause, waiting to make sure I'm alone. The surrounding area falls silent without a hint of tension.

I roll the bike out and throw a leg over her, flicking on the engine. She purrs to life like she's been waiting for me, and the rumble between my thighs feels like an unstoppable energy.

I twist the throttle and drive through the silent structures, finally reaching the quiet main road. Then I take her wide open.

The wind and rain battle me, battle us, but we stay the course.

Freedom rushes through me. This feeling—I'll never lose. Not again. Not a chance.

I'll take them all out, reclaim my birthright, put Rosalie in place, and then live my life.

At any cost.

ELEVEN
Rosalie

Having finished my breakfast of one healthy apple, I precariously balance my latte in one hand and my briefcase in the other as I approach my office door, before Joseph Cage slides out of a conference room down the hallway.

He moves toward me, his gaze sweeping me head to toe. "Rosalie, good morning."

"Good morning," I say, the hot coffee beginning to burn my hand through the cardboard wrap.

He looks me over again. "You look fantastic today."

I'd hurriedly tossed on taupe-colored slacks and a white blouse, hoping I remembered to leave a blazer in my office just in case I unexpectedly get called into court today. I'm wearing a simple angelite mirrored pendant and matching earrings because Alana had once told me that angelite is my stone. "Thanks." I begin to move past him.

He grasps my arm. "Would you like to accompany me to dinner tonight?"

I look up at his handsome face. "We tried that. Remember?"

"Yeah, but," he looks me over again, "I don't know. You seem different."

I try not to blush, I really do, but heat fills my face. I do not want to think about why I look different. "The answer is no." I move past him and walk into my office. I can hear him hesitate in the hallway, his breath nearly ragged, and then he stomps away.

"What a jackass." A familiar head emerges from the other side of my desk.

I gasp. "Alana?"

"Yeah." She shoves herself out from where she's apparently been hiding beneath my desk. "How are you?" She smiles wide and hurries around toward me.

"Good. Let me put this coffee down before I burn one of us." I place the mug on my glass desk and drop my briefcase before embracing my best friend in a hug. I then look surreptitiously around. "Wait a minute, you're here without bodyguards."

She snorts. "It took me a while to evade them, but I finally made it." She grasps my hand and pulls me over to the small area holding a leather sofa and matching chair. "How are you? I feel like I haven't talked to you in forever."

"It's been a week." I smile and take a seat. I've missed her. Her sparkling, greenish-blue eyes light with mischief, and she's pulled her mahogany hair up in a ponytail. For her escape today, she's wearing jeans and a simple white sweater.

"I don't even have my phone," she says, smiling.

I laugh. "You're not going into withdrawals?" As the face of Aquarius Social and now, somewhat, Malice Media, the woman is always on social media.

She nods. "Oh, yeah. They can track you through phones, you know. Besides, Cousin Scarlett is taking on a lot more of the Aquarius Social work now that I'm engaged to Thorn, and I even have her charging some of the crystals just in case. It's difficult going back and forth."

"I can't imagine," I say honestly. The two corporations are clear rivals, and she has to feel torn once in a while. There's not a doubt in my mind that she'll choose Thorn if it comes down to it, which is probably why she's training her cousin Scarlett to take over for her. "Does Scarlett have half of the power you do with charging the aquamarines?" Aquarius, of course, runs on aquamarine crystals.

Alana nods. "Actually, she's much better than I would've thought. The more she works with it, the better she'll get. Thorn and I are thinking about taking an extended vacation after the wedding, so we'll need to leave other people in charge of the corporations."

"That makes sense." Of course, she has been hiding beneath my desk all morning waiting for me. It's a good thing she doesn't want to escape Thorn for long . . . because I'm not sure she can.

She studies me. "You look different. What's up?"

Seriously? I appear different to everybody after having just one mind-blowing orgasm that morning with Alexei? "I have no idea," I say. "Maybe I got extra sleep last night." More heat climbs into my face.

"What are you hiding?" While Alana looks like a simple party girl if she wants to online, she's actually one of the smartest people I've ever met. It's impossible to get anything past her.

"I'm not hiding anything," I say smoothly, definitely not wanting to discuss Alexei right now. "I would like to know how you got in here. It's not a surprise to me that you escaped your bodyguards, but last time I checked, we have security on the main floor."

She shrugs one delicate shoulder. "Oh, please. I smiled at your security guy, and he knows we're best friends. It's not like he doesn't follow me on social media."

"Good point." I have missed her. She's been so busy the last week, as have I.

She leans toward me. "Is it true that you got Alexei Sokolov out of prison?"

I nod. "For now. I'm sure there'll be another trial, and I'm awaiting the prosecution's filing on that."

She clasps her hands in her lap. "Rosie, I don't know. He seems dangerous."

I burst out laughing. I can't help it. "Unlike Thorn Beathach?"

She rolls her eyes. "I'm not saying that Thorn is a safe kind of guy, but . . ."

"But what?"

She chews on her lip. "But we're on the same side now. Are you and Alexei on the same side?"

"Most certainly not," I say instantly.

She leans back and studies me. "What aren't you telling me?"

My phone buzzes on my desk, but I don't want to leave the comfort of the sofa. "Yes, Eloise?" I call out.

"There's a Miss Rendale here to see you," my administrative assistant calls back, having no problem bellowing through hallways.

"Send her my way," I yell. I look at Alana.

She shrugs. "I may have texted Ella that we'd be here."

Ella soon fills the doorway. Well, it's more accurate to say that Ella soon stands in the doorway. At five feet tall and probably one hundred and five pounds soaking wet, she looks more like Tinkerbell than the dangerous computer hacker we both know her to be.

"Alana," she cries out and rushes forward, almost tackling Alana into the sofa. "It's been forever." After hugging Alana, Ella turns to me. "I just saw you a couple days ago, but I miss the three of us being together."

"As do I," I say. Before Alana and Thorn had gotten together, we'd meet often, late at night in a secret basement room of Alana's apartment building to work on charitable programs. "I miss our late nights," I add. How much ice cream had we eaten during those nights, anyway?

Alana's face falls. "I do, too, but I no longer need to sneak money from my trust fund in order to pay for all of these charities. Thorn is more than happy to do so." Even though it's a kindness, she looks forlorn.

"We'll figure out something the three of us can do." Ella plops herself on the seat facing us. "I'm not sure what, though." She glances at me. "You need any help? Rumor has it you got the Sokolov heir out of prison. You want me to put him back in?"

"Maybe," I say, thinking of that morning and how he forced an orgasm on me. Yeah. That's what had happened. "First, I need to figure out who set him up, and then we'll see."

She leans forward. "Are you serious?" Her blue eyes sparkle.

"No," I grumble. "I'd never put an innocent person in prison."

"All right, what's going on?" Ella studies me.

Alana chuckles. "For a lawyer, you really don't have a very good poker face."

"Fine." I relent and tell them about the events of the morning. Alana's mouth gapes open while Ella's shuts tight, making her lips almost white.

"We should kill him," she finally says.

Alana snorts. "I don't know. I've never seen Rosalie look this relaxed."

I punch her in the arm, not too lightly.

"Ow," Alana says. "See what I'm saying?"

Ella frowns. "Is he charging the crystals at Hologrid Hub?"

"No," Alana and I both say in unison.

"He's not," I add quickly.

Alana shakes her head. "Please do not create another virus. You nearly killed Thorn."

Ella doesn't look the slightest bit abashed about the situation. "I didn't know you were going to fall in love with him," she protests. "If I had, I wouldn't have tried to kill the guy." She shifts her gaze to me. "I can, however, take out Alexei once he starts charging the Hologrid Hub crystals if you like. I mean, if he starts charging their amethysts."

"I will absolutely keep that in mind." I mean it. Ella discovered how to poison a crystal so it would then poison the person charging it and had nearly killed Thorn. Of course, we all considered him an enemy at that point.

Alana clears her throat. "I really can have Alexei taken care of if you want."

I cut my eyes at her. "I do not want Thorn killing Alexei. At least not tonight. I have a job to do, and this will get me that office on the top floor. Plus, I do believe the man was set up." I took an oath with my law license to right wrongs.

Today, Ella is dressed in a cute green dress with light silver pumps. She crosses her legs. "I like your outfit, but the jacket sleeves are a little too long."

"I haven't had a chance to trim them," I say easily.

Alana shifts her weight. "Do you need a loan?"

"No, but thank you," I say. Alana has always been generous with her money, and I've worked overtime to keep from taking advantage from her. Now the money would actually come from Thorn, and I don't want to owe him a thing. I assume the head of the Irish mob has no problem calling in dangerous and possibly illegal favors. Ella hasn't had a lot of money, either. Her stepmother paid for her boarding school and college, and her trust fund allotted her a set amount each year until her stepmother decided to end the trust.

As if following my train of thought, Ella sighs. "If I had any extra, I'd give it. In fact, it's time for us to sue for my trust fund."

I nod, already having had drafted the documents a year ago. But why now? "Do you think you're in danger?"

Ella shrugs. "I don't know. If anybody makes a move on me, it will be too obvious who. Yet sometimes I wonder, you know? She'll come for me someday, or maybe I'll go for her."

I believe that Ella has plans to take out her stepmother and stepsisters, at least financially. She's the smartest hacker around and she's trained all over the world. She has, however, neglected to share any plans with us. It could be because someday, I'll have to serve as her lawyer, and I can have no prior knowledge of her planning to commit crimes. At least that's what I tell myself.

There's a rustle and then a murmur down the hallway,

and then a couple of shouts. "Ah, crap." Alana shakes her head. "Well, this was fun. I enjoyed seeing both of you."

I look up to the doorway as Thorn Beathach strides inside. Even after watching him and Alana be together for the last three months, the sight of him catches me off guard. He's tall and broad and was probably quite handsome before being scarred completely across his face and down his neck. I have to admit to myself that he's still handsome.

Right now, his eyes are pissed. "Alana?"

She stands and smiles. "I just went for a walk. I have no idea where the bodyguards got to, Thorn."

He lifts one dark eyebrow, and the air in the room chills. I have to admire her bravado though. Not much scares Alana. "I see. We'll discuss this at home." Thorn takes two graceful steps inside my office, ducks his head, and instantly tosses her over his shoulder.

"This is absolutely not necessary," she says, her long hair hanging down before she punches him in his upper thigh.

"I believe it is." He smacks her butt hard enough to echo around the office.

"Want me to try and kill him again?" Ella offers.

Alana chuckles.

Thorn turns his dark gaze on her, and she gulps. "I believe our deal was for you to do some work for Malice Media."

"I did for almost two weeks." She lifts her chin. "Your brother chased me off."

"Huh." Thorn looks incredibly dangerous in my doorway. "Keep away from Justice. I think he wants to return the favor of you trying to kill me."

"I know he does," Ella spits. "You keep your brother

away from me. I have better ways of getting to people than just by messing with their crystals."

I have to give her props. I don't know many people who would dare threaten Thorn. Of course, he currently holds our best friend over his shoulder.

"I'll have Justice contact you," he says smoothly and with a smile that is anything but.

She faces him but remains silent.

He nods to me. "Rosalie, if you need any help with this Alexei issue, let me know. I'll have it taken care of." With that, he turns and strides out of my office with Alana over his shoulder.

Ella shakes her head. "You know, sometimes I think I should probably infect his crystals again."

"Alana loves him," I remind her.

Ella drops back into her chair, her lips turning down. "Yeah, I know. I don't get it. Do you?"

Truth be told, I hadn't. But after this morning, I think I have an inkling.

Another rustle echoes down the hallway. "What now?" Ella pales. "You don't suppose that stupid Justice is coming after me?"

I stand. "I hope not." As Alexei Sokolov completely fills my doorway, I change my mind. I do wish Justice Beathach was standing there. My knees wobble and my chin shoots up so I can better glare at him.

His smile holds so much sin, butterflies rip through my abdomen.

TWELVE
Rosalie

My breath catches and I stand as Alexei walks inside, followed by my secretary, my paralegal, and a couple of junior attorneys.

"Sir, you cannot just barge in here," Eloise sputters.

"It's okay." I have to admit, she's looking at him with more curiosity than anger, as are the other three. "Mr. Sokolov is a client, and he's welcome anytime. Everybody return to work." I infuse my voice with as much authority as I can manage, considering I'm now blushing head to toe, at least I assume I am from how heated my skin gets.

Ella stands and partially puts her tiny body between me and Alexei, as if instinctively knowing to do so. I introduce them.

He smiles, all deadly charm, looking dangerous in his leather jacket. "Miss Rendale," he says, "it's nice to meet you. Rumor has it you were once the heir to TimeGem Moments."

"I'm still the heir." She briskly shakes his hand.

TimeGem Moments is currently ranked fourth out of the big social media companies, and it allows users to share memories in real-time. It's pretty fascinating, really, and if Ella ever manages to wrestle the company away from her stepmother and stepsisters, she'll take the entire platform to mighty heights.

She looks back at me. "I'm busy tonight, but should we hit a couple of clubs tomorrow?"

"Sounds good," I say. "It's been too long. We'll see if we can get Alana out without a million bodyguards."

"Ha. Good luck with that, but we'll still try." Ella turns around and hugs me before heading toward the door. "Call me if you need me."

"Thanks." I don't blame her for fleeing.

She's great at computers, but not so wonderful with people. She gives Alexei what could only be considered a warning glare before turning and stomping out of my office.

I cross my arms. "I don't believe we have an appointment."

His smile barely moves the hard planes of his face. "Like you said, I'm welcome anytime." He glances around my office. "We should start preparing my case."

"I've already created a trial binder." Even in the generic but bad boy clothing, he somehow appears wealthy. As if he's just dressing down for the day. I have to admit, he's mouthwateringly sexy. "Follow me." I reach for my now cooled-off latte and walk toward him, my knees trembling. "I have a war room set up in the smaller conference room down the way."

He moves to the side and allows me to pass. The heat from his body washes over me, and I shiver, masking the obvious tell by taking a drink of the coffee. He follows me silently down the hallway, and I turn into the smallest conference room where my paralegal organized stacks of files with trial transcripts, depositions, evidence files, and pictures already taped to a board.

"What's your plan?" He shuts the door, enclosing us.

Heat swells from him and instantly charges the room.

"First, we need to get a couple of issues straight. One, you're moving out of my place. Two, you're never to touch me again. Got it?" I move to cross around the table.

He grasps the side of my waist with one hand, lifts, and easily plants me on the table. "No."

My jaw drops open, and I set the coffee roughly down. How did he do that with one hand? My breath catches and not in the way I want. So I clear my throat. "I'm not giving you a choice."

He moves in, his hips spreading my thighs, and leans over me until I fall back onto my elbows. What in the world is he doing? We're at my office and anybody could walk by the conference room windows.

His eyes glitter. "You might want to rethink your approach. If bringing you to orgasm is the only way to gain your cooperation, I'll get to it right now."

I stare up at his onyx eyes, feeling devoured. The man makes up his own rules and society's be damned. My lungs stutter, and even with my body lighting on fire, a new fear fuels through me.

A light flickers in those eyes. Just for a fleeting second. "You want a choice in this?" he rumbles.

I gape at that statement. "I-I do have a choice in this." What an asshole.

"You really don't, but I'll let you get there yourself." He steps back and gently tugs my skirt back down almost to my knees. "Nothing goes farther between us until you ask for it." He moves away, and an irritating coolness washes over me.

I push myself off the table and shove hair out of my face. It's time to regain control of this situation. "I want to go over your version of what happened the night of David Fairfax's murder." My nipples sharpening, I stride around the table and roll out one of the plush brown leather chairs. "Then we need an alternate theory of who killed David."

"I have a lot of alternate theories." Alexei pulls out a chair across from me.

Good. So he's going to be somewhat agreeable.

"Also," I clear my throat, "since we now understand the agreement between us, and I'll never make a move, you need to find a different place to stay."

"I've already given you the parameters. I'm staying with you, and when you make the choice, there's no going back. So take your time," he says mildly, cocking his head to look at the pictures Eloise taped to a board of him, Blythe Fairfax, David Fairfax, Garik Petrov, Hendrix Sokolov and Cal Sokolov. Off to the side are taped pictures of the prosecuting attorney, the judge, and Miles Molasses from my firm.

I take a deep breath—one fight at a time. "You mentioned that Miles Molasses from my firm was dirty?"

Alexei's upper lip quirks. "He must've been because he sucked as a lawyer."

Miles had made mistakes in trial, but nothing horrible. "Any other reason you made the accusation?"

"I said Miles worked with the prosecuting attorney and judge to get me convicted. I had a feeling at the time because he didn't do a very good job, but rumors abound in prison. When the judge and prosecuting attorney were taken down, those rumors flew wild. The three were friends."

"I'll need to hire a private investigator to look into this."

Alexei settles back in his seat as if he owns the room. "First thing we do is release my financial accounts."

I nod. "I'm having my paralegal draft up the paperwork right now. We have a good argument that you need the funds for a decent defense."

Apparently, the trust holds a morality clause, and so when Alexei had been convicted, Lillian had been able to freeze the funds. Now that he's been freed, I should be able to make those available to him.

I reach for a legal notepad. "How much are we talking about?"

He lifts one careless shoulder. "It depends on how well the fund has done while I've been in prison. I haven't received statements. But there were about two billion dollars in it before then."

I cough and look up, my eyes wide. "Two billion?"

He shrugs as if that kind of money is no big deal. "Yes."

"Man, we live a different life," I mutter, making notes on the notepad. "All right, in your own words, tell me what happened from the night before to the morning that David Fairfax was killed."

Alexei, quite understandably, had not testified, nor had he said a word to the police, according to the police reports I have already read through.

His fingers drum quietly on the heavy mahogany conference table, and he looks up to stare at Blythe Fairfax's picture. "I worked with Garik at the bar that night. We were drunk. We sang some tunes. Blythe met me there, we went back to her place, and I stayed the night."

I lean back in my chair, inexplicably and unreasonably jealous. "How long did you date?"

"Date?" He chuckles. "We didn't exactly date."

I hold on to my patience with both hands. "All right. How long did you have a sexual relationship with Mrs. Fairfax?"

He sighed. "I don't know, maybe three months. It wasn't serious."

"Three months is a long time for you, as far as I can tell from my research," I say. "The relationship must've been somewhat serious."

He glances away from the picture and back at me, piercing me with those dark eyes. "Maybe. I wasn't planning on marrying her or anything, but there was something more there than usual."

I ignore another unreasonable spurt of jealousy. "What happened that night?"

"Like I said, we went back to her place, fucked all night, and I got up and left in the morning." His voice hardens.

Does he still care for her? "How did you get home?"

"My bike. I followed her from the bar to her place."

I cock my head. "You ride a motorcycle?" Not only hadn't I read that fact in any of his files, I never noted it in media write-ups about him.

"Yes." His jaw appears made from stone.

So the bike is a sensitive issue to him? Who is this man? "Where was Mr. Fairfax while you were fucking his wife all night?"

My crude repeat of his words has his lips curving again. "Fairfax was out of town at a business meeting. Well, at least we thought," Alexei says evenly, looking like a lounging panther in a chair. One not quite tame.

I take a calming breath. "Okay. What time did you leave that morning?"

"Around six. I headed to my place, showered and

changed before going to work and charging the crystals at Hologram Hub."

"How often do you need to charge those crystals, and how long did the process take that time?"

He looks up and to the left, as if trying to remember. "The crystals require recharging every two weeks, absent a cyberattack or a system overload. Then they require more attention, obviously. That time? I stopped in my office, read through some financials, then went down and charged for about an hour."

"So we're talking, what, maybe about eleven o'clock is when you finished?" I scribble the timeline into my notes.

"Around that," he says.

I look up, curious. Alana has always remained tight-lipped about the process, and Alexei seems more open to discussion. "Does charging the stones drain you?"

"No. It's an exchange of energy, meaning I end up charged as well. I feel stronger the second I connect."

Fascinating. "What happened after you charged the amethysts that day?"

"Then I received a text from Blythe saying she was at Pilates and asking if I wanted to meet her at her place for lunch."

The way he said the word caught my ears.

"Lunch," I say sarcastically.

His grin shows sharpened teeth. "We would have eaten at some point."

This guy really is an asshole. I fight the urge to pinch the bridge of my nose because a headache is definitely coming my way. "So what then?"

"Since this was a customary practice of ours, I jumped on my bike, and I headed to Blythe's."

"Was she at home when you arrived?"

He steeples his fingers beneath his chin, giving him a contemplative look that somehow appears dangerous. As if he's plotting. "You know she wasn't, if you've already read the files."

"Then how did you get in?"

"I knew the gate code," he replies smoothly. "I opened it and drove up to the front. I also knew the front door code, and I walked inside."

So they were closer than he'd insinuated. "Then what did you do?"

He shrugs. "I called out for Blythe, realized she wasn't home yet, and so I went to the kitchen to get myself a drink."

I pause, waiting. Years ago, I learned a good interviewing technique is to just pause and let people talk. Alexei stares at me, not saying a word. Perhaps he knows the same technique.

"Continue," I prod curtly.

"Then I found Fairfax stabbed to death on the kitchen floor." Alexei looks away as if remembering. "There was blood everywhere. So I took a step back, planning to leave, and the housekeeper walked in through the garage door, her arms full of groceries. She screamed, dropped the groceries, and ran back outside before I could stop her."

I gulp. "What would you have done if you could have stopped her?"

"It doesn't matter. The front door opened, and Blythe came in, running toward the kitchen after having heard the screams."

"How do you know she wasn't there before you?" I ask quickly.

He shrugs. "Her car wasn't in the drive when I arrived but was when the police escorted me so nicely out."

"Do you think she could have killed her husband and then cleaned it up?"

"I don't know," he admits. "It wouldn't surprise me. She inherited his entire estate upon his death. If I recall, it was fairly lucrative."

"Yeah, like millions." I shake my head. "So the housekeeper called the police and what did you and Blythe do?"

"Blythe paled and almost passed out, so I took her into the other room and sat her down. Got us both a bourbon and we drank them quickly as we waited for the police."

I reach for a file folder and flip it open. "Your fingerprints were found all over the counter and on the fridge."

"No shit. I was there a lot."

I turn a page. "The murder weapon was a knife from their utensil drawer. It was found thrown in the pond out back."

He snorts. "I didn't touch that knife that day, and I sure as hell didn't throw it in the pond out back."

"It has your fingerprints on it," I say, reading through.

"Rosalie," he says softly.

I look up at him.

"Do you really think I was stupid enough to leave my prints on a murder weapon and then throw it in a pond located on the estate of the deceased?"

I truly don't, but maybe there hadn't been time between the housekeeper calling the police and their arrival. I read through more notes. "Blythe said you left her while she was drinking her bourbon."

He runs a rough hand through his hair. "I went to check on the housekeeper because she was shrieking at the top of her lungs, still in the garage. The woman had actually grabbed a mop to start cleaning up. I stopped her, I sat her down on the steps in the garage, and then I returned to check on Blythe and wait for the police."

I read through the notes again. The investigating officer had been a Detective Battlement, and he had precise, neat penmanship. "So there was time for you to take a knife and throw it in the pond."

"Sure," Alexei agrees, "but like I said, I wouldn't do that. That was stupid."

"Maybe you panicked."

His chin drops slightly, and he stares at me. "Unlikely."

Alexei Sokolov does not seem like a man who would panic, even back then.

"If you didn't kill him, who did?"

"That's the question, isn't it, Peaflower? I have a feeling we're going to need to figure that out if we're going to get anywhere with this."

The man has a point. I reach for another file folder. "Let's discuss the judge and the prosecuting attorney. Who could have bribed them?" I need to figure out exactly what they did to ensure Alexei's conviction, and then I should investigate my colleague, Miles. "What do you think?"

Alexei shrugs. "That's a long list. That would include everybody from my family to anybody I pissed off, to the rival social media company owners. We better unfreeze those funds fast."

I nod. "We're going to need more than one private investigator."

He smiles. "All right. This has been productive. How about you and I go grab lunch now?"

There's no doubt in my mind he does not mean *lunch*.

THIRTEEN
Alexei

Hot, red, poisonous biting ants are crawling beneath my skin, shredding layer after layer as they tunnel through my flesh. The elevator door opens, and I manacle Rosalie's hand, yanking her into the quiet parking garage.

"Hey." She tries to pull away, surprise in her tone.

I'm done. Finished being inside four walls. Any walls. We ordered lunch in and worked on my case until about five, and then my throat started to close. So I keep her hand. Her skin is soft and cool, calming enough to tether me to this world. For now.

"Alexei." She sets her feet to stop me. "I forgot my phone upstairs."

I keep us moving, maneuvering between cars until reaching my bike. Replaying the day that my freedom ended, over and over for her today, had an inferno boiling in my gut. Relating my unfortunate vulnerability to Rosalie specifically had poured oil on those flames. "Get on."

"No." She uses her free hand to push against my ribs.

I turn, lowering my head toward hers, fire burning

through me. "Get. On. The. Bike." My voice is a low growl, and even I don't recognize it. Then I straddle the bike, still holding her hand.

Her blue eyes widen, and her pupils contract. "I don't—"

I twist my torso, snatch her waist, lift her, and plant her on the back in one easy motion. I can't breathe. Can barely think. Yanking the key from my front pocket, I slam it into place and twist. The engine ignites and roars awake between my thighs. I enable the launch motion with my right thumb, use my left hand to pull the clutch, and engage the first gear with my foot for a fast takeoff.

Rosalie yelps and grabs my ribcage under my jacket with both hands, scooting closer to me.

I zip through the parking garage and out onto the street, letting the bike have her lead.

Wind whips against my face, and I partially lift, feeling freedom. Finally, I can take a deep breath. Cars honk as I zip between them, noting how perfectly Rosalie fits her legs against mine.

The woman is a natural.

When I move, she moves. Perfect unison. I steer away from the busy street onto side streets, leaving the city. My heart finally slows to a normal rhythm. As the sound of horns and screeching brakes fade away, I notice her yelling at me. Well, against me, her mouth to the back of my jacket.

When we reach a quiet warehouse district, I slow and partially turn my head. "What are you yelling about?"

"You fucking fuck head," she screams, digging her nails into my skin.

Fascinating. I turn another corner and slow down near a rusting metal warehouse labeled 'Bob's.' I have no idea who Bob is, but he's definitely not around right now. The garage doors are shut tight, and darkness shows through the grimy window of the man-sized door. Water drips from the roof to the battered asphalt from the rain of last night, the sound forlorn.

So I pull to a stop.

She retracts her nails, pulls her hands free of my jacket, and then smacks my back. "You're such a complete dick." Grasping my jacket, she swings off the bike and takes several steps away, her chest rising and falling rapidly.

Fuck, she's beautiful.

Her black hair is a wild mess around her flushed face, and the blue of her eyes defies description. Somehow, her white blouse and tan trousers still look pressed.

"What's wrong?" I drawl, twisting the key and silencing the powerful engine.

Her chin drops. "Wrong? What's wrong?" Her mouth opens slightly as she tries to draw in air. "We don't have helmets," she says in a rush.

Helmets? Amusement clashes through me. The real kind. I blink the sensation away, because liking her isn't a risk I'll take. Oh, she'll be mine in every sense possible, and I'll protect her with my life. But liking her isn't going to happen. "You're safe."

"Safe?" she screeches.

I hold back a wince. That's an impressive decibel she hit. "Yes."

She looks erratically around. For what? Safety? There isn't any from me. "You prick," she snaps.

"There's nowhere to go."

"I'm looking for something to hit you with," she snarls, her teeth a flash of white between her cherry-red lips.

My dick goes rock hard. "Use your fists," I say softly.

She blinks.

Smart girl.

I keep her in my sights, noting everything from her rapid breathing to her parted lips. She's scared. And aroused. Confused about both feelings. "Come on, Rosalie," I coax. "I'll give you one clean punch. Won't even try to stop you."

She swallows and looks at my jaw. It's not made of glass, and she'll probably break her knuckles if she tries. Her sense of preservation must be pretty decent, because she doesn't.

The hair on the back of my neck rises. Slowly, I turn to look the way we came. Silence. Heavy silence.

"Get back on the bike." I twist the key, going cold.

"No," she yells, stomping one foot.

A car careens around the farthest warehouse. It's a nondescript brown Chevy with the windows tinted dark enough to hide its occupants. The same one as the other day when I was shot.

"Now," I yell.

She looks at me, at the car, and then barrels into motion, jumping on behind me.

I launch the bike nearly into the air, driving out of Bob's alcove away from the car. A bullet whizzes by my ear. Shit. I turn between two warehouses, increasing our speed, turning again as soon as I can. I keep to the narrow alleys between warehouses, and the car holds pace, the passenger shooting as it speeds by at the far end. There's only one way out of this area, and I'm sure somebody remained behind in case we make it that far.

I flip around a broad, gray warehouse into an even smaller alleyway, pivoting at the last building and seeing what I need. I zip in front of several warehouses and right into an open doorway before immediately turning off the bike. Silence echoes around us. Turning to wrap an arm around Rosalie's waist, I swivel us both off the bike.

Moldy and torn boxes line one filthy wall, while only dirt and garbage cover the crumbling concrete floor.

"Stay here." I can hear the car coming closer, so I run outside and shut the door before she can answer. It hangs haphazardly in place, not coming close to fully closing.

My gun already in my hand, I careen toward a burned-out steel building that only retains a shallow shell.

The car's brakes squeal as it turns around a building and then heads straight for me. I drop and roll on the pavement, coming up and firing rapidly at the driver. The front windshield explodes, and the car jerks wildly to the side, smashing into a stone pillar that crumbles almost instantly. I jump to my feet, lift my gun, and keep firing toward the passenger-side window.

Nobody moves.

The car's engine continues rumbling as the wheels turn uselessly, burning rubber.

I keep my back to the building as I angle closer, gun out, wishing for a blade in my boot. I'm out of bullets. Reaching the car, I use the bottom of my shirt to pull open the passenger-side door. A man falls out, and I step back, letting his head and shoulders hit the ground. His eyes are wide in death, and blood covers the lower half of his face and chest. I glance to see the driver slumped over the steering wheel, the back of his head a bloody mess.

They both wear black suits and bloodied pants, and neither is breathing.

I glance quickly into the back seat to find it empty. Tucking my weapon at my waist, I scan the area. It's desolate and deserted, and right now, the only sounds are the engine and the drip, drip, drip of forgotten rain off rooftops compounded by the eerie whistle of wind.

Using my boot, I kick the guy on the ground to partially roll him over onto his shoulders. His legs remain in the car. I frown and squint. I know this guy. Dmitry Egorov. In his late sixties, at least, he's a Shestyorka—a low level errand boy. Who sent him to kill me? Hendrix or his mother? Or is somebody else in the organization making a move? Now would be a good time, since Hendrix and I will blame each other. This man is not an inspiring choice. Nobody will miss him.

Is there a contract out on me? I'm not surprised if there is more than one.

I claim his Makarov pistol from his limp hand and check the clip. Eight rounds. It must be a fresh clip. Excellent. I slam it into place before walking around to the other side of the still-running car, the engine grinding noisily.

Using my shirt, I open the other door and shove an elbow into the driver's face, pushing him back. I don't recognize this one. His black hair has gray at the temples, and if he's in the local Russian mob, I should know him, but I don't. I don't like that. Several shots had hit his face, but still, there should be something familiar about him. I push him to the side and look down at his back pockets, not surprised to see them empty. These guys didn't bring ID.

Grunting, I twist the keys and shut off the engine.

I crouch, and still keeping my hand covered by my jacket, click the button to release the trunk. I'd search these guys, but no way do they even have a phone, so I stand again and walk around to find two AK-47s in the trunk, along with several soiled and oil-covered rags.

Using the rags, I lift the AK-47s and look around. I'm not comfortable carrying these on the bike, so I lope into a jog toward the end of the warehouse district, find one of many abandoned warehouses, this one with a pink roof that was probably red metal at one point. I kick open the door to find it empty, save for battered and dented appliances scattered throughout. I hide the AK-47s behind a scratched light-blue electric stove before emerging outside again.

This time I move quieter toward a taller warehouse with a rickety ladder on the backside. Using the rags to cover my fingerprints, I climb to the top and then shimmy on my belly toward the other side. Then I wait. The exit to this warehouse area is barely two lanes with scrub grass and shrubs on either side.

I take a deep breath and then exhale, calming my senses, and then I wait and I watch. Finally, something moves to the right. I wondered how long the lookout would wait. Surely he had heard the firefight, and his friends had not returned.

He finally stands and looks around.

I recognize him. His name is Igor, and his father is the dead passenger. I remember him as a kid. He's about three years older than me and has always been an asshole. Lifting a phone to his ear, he speaks too softly for me to hear.

The phone has to be a burner.

Tucking it into his front pocket, he looks around and lights a cigarette. Not only is he an asshole, he's a moron. Even if I reclaim ownership of the local Russian mob, I don't want this guy.

We're close enough he should be looking up to make sure he's not being watched. He doesn't bother. I pull the Makarov to the side, balance the weapon on the edge of the roof, and fire twice.

His head explodes like a melon, and he falls.

I wait a while longer, but there's nobody else out there. Even so, I crouch low as I turn toward the ladder to climb down, again keeping my prints safely covered by the oily rags. Just as I reach the bottom, I turn and see Rosalie standing in the road, her jaw slack, her face pale, and her eyes wide as she stares at the man I just shot.

Well. Shit.

FOURTEEN
Rosalie

Bile rises in my throat, and I swallow rapidly, trying to keep lunch in my stomach. It's impossible to think clearly right now. I won't say my upbringing was sheltered, but I haven't seen violence like this. The body by the road doesn't move. His head exploded like he swallowed a grenade.

No way is he still alive.

There's no expression on Alexei's face as he stares at me, a gun in his hand. I blink. This isn't happening. Slowly I start to back away. He releases the ladder, his gaze intense as he prowls toward me.

I trip over uneven gravel and kick my foot back to regain my balance, my left heel hitting a concrete block. I want to run, but I can't move. His eyes are dark pools with no emotion. Not a speck of blood mars his dark jacket.

"You killed them." I try to shake myself awake.

"Get back to the bike," he orders.

The bike. I'd forgotten all about the bike. "No." I look

frantically around for an escape as adrenaline floods my body through the shock.

He shoves what looks like dirty dishcloths into his pocket before slipping that gun in the front of his waist-band. "Rosalie, we have to get out of here." Without waiting for a response, he grabs my arm and starts pulling me back toward the car of death, his grip relentless.

"No." I panic, pushing against him, kicking him. His stride doesn't shorten, and I have no choice but to follow him before I trip. If I fall, he'll just drag me. I push loosely against him. "Alexei, you killed three men. You're not even supposed to have a gun." I haven't secured him a new trial yet. He's not a felon since the court overturned his conviction, but I bet that gun is not registered.

"We're lucky I have one," he says grimly, so much taller than me that I feel truly vulnerable for the first time.

We reach the vehicle, and he stops before finally look-ing me over head to toe. "What did you touch? You're covered in blood."

"Everything," I explode. "I was trying to find a phone." I checked the two men in the car who were dead and couldn't find any sort of phone to call for help. The images of their wounds and so much blood will haunt me forever, and I try not to look at them now.

Alexei's gaze sweeps me. My hands and white shirt are covered in blood since I tried to stem the bleeding chest of the man half out of the car. Trying to help him had been an instinctual response. When I realized he was dead, I tried to run, keeping close to the warehouse buildings. I hustled toward the main road, hoping I was running in the right direction. I saw the man standing, smoking a cigarette, and then two shots echoed from above me. From Alexei.

He'd killed so easily. So expertly.

He drops his head for a moment and closes his eyes. "You touched everything? You mean your fingerprints are all over that car?"

"Probably." I punch him as hard as I can in the arm, and his grip remains tight.

He waits until I look up at his eyes before he releases me. "Why the hell were you looking in that car? They're obviously dead."

I had tried to save one guy first. "I was looking for a phone to call the police."

Alexei blinks once, very slowly. A pit of dread drops into my stomach.

"The police?" He slowly shakes his head. "Goddamn it, Rosalie." Red spirals across the top of his finely cut cheek-bones and fury lifts his eyes, but his voice remains deadly soft.

I gulp and want to explain myself. But that's just wrong, so I remain silent. Who is this man? I scan for an escape route and only see dilapidated buildings and torn-up asphalt. There's nowhere for me to run.

"Stay here," he orders and strides toward the last man he killed.

My legs wobble and I look around. Wait a minute. The bike! I can't remember if he left the key in the ignition or not. If he did, I can escape on the motorcycle.

I run as fast as I can back to that hidden warehouse, dodging inside and scrambling for the vehicle. No key. My heart absolutely sinks. I have no idea how to hot-wire a motorcycle.

I look around for a weapon and spot what looks like a rusty old tire iron in the corner. It's better than nothing. I scramble over garbage and a couple of torn, gray boxes to reach the makeshift weapon. The dirty metal is heavy and scratches my hands.

Then I hurry outside looking for Alexei, reaching the wrecked car and dead bodies. Even if I can reach a main road, we're in the middle of nowhere. But I have to get away from him. I look up to see him walking toward the car with the body of the third man over his shoulder. He opens the back door and shoves the guy inside. What in the heck is he doing?

Turning to glare at me, he throws the rags inside and returns to the trunk where I can't see him. It's open, and the lid hides him, but smoke soon spirals from both sides. He must've taken the lighter from the smoker.

Now might be my only chance. So I turn and begin running in the opposite direction, my kitten heels sliding on the uneven ground.

He's on me before I even know he's coming. "You're not going anywhere." He snags the nape of my neck and yanks me to a stop. Heat flares up my esophagus, and I whirl, swinging the tire iron with all of my strength.

He grabs my wrist, but the end still hits his jacket with a satisfying thunk. "Damn it." Wrenching the rusty weapon out of my hand, he drags me toward the now burning vehicle.

I uselessly try to punch him, but my fist glances off his jacket.

We reach the cinder block where I'd hit my heel. The one that had stopped me before.

"Knees," he snaps.

I blink. What is he saying?

One sharp hand smacks the back of both of my knees, and I drop, more out of surprise than pain.

"Cross your ankles," he snarls.

I do so, my mind spinning, knowing the vulnerable position will keep me from moving fast. Is he going to kill me, too? What had I been thinking taking this case?

Trying to free a killer? He might not have stabbed David Fairfax to death, but he certainly killed the three men in the now smoking car.

He releases me. "Move and you'll fucking regret it."

I watch his boots stride away.

Blinking away tears, I look up, remaining in place. More smoke begins to rise around the car. His face set in a grim mask, he walks to the passenger side of the vehicle and lifts the heavyset man back inside, flicking a silver lighter. It's the one I saw the guy at the end of the road use to light a cigarette.

Alexei leans down. Soon more flames and smoke become visible. He walks around to the other side and lights the driver's shirt on fire. Then he ducks between a couple of warehouses and returns with what looks like a bunch of dried leaves and grass that he throws in the back seat.

I'm frozen in place and can't move. All I can do is watch. He ignores me, entering and emerging from several of the abandoned warehouses, and returning with more cardboard and discarded materials to throw on the front seat of the car, which is swiftly becoming engulfed in flames.

He almost too easily kicks open the doors to two more warehouses on my side. Smoke is billowing big black rolls into the sky, and he's still not appeased. Finally, he exits one of the warehouses with two bottles in his hands, his expression intense. What are they?

My head and knees both hurt, and my temper is beginning to finally return.

The hood of the car has popped open, and he smiles,

pointing the cans and squirting a liquid. Fire immediately roars from the engine. He tosses the two cans into the vehicle and then turns, stalking rapidly my way.

My stomach rolls over. I make a small sound of fear in my throat and hope he doesn't hear it.

He wraps one hand around my bicep and pulls me to stand before yanking off his jacket. "Put this on."

"No," I say, my hands lifting to ward him off as I back away.

He moves toward me as if not caring, grabs me, and forces my arms into the jacket before he zips it. "You're covered in blood. You need to at least hide that."

I blink, finally coming awake. "I'm not going with you."

"I don't have time for this." He ducks his head, tosses me over his shoulder, and breaks into a run.

My stomach protests as his movements batter against my lower abdomen. I shriek and pound the bottom of his back. This can't be happening. The fire and the smoke are choking the entire area, and my eyes start to water.

We reach his bike. He slides on before putting me on the back and ignites the engine smoothly. "We have to get out of here," he mutters as he swings the bike in an arc.

I numbly wrap my arms around his torso and hold on. He's just wearing the thin T-shirt, and I can feel the taut muscles of his abs. I turn my head to the side and rest my cheek against his back, my entire body exhausted. I can't believe he just killed three men. They were shooting at us, but we could have gotten away. I think.

We drive right by the burning car, and I close my eyes from the devastation.

An explosion echoes loudly behind us as he roars onto the main road and opens the throttle. All I can do is hold on and try not to throw up. I've never seen such casual violence. In fact, I hadn't realized violence could be casual.

We ride for what has to at least be an hour.

Alexei breathes calmly beneath my hands, and I partially slide my hand up to feel over his heart. Just curious. The organ is beating steadily, not wildly. He's as calm as if we just had a nice lunch by the river.

I can't believe this. It's my job to make sure he stays out of prison. There isn't a doubt in my mind that's exactly where he belongs. Even if this can be considered self-defense, which frankly, I'm not sure he needed to kill those men, he's far more dangerous than I realized.

I know I'm still in shock, but there's nothing I can do right now with his big body controlling the motorcycle. I have to plan. I'm a planner, so I try to force myself back to reality.

How can I call the police? Will that be an ethical violation? He's my client, and the crime is already over. I have a duty to inform the police if I suspect a crime is going to be committed, not afterward. Yet I'm a witness to this one.

I open my eyes to discover we're in a wooded area way outside of Silicon Valley. I assumed he wanted to head back into the city.

He drives around several trees on a dirt road until he reaches what looks like a small camping area near a trickling creek. He pauses near a picnic table and cuts the engine before tugging me off of the bike. My feet hit the ground, and I start to backpedal away.

He swings his leg over. "Stop."

My body stops. I don't know why. I need to run. Is he going to kill me, too? "I can't say anything because I'm your lawyer," I say, noting the key still in the bike.

"I know that." He reaches for me, and I shrink back. A small chuckle emerges from his chest as he sticks his hand in his jacket pocket that I'm wearing and pulls out a phone. "I borrowed this from our friend along with his lighter."

Our friend. The third man Alexei had so easily murdered.

"What are you going to do?"

He lifts the phone to his ear, waits a second, and then issues a series of what sound like orders in Russian. The words barely free of his mouth, he clicks the phone shut and tears the device apart, dropping it to the ground and stomping on it. "It's a burner. But even still, we can't be too careful."

I stare at him. "I don't know what you just said." My friend Alana can speak several languages. I, however, only speak English.

"I called for help." He unzips the jacket that's keeping me warm.

I let him take it and try not to look down at the blood covering my white blouse.

He throws the jacket into the pit of a long-dormant campfire before turning to stare at me. "Take off your clothes, Rosalie."

FIFTEEN
Alexei

The woman glares at me and stomps to the worn picnic table.

"Don't touch anything," I say. She rolls her eyes, steps up on the seat and plants her fine ass on the top of the table. While I like the act of defiance, I do note that she keeps her hands together and in her lap. She hasn't actually left her prints anywhere.

"What exactly is your plan here?" she asks, her voice calm even though her pupils have widened. I admire that she hasn't gone into shock yet.

"We have to get rid of these clothes." It will take Garik at least an hour to arrive, so I was partially joking about getting her naked, although an hour is a good amount of time I'm happy to fill with her.

She shakes her head, looking lost on the barren table. "You didn't have to kill all three of them."

"Unfortunately, I did." If I had been alone, I probably would've kept one of them alive long enough to get some answers, but with her there, I had to strike swiftly.

She draws in air, her face pale and her wide cherry lips trembling. "Who do you think is trying to kill you?"

I look back toward the barely there road through the trees. "It could be any number of people." She crosses her arms and then rubs her shoulders as if trying to get warm. "You can put the leather jacket back on if you want." I smell rain on the wind, but it's still fairly warm out.

She shakes her head. "No, I'm not cold. It's just a reaction. Did you recognize any of the three men?"

"No." I lie easily. There's no need to get my lawyer involved any more than she already is. "Since the crime is finished, you also can't say anything," I remind her.

She swallows and her chin lifts. "I don't know about that. I'm actually a witness."

"You're here as my lawyer," I say. She swallows again, as if nervous. We're at a bit of a stalemate, but I can't relent. "In fact, this entire evening is covered by attorney-client privilege." I have no idea if that's true or not. A warning of thunder sounds in the distance and darkness begins to fall.

She shakes her head again as if trying to deny reality. "Don't you think we should let the police know that somebody's trying to kill you?"

I cross my arms. "The police don't care if somebody's trying to kill me." How much does she know about my family? "You do understand the four social media companies and the strength of each family behind those, correct?"

She nods. "Yes, and I know how the crystals charge the servers. In fact, I understand that the four families have been in power through generations, centuries, and kingdoms."

I wonder where she learned that. It had to be from either Alana or Ella. I hadn't realized they were close enough for them to reveal secrets we've all vowed to force into silence forever. I wonder how much I should tell her, but she does need to properly defend me, and she also has to understand the world she's now entered.

"What do you know about the Russian Bratva?" I ask.

Her head jerks up. "Why?" I just stare at her, waiting for an answer. A light pink filters across her cheekbones, and I'm pleased the color is returning to her face. I have no doubt her temper will arrive swiftly. I like that about her. Again, I don't like that I like that about her. "Why do you want to know about the Russian mob?" she asks.

I sigh. "The headquarters for the Russian Bratva is in Russia, of course. However, there are several contingents, shall we say, scattered throughout the world. Until I went to prison, I led one of the strongest ones."

She blinks once and then again. "You're in charge of the Russian mob?" she blurts out.

"I don't exactly like to hear it put that way, but close enough." I nod. "At least the local contingent, which of course includes most of the United States."

She gulps. "So what happened when you went to prison?"

"My brother took over." It was probably a combination of my brother and his mother, but I believe all of the soldiers answer to Hendrix.

Her gaze flicks to the quiet forest and then back. "Were those men Russian?"

"Yes," I tell her.

She nods. "So your brother's trying to kill you."

"It's possible, but this would also be a good time for anybody in the organization to make a move. Hendrix could be in as much danger as am I right now."

Thunder sounds again, and she rubs her shoulders. "I

think if somebody is trying to kill you that we should at least alert the police. Don't you?"

"No, and that's my final word on it," I say softly.

She looks down at her hands, and her shoulders visibly tense. "I have blood all over me." Leaping off the table, she stomps toward the creek, her little heels sticking in the soft ground as she goes.

I watch her bend down and remove all the blood from her hands and one of her wrists, taking note of her position the entire time. Finally, she stands after having scrubbed her hands a deep pink.

Irritation clocks through me, and I ignore it.

She walks slower this time, back to the table to sit. I wait until she has settled herself and then stride over to the water and kick any rock she may have touched to the middle of the creek. I learned a long time ago that being paranoid isn't necessarily a bad thing.

Returning, I note that color has returned to her pretty face, yet she's still rubbing her arms. "Would you like to put the jacket on until Garik brings us clothing?" The jacket is marred deep red, which is why I had her remove it.

"No," she says. "I don't."

The woman reminds me of a cranky kitten. Cute with claws. I lope her way and then also sit on top of the rough wooden table.

"I'm sure you at least knew one of those men," she says quietly.

"I'm not discussing this with you."

Her nostrils flare as she visibly fights her temper. I like that about her. I shouldn't, but I do.

Her hair flies into her face, and she pushes it away. "I'm an attorney, Alexei. As such, I'm uncomfortable with even the thought of working for the, well, the mob."

I understand that concern. "The mob has always existed, and getting rid of it is impossible since the organization is woven into society. Somebody has to lead it."

"But you break laws."

"That's true, but I'm trying to fix some of that." The life isn't an easy one, but having protection in place is mandatory for my peace of mind. "Where are we on getting my funds released?" I change the subject.

She took several calls while we studied my case file. In fact, she partially dictated a brief in favor of her motion to release my funds while also organizing files at the same time. The woman is impressive.

"The hearing's set for tomorrow morning," she says. "I believe your stepmother is going to contest the motion. Otherwise, we wouldn't even need a hearing."

"Is my presence required?" I keep my senses tuned to our surroundings.

She glances over at my jeans and shirt. "Yes, but only if you can find something nicer to wear. I need the charming Alexei and not the killer. Can you manage that?" Her sarcasm is amusing.

I expect her to be angry and in shock after the violence at the warehouse. This spunk and the obvious intelligence she's shown all day have been a surprise. I underestimated her when she visited me in the jail, a fact for which I am actually grateful. I require a smart mate.

I hear an engine first and then the crunch of tires on gravel, so I push myself away from the table and withdraw the gun from the back of my waist. Garik's battered truck soon comes into view, and I relax, dropping my arm but still keeping a grip on the weapon.

He pulls to a stop near the firepit and jumps out of the old Ford with a backpack slung over one shoulder that he tosses to me. I catch it easily with one hand as he reaches back into the vehicle and emerges again with a long box of matches and an impressive can of accelerant.

I reach into the backpack and draw out sweats and a sweatshirt to toss at Rosalie. "All your clothes. I mean everything."

She glares at me, gives Garik a look for good measure, and then pushes off the table to stomp toward the tree line. Amusement takes me again. Damn, she is likable, whether I appreciate that fact or not.

I yank off my shirt and kick out of my boots, jeans, and boxers before pulling on a long-sleeve shirt and a pair of ripped and worn jeans.

"You have to get rid of the boots?" Garik asks. "Those are fine."

Again, paranoia is a good thing. "Yeah."

"I didn't bring you shoes," he says, wincing. "I'm sorry."

"No worries. You brought socks." I tug out socks to cover my feet. I never considered how fortunate it is to have a friend or a best friend or an only friend about the same size as me. I'm taller than most.

He squirts the accelerant onto the clothing and then flicks a match. Flames instantly rise.

Rosalie emerges from behind the trees and strides gracefully toward the fire to throw her bloody clothing into the flames. I note a pretty pair of pink panties with a matching bra before the fire engulfs them. I need to buy her new clothes after this.

I look down at her feet. "The shoes too."

She takes a step back. "No way. These are my favorite kitten heels. I got them on discount. I'll wash them really good when I get home."

If I can get my funds released, I'll buy her all the kitten heels she wants. Whatever the hell a kitten heel is. "Now, Rosalie, or I'll take them from you."

Garik wisely takes a step away from her before squirting more accelerant onto the fire. We all know not to get between a woman and her shoes.

He chews on his gum and blows a loud bubble.

Rosalie visibly jerks. "Fine." She leans down and tears off the dainty heels to throw onto the fire, her face flushing and her lips pressed tightly together. The cute shoes land in the middle of the flames and instantly begin to curl and burn.

Garik sprays more accelerant, and we all take a step back. He blows several more bubbles, and the scent of mint competes with the smoke for just a second.

Rosalie jerks again and looks away. My instincts rise. Something is up.

The fire is warm and has definitely reddened her cheeks. Her long black hair falls down her shoulders, and she looks like a lost kitten in the oversized clothing. She rolled Garik's sweats up several times to her ankles, and while it appears she attempted to roll the sweatshirt sleeves up, they keep falling down. The top hangs nearly to her knees.

"Now what?" She looks down at her bare feet.

I reach into the bag and pull out another pair of large gym socks. "Put these on." I hand them to her.

She doesn't argue this time and instead bends over and puts the socks on, pulling them up past her knees and then letting the sweats fall back down. "All right, socks on," she says, her voice snippy. "What now?"

I catch a glimpse of amusement on Garik's broad face. He shrugs and then looks away as if not wanting to get involved, popping his gum several more times.

Rosalie visibly flinches again and then looks away.

"What's up with you and gum?" I ask.

"Nothing," she says, her voice low.

I look at Garik. "Pop your gum again." He does so, and while she doesn't jerk this time, her ears turn red. "Rosalie, what's wrong?"

She shakes her head. "It's stupid and you wouldn't understand."

"I understand more than you think. Do you have some sort of gum phobia?" The smoke has obliterated the minty smell already.

Her chin jerks up, and she looks at me before rolling those spectacular eyes. "No, I don't have a gum phobia." She kicks at a pebble that rolls toward the fireplace. "I have something called misophonia. It's a fight or flight reaction to certain sounds, usually mouth and nose sounds. Most people don't get it."

Garik looks at her. "You mean like when you're at the movie theater and someone crunches their popcorn behind you? That drives me crazy, too."

She nods. "Yeah, kind of like that, but it's different. Like telling somebody who suffers from OCD that you also wash your hands a lot and thinking it's the same thing. That a guy crunching ice by you at a restaurant is annoying. For me, it's like getting stabbed in the solar plexus." She hunkers down even more in the overlarge sweats, looking fragile. "Most people don't understand or even believe me. There's an institute now in California, and they're studying the condition. I can't explain misophonia any better than that."

"No nose sounds?" Garik asks. "You mean like sniffing?"

"Yeah. Sniffing puts me through the roof." She sounds

vulnerable, as if she's giving us a weapon to use against her. Maybe I should tell her what the plans are for her future, but probably not with Garik here.

"All right," I say. "I'll take Rosalie to claim her vehicle at her law firm and then meet you at the bar, Garik. Don't leave until the clothing is nothing but ashes." I need to know more about the three men I just killed, and hopefully Garik will have some information.

He squirts even more accelerant on the fire. "Sounds good."

I grasp Rosalie's arm through the thick cotton. "Are the socks protecting your feet enough? I can carry you."

She jerks free and pads toward the motorcycle. "Not a chance."

Cute. Definitely cute. She grabs the waistband of the sweats to keep them up, obviously trying not to trip over the bottom that has now unraveled.

Infinitely fuckable. For the first time in much too long, I anticipate a future. A good one. In doing so, I make a mental note to ban all gum chewing in my organization from now on.

SIXTEEN
Rosalie

Hours after watching the casual murder of three men, I scoot myself back in the booth and drink my fourth apple martini. "This was a good idea." I look at my two best friends. Alana sits to my right and Ella to my left, and both of them seem to be shimmering in the air. I should probably slow down with the alcohol.

Alana leans forward, her hazel eyes blurry. "I can't believe you haven't called the police."

Ella shakes her head, her blonde hair piled up high tonight. In a light-green dress, she looks more sprite-like than ever. "You can't, right? I mean, you're his attorney and there's no imminent threat."

I pluck the apple slice from my now empty glass and pop it into my mouth to enjoy the sweetness. "I think that's right. Even though I'm a witness, I don't think I can say anything. Besides, they were shooting at us first."

"There is that." Alana is dressed in her signature aquamarine-colored dress. We're drinking in the VIP lounge of the hottest new nightclub in town, Dark Mirror Lounge. I note multiple security guards at several points. They're all here for Alana.

"I'm surprised Thorn let you out," I joke. "What, are there only ten armed men in here?"

Alana snorts delicately and finishes her margarita. "Are you kidding me? Those are only the men you can see." She blows a kiss to a security camera in the corner.

My mouth drops open. "He hacked into the security system?"

She shrugs. "Most likely. But that makes it easy for me to go out for a while, you know?"

I actually don't know. Thorn seems to be a bit much for me. Although, I'm now somewhat of an accomplice to a man just as dangerous. Why are dangerous men so sexy? There's something wrong with the female brain. "What is it in us that's drawn to bad boys?"

Alana shrugs. "I like feeling safe. If anybody so much as flicks my ear, Thorn will cut theirs off." Her eyebrows draw down. "Wait. That seems wrong. Right?"

Heck if I know. Being safe is definitely an aphrodisiac.

Ella waves for the waiter to bring another round. "My guess is that dangerous bad men are good in bed."

That's probably true. The memory of the wild orgasm Alexei forced on me flashes through my brain. My sex clenches. That's it. My body is a moron not listening to my brain. But don't hormones and sexual attraction come from the brain? "I'm losing my mind."

Alana snorts. "Welcome to the club."

Ella smiles as a cute waiter brings over three more drinks for us. "I kind of like having security in place." She looks around at the thick mahogany tables and tasteful and somehow flowery decor. "I feel like nobody—even my evil stepmother—can get to me here."

Alana reaches for another margarita. "Believe me, nobody can get to you here. Thorn has every exit covered." She sounds happy, so I don't give her too hard of a time. I can't imagine ever giving up that much of my own freedom, and my thoughts fly unerringly to Alexei. He does seem to be rather bossy, and I need to set limitations soon. Although I'll never admit this to anybody, but I slept peacefully for the first time in eons with him in my bed.

Ella kicks me lightly beneath the table with her high-heeled pump. "What is that look on your face?"

Heat instantly fills my cheeks. "I don't know what you're talking about."

"Oh, yes you do," Alana says. "Come on, dish it. I've seen Alexei. He's seriously hot. You've only told us part of the story, right?"

While I'd told them about the events of the day, I hadn't told them that he's staying with me.

"Come on," Ella coaxes. "You never could keep a poker face, at least not with the two of us." This is true.

While I can bluff in court plenty, I can't lie to my two best friends. "Fine." I give them a full lowdown on how he's staying with me.

Ella's head jerks, and her blue eyes widen. "Are you serious? You let him stay the night?"

"I didn't have much of a choice." I shrug. "He doesn't have anywhere to live."

Alana tips back half of her margarita. "That's the lamest excuse I've ever heard."

I cut her a look under my lashes. "Oh yeah? I remember you coming up with some pretty lame excuses about Thorn Beathach."

She chuckles, the sound happy. "Yeah, that's probably

true." Then she sobers. "But you're not going to get involved with Alexei, are you? I mean, come on. He's a murderer."

"Like Thorn isn't?" Ella instantly snaps. "We were just talking about sexy bad boys."

Alana's mouth tightens. "Neither Thorn nor Alexei are boys. Don't forget that."

I immediately try to squelch any argument. "Come on, Alana. We all know that Thorn runs the Irish mob."

"I know." Alana looks at Ella. "Right now, you're under his protection, which you need."

Ella reaches for her rum and Coke and takes several drinks. "I'm not entirely sure I am under his protection. His brother wants me dead."

Alana rolls her eyes now. "Oh, come on. Justice doesn't want you dead. Maybe excommunicated to a faraway island, but not dead."

Ella laughs. "That's fair. I did almost kill his brother, but I didn't know you were going to fall in love with the guy."

Alana smiles. "I know. I'm not mad about it. I think you were pretty brilliant. And plus, that's a skill we may need someday," she flicks a glance at me, "just in case we need to kill Alexei."

I shake my head. "He's not charging the crystals. If you infect the amethyst crystals that power the Hologrid Hub servers, you'll end up killing Hendrix, not Alexei."

"Hendrix is an ass." Alana reaches for a bowl of miniature pretzels. She slides a pretzel in her mouth and chews softly so as not to bug me. Guilt instantly flushes me that my friends can't enjoy a pretzel without trying to be quiet about it. It's not my fault, but I still feel like an asshole. Alana doesn't seem to mind.

She glances at her aquamarine-and garnet-encrusted

watch. "I have about a half an hour more, and then I need to go create posts for Aquarius Social. It's almost midnight."

I'm not up to my usual state of holding the phone for her while she posts. I'm a little wobbly, to be honest. "Alana? How do you deal with that? The fact that Thorn runs the Irish mob?"

She sobers. "I accept all of him. Plus, I trust him to control the organization better than anybody else. I trust *him*."

Is it possible for me to trust somebody that much? To ignore the danger and crime associated with Alexei? A shadow crosses our table, and I look up to see dark blue eyes and thick blond hair. "Hendrix," I murmur. It figures he's at the hottest new club in town.

"Hello, Miss Mooncrest," he says, smiling. He has perfect teeth. I've always admired people who have perfect teeth. Mine are close but no cigar. "I was hoping I could have a moment to speak with you."

Alana draws back. She probably does feel weird, considering she was the last person to see his brother alive, and Thorn probably killed the guy. Of course, Cal Sokolov was a complete ass.

"No," Ella says for me.

Wait a minute. I'm a lawyer on a case. Maybe Hendrix has been drinking. "No, that's all right." I scoot from the booth and waver on my four-inch heels.

Hendrix grasps my elbow. "Are you all right?" He leans down, smelling of dusky cologne. He has to be a good six-foot-two and is well muscled. The rugged planes of his face are rather attractive.

"Yes, I'm fine." Besides my kitten heels that had been unfortunately destroyed by fire earlier that day, these four-inch Louboutins I snatched at a secondhand store last month are my favorite.

"I'll bring her right back to you." Hendrix winks at Ella.

She glowers at him. I've always liked her overprotective side. She looks tiny and defenseless, but she could destroy his life with a couple of keystrokes if she wanted.

Hendrix leads me graciously across the VIP area to a quiet booth where he settles me before sitting across the glass table.

"Can I get you a drink?" He lifts one finger to signal the waitress.

She hustles up, her bosom swaying, and practically shoves both boobs in his face as she leans over. "Can I help you?"

Crap. If she gets any closer, she may smother him.

He leans back slightly. "The lady would like an apple martini with two apple slices, and I'll take a Balvenie Old Port Wood on the rocks."

I've never liked scotch, but it seems like such a manly thing to order. I blink several times in an effort to clear my vision. "What can I do for you, Hendrix?" I only slur his name slightly.

His smile makes him appear even more handsome. While his younger brother had been slick with the good looks, Hendrix is smooth. I like that about a guy.

He taps his fingers on the table. "I feel we should discuss Alexei and your representation of him."

"What would you like to discuss?"

"Your safety," Hendrix says calmly. "I won't be able to sleep if I fail to at least warn you that he's a very dangerous man."

Well, no kidding. I learned that today firsthand. "I appreciate the warning."

"He killed David Fairfax." Hendrix leans forward. "You need to understand that fact. He actually killed the man in cold blood."

"He says that he was set up," I mumble. There's a ring of truth as well as anger in Alexei's eyes every time he talks about the murder.

Hendrix purses his lips as if he's just sucked on a lemon as the waitress deposits our drinks, once again pushing her boobs toward his face. I don't think the guy looks like he needs to breastfeed at the moment, but what do I know? She pats his shoulder and then turns, her butt swaying seductively as she walks away on four-inch spiked boots. I admire that. I've never mastered the sway in high heels. Both Hendrix and I watch her go, then he turns back toward me.

"He is a killer."

I'm well aware that he is a killer, but I don't think he killed David Fairfax. "I don't see Alexei being dumb enough to hide the murder weapon in a pond right outside the back door of a mansion," I say. "Do you?"

Hendrix sighs. "As I understand it, there wasn't a lot of time to do anything else. Alexei has always been very — shall we say — seductive. I'm sure he thought he could charm his way back into the crime scene and fetch the knife before anybody found it."

That makes zero sense. The police didn't release that entire scene until they were done. "Is that all you have for me, Hendrix?"

He takes a drink of his scotch. "No, I have more for you."

I reach for my martini and lift the glass, noting it seems heavier than my last drink. That's a sure sign that I've had too much to drink. "What do you have?"

"Money," he says directly, taking another gulp and then putting the glass on the table.

I lean away from him, studying him. Tonight he wears

a perfectly pressed peach-colored button-down shirt and black slacks. The lighter colored shirt makes him seem even more dangerous. "Are you trying to bribe me?"

He carelessly lifts one shoulder. "You can call it whatever you like, but Hologrid Hub is looking for an in-house attorney. Starting salary is $1.2 million with a $1.2 million signing bonus. Full benefits, 401k, golden parachute, you name it. As well as two months off a year and the use of both the corporate jet and any of our vacation properties anytime you want."

Heat flashes down my throat. "That's quite the offer."

"You're quite the attorney." His eyes sparkle. "In addition, I understand that you're having financial difficulties. This would take care of your problems, don't you think?"

My temper spirals somewhere from the base of my spine and up, although I'm a little numb right now.

He holds his drink up and then clicks it lightly with mine. "Cheers."

"Cheers," I say automatically and take a sip. It's the good stuff and I enjoy it. "Hendrix, you have to understand that if I am taken off of your brother's case, another attorney will be assigned. The case won't go away."

"He's not my brother," Hendrix says instantly. "Please don't refer to him as such."

Man, this family has some serious problems. "Fine. That fact doesn't change my analysis." I take another sip.

"I know, but from my research, you're the best litigator they have. Even the full partners don't come close." He winks. "In addition, you're beautiful and smart. I've never thought of myself as much of a savior, but if I can save you from Alexei, I'll do it."

I blink twice. "You think he'll kill me if I lose?"

"No, I think he'll seduce you so you win. If he's going to take over our, well, company, he's going to want to appear mature and settled. With a wife. In fact, I wouldn't be surprised if he hasn't already tried to get into your bed."

The image of Alexei in my bed that very morning flashes through my mind. Apparently, Hendrix does know his brother, even if he won't claim him. "Is there any chance for a peace between you two?" I ask curiously, grasping the little sword in my drink and pulling out the apple slices to delicately nibble on one.

Hendrix watches my movements, his gaze on my mouth. His eyes flare. Oh my. I put the other slice back in the liquid. "No peace," he says. "We will never have peace."

So that's one question answered. "Why do you want him in prison so badly?"

"I didn't say I want him in prison. Did I?"

I cock my head to the side. "But you do."

Hendrix finishes his drink. "Yeah, I do. He belongs in prison. He killed that man merely because the guy found out about the affair. That's cold-blooded and that's evil." His eyes glow with intent and purpose. He truly believes what he says. "Do you ever wonder how the Fairfax security system was fried that day so the interior security system didn't record the murder? Alexei has a way with computers."

I sober slightly. "Security system?" I'd gone through all the evidence provided to the defense and hadn't seen a hard drive.

"Yes," Hendrix says. "Surely you're aware of that fact."

"I'm not." I make a mental note to visit the police station first thing in the morning. Well, after my hearing. Oh yeah, I have a hearing. I should probably stop drinking. Even as the thought crosses my mind, I finish my martini.

"You're very charming, Hendrix, and I appreciate the offer, but I'm going to have to decline."

I start to scoot from the booth. He plants one hand over mine, holding me in place. I jolt and look up. His face loses the pleasant expression, and I see the animal behind the facade. To be honest, he looks more like Alexei than I would've imagined.

His voice drops low. "I don't think you understand. I'm offering you an easy way out. If not, you're going to lose everything."

"Is that a threat?"

"You can take it any way you like, but you're three months behind on your mortgage, and I'm about to own your home."

My heart stutters. I can't lose that house. I have seven elderly men to care for. "I don't appreciate the threat." I glance across the bar to where my friends are watching me. "If I need money, I can get it and you know that."

He releases my hand and follows my gaze before looking back at me. "That's true. Although I believe you have too much pride to ask those silly heiresses for help."

I normally would, but when it comes to taking care of my boarders, pride can get lost. I just lift my chin and glare at him.

He shrugs. "Very well. Perhaps I can't take your house, but I know how much you care about Merlin and Felix and Percy. Shall I name all of them?"

Fire finally lances through me, and I keep my hand in place on the table, leaning closer to him. "Try me, Hendrix. You don't want me for an enemy. Trust me." With that, I stand, turn, wobble only slightly on the heels and stomp my way across the bar.

"What was that about?" Ella asks as I slide back into the booth.

"It was a bribe and a threat," I say.

Alana glances back at Hendrix who's now watching us. "I don't really like violence, but if you want—"

"No," I say before she can finish a thought. "I don't need Thorn Beathach to do my dirty work. I can handle myself." I wave to the waitress for one more drink.

Ella cocks her head. "Are you working tomorrow, Rosalie?"

"I am. I have a hearing at nine in the morning," I say.

"Oh." Alana waves at the bartender. "Then we only have about a half an hour to do a couple of shots."

For some reason, that sounds like an excellent plan to me. Just how drunk do I want to be when I return to my bedroom tonight?

SEVENTEEN
Alexei

At the Amethyst bar, I sit on a bar stool with a shot of vodka that I raise to the assembled men in the room. "To our future," I say, tipping it back. They repeat my phrase and all drink. There are only eight men here. I recognize most of them, and it looks like we've gotten a few new recruits—fresh from Russia. They are not happy with Hendrix.

In the crowd that ranges in age from sixteen to seventy, there are two torpedoes who serve as hitmen and hired muscle, several Boyeviks, foot soldiers, and even a couple of Vor v Zakones who are high-ranking and highly respected members. I'm surprised to even have one Obshchak Keeper, who's a keeper of communal funds. Hendrix will have them all killed if he discovers this meeting.

"What else has gone wrong?" I ask. They've already gone into some length about Hendrix playing with daughters and promising marriage and then backing out after using them.

Vsevolod Nikiforov kicks back in his chair. "Are you serious about no trafficking?"

"Absolutely," I say, meaning it. "I want nothing to do with trafficking people. Why? What do you know?"

He flushes. "I know that Hendrix is well involved in it and is making a lot of money."

Anger flows through me. Our father may not have been the kindest of men, but he had set rules, and that was one of them. We don't mess with women, and we don't mess with kids. I don't see myself as any sort of hero, but I do believe in karma and protecting the most vulnerable.

Yet I know how to explain my position to these men. "Trafficking is unacceptable. The authorities are finally cracking down on organizations, and I want to be free of exposure. If anybody feels differently, you can leave now." I'll probably kill them later, and they should know me well enough to understand that fact.

Nobody moves. "Good. Plus, I do believe in karma." I cross my arms and look toward Garik. "I'm retaking the organization, and I value your loyalty. Garik is my second in command, and that decision is final."

A couple of men frown, and an older one, a former assassin named Jac, shakes his head. "He's not from a main family."

"He's my family," I state calmly.

Garik doesn't move and reveals no expression. Good.

"Any more discussion?" I ask softly.

Several heads shake. I clear my throat and glance at Garik. "Do we have anybody with computer expertise?"

He shakes his head. "No. Anybody with computer skills is paid well by Hendrix. They'll be loyal to him for now." He cocks his head. "However, your lawyer has a good friend who's one of the best."

"Ella?" I ask, my eyebrows rising. I do remember

hearing something about her being a phenomenal hacker. She even trained in the motherland briefly.

"Do you want me to take her?" Garik asks.

"Probably," I note. "Let's wait until we have a decent setup." The first job I need her to do is figure out who framed me for David Fairfax's murder. How had anybody found time to throw that knife in the pond—and make sure my fingerprints were on it? They might've been planted, or perhaps that was just bad luck since I was there so often. It had to have been somebody investigating the crime, who worked with the judge and prosecuting attorney. As well as my dead attorney. "How good is she?"

Garik shrugs. "I don't know. Just heard rumors, but say the word, and I'll have her available to work for us."

Power finally begins to flow through my veins again. I don't think anybody knows about my need to get back to my servers. I'm sure Hendrix has them well protected now that he knows about my backdoor tunnel, and it's going to be all-out war. In this game, at least from the outside looking in, Caine is going to kill Abel again.

So be it.

I look around. "I'm sure I'm being watched, and Hendrix will know you came here. You're all in danger."

Not one of them looks scared or even bothered. Jac speaks for the group. "We're taking precautions and are ready for war. There are many inside the organization who will make the jump and return to you if there's a show of strength."

Meaning I need to kill Hendrix. I don't like the idea of murdering my father's son. We do share blood, after all. "I understand."

The group stands and files out, all heavily armed and

watching for threats. I like that. Jac is the last to leave, and he hands me a folded piece of paper.

I take it. "We're passing notes now?"

He shrugs. "It was taped to the front door of the bar. I read it. Doesn't make sense."

Ah. The kill list from Urbano Reyes. I've been waiting for this. "Don't worry about it." I shove the paper into my pocket to read later.

Jac nods, following the others out and leaving Garik and me alone.

"How many of them do you trust?" I ask.

"About half. I'll make a list of who we want to watch—who I think Hendrix might've sent. But betrayal always comes from the inside."

True words.

We have a couple of drinks of the good vodka, and both of us turn when the front door opens. I sit back and blink. Well, this is a surprise.

Lillian Sokolov walks inside dressed in a casual black dress with her hair down and a lot grayer than I remember. Her jewelry sparkles with more diamonds than I can count, and the flats she wears look comfortable. However, her shoulders are slightly stooped and her skin looser than I remember. She has not aged well these last seven years.

"We obviously need to talk," she says, moving behind the bar and looking more like a grandmother than the bombshell I remember.

Garik leans down and lifts up the good bottle of vodka. With a look at me, he turns and strides through the back door where I can hear his footsteps ascending to the apartment.

Lillian pours two glasses and nudges one toward me. "Welcome to freedom."

I lift my glass and down the contents as she does the same. "What do you want, Lillian?" I fear that every exit to my place is now covered by men with automatic weapons. Even so, I have to admire her grit in walking in alone. I could kill her with my bare hands and she knows it.

"I thought we could end this thing for now. For good," she says, her voice trembling slightly. Apparently, losing her youngest son has taken a toll I haven't considered.

I cock my head to the side. "You're ready to give up Hologrid Hub?"

"Of course not." Even in obvious mourning, she's all woman, and I can see what my father saw in her. Although their age difference had created quite the fodder for the gossip rags. She has blue eyes and a delicate bone structure. Both of her sons inherited much of her attributes—including ambition. She'd become pregnant right away with Hendrix and then Cal to better secure her place with my father.

"Leave town," she says. "I will release your trust funds and you'll have billions to go play with. You can go any-where in the world, but it will be out of this country. Please, Alexei. Grant me some peace."

She looks as out of place behind the rickety old bar as a princess would in a dungeon. Yet, I know of her humble beginnings, and she has risen high above them by marrying my father.

"Hologrid Hub is mine." I try to keep the need out of my voice. If I don't get near the large amethysts again soon, my skin is going to fall off.

She shakes her head. "Hendrix is doing a good job branding the corporation."

"Actually, you're in third place, maybe fourth now out of the four social media companies," I say smoothly.

"Aquarius and Malice are helping each other out, which I think brought Aquarius up to second and dropped Hologrid Hub to third and TimeGem to fourth."

I don't have the numbers yet.

Her nostrils flare. "I had planned a merger between Cal and the Aquarius Social heir that didn't work out. However, they have a new heir with some long-lost cousin."

This is new information for me. I take it in to roll over in my mind later.

"Or." She taps a chewed off fingernail on her lips. "There's always little Ella. She's the rightful heir of TimeGem Moments, you know?"

An interesting thought, Ella with Hendrix. It would be quite the merger, and I can imagine the young Rendale heir is interested in reclaiming her birthright. I might have to kidnap her sooner rather than later to gain her hacking skills. For a short while, of course. Unless she's helpful, then I'll keep her forever.

I stare at my stepmother. "I do appreciate the bribe and the offer to avoid war, but I want what's mine."

Her chin goes up. "You lost what's yours when you killed David Fairfax. You belong in prison, and we both know it."

"Did you set me up?" I ask. "Are you the person who arranged for the evidence to be planted?"

"Of course not," she says. "I always knew if I gave you enough rope, you'd hang yourself, and you did exactly that, Alexei. You have nobody to blame but yourself for this predicament. A jury convicted you once and they'll do so again." Even looking sad and lonely, her voice holds strength.

I smile. "Not without the help they had last time."

"Your prints were on that knife, and it is the murder weapon. Correct?"

The newspapers had had a field day with that fact, which still bothers me greatly. I can't see from what direction that betrayal had come. "Did you bribe the police or an officer along with the judge and prosecutor?" I ask.

She frowns. "I don't know what you're talking about."

I try to search her gaze for truth, but I can't tell if she's lying or not. There were several people who could have set me up. I was quite the asshole back then and had slept with more than one man's wife, but she and Hendrix had the most to gain from my going to prison and having my funds frozen. I know with certainty that Hendrix had hits put out on me in prison, which is why I had to make the deal with Urbano Reyes. That must've infuriated my so-called brother to no end.

"Did you send a squad after me the day I was let out and also this morning?" I ask.

"Squads?"

Maybe Hendrix doesn't share his business with his mother. I cross my arms. "I'm armed and ready to kill, Lillian. Make sure Hendrix understands that. If he considers having anybody tear in here later tonight to take me out, I would tell him to think again. You don't want war with me." It's the last olive branch I will extend to her.

She smooths a lock of hair off her forehead. "Nobody wants a war. Hendrix would not resort to violence."

I wonder if my own mother would've been blind to my many faults. "Turn over my company to me, unfreeze my funds, and we'll both go on our merry ways. Like you said, you also have plenty of money to go live a good life. Take Hendrix with you. He doesn't have the connection with the crystals that I do. It's a fact."

"Right now," she says, finally showing some emotion.

Anger looks good on her. "If you die, you and I both know that power will increase in him."

Another fact. We don't know why, but usually one person can fully charge or use the crystals out of the four families. Right now it's me. If I die, his power will increase. It's something we've never understood and haven't really bothered trying to solve.

"If he dies, mine will increase as well," I say evenly. "I suggest you heed my words. I really don't want to kill your son."

Her hand trembles as she pushes back her hair. "It's nice to know where you stand." Her head held high, she walks around the bar toward the door. "It's too bad, Alexei. Your father would be so disappointed in you." She opens the door and sweeps out.

I free my gun from the back of my waist and wait patiently for about an hour. Apparently, they're not coming for me tonight. Sighing, I pour myself another shot of the vodka and down it before pulling the folded piece of paper out of my pocket. I open it to read a series of numbers. I lean over the bar and scramble for a pencil. I use Reyes's code to decipher the first three names. I don't recognize these people I've promised to kill, so they must be from Reyes's gang. The fourth name gives me some pause, as it's a prominent businessman in town.

I'll do the job because I promised, but I'm going to find out why Reyes wants each of these people murdered. I slowly write the last name and then sit back. Well, this is unexpected.

The final person on Urban Reyes's termination list is Rosalie's best friend, little Ella Rendale.

EIGHTEEN
Rosalie

I'm a little embarrassed to admit, even to myself, that I'm disappointed to find my bed empty when I tumble onto it. I haven't been able to banish the memory of that spectacular orgasm, and I want an excuse to tear up the sheets again with Alexei.

Is that stupid? Yes, definitely.

Is that a violation of legal ethics? Without question.

Have I been spared? Of course.

Groaning, I turn onto my stomach, my ankles hanging off the bed, and tell myself to get up, wash my face, and disrobe. But I don't move. Even with my eyes closed, the room is spinning around me. Just how many drinks did I have, anyway? Thank goodness Alana had both picked me up and dropped me off in her chauffeured car. While I won't take advantage of my friend's wealth, sometimes her good fortune comes in handy. Although ending up with Thorn Beathach might not be good fortune. He's dangerous.

Like Alexei.

I snooze for a while and awaken with the room still

dark and my clothes still on. Heat flashes into my face. Thank goodness my half-admitted and definitely moronic plan to escape reality for a night had not come to fruition.

Fingers dance along my ankle and smooth off my high heel.

I jump and flip over, partially sitting up. "What?" Then I stop breathing. Alexei stands in front of me, his scarred torso bare, his face blanketed by shadows. Moonlight streams around his strong body from the window behind him, caressing him while leaving his front in darkness. Like an apparition. One with cut muscle and long-ago healed wounds.

I swallow.

Without speaking, he reaches down and removes my other shoe.

I scamper away from him, sitting all the way up.

He cocks his head, but I can't see his face. His eyes glow an unholy hue. "Why are you on the bed clothed?"

Barely clothed, really. The silk skirt has ridden up to the top of my thighs, and the slender straps of my tank top are halfway down my arms. My vulnerable state penetrates my still foggy brain. "I fell asleep."

"I see." Without seeming to move, he sets his body between my legs, flush against the bed. One finger tugs my strap down more. "You been drinking, Rosalie?"

"Yes." I swallow, tucking my elbows to my ribs to prevent the top from falling. Why had this seemed like a good idea?

His other finger finds the other strap. "Did you mean to get drunk?"

"Yes," I whisper.

He pulls and the straps slide down my arms while the

tank drops to my waist. "You never need an excuse with me, Kotik." With his fingers still wound around the straps, he also clasps the bottom of the tank and pulls everything over my head. Cool air brushes my breasts, bringing me back to reality completely.

I hold up a hand. "Wait a minute. You know I've been drinking."

His chuckle heats the room. "I do." He plants one hand on my upper chest and pushes.

I fall back on the bed, and in a second, he swipes the skirt and thong down my legs to toss on the floor. "Wait-wait a second."

"No." He drops to his knees and presses his face into my pussy, breathing deep. "I've craved your scent all fucking day."

Wetness spills from me. That should not be a turn on. It's wrong. He's all wrong. I've screwed up big time. "All right." I use one hand to push myself to sit again and try to close my thighs.

He looks up, frowning like a treat has been taken away. Keeping my gaze, he sinks his teeth into my thigh.

The erotic bite sends pain and then a burning pleasure through my body. I slap his head. "What is it with you and biting?" Without waiting for an answer, I tunnel my fingers into his hair and grab a good chunk. "You need to listen to me."

He turns his head, scraping me with the bristle on his jaw. Then, shocking me, he leans back, still crouching between my legs. "I'm listening."

My throat closes and I release him. He's listening? Even with his face shrouded by darkness, his eyes gleam. "Um. This is a mistake."

"This is inevitable." Even the dark confidence in his tone is arousing.

I scrub both hands down my face. I did this on purpose. I want him. Have I ever wanted a man this much? Is it the danger? Or am I just curious? "This is just sex," I murmur, relaxing. Okay.

"This is more," he returns.

I jolt and drop my hands to the bed, curling my fingers into the plush comforter. "You don't need to say that." I'm sure he's full of the perfect expressions to get women into bed with him. I'm just a number, and I'll make him that as well. A little voice in the back of my head calls me a liar. He's one of a kind. Good or bad, right or wrong, he's unique. "I don't need lies."

"You were made for me, Rosalie. Whether you like it or not." His hands land on my legs, his thumbs digging into my inner thighs.

Romantic words that I don't require. Or want. "I don't need a seduction, Alexei." We have to be on the same page.

His thumbs dig in more, certainly bruising me, and he spreads my legs. "You think this is a seduction? Baby, you've been with the wrong men."

I tighten my hold on the comforter to keep from falling back. "Then what is this?"

He ducks and runs his face along my abused thigh, ending right back up where he started, sucking my clit into his mouth.

Electricity arcs through me, even singeing my ears. Then he goes at me with teeth, tongue, lips, fingers—showing absolutely no mercy. My arms begin to tremble and then give out. I fall onto my back.

With a pleased hum against me, he grips my butt with

both hands, squeezing and bringing me off the bed to his mouth. It's too much. I'm so close, God, he's good at this. I can't think. Every time I'm right there, he changes his angle or bites me, stopping the orgasm right as it awakens. He's brutal. Devastating. Infuriating.

My head thrashes on the bed, and I blindly reach for a pillow to shove over my face. The men in my boarding house might be mostly deaf, but I'm about to scream. I know it.

If he lets me.

At least three fingers inside me, twisting and turning, he bites my clit.

I shriek into the pillow, detonating into shards of me that might never fit back together again. Shocking wave after wave barrels through me, sparking the world into fire. He forces me to ride the flames until I finally come down, my body limp and weak. Even then, he licks me, getting his fill. I shudder, unable to move. Unable to stop him. Finally, he releases me and stands, removing his belt. Then his jeans and boxers.

I can't think.

He grasps my thighs and flips me over, yanking me back onto my knees. My hands struggle to find purchase on the destroyed bedspread. His fingers bruise my hips. "Rosalie? You asked what this was." He shoves into me with one brutal push.

Pain that rapidly turns to white hot pleasure explodes throughout me. One I've never felt before. God, he's huge. Overwhelming me.

He leans over, his mouth at my ear. "This is a claiming." He bites the shell of my ear and stands, gripping my hips. Then he doesn't move. Just stands there, in full control of us both, his cock pulsing inside me. I can feel the demand. The control he has is terrifying. A shiver licks up my back, trying to warn me. But it's too late.

Deep inside me, deeper than he is, I know it's too late. For what, I'm not sure. Not yet.

Need builds inside me, and I can't believe his strength. Control is the only word for it. How is he not moving? I can help but clench around him.

A growl emerges from behind me, and a light triumph fills me. I do it again.

He pulls out and pounds back inside me. Once and again . . . then stops.

On all that's holy. He's not human.

It has been at least seven years for him, and he's ruling his body. And mine. I could never do that. I clench again, trying to get him moving. The need inside me has stolen my breath, and I ache in a way that can't be healthy. "Alexei."

He leans over again, licking the slight wound he left on my skin. "What is this, Rosalie?" he rasps, his warm breath heating my ear.

I shiver. No. Nope, Not playing that game. Nope. I clench again. I can't let him win this one. It's too important, even though I barely understand the parameters. It isn't a game. Gut instinct tells me that. If I can just get him moving, he'll be swept away as fast as me. I know it. I move forward and then slam back against him.

His sharp intake of breath gives me hope.

Then he grabs my hair and yanks back, forcing my head up and my back to bow.

I can't move an inch. Not at all. From this angle, I feel him even deeper inside me. His grip unrelenting, he reaches around me with his free hand and palms my breast before pinching my nipple.

Hard.

I gasp, my thighs dampening. No. Not me. I'm not a girl who likes pain.

He reaches over and palms the other breast. I suck in air, holding it. He chuckles and the sound is dark. Then he pinches, twisting viciously.

I cry out and then quickly bite my lip. All I need is for somebody to hear me and come looking. Burning fire flashes from my breasts to my pussy. Nothing matters except how I feel right now. What I have to have. There is nothing else. Need has turned to a desperate craving. I don't know myself right now. That hurt . . . and I liked it. At least my body did. "Alexei," I whisper jaggedly.

His free hand descends onto my ass. Hard.

I gasp.

Once and again. The erotic pain digs deep beneath my skin to where he pulses inside me. "Not going to ask again."

"Claiming," I blurt out. "It's a claiming."

"Good girl." The praise fills something inside me that'll embarrass me later. Right now, there's nothing but him. Still holding my hair, he grips my hip and pulls out before powering back inside me.

Then he lets loose. Finally.

His savage thrusts rock the bed even as he holds me in place. Right where he wants me. I want to lower my chin and bury my face in the comforter, but he keeps me at that vicious angle. Head up, back arched, butt in the air. He pounds against me, hard and wild, and I start to climb again. A stirring begins inside me, sparking into a live wire that uncoils deep and then explodes. I shut my eyes and bite my lip to keep from screaming as my body gyrates with a wild orgasm that sucks every ounce of energy I have away. Sobbing, I come down, trying to breathe, my lungs shrieking for air.

He doesn't even slow.

The sound of flesh slamming forcefully against flesh fills the room. I mumble something but am not sure what.

In response, he releases my hair, grasps my nape, and pushes me down. I turn my head at the last second on the bed so I can breathe, held down and held open by him.

He's relentless.

I soften, unable to do anything else. I'm spent, and he's still rock hard, drilling into me. A spark ignites where we meet. No way. I blink. Three times in one night is a record. His hold tightens on my neck.

Then his free fingers find my clit.

I try to shake my head, but he has me captured. "No, Alexei," I whisper brokenly. "I can't. Really." I'm swollen and sore. Three times is a miracle for me. I usually don't make it to one. "Stop."

For answer, he pinches my clit.

I suck in air, too startled to scream. The pain is unreal. His finger wipes along my wet thigh, and then he's gently rubbing my abused clit. My body starts to move in rhythm with his finger. "No. I can't," I whisper brokenly. "Please." Now I'm begging.

He ignores me. Flicks me lightly. I shudder, opening even wider for him.

Somehow, his finger is at my mouth, and he shoves it in. I taste myself on him. Then he pulls out, and his wet finger slides against my clit again. I tremble, wide open to anything he wants to do.

He pounds harder, holding me in place, and then scrapes his nail against me.

I fly away into an orgasm that has me silently screaming, my mouth open, no sound coming out. My body jerks and flails, held in place by him. Fire blasts through me, and I shut my eyelids, the blood pounding through my head so loudly, it's the only sound in existence. Just as I come down, finally, completely broken, he stops inside me, holding tight as his body jerks against me.

His climax takes forever.

Finally, he releases me, pulls out, and flips me back over. His hands on my hips toss me farther up on the bed, and then he's on top of me. "It's been a long seven years, Peaflower. You're not gonna get a lot of sleep." His mouth takes mine.

Hard.

NINETEEN
Rosalie

I have nobody but myself to blame for what happened last night. Mentally chiding myself, I finish fastening my little mirror earrings as my gaze catches on the sketchbook in the corner of my bedroom. The pad is resting against the wall by the chair, next to the bag. Casting a guilty look at the bathroom door, I move and reach for it, flipping open the top.

It's me. I'm staring out, my eyes blazing and my hair all over the place. I expected to find a drawing of trees, or I don't know, a car. But not one of me looking all wild and kind of sexy.

The bathroom door opens, and I drop the sketchpad, turning guiltily.

One of his dark eyebrows rises.

"You drew me," I whisper, trying not to be touched.

He shrugs. "Couldn't sleep."

This is way too much sensory overload. "I need to get going." I hurriedly move to open the door.

He's behind me, letting off heat.

Trying to ignore that masculine warmth, I walk gingerly down my private stairs from my suite to outside, sore in places I hadn't realized existed. He bruised and bit me, leaving his mark everywhere on me. Head to toe, I wear him. I'd gotten about thirty minutes of sleep and had to spend extra time on my makeup to mask dark circles under my eyes and razor burn across my chin. The burns on my thighs would just have to heal on their own. Right now, I'm acutely aware of Alexei behind me. Things have definitely changed, and it is my fault. I had purposely gotten drunk.

Why?

My mind spins. I watched him kill three men yesterday. Why would I then get drunk and put myself into a bed with him? Was it some sort of biological mode of self-preservation? Do I want to mean something to him since I know he killed somebody? Or is it that the casual violence somehow ignites something in my blood, something primitive? Or even worse—am I just horny? I'm afraid that may be the answer.

But last night was more than sex. He was right. Even now, in the morning light, I'm too chicken to ask him what he meant by a claiming. I want to convince myself that he was just being dramatic or even romantic, but I know better. Alexei doesn't mess around. The carefree young man in those videos I watched is long gone.

This man chooses his words with deliberation.

I smooth down my blouse and shiver as a biting breeze snaps at me when I walk outside. Bulbous clouds cover the sky, looking ready to open up any second. A thought occurs to me, and I stop cold.

"What?" He's right behind me.

"Um, well, I think I should tell you that I'm on the pill." It's a little too late to have this talk.

He runs his hands down my arms, his body warming me from behind. "I know. Saw them in your cabinet." He kisses the top of my head. "I'm clean, just so you know. Had a checkup right before being arrested and haven't been with anybody in seven years."

Heat spirals into my face. The man either pinched, kissed, licked, or bit every inch of me the night before, and *now* I'm embarrassed? I hurry around the corner to where I parked my car at the curb, wishing Alexei would just peel off without a word. I look up to see my beloved vehicle and stop short. "Oh my God."

He walks to my side. "Go back inside."

"No." I hurry toward my now destroyed vehicle. It looks like somebody has taken a bat to it. How had I not heard anything? Heat flushes my face. Oh yeah, I was busy last night. All night.

The windows are smashed in. The tires are slashed, and dents are everywhere. Scrawled black paint very clearly reads, "You will die, bitch."

Oh my God. I take another step back and look up at Alexei.

His jaw firms and fire flashes through his eyes. Unlike me, he appears well rested and solid. As if he had a great night's sleep. "I told you to go back inside." He moves toward the vehicle and peers through the broken windows. I step up to do the same to see all of the leather slashed into pieces. 'He's a killer' is carved into the driver's seat.

I take a step back.

"Rosalie? What happened?" Yells an older male voice.

I look up to see Felix turn the corner and run toward

us, his seventies-style jogging outfit brightening the entire day.

I shake my head. "Doc, you shouldn't be here."

He lets out a shrill whistle. As if on cue, elderly men pour out of my pink boarding house. I glance up at Alexei. This is a disaster. He needs to go.

A cacophony of exclamations arrive as they all bustle toward us dressed in everything from a bathrobe to a business suit.

"What happened?"

"Oh no."

"Oh my."

I drop my chin and then shake my head.

"Who the hell are you?" Merlin glares up at Alexei. Although early in the morning, Merlin is already dressed in a three-piece suit with a bow tie. I hadn't realized he was going out today.

"I'm Alexei. Who the hell are you?" A slight grin tugs at Alexei's full mouth. His gaze sweeps the group of elderly men.

I take a deep breath and hope my face isn't as flaming red as it feels.

"Alexei Sokolov, please meet Felix, Kenny, Merlin, Ozzy, Percy, Wally and Yardley." I swallow. "They're my boarders." More like my family.

Merlin holds out a hand and shakes Alexei's, grunting as he obviously puts an effort into squeezing Alexei's hand. Alexei looks over his head at Percy, who's staring right back. Something passes between them, and a shiver skates down my spine.

"What's going on?" I ask.

"Nothing," Alexei says smoothly. He's dressed nicely

in gray slacks and a white button-down shirt he borrowed from Garik. It's good enough for court, but the shirt is a little tight. He shakes the hands of the men and pauses with Percy. "Percy, did you say?"

"I surely did." Percy is about six foot two, but old age has bowed his back. His eyes are a luminous black and his hair a thick silver. He was one of my first boarders, and I think he once worked as an accountant. Many years ago.

Alexei releases him. "It's a pleasure to meet you all. Did anybody hear anything?"

The assembled group walks around my brutalized vehicle, all of them mumbling and shaking their heads. I'm sure most of them had already taken out their hearing aids for the night when this happened.

"Where did you come from?" Wally asks, his slight Welch accent emerging. That only happens when he gets angry. He normally stays inside and rarely ventures into the world. I believe he was once a traveling salesman, and that's why he prefers to remain indoors these days.

"I'm a friend of Rosalie's," Alexei says. "Do you have any idea who could have done this?"

Percy puts his hand on his hips. He's wearing loose khaki pants and a stained red polo shirt today. "No. Although reading the message cut into the leather, it's obviously about you. You are a killer, are you not?"

"Rumor has it." Alexei sighs. "I'll give you a ride to the courthouse, Rosalie."

I'm suddenly grateful I'm wearing my navy-blue suit with pants instead of the skirt, although every time I move, my clit cries. She probably deserves it, getting drunk and all, but Alexei hadn't been gentle with her last night. Apparently, I don't like gentle. I am so screwed up. He sees something in me that I haven't realized is there. A need for darkness—for what he can provide. "I do have to get to court." Being late to Judge Lahaska's courtroom is to be avoided at all costs. She lacks any semblance of patience.

"Should we call this into the police?" Felix asks, his headband a multitude of colors across his forehead.

"No," Alexei says. "This is about me, and I'll handle it."

Wally looks at me. "What do you think?"

"I think we call the police for vandalism," I say.

Alexei shakes his head. "Nobody saw anything. Nobody heard anything. You'll be wasting the police's time. This is about me, and I will figure it out."

Surprisingly, Percy nods. "I agree. Anybody who could do this without making enough noise to awaken us avoided all cameras in the area."

I blink, surprised. Percy is usually a by the book type of guy. It seems odd for him to agree with Alexei.

"I'll think about it." I look around at the many places for a bad guy to hide.

Merlin straightens his tie. "You have insurance, correct?"

I wince. "Just liability insurance." The cheapest amount I can afford. As they all exclaim and Merlin draws in air for a lecture, I look for help from Alexei. "Where is your motorcycle?"

"It's around the block." Alexei takes my hand, and the only reason I don't jerk free is because I don't want to get in a scuffle in front of the men. One of them will step in and get hurt.

"I'm sorry about this," I say to everybody in general. "I'll handle it later. I need to think."

With that, I follow Alexei around the corner to where he has his motorcycle hidden behind a crop of trees.

"You're a little paranoid, aren't you?" I ask.

He glances back the way we came at my now demolished vehicle. "Do you blame me?"

"No." Something in my stomach hurts. I loved that car. I don't know when I'll be able to afford another vehicle. Hendrix's offer the night before filters through my brain, but I won't take that job. He only wants me off Alexei's case, and then he'd probably fire me. "Hendrix threatened my boarders last night if I don't take a job offer from him."

Alexei straddles the bike and holds out an arm to help me on. "Hendrix doesn't want to lose control of Hologrid or the mob. I won't let anything happen to your boarders."

"Thank you." The mafia scares me, but I like that Alexei will use it to protect the elderly men. I swing my leg over the motorcycle as if this is a normal morning and I'm used to riding on a bike, seated behind an alleged killer, to court. The second my sex hits the seat, I wince and gingerly try to find a comfortable position. I can't. Even my butt is sore. I'd barely been able to put a bra on my sensitive nipples.

"Something tells me they can handle it." He backs us out of the trees. "This will mess up your hair."

My hair is the least of my worries. "I don't care." Right now, this bike is both killing my clit and waking up the bitch. I do not like pain. If I repeat that mantra enough, perhaps my body will listen. Men usually bored me before too long. Not Alexei. He was too much. Or was he? Did he just tap into a part of me I want to deny? Vulnerability whispers through me.

Alexei looks down the street before walking the bike into the open. "We should get you a helmet."

"I don't want a helmet." I'm pissed off and angry at the world.

"You seem to be pulling an attitude with me today, and that might be a mistake."

Irritation heats from my chest to my face. "Oh, really? Why is that?"

He turns his head, watching me from the corner of his eye. "You have to be sore, and I have no problem tossing you over my knee and making sure. Is that what you want?"

Not in a million years. "Last night was a one-time deal." I blurt the words out, lifting my chin for emphasis.

He stops moving, turns, and wraps an arm around my waist. With a quick pivot, he plants me in front of him on the bike, facing him. I try to lean back to take the weight off my sex. He slides a hand beneath my blouse and under my bra, palming my breast. "Do you really want to do this now?"

I gulp.

He balances the quiet bike with his strong legs while his other hand unzips my pants.

I grab his wrist. "Wait."

"No." He tunnels inside and slides a finger inside me. I'm a little embarrassed to be wet. "This belongs to me. Not a one-time deal. Got it?"

I blink.

He plucks my already sore nipple. I gasp from the pain, even as I dampen his fingers.

He shows his teeth. "This is mine." He plucks again. "Right?"

Numbly, I nod.

"And this." His thumb presses on my clit. "Right?"

We're nearly in the street. Anybody could see us. He doesn't care. I have to get out of here. Worse yet, I'm getting even more aroused. I give a quick nod.

He shakes his head. "More, Rosalie. You pushed, now you pay."

I hate him. And kind of want him. Wouldn't mind another orgasm, even though I'm so sore. He flicks my clit. "Fine. I'm yours," I whisper. I'll kill him later. Yeah. That's a good plan.

"What's this?" He leans in, his nose almost touching mine as he twists his fingers inside me.

"Yours," I whisper, out of my element completely.

His gaze searches mine. "Good girl." Whatever he sees in my eyes, which has to be a plan to kill him, makes him smile. He fixes my clothing and then swivels me back around behind him.

With that, he twists the key and the engine roars to life.

My clit lights and I suck in a breath, biting my already sore lip. It was a little swollen, and I'd managed to find a soothing cream-type of lipstick. The bites on my breasts still ache, as does my entire body. I try to convince myself that he's just playing a game and doesn't really consider us together. Consider me as belonging to him. I can't go around with bite marks all the time. Or bruises. Even if they are in erotic places. "We need to talk about this."

"We just settled everything. Stop pushing me." If anything, he sounds bored as he opens the throttle.

When did everything get so out of my control? I wrap my arms around him and lean in, holding tight. His rain and oil scent fills my senses. I shiver.

His low chuckle echoes back on the wind.

TWENTY
Alexei

I like the efficiency of the court's docket. I sit in the seat next to Rosalie as she stands and argues to have my conviction overturned with prejudice instead of the way it was—meaning they can't try me again and I'm free for good.

She looks stunning in the navy-blue suit with light-pink shell, her hair up. It was a glorious mess when we arrived on the motorcycle, so she pinned it up smoothly, her gaze not meeting mine. I'm fine with that. She'll accept her fate soon enough. We definitely fit.

Last night had cemented both of our fates. I've been with hundreds of women, maybe more, and she has permanently made me forget all of them. From now until my end, there will only be Rosalie.

I glance over at the prosecutor, who's a young guy with blond hair. He might be pushing thirty and wears a gray Armani suit with a red power tie. I try not to pull against Garik's shirt. The worn cotton is the nicest one he has, and it's too small for us both. If today goes well, I will change our status. In fact, I need funds to pay the men who had agreed to be on my payroll, at great risk to their own lives.

Rosalie flips her papers. "There's no other solution here, Judge," she says. "The corruption of Judge Sower and the prosecuting attorney has been well-documented and well-proven. While Mr. Sokolov's conviction has been overturned, granting him a new trial, I must argue that said order should've been granted with prejudice. The state must not be allowed to try him again. I've just given you more evidence, but you already know there's no other option but to overturn the conviction . . . with prejudice."

The judge flips through her file folder. The prosecuting attorney already argued that I received a fair trial, and will get another one, but the judge questioned him rather harshly about the corruption.

The prosecuting attorney seems young and earnest, so I doubt he worked here seven years ago. We have no actual proof that the judge was dirty in my case, but so many payments were logged into his offshore accounts that it is impossible to tell where the money came from.

I bet Hendrix paid him plenty to rule against me the way he had on every motion or objection my lawyer had issued—not that he did much.

Judge Lahaska looks up. She's a woman in her sixties, and her gaze lands on me. There's no softness or kindness or even understanding in her blue eyes. Her lips are pursed and her jaw is tight. Even so, I can read her easily. She can't stand me.

"All right." She clears her throat. "I agree with the order overturning Mr. Sokolov's conviction without prejudice."

That figures.

The prosecuting attorney leaps to his feet. "In that case, the state fully intends to retry the convicted felon."

Rosalie turns to face him, her eyes sparkling and her color high. "My client is no longer a convicted felon, so I suggest you watch your mouth, Counselor. I've been looking for a good slander case to take on."

Pride filters through me and I smile, allowing her to see my amusement. Her intelligence is impressive, and I find that I like that more than I expected.

The judge taps on a keyboard. "All right, why don't we go ahead and set this thing for a preliminary hearing. Counselors?"

The judge and prosecuting attorney land on a preliminary trial date, three weeks from today.

Rosalie nods. "That's acceptable, although I'm giving the court notice that Mr. Sokolov is going to appeal the court's ruling denying the motion for an overturned conviction with prejudice. I doubt I'll be heard by the trial date."

The judge sighs. "Let's leave this on the docket for now and file a motion for a continuance when you have more information."

"Of course." Rosalie smiles.

The prosecuting attorney glares at her, at me, and then turns and bustles out of the courtroom.

"That was fun," I whisper to Rosalie.

"Behave yourself," she whispers back. "We're not done yet. I like that we're getting all of my hearings done in one morning. If anything, the judge is efficient."

I glance to my side as Lillian, dressed in a loose-fitting long skirt, walks inside next to Samuel La Vinci, who's been her attorney for as long as I can remember. Apparently, her days of wearing tight dresses are over. She looks at me evenly, glances at Rosalie, and then takes her seat. The woman seems smaller than I remember.

"All right," the judge says, shoving folders to the side before grabbing another one, this one gray, unlike the other blue ones. Must be an easy way to differentiate between criminal and civil matters. "Let's take out the civil motion to unfreeze the funds of Alexei Sokolov."

"Thank you, Judge." Samuel stands, his voice firm and strong. The guy's around fifty and there's heated warmth when he glances at Lillian. So they're more than business acquaintances? Not that I care. He gives a pretty decent argument about my days as a playboy and how I wasted money, and he adds the fact that I'll be tried for first degree murder again, so the money should be preserved.

Rosalie makes a couple of objections, and the judge mostly rules against her. I lose interest in the byplay until Rosalie stands up and starts to speak.

"I find it unnecessary to address the fact of whether or not Mr. Sokolov wasted money, considering it was *his* money." She looks down at the documents. "Your Honor, as it stands right now, my client has been charged with a crime. He has not been convicted, and there's a good chance he'll never be tried again once I appeal your earlier ruling."

I hide a smile. It's enjoyable watching her poke the judge. Though I really do need money. Sooner rather than later.

"Therefore, there's no legal reason for Mr. Sokolov to be cut off from his own money." Rosalie then launches into a series of legal terms that bore me, so I start to plan the rest of my day in my head. Finally, she sits, her scent of vanilla wafting toward me.

My cock wakes up, wanting another taste of last night.

The judge ruffles through several file folders and a couple

of books before looking up, her eyes sparking again. Man, she really doesn't like me. It's rare. Most women do. She's probably read the trial transcripts. Truth be told, I look guilty, but many people had conspired to make that happen.

The judge once again looks like she is chewing on lemons. "I agree with Mrs. Sokolov that irreparable harm might come to the funds if the court allows them to be wasted. However, Mr. Sokolov makes a good point that the funds are his to waste. Thus I grant the motion."

Relief relaxes my spine.

The judge grabs her gavel and slams it on the counter. "The court's adjourned." Standing, she slips out of the courtroom without looking at any of us.

Rosalie turns. "Apparently, you're loaded again."

Lillian and her attorney disappear down the corridor, and he has an arm over her shoulders in a protective stance.

We follow slowly into the hallway, and I make plans to head to the bank immediately after we leave the courthouse.

A uniformed officer breaks off from a group whispering quietly, a box in his hands. He winks at Rosie. "Hey, Rosalie. I brought you copies of the evidence from the Sokolov case, although your firm should already have it all."

I find I want to smash it in his face.

She reaches for the box, and I take it before she can, noting it's fairly heavy. "Thank you for bringing this over, Saul. I planned to drop by the station later today."

He sniffs and doesn't notice the slight jerking of her head. "No problem." He glances at me. "I hope you're free for lunch."

The whispering gains volume from the group.

She nods her chin toward the uniforms. "What's going on?"

He leans in too close to her. "There's a gang war. The head of Twenty-One Purple was gutted last night."

"Oh," Rosalie says. "Are the streets going to become unsafe again?"

He tucks his hands in his belt and puffs out his chest. "We're planning for a war. Twenty-One Purple is accusing a rival gang, but who knows?"

Rosalie chews on her lip.

Saul glances at me and looks at her. "Are you okay? You want me to escort you back to the office?" He sniffs again. Loudly. "Damn allergies."

"I've got her," I say smoothly. "You should get yourself a fucking tissue. The sniffing is annoying as hell." For Rosalie, anyway. I grasp her arm and pull her away from him.

"Thanks for the evidence box," she calls back.

He watches us go, and all of his buddies turn to do the same.

The sense of possession, of absolute ownership I feel right now makes every inch of me hot. "Is he someone you dated?" I ask mildly.

"We went out a couple of times," she murmurs, her heels clicking on the tile flooring as we move. "There was no spark, so I let the whole thing fizzle."

"Did you sleep with him?"

Her stride hitches and then she regains her gait. "That's none of your business."

"Wrong," I say. "Dead wrong. Answer me or I'll go ask him." I'm not joking.

Her sigh is full of exasperation. "No, I didn't sleep with him. Like I said, there wasn't a spark. When there isn't a spark, you're not going to find one by getting naked." She tries to yank her arm free, and I don't allow her the freedom. "What if I had?"

I shrug. "Don't know. But I wouldn't want to be the only one in the dark in a conversation between you two."

She shakes her head, and some of that glorious dark hair falls out of the clip, framing her heart-shaped face. "Last night was just one night, Alexei. Don't start acting like we're a couple. I know your past."

The woman might know my past, but she's my future. "Everything about you is mine, and the sooner you learn that, the better. We are a couple, and that's final."

The sound she makes is a soft one of disbelief. Actions speak louder than words, so I'll just have to show her. "No more lunches with Saul."

"I'll lunch with whomever I want." We walk outside into a sunny day. "That crack about his sniffing wasn't necessary."

"Watching you flinch like you're being stabbed in the ear isn't something I'll accept. And if you lunch with Saul again, they'll never find his body."

Since she can't pull her arm free, she makes do by side kicking me in the shin. Her heel glances off, and I barely feel it. Man, she's cute. Never in my life have I seen cute and sexy combined in such an intelligent package. "Kick me again, and you'll regret it."

Her sharp intake of breath sounds heated. "Stop threatening me. Also, leave Saul alone. We don't lunch anyway."

Good to know. I'd hate to kill good old Saul, like I had Paco Gomez last night, slitting his throat, leaving not a trace from myself or any other gang. His former gang must be looking for a good fight. Considering the guy was trying to lure a thirteen-year-old girl into his car when I came up behind him, I didn't think twice at crossing off the first name on Urbano Reyes's list.

The other two gang members on the list don't bother me much, but I need to investigate the businessman. All I know is that he owns one of the Silicon Valley startups.

Then there's Ella Rendale. Rosalie's friend. I'd like to figure out why Reyes wants her dead.

Unfortunately, a deal is a deal.

TWENTY-ONE
Rosalie

Back in my office after a quick lunch, I'm still chafing at Alexei being so bossy about me not leaving today until he picks me up. Yes, somebody vandalized my car, but it was because of him, not me, clearly. But he made me promise, and I don't really want to break a promise to anybody.

It's not that I'm afraid of him or afraid of what he'll do, or at least I comfort myself with that thought. I hit speed dial on my phone.

"Yo," Ella says. "What's up?"

"Hey, I need a favor. I have a damaged security disc, and I was hoping you could do your magic."

Papers rustle over the line. "Security disc? From the last decade?"

"Well, seven years ago," I say.

"Tell me more," she says. "Is this about Alexei? Do you want me to get him convicted? I can do anything with a disc."

I'm thankful she's on my side in life. "No. I actually want you to fix it, like run one of your fancy programs or something. The recording is of the interior of the Fairfax house, and it might show the murder. But it's corrupted."

Her laugh is low and entertaining. I smile. There's something about her laugh that has always been contagious.

"I don't know what I'll have to do, but I'm happy to look at your corrupted disc and see if there's a program I can create or use, to get what's on it. Though, I need to ask you, what if I find a video of Alexei killing David Fairfax?"

"You won't," I say. "There's really no question he was set up, and if we can get the person who actually killed Fairfax on record, I can get this thing dismissed."

"You sure you want it dismissed?"

I roll my eyes. "Yes, I'm absolutely positive."

Her silence has weight until she speaks. "I'm worried about you. You seem different."

"I'm always like this with a case," I protest.

She keeps quiet again.

"Fine," I say. "Yes, there's something going on, but until I understand it, I can't explain it."

She loudly blows out air. "Oh, sorry," she says.

"No, it's okay. Air doesn't bug me. If you start chewing chips though, we're going to have a problem."

"I would never do that," she exclaims.

I believe her. She truly would never do that.

She clears her throat. "I lost Alana. I can't lose you to another mob boss." Her fear of abandonment has always been right there, and my heart aches for her. The death of her father wounded her deeply, and then her stepmother pretty much cast her out to the boarding school where we met. My grandfather had worked as the janitor so I could attend the classes.

"First of all, neither one of us has lost Alana," I say. "We all had to grow up someday and maybe get married."

"You're not marrying Alexei Sokolov, are you?"

The thought sends a very stupid thrill through me, and I quench it. "Of course not," I say. "Come on, Ella. Even if I do get married someday, you're not going to lose me. You're not alone."

"I know," she says. "It'd just be nice if my friends were here when my stepmother comes to kill me."

My head snaps up. We joke about that sometimes, but there's a ring of truth in her tone now. She seems more somber lately, and I'm wondering what she's planning. I know her. She's a planner. "You really think she will want you dead?"

"I don't think I'll give her a choice," Ella says softly. "I'm going after the company, and soon, and she'll have to fight back."

"I'll be at your side. I promise." No way will I let Ella face that evil bitch on her own.

"I know."

I twirl a pencil through my fingers. "Why haven't you made a move yet?"

"Their firewalls are too good," she grumbles. "I'm close, but it'll take me a while to hack, and I can't really do anything until I control the servers of TimeGem."

I might have to prepare a defense for corporate hacking, just in case. I'll have a paralegal start researching that immediately. "If I can do anything to help you, you know I will."

"I have a program running 24/7. I'm getting close," she says. "Very."

A pit drops into my stomach. She's not kidding about her stepmother. She's evil and greedy.

But I only have the mental bandwidth to work on one trial at a time, and I need to get Alexei set free for good. "I'll get the disc to you tomorrow. I have a full day. What do you say about popping by around dinnertime?" I should be able to scrounge up enough money for pizza.

"If dinner is on you, I'm there," she says. "We can ask Alana to meet us."

"That's fine. Give her a call. Oh, and I need my gold earrings back. They would've gone perfectly with my outfit today."

She borrowed them months ago. "Sorry, I forgot to give those back to you," she says. "I wore them on a date the other night."

"How did it go?"

"Horrible. He spent the whole time telling me how close he is with his mother."

I wince. "That's not good."

"No, but that's okay," Ella says. "Honestly, men are boring."

I had actually thought the same thing until very, very recently. "Hmm." I say noncommittally.

"I'll get to the bottom of that hmm tomorrow. Talk to you later." She ends the call.

A shadow crosses my office door, and Joseph Cage walks inside to set down three heaping boxes full of file folders and trial notebooks on one of my guest chairs. "I brought you the Miles casefiles for the last ten years."

"Thanks." I need more time in a day.

Cage leans against my desk, a little closer than usual. "Do you think the eldest Sokolov was set up?"

"I think it's possible his brother or stepmother bribed the judge and the prosecuting attorney." I look over at the box of files. "Those were all Miles's?"

Cage's gaze remains warm on me. A little too warm. "Yeah—just from the last ten years. You said you wanted to look into his cases. You don't believe he was dirty, too?"

"I really don't know, but we should find out," I say. "Just in case."

"If you want a project, you just found one." Cage reaches out and brushes a lock of my hair off of my face. "How about dinner tonight?"

I blink, startled. "Um, I thought we decided us dating was a bad idea." We only went out a few times and had a few kisses that basically didn't do a thing for me.

"I think we should try again. I can't stop thinking about you."

"Why?" I shake my head.

His gaze drops to my chest. "I don't know. Lately, there's just something about you, something electric."

That something about me is named Alexei Sokolov but I can't say that. Sleeping with a client will get me disbarred. Cage is a good-looking man, but apparently, I like sizzle. Dangerous, deadly, over-the-top sizzle. But it's not just that. Alexei has unlocked something in me. A wildness that contrasts with my need to be in control. Letting go as someone else takes control is addicting. Nobody else has ever figured me out like that. "It's not a good idea, Cage. I like my career as it is."

My phone buzzes and I pick it up. "Hi, Eloise. What's up?"

"Blythe Fairfax is here to see you," she says.

I have been calling Mrs. Fairfax for days to set up an

appointment. Apparently, she likes to set the tone. "All right, send her back. No problem."

Cage pushes away from my desk and looks down, today dressed in a nice black suit. "How about you think about it? I would love another shot with you."

"I believe I've already said no twice, Cage," I murmur. Besides being a risk to my career, the guy is at least twenty years older than me. It's just not a good idea. There's a knock on my door. "Come in," I say, surprised when Blythe Fairfax walks in with Jaqueline Lion on her heels. Oh, this is going to be interesting.

Cage looks at the women. "Are we having a meeting?"

"No." Jaqueline looks from me to Cage, her black hair up in a bun and her suit a red Chanel. In her mid-fifties, she has a spectacular body. "Why are you in here with the door closed?"

"I have a case with Rosalie," he says smoothly.

Jaqueline's eyes narrow, and she looks at me. "I see. We're here for a meeting."

I sit back and look at the women. "Do we have a conflict of interest?"

"No," Jaqueline says, taking a step to the side. "Cage, if you'll excuse us."

"Very well." He walks by them, condescending irritation in his wake.

Jaqueline shuts the door. "The firm does represent Blythe, but she's a witness in the case we've given you, so I wanted to be here while you interview her."

This is weird and probably inappropriate. "If there's an issue with Mrs. Fairfax's testimony, she should seek outside counsel, since we're representing Alexei," I say calmly.

Blythe is a beautiful woman, and I can see what Alexei

saw in her. Today she's wearing a light-gray suit with spectacular gold jewelry, and her hair curls around her lovely face. She lifts one eyebrow. "It's Alexei, is it, instead of Mr. Sokolov?"

Considering I carry his bite marks on several places of my body, yes. "Mrs. Fairfax, would you like to sit down?" I gesture to the chairs on the other side of my desk. She smiles, even as her eyes narrow and she takes a seat. Jaqueline sits next to her.

"Like I was saying,"—I can't believe I have to explain this to my senior partner—"if there's any issue with Mrs. Fairfax's testimony that could get her into trouble, or if there's a possibility she committed a crime, we need to obtain outside counsel for her."

"I don't want outside counsel," Blythe snaps. "Jaqueline's been my attorney for years."

"Well then," I say. "I'll have to advise Mr. Sokolov to obtain outside counsel."

Blythe's gaze rakes me from the top of my head to my chest and then back up. "Somehow, I don't think he'll agree. He's hell in bed, isn't he?"

I keep my expression stoic. "I wouldn't know."

She laughs, the sound, tinkly. "Oh, honey, believe me, you know."

Jaqueline crosses her arms. "Rosalie, you've slept with a client?"

I face her directly. "Of course not." Apparently, I have no trouble lying to my boss. I'm not under oath, and if she finds out it's true, she'll fire me anyway.

I've known Alexei Sokolov for less than a week, and I'm already lying to people and changing my morals. I need to get him out of my life, and the sooner the better. "I think it would probably be best if we recommend that Mr. Sokolov retain outside counsel."

Blythe chuckles. "I have a feeling he'll decline that invitation. You're quite beautiful and probably the perfect woman to have on his arm to look respectable."

"Finding him alternate representation isn't his choice," I murmur.

"Ha. You have to know him better than that already." She crosses her legs, hitching her gray skirt up higher on her toned thigh.

Jaqueline sighs. "If they agree, we can continue representing them both. It was a blow to the firm when we lost his case."

I look from one to the other. "Did we represent Mrs. Fairfax at that time?"

"No," Jaqueline says. "We've actually only represented Mrs. Fairfax for three years."

Relief fills me. That would definitely have been a breach of ethics if the firm had represented the widow, most likely the estate, and the accused. I'm tired of these games. I look at Blythe. "How long did you and Mr. Sokolov see each other?"

"About three months. Like I said, he was hell in bed. Told me he was in love with me, that I was the only woman for him." She smiles. "Has he told you that yet?"

I ignore her. "Who do you think killed your husband?"

Her eyes widen. "I think Alexei killed my husband. All of the evidence pointed to him."

"I understand that," I say. "But we have fairly good evidence that the judge and the prosecuting attorney were bribed, and the security disc from your home of the day in question is corrupt. Can you explain that?"

"Yes," she says smoothly. "Alexei had access to the security system. He messed with it often, so my husband wouldn't know he was there with me."

Warning ticks down my spine. "How many people had access to your system at that time?"

She shrugs. "Just people who worked there. Of course, the police confiscated the disc after the murder. They were the ones who told me that all the data was corrupted."

I still need to obtain a list of all the police officers who worked on the case. "How much did you inherit when your husband died?"

"Rosalie," Jaqueline snaps.

Blythe lifts one shoulder in a half shrug. "I don't know, just south of two hundred million."

"That's quite the motive," I murmur.

She looks around my office and at the pretty mirror to the side before smirking. "Yes, except I wasn't in the house when he was killed."

"We don't know that, do we?" I ask.

She rolls her eyes. "Phone records show I called Alexei when I left the Pilates class."

Sure, but she could've killed her husband and then gone to Pilates. "The murder weapon was a steak knife from a set?"

"It was a steak knife—we had many different kinds, most not a full set by that time. My husband liked very sharp knives, and he'd just throw one away if he couldn't get it just right. I swear, I bought more knives for that man."

I'd reviewed the crime scene photos, and somebody strong had killed David. Someone angry. Was she strong enough to have plunged that knife in so far? "If Alexei didn't kill your husband and neither did you, who would you suspect?" I find hypotheticals often work best with clients.

She smooths her hands on her skirt, showing several beautiful amethyst rings. My gaze catches on them. She smiles. "These are gifts from Alexei. He loves amethysts, as you know." She looks at my unadorned hands. "He hasn't given you a gift yet?"

I'm about to punch this woman in the face. "You have no idea who else might've killed your husband?"

"Oh, I don't know." She waves her hand in the air. "David was a stockbroker. He had happy clients, unhappy clients, but no one who would kill him in such a savage manner. Being stabbed to death like that required both anger and precision." She smiles again. "Two words I think we both can associate with Alexei Sokolov. Don't you agree?"

TWENTY-TWO
Rosalie

I finish the sandwich Ella has brought me for dinner and crumple up the paper to toss in the garbage can in my office. It's embarrassing to admit that I couldn't find enough money to buy pizza, and I'm afraid she knows it. Worse yet, she isn't rolling in money right now, either. "Thanks for the food. You shouldn't be spending your funds on me." I feel a little hypocritical considering my belly is now full with turkey, Swiss cheese, and excellent sourdough.

She waves a hand, sacked out in one of my guest chairs, quietly drinking a soda with a straw. "I set up and manage the website for Hal's Deli, and they pay me in food. It's all good." Per her usual arrangement, she looks adorable in a blue jumpsuit only women about five feet tall can get away with wearing. Her blond hair is back in a ponytail, and her smooth skin lacks makeup. Not that she needs it.

I nod at the bag holding the security disc of the Fairfax mansion that hopefully will show the day of the murder. "I need you to fix that."

"I'll do my best."

While I know she's brilliant and tough, she sometimes looks so fragile I'm not sure what to do. I feel a clock counting down for her, and part of that is her plan. "I've read through TimeGem's formation documents, updated bylaws, employee handbooks, and tax returns that I don't want to know how you acquired. I've also gone through your father's last will line by line."

Her shoulders slump. "Anything helpful?"

"No." I owe her honesty—as well as free legal advice. "The will leaves everything to your stepmother." Most folks don't understand that anybody can disinherit their kids . . . but usually not their spouse, absent an agreement like a prenup. There was no prenup in this case, that I've found.

She sighs. "The will is a fake, but I can't find the real one. I know, without question, that my father would not have left me out of the will. I think he granted me the corporation and left Sylveria with financial security."

That sounds about right to me. "If there was another will, I'm sure she destroyed it," I say thoughtfully. "But if we can find the attorney who drafted it, they'll have a dated copy."

She nods. "I know. I've hacked into most of the big law firms in Silicon Valley and am now spiraling outward to other big cities in California. It's taking some time."

"Hacking is also illegal." I haven't brushed up on the most recent criminal statutes and guess I should start.

"Please. They can't catch me."

I take a sip of my soda. "Says every convicted hacker ever." I tilt my head. "If she had a falsified will created, why do you think she left you a trust in it?"

"Because it takes some suspicion off her. Everybody who knew my father wouldn't have believed he left me with nothing. But the trust just took care of my schooling until I finished college. My stepmother isn't stupid." Ella sounds more thoughtful than angry, which is good.

I nod. "As I understand your plan, you're trying to find a valid will. In the meantime, you're hacking into the TimeGem Moments server. At least, you're trying to do so."

Now her eyes gleam. "Yep. Sylveria is actually pretty good at charging the diamonds that help power the servers, but our true connection is with citrines, and she can't touch those. They're mine. If I can get into the system, I might be able to attack the diamonds, leaving TimeGem completely vulnerable and in need of the citrines."

As a plan, it's good. And criminal. "They have to know you're coming."

She nods. "I know. But there's hints of a fifth player making a move soon, and I'm covering my ass by adding to the rumors."

My eyebrows rise. "So is there really a new social media company gaining traction?"

"Definitely. There are ghost rumbles across all four companies, meaning someone is conducting research, and we've all been hit with attacks and several viruses. So far, nobody has traced the accounts back to a source."

Fascinating. "I'm worried about your safety."

"I've moved my computer base several times, and very few people know where I live. Plus, any time I'm out with Alana, bodyguards are everywhere. Something tells me good ole Alexei isn't too far from ordering guards on you."

I roll my eyes. "Please. I'm his lawyer. He's probably already moved on to another woman." The thought shouldn't hurt, yet my chest aches. I need to wake up and get a clue.

Ella stands. "When I finally find the real will, we'll want to move fast with filing suit."

"Of course. I have the documents ready to go, including the preliminary injunction to freeze TimeGem's activities until a trial conclusion."

Her sneakers are silent on my antique rug as she heads to the door.

"Ella?"

She turns.

"When you attack the servers, you're not infecting the diamonds with a virus that'll kill Sylveria, are you?" It's a question a criminal defense attorney should never ask. But she's my best friend.

Her delicate jaw hardens. "No. I want to win this one in the courtroom." She winks. "Besides, I'll only kill for you or Alana."

A chill skates down my spine because I know she's telling the truth. I take a deep breath. "Ditto." So am I. Perhaps I can understand the family structure of the mafia.

She quietly exits, and I return to drafting a document for a sale of a car dealership that I've been ignoring for too long. The parties are both currently in the Bahamas, but they'll return soon.

After a couple of hours. I'm done.

I've had it with waiting for Alexei, and I'm just about to leave my office when Lillian Sokolov appears in my doorway.

My paralegal rushes up the hallway. "I'm sorry. I didn't see anybody come in."

"That's okay. It's after seven, Eloise. Go ahead and go

home." I cock my head and stare at Alexei's stepmother. "What, no kidnapping today?"

Her smile doesn't reach her sad eyes. She's dressed in a too tight but lovely pink Chanel suit with Manolo Blahniks and enough diamonds to choke a horse. Her hair looks limp today. "I said I was sorry about that. I really am, but it was kind of fun to be the bad guy."

That's surprisingly understandable to me. "You didn't need to get so pretty on my account." I push an unopened stack of bills away. I don't get paid until Friday.

Lillian takes a seat across from me. "I want to avoid another trial for Alexei if possible," she says, crossing her legs. "Tell him if he pleads guilty and serves ten years, I'll turn Hologrid Hub over to him when he's out."

"I don't believe you." Has Hendrix sent her here with this silly offer?

She blinks. "I'm telling the truth. I'm unable to charge the amethyst crystals strong enough for our servers. And sweet Hendrix? He works hard, and we're keeping running, but he's not going to get any better."

I steel myself against her pleading look. "You mean while Alexei is alive."

"Maybe, maybe not." She shakes her head. "There's no guarantee that the death of either of them will lead to more strength for the remaining one. It may work, it may not. But it's not worth it." She sets her bag down on the floor and leans back. "Do we have a deal?"

"I'm sure we do not," I say. "There's no way Alexei is returning to prison. If you want to reach an agreement with him about the company, why don't you just do it above board? If Hendrix isn't charging the crystal strongly enough, I'm sure Alexei would love to get involved again."

She tsks her tongue. "Alexei is dangerous and will kill both my son and me if he remains on the outside. It's who he is. Be a smart girl and at least see that much."

I do know that he can kill, but I don't think he would just murder them for power and money, although the crystals might be another draw. I've seen the craving in his eyes when he's talked about them, though I've pretended I haven't. I'm well aware of how badly Alana needs to charge the aquamarines, even though she seems to be turning some of that over to her cousin. I can't help but wonder if she's able to charge garnets with Thorn, but that's a question for another day.

Lillian takes a deep breath. "I've made a good offer. Don't make me testify against him again. That was grueling the first time."

"This is an insane offer," I mutter. "No way will he agree to return to prison."

Her chin lifts. "He killed David Fairfax, Rosalie. The evidence convicted him, and nobody bribed the judge or prosecuting attorney. Not for Alexei's case, anyway. He's handsome, but the jury will see the killer lurking beneath the surface."

I need to read over her testimony again. It had been disastrous the first time.

"Please talk him into taking Hendrix's deal." She stands, grasps her purse, and plunks it on my desk. "It's not right, but Hendrix is buying the loan for your home."

"The mortgage I took out?" I ask.

"Yes."

What a jerk. "That's fine, but I'm almost current with payments. So he can own a loan all he wants, but I will pay and keep my home." How am I going to get caught up?

She winces. "I'm sorry, but Hendrix believes there are a couple of acceleration clauses in the original contract."

That's true. I had really needed the money, and I hadn't qualified for the best of loans. "This could be considered blackmail or extortion," I say quietly. "If you think I won't have Hendrix arrested and charged, you have not read me correctly."

She shakes her head. "Just think of you and all those old men out on the street. If I were you, I would convince Alexei to take the deal. Ten years of his life, and then the company's his." Which would give Hendrix a decade to raid all of the company funds and quite possibly put a hit out on Alexei in prison. I don't know a lot about hits or how they work, but I'm afraid Hendrix is capable of it.

Lillian grabs her purse, and it opens, spilling contents across my desk. "Darn it," she says, reaching for two gold-plated lipsticks and a small pill bottle.

I read the label. "You're on prenatal vitamins?"

She shoves everything back into the bag and steps back, pushing her hair out of her face. Her very red with a hot-looking-blush face. "That's really none of your business."

I think of the interaction between her and her attorney in court earlier. "I guess I should say congratulations?" I look at her. "Are you sure?"

"I'm only forty-five," she says, and she stops talking as if not quite sure what to say. Wow. She truly does look older. Losing her son must be why. Obviously she wants to keep the pregnancy a secret. The baby isn't related to Alexei, so he or she won't have an affinity with the amethyst crystals that run in his blood. Perhaps she really does want to be free of the company to start over somewhere else.

"I'll extend your offer to Alexei, but I believe his answer will be no," I say. "Sorry, Lillian."

"Please try, Rosalie," she implores. Then she turns and bustles out of my office.

Man, I can't imagine what it was like for Alexei growing up with that family. I shudder and then grasp my purse and stride out the door, shutting off the light before heading to the elevator. I'll have to get a taxi home.

"Rosalie. Hey." A mammoth of a man looks up from the waiting area and tosses a magazine onto the table. I look at the vacant reception area and then back at him, my heart rate rocketing. He holds up a hand. He's dressed in faded jeans and a black T-shirt.

I squint closer. "Garik?"

He smiles. "Yes. Alexei has some business to take care of tonight, so I'm on you."

I blink. "You're on me?"

"Yes. I have a car. I'll take you wherever you want to go."

I find the high-handedness of Alexei irritating. "That's all right. I can make my own way." I stride to the elevator and push the button. Unsurprisingly, Garik steps next to me and enters the elevator.

"I don't need or want a ride home, nor do I need a bodyguard." I look up a good foot to his hard-cut face. His nose has been broken before, but it's still impressively straight with maybe a slight bump. "Go away."

"I don't think we have a choice in that," he says mildly. "I have one job, and that's to make sure you get home safely." He shrugs. "It's up to you how I accomplish this feat."

"Fine." I am just too tired to deal with this. At least I had a nice meal with Ella earlier when I gave her the disc that she promised to decipher. Right now, I'm unsure I want to help Alexei avoid another stint in prison. I'm starting to think he deserves it.

Garik and I ride down the elevator to the street level, where he escorts me outside to a waiting black town car. A Mercedes. I look at him and then back at the vehicle. He shrugs. "Alexei went shopping after his funds were released."

"Apparently so." Garik opens the door for me, and I slip inside and sit on the buttery soft seat. I have to admit the new car smell is relaxing. Garik slides into the driver's seat and maneuvers the luxury vehicle through town, taking me to my pretty pink house. He's out of and around the car in a heartbeat to open my door to help me out.

"Thank you," I say.

He straightens, his gaze scanning the surrounding area. "No problem. I'll be here all night unless Alexei gets back."

"He's going to be gone all night?"

Garik shrugs, no expression on his hard face. "I don't know. But if he is gone, I'm here. If you need anything, call me."

I glare. "I don't need anything." I don't like the mystery, and I don't like caring where Alexei is. That just angers me. I'm not in the mood to deal with any of my boarders, and they surely had dinner without me, so I climb my private stairway up to my suite, open the door, and shut it before flicking on the light. I gasp.

Shoe boxes are perched everywhere around the small seating area.

I look around wildly. Nobody's here. I walk forward and tip open the top of a pair of Louboutins. They're kitten heels—so cute like the ones I lost, except much nicer. Trying not to smile, I toss open a couple other boxes. All sorts of kitten heels in every color from every designer soon fill the room. I don't want to be delighted, but I am.

Laughing, I try on a pair. They fit perfectly. The shoe boxes lead into my bedroom, where there are more shoe boxes. These are more shoes than anybody could ever want.

I open the top of a feminine flowery pair made out of hand-sewn crystals and sigh. They're absolutely beautiful. Maybe I've been wrong about Alexei. This is a sweet gift. Perhaps he is the right man to handle the mob. Plus, he did sketch my face. That's romantic, I'm pretty sure.

Although, I do wonder what business is keeping him out all night.

TWENTY-THREE
Alexei

I've brought Miguel Cruz down to the basement of his one-bedroom tenement on the outskirts of San Jose. Oddly enough, the place is already soundproof with plenty of cement blocks set against the walls. Blood sprays show on many of the blocks as well as on the dirt floor.

"You're not going to get away with this." He spits blood out of his mouth.

"I actually am." I sound as bored as I feel. He's tied to a chair, and I've cut ribbons of his skin, but I have to admit, he hasn't broken as quickly as I would've thought. I stab him again, casually in the shoulder, and his jaw clenches.

He has to be around thirty with several tattoos across his face and neck. Some of it's pretty decent ink. Some of it looks like he did it himself. I've cut off part of his right ear, and so I stick to the left side so he can hear me. "I could keep playing all night," I say casually, twirling the knife in my hand. The blade has always been my favorite device, and apparently I haven't lost any of my skill with it. I've removed his shirt, and his jeans are in tatters. His knees are bloody.

"What do you want, man?" he asks. It's been a couple of hours, and that's the first question he has asked. Good. We're getting somewhere finally.

"I want to know why Reyes wants you dead." I cross in front of his vision.

His gaze remains on the bloody knife. "I don't believe you. Urbano Reyes does not want me dead."

I crouch so I'm meeting his eyes. One's filled with blood. "I have a kill list, Miguel. You're the second name on it. You will tell me. You might as well make it quick." I have no sympathy for him because I know his type. I'm certain plenty of the blood on the walls was spilled by him.

He swallows. "I don't believe you." His eyes widen and more blood drips out of the right one. "Did you kill Paco?"

I smile, and he shrinks back. "Yeah, I did." His mouth gapes open, and he's missing several teeth. I've only taken out two so far. I don't know how he lost the others.

He shakes his head wildly, and blood sprays. "Why would you kill Paco?"

"He was number one on the list."

Miguel's chest sinks and his shoulders slump. There we go. We're almost there. His breath wheezes out. "How did he find out?"

"He's Urbano Reyes," I say. "He's the head of your organization."

"He didn't tell you why?" Miguel asks.

Just as he draws up his chin to be defiant, I stab him in the thigh again. He cries out. "Nope, but you're going to tell me everything." I look around at the cinder blocks. "You did a good job soundproofing this basement."

"Thanks." He coughs up more blood. I rip the knife out. The sound he makes is indescribable. I've been stabbed before. I know how it feels. He swallows rapidly. "You're going to kill me."

"Yep," I say. "It's up to you whether I do it in the morning or right now."

He reaches the bargaining part of the dance. "How about we come to a different agreement?"

"I'm listening." I have no intention of reaching any other conclusion, but I find that giving somebody hope in their last hours is not a bad thing to do.

"I have money. About two hundred thousand dollars. We'll split it."

Considering my funds were released earlier, and I already went shopping, that's a piddly amount. But I smile. "Right now, I want information. Why does Reyes want you dead?"

He swallows, and more blood gurgles out of his lips. I think I may have punctured one of his lungs because he's wheezing. "He must've found out Paco was making a move to take over Twenty-One Purple, and I'm one of his lieutenants."

"Yeah, but that's not all." It's expected that somebody will make a move. "What else?"

Miguel shudders violently. Yep, definitely nicked a lung. "I don't know how he found out. There's no way she talked." Miguel's eyes get a faraway look as if he forgets my presence.

I'm sure it's the brain's way of protecting itself. "Who?"

He jerks. "Reyes's old lady. Juan, Paco's other lieutenant, made a play for her. She wasn't receptive. He didn't care."

I sit back. "What does that have to do with you?"

"I helped him cover it up. I threatened to kill her if she said anything." He spits out blood. "I meant it. She has no protection now that Reyes is gone. She should've taken Juan's offer."

"Doesn't sound like an offer to me," I say. Juan is the third name on my list, so at least now this makes sense. "Where does she live?"

He rattles off an address that's three blocks away. "She ain't going anywhere, man. She lives here. Reyes makes sure she has enough money to live and feed that kid, but she'll never get out of here. Like I said, she should've taken Juan's offer."

"Where is Juan?" I ask nicely.

Miguel's eyes look up, cloudy and brown, the bloody one looking darker than the other one. "Why?"

"He's third on my list," I admit.

"Whoa, whoa, whoa. No. If you and I are going to split the money, part of the deal is Juan lives."

Interesting. Loyalty among assholes. "Why?"

"Because he's the man. I'll take you to a party on seventh so you can meet him tonight. Now that Paco's dead, Juan will take over. He's got some great ideas, and he's always been our best bitch trafficker."

Yet another reason I'm going to kill Juan. It occurs to me that the man I'm killing them for is probably worse than the three of them put together, but right now he's safely in prison, and I don't have to worry about him.

"You've been pretty helpful, Miguel. Thanks." He's bleeding out, and I wonder how much time he has left. He isn't noticing that he's losing blood faster than he can make it. The guy's not the brightest.

He's bald with even more tattoos across his skull.

There's actually one of a skull with the word hell spelled with three l's beneath it.

I make sure there isn't too much blood on my jeans. There's a fair amount, damn it. "Tell me about Howard Fissure."

Miguel blinks. "Fissure? Why? What do you want to know about him?" He pales beneath his brown skin. "Oh God, Reyes knows about Fissure?"

"Yep," I say. "Who is he?"

"He's the owner of Nero Tech. It's some startup that has to do with the web." Miguel hangs his head. "Is there anything that Reyes doesn't know?"

"Probably not," I say agreeably, wiping off the knife on a clean spot on his jeans. He works to loosen the ropes behind his back, but I know how to tie a rope.

He gulps. "Shit. No wonder Reyes wants us dead."

I'm getting a little bored. I hear something, and I lift my head. It's thunder in the distance. "Tell me about Howard Fissure."

"Fentanyl," Miguel says quickly. "He can get great quantities of it through connections he has in China. We arrange to transfer it over the border, and suddenly it's here."

I assume Reyes is more pissed they've cut him out of a deal than that they're bringing poison into the country. "You split the profits?"

"Seventy-thirty." Miguel's lip curls up in a sneer. "I want to change that, but it's the best Paco could do."

"I see. Does Howard Fissure have a family?"

Miguel screws up his face, appearing as if thinking hurts him. "Um, ex-wife, maybe two. I don't know. We don't go to barbecues together, man. It's a business arrangement."

"An arrangement you made without Urbano Reyes knowing?"

"Obviously," Miguel says.

Oh good, he is getting some of his spirit back. "Where's the money?" I ask.

He looks up. "I ain't telling you that until I'm free."

"Where's the money?" I ask again.

"I'm not telling you." I stab him in the shoulder and tear down. He cries out with the most high-pitched sound he's made. He must have an old shoulder injury. The knife didn't go through as easily as it should have. Scar tissue impedes blades.

Bloody tears flow down his face. "Fine, fine. It's upstairs beneath a board in the second bedroom."

"That wasn't that hard, was it?" I ask him. He doesn't answer and instead tries to sniff a snot bubble up his nose. It occurs to me how much that would annoy Rosalie. Well, she probably wouldn't like the blood either. "Now, tell me about Ella Rendale," I suggest.

Miguel blinks. "Ella Rendale? From the society pages?"

"Yeah. Why would Reyes want her dead?"

Miguel sits back, his eyebrows rising. One of them is heavily scarred. "Dude, I have no idea. We don't have anything to do with the society page. Reyes must have a contract I don't know about."

Most entirely possible. "You better not be lying to me." I lift the knife.

"I'm not. I'm not," he says quickly. "I promise. I don't know anything about Ella Rendale."

Probably truthful. He did give me the information on Howard Fissure pretty easily. "So Juan Gomez?" I ask. "Why are you two so tight?"

"He saved my life more than once," Miguel says. "I'll split the money upstairs with you, but you have to leave Juan alone. We need someone to lead since Paco's dead, and Reyes ain't getting out of prison anytime soon."

"Fair enough." I walk behind him and reach down for the ropes tying his wrists together. His shoulders relax. In that split second, I lean around him and slice his jugular. Blood spurts across the room, and he jerks several times, finally going limp in death. I manage to keep most of the blood off of me, and the cheap gloves I wear will be easy to burn. I wipe the knife off again on him and then stab it into the ground next to his foot. It was his knife, so he should keep it.

I exit the room silently and carefully walk upstairs, listening for noise. Nothing. I make it to the second bedroom and tap on the floorboards until I find a loose one. Making sure my gloves remain in place, I lift the fake wood to find a knapsack that I pull out and open. The little bastard lied to me. There's at least three hundred grand in the duffel bag.

Slinging it over my shoulder, I walk out the back door and through many sad-looking, forlorn backyards until I reach my motorcycle. I pause and then decide to walk the other block. I have the bike hidden neatly between two old sheds, and starting her up will just create more noise.

So I walk the other block and knock on a door. Nobody answers. The house is one story with falling shutters, and it may have been green at one point. Now the color is more of a dingy gray fronted by a small patch of burned-out grass in the yard. I knock louder.

The porch light flickers on, and the door opens to reveal a girl who can't be any older than seventeen. She has at least a two-year-old on her hip. "What do you want?" She's pretty, though bruised. She has a black eye and marks on her neck. Her hair is long and black, and the baby's adorable with her little thumb in her mouth.

I drop the knapsack next to her feet. "There's enough here for you to take off and don't look back." She looks at me suspiciously and takes a step back. "Paco and Miguel are dead and Juan is next," I say. "Reyes is not getting out of prison anytime soon. Take the baby, take the money, and go."

Turning, I leave her on the porch staring at me. It's up to her whether she takes a chance at freedom or not. My gut feeling says that she will. I make my way back to my bike and roll it for almost a mile away from the shitty neighborhood before jumping on and starting the ignition.

I find Jose with a group of his buddies partying at a house about fifteen blocks away on Seventh, exactly where Miguel had said. I park in the distance and watch, waiting until Juan comes into sight. I tracked him through Facebook and know exactly what he looks like. He laughs and jokes with buddies, a gun visible at his hipbone.

I stand in the darkness across from the street in a lonely stand of pine trees in front of an abandoned house. He kisses a tall blonde and then saunters down the walkway around four in the morning. The blonde tries to follow him, and when she gets close enough, he turns and punches her in the face. She falls hard on the unforgiving ground.

"I told you, you can't come home with me. Melissa's there." He turns and starts whistling again as he struts down the sidewalk.

I follow on the other side of the street until we reach a more deserted area, and then I let him get ahead of me several yards before I silently cross to his side. The wind has picked up, and a light rain is beginning to fall.

I'm on him before he knows it, and I take him out quickly with a knife I snatched from Miguel's kitchen earlier. I have all the answers I want. I believed Miguel when he said he didn't know about the hit on Ella. That had come from Reyes specifically, and I bet he has accepted a contract for her life.

Leaving Juan drowning in his own blood, I move silently through the night back to my bike before I take off the gloves, turn them inside out, and tuck them in my pocket. I'll burn these clothes even though it's unlikely the police will do too much forensic testing on these men.

I think idly about dropping by Howard Fissure's house, but I need to know more about him before I make a move. He probably has security.

I left Garik on Rosalie all night, and now that I have enough money to fund my payroll, I'll make sure there's a rotation of two guards on her at all times. The warning on her vehicle was for me, but I can see someone hurting her just because she's my lawyer. They have no idea what else she is to me, and I'll keep it that way for now.

So long as she understands who she belongs to.

TWENTY-FOUR
Alexei

I arrive back at Rosalie's around dawn and hide my motorcycle between the trees before moving toward her house. A dark shadow waits for me, and I'm not surprised. I keep my hands loose at my sides as Percy Jancovic slips out from his hiding place.

"I was surprised to see you out and about," he says, a nine millimeter pointed at my chest.

"I have a good lawyer," I murmur.

He's aged in the seven years I've been in prison. Frankly, he was older than dirt before that.

"So I guess you didn't quite die in that car that blew up," I say wryly.

"Doesn't look like it."

I step closer to him. Will he actually shoot me?

"That's far enough. We both understand I know how to kill," he says.

"I would assume killing people is in your past."

He's wearing a pink polo shirt that covers his sunken chest and old-man pants that are held up by a belt over his belly. Grizzly gray and white hair sticks up all over his head, and his eyebrows are so bushy I'm surprised they don't crawl across his face. His eyes are a cloudy brown and his ears much larger than I remember.

"Why did you fake your death?" I ask.

"I wanted out," he says. "Your dad was dead, and that just changed the entire organization. Lillian doesn't know what she's doing. Or rather she does, and I didn't like what she was doing, and Hendrix is no better. You were an asshole, and I didn't see you ever making anything of yourself. So I decided to die." He shrugs. "I ended up here, and I was her first boarder. Once I got here, once I got to know her, I couldn't leave."

Rosalie. She does seem to draw men to her like butterflies to the perfect flower.

I shake my head. "Why would you even remotely stay in this area if you wanted out?"

"Rosalie. Plus, I don't go anywhere. Look at this." He sweeps his free hand out toward the multitude of bushes, flowers, and plants. "This is what I do. I'm the gardener here. We all have a role."

"None of them know who you are or what you've done."

"Of course not. Rosalie thinks I'm a retired accountant, which I kind of am," he says.

My chin drops. "You're an assassin."

"Well, I counted bodies, and sometimes I helped with the books," he says defensively, his voice croaking.

I look at the gun. "What's your plan?"

"What do you want with her?" he asks.

I cock my head. "She's a little young for you."

Red flushes over his cheeks. "It's not like that. She's like a granddaughter to all of us."

I can see that. She obviously cares for them. "She's going broke feeding all of you."

"We try to help," he protests. "It's not like you get Social Security for working in the mob. Plus, don't you have a lot of money now? Rumor has it your funds were released."

I cock my head to the side. "Rumor has it, huh? So you do have a couple of people still in the organization who know you're alive."

"Yeah, but I'll never tell you who they are."

I believe him. He's legendary. Some men just don't crack. "That's fine. But Hendrix and Lillian have no idea you're alive."

"Of course not," he says, "or I'd be dead." He snorts. "Rumor has it you're stepping back up."

"Rumor's true," I say quietly. "You want back in?"

His gaze is hard. "No. I'm eighty-two years old. I want to be completely out." His hands shake slightly, and I hope he doesn't accidentally shoot me. "But if you do anything to hurt Rosalie, I will kill you."

I read the sincerity in his eyes. "She cares about you, and I don't want to kill you," I return easily. "She is my future, and I plan to rebuild my entire organization. If you have a problem with that, you should probably shoot me right now."

He gulps, and the saggy skin around his neck moves. "What do you mean she's your future?"

"Exactly that," I say. "I'm keeping her, Percy. I'll make sure she's safe and well taken care of. She'll never worry about money again."

"When the hell did you decide that?"

Probably the first time she glared at me in that prison meeting room. "Doesn't matter."

He stares into my eyes and reads something there that finally has his arm lowering. "I don't know that she wants that kind of life."

"Too bad. That's the life she's going to have."

He tucks the gun at the back of his waist. "If she asks me to kill you, I'll do it."

I smile. "Fair enough. Are we done?"

He nods. "For now." He starts to walk away and then turns. "You've changed."

"I hope so," I say dryly. "I really was an asshole back then."

He gives one short nod. "How many men do you have?"

"About ten," I say. "I won't give you names."

He stands straighter, still stooped over. "I can get you a few more," he says. "Hendrix is not well-liked."

We'll still be outnumbered, but that'll be a good start. "I appreciate the assistance."

"I expect to be paid," he says instantly, looking around at the flowers.

"Of course. I wouldn't have it any other way." I turn and head toward the private entrance to the top floor. I walk up the stairs, for the first time taking a really good look at the keypad next to Rosalie's door. Oh, I know the code because I saw her key it in, but it's much nicer than I expect at this little house.

In fact, it's absolutely top of the line. How does she afford this?

I key in her code, open it, and walk inside to see the shoe boxes neatly lined up against the far wall. I smile. I hope she enjoyed the treat. I hear a shower running, and my blood starts to hum. But as I walk by the little kitchenette, I note her purse flopped over. Looking closer at the desk, near her little fireplace, I see her phone plugged in.

I grab the device and lift it. The screen wants her face, not mine. But I saw her type in that code, so I open her phone and scroll through several of her texts. Apparently, she likes chai tea lattes from a place called Bernie's. I read through several more, and then I find the number I want, keying in the text message.

When I'm finished, I wait. An answer comes almost immediately. I read it and then shut the phone, plugging it back in. With that, I strip off my clothes on the way to the shower. I might as well join her this morning.

There's so much steam when I enter the shower that I can barely make out her form. Pulling open the glass door, I move inside.

She jumps and turns around, her hands to her neck and her elbows covering her breasts. It's an instinctual and primal reaction to a threat. She blinks and then her body relaxes. "What are you doing here?"

I look down her naked and wet form. She has all the right curves, plenty of them, in all the right places. I like that. Have never gone for stick thin or fashionably skinny women who don't eat. "For now, I live here."

Her chin lifts as wet and dark hair sticks to the side of her face. "For now? That's over. You have your own money now and can afford to own Silicon Valley twice over." With the steam dancing across her, she looks like a mysterious angel.

"*For now* because you're moving somewhere more secure as soon as I find a place." I place one finger on her cherry-red lips and trace down, taking my time, sliding over her chin to her clavicle and between her breasts. Her abdomen clenches as I continue the journey until I find her and press that finger inside her. I like that she waxes everything. She's wet and hot. Scalding.

Her eyes flare. Need and anger. A little fear. She grabs my wrist with both of her hands and pushes it away, taking my finger from its home. "I'm not moving anywhere."

Ah. I'm not the best at communicating anything other than threats, and that's not the route to go with her. At least not unless it's absolutely necessary. "Have you ever felt this way with another man?"

"No," she says, giving me such an innocent honesty that my chest fills with something heated. "But I'm not sure *this* is good. It's certainly not safe."

God was beyond generous when he gave her both this body and that brain. "Baby, your safety will never again be your concern. That's mine." I'm about to control one of the most dangerous forces in the world, and every single one of those men will take a vow to protect her to the point of their own death. As will I. I indulge myself and sweep that thick wet hair away from her stunning face.

She shakes her head but doesn't back away from my touch. "Alexei. Be serious. I know this it hot and thrilling, probably stupid and dangerous. But we just met. Stop talking like we'll be rocking on chairs on a front porch together eighty years from now."

There's a new vulnerability in her cerulean-blue eyes. One I don't mind. She's starting to care more than her intellect says she should, and that must be terrifying. Especially since I'm, well, me.

So I wrap that glorious hair around my hand, twist, and lift her face for a kiss. I take her deep, already lost in her. She makes a sound of surrender deep in her throat, and it tunnels through me to land in my heart. Hard. A warning ticks in the back of my head and I ignore it.

Finally, I release her mouth to allow her to breathe.

She blinks, her eyes stunned and her lips already a little swollen.

"You should probably thank me for the shoes," I suggest.

Her eyes refocus. "Oh." Delight dances across her face and she banishes it. "The shoes are beyond beautiful and way too many." Yet she's touched and she doesn't hide that from me. "They were very, ah, unexpected."

I'm sure. In addition, I'm still surprised by how much fun I had in choosing them. For her. "There's another gift in the dresser by your bed." It's an amethyst pendant that I spent a wondrous time charging. "You need to choose a new car. Do you want the same kind?"

She swallows and her spine stiffens. "Absolutely not."

I kiss her nose. God, she's adorable. "Okay. How about a BMW?"

She plants a hand on my chest but doesn't push. "No. No car. No other presents." Confusion wrinkles her face until she smooths it out. "I'm not . . . I'm not a mistress. I can't be bought."

Unexpected humor takes me, and I chuckle. She's been watching too many mob movies. "Mistress? No. I'll marry you right now, if you want."

Her mouth drops open, and she tries to take a step back. I keep her in place. "What kind of game are you playing?" Her voice trembles.

I dig deep for patience. "The only games I'll ever play with you are in the bedroom. Other than that, you can take me one hundred percent at my word."

She shakes her head, and I loosen my hold so she doesn't hurt herself. "We just met."

"You admitted I claimed you last night. We both meant the words." Then, before she can argue, I kiss her again, lifting her up against me. I know from the calendar on her phone that she has early meetings scheduled, so we don't have much time to play.

This is the only way to start a morning.

TWENTY-FIVE
Rosalie

Considering I'm not straddling a motorcycle this morning, I wear a light-green pencil skirt, a pink and green blouse, and new kitten heels—a green pair that look absolutely perfect with the outfit. I should feel guilty accepting the shoes, although Alexei hadn't exactly given me a choice.

I shiver as I think about the morning in the shower. What am I going to do about him? I've known the guy less than a week, and he's planning our future. Worse yet, I'm tempted to jump right into that future, which I know will be a disaster.

Around my neck, I wear an absolutely gorgeous amethyst pendant, which I should not have accepted. Not that he gave me a choice. He'd already left the apartment when I found the gift in my dresser. I considered not wearing it because it's just too much. I can't imagine what it costs. And yet, there's something in me that doesn't want to hurt his feelings, and I think that would.

Why am I concerned about Alexei Sokolov's feelings?

I slap my hand against my forehead as I walk down the steps toward my driveway and then pause as I note three men waiting for me. "Good morning, Merlin, Percy, and Wally," I say, my instincts humming. "What's up?"

Merlin's dressed in a three-piece suit with a gold-colored bow tie that he tugs on. His cloudy blue eyes narrow on me. "We need to talk."

I glance at Percy, who's my favorite gardener in the world. "Okay. Do we need new mulch?"

Percy sighs, moving his narrow frame. "Before I retired, I worked for the Russian Bratva. In fact, for more than five decades, I worked for Alexei's father."

I step back, my body seizing. "You were a mobster?" Percy is one of the kindest and sweetest men I've ever met, and he's a god with rosebushes. "Are you kidding me?"

He gulps. "I was just an accountant, but I know who Alexei is, and I'm not sure you do."

Merlin looks down at his scuffed shoes. "Oh, I need a polish." Then he shakes his head as if bringing himself back to the present. "I hacked into his prison records, and I have to admit Alexei was a model prisoner, although he was heavily covered by the Twenty-One Purple gang. They don't do anything out of goodwill. You know that, right?"

"Actually, I'm not all that familiar with gangs." I look at Wally. "What do you have to do with this?" As far as I know, he worked as a salesman his entire life.

He shifts his feet. "Since we're all being a little bit honest here, I think we should update the security on this entire house."

I pat his arm. Unlike the other two, he's shorter at about five-foot-six and weighs over two hundred and eighty pounds. I've tried to work out with him because I'm worried about his heart. But so far, according to Doc, his numbers are all good. I know he takes blood pressure and cholesterol medicine, and I make a mental note to buy him some CoQ10, which is a vitamin everyone who takes a statin should use to protect their joints.

"I'm a little short on funds," I tell Wally. "I can't afford to update the system again." He has friends who own a security business, which is how I received a deal on the system we have now.

He reddens slightly, and his jowls jiggle. "I worked in security for years."

"Tell her the truth." Merlin elbows him in the ribs.

Wally winces. "All right, I was with MI6. I can create and install any security system you want."

The reality of the statement crashes through me. "Wait, wait, wait. Wait a minute. You're telling me that you were in the mob—" I point first at Percy and then at Wally— "and you worked for MI6? Are you kidding me?"

"No," Wally says glumly. "After Percy found you, he kind of reached out to several of us who were looking for a good place to live. We all had dangerous jobs and didn't plan on living until retirement."

I glance at Merlin. "I already know you were a hacker, you spent some time in prison and then worked for a government agency, but that's all I know."

"That's all you'll ever know." Merlin smiles.

I think of my other four boarders. "Is Felix really a doctor?" He has been giving me medical advice for quite some time.

"Of course, he's a doctor. Otherwise, he wouldn't be able to write you prescriptions," Merlin says. "Now, Rosalie, concentrate on the moment at hand. We don't have much money, but we still have great contacts. I can get you out of town into a safe house in no time if you want."

I can't believe this. It's doubtful my other boarders have any idea about these men. "How dangerous are you guys?" I ask, more out of curiosity than fear. They're family, as far as I'm concerned.

"Considering we're all over eighty, I wouldn't worry too much," Percy says dryly. "But if the occasion rises, we can protect you."

This is too much. "I appreciate that," I say, "but I can protect myself." I look down the driveway, where Garik awaits patiently next to the Mercedes.

Percy follows my gaze. "Rosalie, if you want a life outside of the local Russian mob and away from Alexei, now is the chance. You probably won't get another one."

His words rattle me, but I'm not leaving town. "I appreciate your concern, but I can take care of myself."

Relief crosses Percy's face. "All right. Looks like your choice is made. I'm glad. I didn't want to move."

My heart warms. "You would've moved?"

Merlin nods. "We'll all move with you if you go somewhere. So consider it, all right?"

My heart thumps. It feels good to have family. I miss my grandpa every day. "All right, I'll keep that in mind."

Wally clears his throat. "We're going to try to gather enough funds to up your security system, just in case."

I shake my head. "We're all too low." In fact, several of them still owe me rent. Apparently, retiring from the mob and MI6 doesn't lead to great amounts of wealth. I wonder, fleetingly, if anybody really knows where these men are, and if they're truly retired. Perhaps their businesses were such that disappearing was the only way to go.

"I'll see you all later," I say. "Thank you for worrying about me." I stop to kiss each man on their weathered cheeks. They all three blush, and it's freaking adorable.

My heart feeling lighter than it has in days, I walk down to where Garik opens my door.

"What was that all about?" he asks.

I smile. "Just normal renter stuff. We need a new air conditioning system." I slide into the luxurious vehicle, and he shuts the door. When he enters the driver's side and starts the car, I give him directions. "I have to go by the police station," I say. "I set up a meeting with the detective from Alexei's case."

Garik's eyes meet mine through the rearview mirror. "The police station?" He doesn't sound too happy about it.

I smile brightly. "Yep. Feel free to come in with me, Garik."

He shakes his head. "It's all right. I'll leave you at the door."

"Yeah, I figure. So are you like Alexei's bodyguard or something? I'm not all that familiar with how the Russian mob works." I'm still not sure I'm okay with any of this.

Garik returns his focus to the traffic suddenly surrounding us. "One of the ways it works is you don't talk about the Russian mob," he says calmly.

"I can't get any details from you?"

He makes a right turn down to Main Street. "None whatsoever."

I have to admit, it's interesting having a bodyguard. "I'm thinking that you and Alexei go way back?"

"We do," he says. "We became friends a long time ago when we opened that bar."

"So you know a lot of the women he has dated."

Garik makes another turn. "I wouldn't consider any-body to be really somebody he dated."

"What about Blythe Fairfax?" I ask. "He was with her at least three months."

Garik slows down to let a school bus pass us. "If you want details about Alexei's love life, or lack thereof, I sug-gest you speak with him."

I can admire a loyal friend. "He says I can speak with you."

"Huh," Garik says, clearly not believing me as he pulls up to the front of the police station. "Go in the main door that is in my sight and come out the same place," he says. "Please," he adds at the last minute.

"I can walk from here to my office."

"No."

I shrug. "All right. I'll go in the front door, and I'll come out the front door, Garik." Rolling my eyes, I scoot from the vehicle, my computer bag over my shoulder. I feel his eyes watching me and the surrounding area as I lever up the stairs to open the gleaming glass doors.

Instant coolness hits me as I walk inside, and I head over to the reception desk to give my license and creden-tials. They accept them, check some sort of list on the computer, and then call up to the detective before handing me a visitor's badge. "All right, go ahead. Third floor. Go right," the burly guard tells me.

I walk toward the elevators, quickly landing on the third floor, where a pretty dark-haired woman meets me.

Her skin is a deep brown, and her eyes alight with humor. "Hi there. I'm Louise." She's dressed in casual clothing. "I'll take you back to Detective Battlement."

"Thank you." I note the hustle and bustle of the place.

I walk by a guy slurping soup and shudder before continuing on. I keep AirPods in my handbag at all times just in case, but I can get through this place quickly enough without having to use them. We reach a door at the far end, upon which she knocks.

"Enter," a booming voice yells.

She opens the door. "Here you go. Miss Mooncrest is here from Cage and Lion," she announces. "This is Detective Battlement."

I walk inside a room besieged by file folders, papers, and books that match the harried man behind the desk.

He stands. He's big and burly and has a square face and a hard jaw. "Hello." He shakes my hand. "Please sit down." There's one chair that's clear of debris, and I sit, gently nudging a couple of file folders away from my new kitten heels.

"Sorry about the mess." He looks around as if seeing it for the first time. He has to be in his early fifties, and his wiry gray hair stands up on end. He hasn't shaved in a couple of days, and his eyes are bloodshot.

"Thank you for fitting me in." I look around the cluttered office. "I can tell you're swamped."

"I am." His beefy hand lands on the desk. "There's a lot going on in Silicon Valley these days." He digs under a stack of file folders and pulls out one. "I looked over the Alexei Sokolov case last night to prepare for our meeting, and it was pretty solid, I got to tell you." He's actually a lot nicer than I expected, considering I'm at the moment acting as a criminal defense attorney.

He continues, "I have a notation here that we sent copies of all the evidence over to your office already."

"Yes," I say. "We're hoping to be able to repair the security disc from the date of the murder."

He scratches his head and reads something in the file folder before turning the page. "Yeah, it was pretty corrupted. But that was, what, seven years ago? Technology has probably changed. We can take another look as well."

"That is wonderful," I say, although Ella is the best. I study him. "Do you remember much about the case?"

He focuses on me. "Yeah. I was the investigating detective at the time. Your client's guilty, Counselor." His voice doesn't hold a lot of emotion, and I take that to be more from experience than anything else.

"Why so?" I already read his testimony, but I want to hear it directly from him.

The detective shrugs, leaning back in his chair, which shrieks in protest. He's got to be a good six feet tall and maybe about two hundred and fifty pounds of what I would consider to be solid muscle—beefy and strong. He probably needs to have his suits specially tailored. "Your client was at the murder scene, and his fingerprints were all over the knife that he had to throw in the pond. He was in love with the deceased's wife, and he thought he was untouchable."

"Untouchable?" I ask, just watching him and not making notes. People are less likely to speak freely if they think you're writing everything down, so I listen and make mental notes that I will type later.

The detective nods. "Yeah, he was rich, and he was popular, and he was cocky. Honestly, I'm sure he thought he could get away with it—that money would triumph in the end."

I can see the younger Alexei thinking that, so I nod. "Go on."

The detective shrugs. "Have you looked through all the evidence yet?"

"I've read the reports, depositions, trial transcripts, and his former attorney's notes," I murmur. "Besides the corrupted security disc from the Fairfax residence, I'm still watching the hundreds of hours on a bunch of CDs from the Amethyst Pony."

"Your boy loved that woman," the detective says, "and that's one of the best motives there is for murder. Trust me, I've seen it happen over and over again. You take a cocky, rich playboy who's challenged by another man, and he would've killed him. He did kill him. It's a fact."

It all seems too easy. "Alexei says he was set up, that he wouldn't ever be dumb enough to throw a knife with his fingerprints into a pond that's just off the back of the deceased's home," I say.

The detective smiles. "In hindsight, people think they're a lot smarter than they truly are. I imagine this was your client's first murder. I'm sure he freaked out, and he knew the police were on the way. The kid panicked." The kid wasn't a kid anymore, and he was less prone to panicking.

"The judge and the prosecuting attorney were corrupt."

"I'm aware of that," the detective says, anger burning in his weary eyes. "In fact, I'm one of the people who investigated both. And you know what? There was never any evidence that they threw the trial against your client. You've read the trial transcripts, correct?"

I nod. "Yes."

"The judge ruled against Alexei's attorney several times, who also didn't do a very good job. But it doesn't mean they were bribed. It looked like a fair trial to me, and the primary evidence is the knife. Your client panicked, Counselor. If anybody's offering you a deal, you should probably take it." His voice is sure.

Apparently, he can testify not only as to the case against Alexei, but the case against the judge and the prosecutor. I think through my options. "You don't think Alexei was set up. You're not even willing to consider that possibility?"

The detective shakes his head. "I find absolutely no evidence of that. What I do find is plenty of evidence that your client murdered David Fairfax out of jealousy or ego or both. I don't really know, and I don't really care."

I question him for another half an hour, but he doesn't give me any more that I can use. I stand. "I appreciate your help, Detective." He actually seems like a pretty nice guy.

He stands. "Anytime, Miss Mooncrest. I have to tell you from the investigation I've conducted on your client, you need to be very careful."

I blink. "Why is that?"

"He's ambitious and he's strong, and he has no problem killing. If I were you, I'd pass this case off to somebody else."

It's too late for that. "I appreciate your warning, but I really do think my client is innocent."

The detective bursts out laughing. "Then you're in the wrong business, sweetheart. Trust me."

TWENTY-SIX
Ella

My backpack slung over one arm, I hustle through various crowds to reach my favorite coffee shop. I have no idea why Rosalie texted me earlier to meet here this morning, but I trust her instincts. I keep to crowds, like she told me, until I reach the correct block.

I'm wearing jeans and a light sweater, since I think it's going to rain, and with my Keds and my backpack, I pass for a student. That works for me. I stop and wait for the light to turn before crossing the crosswalk, my mind spinning.

Her text that morning had held certain urgency, and I'm concerned for her. I've already talked to Alana, and we have a plan to get Rosalie out of the country if we need to do so. We'll have to rely on Thorn, and I don't like that, though Alana seems perfectly comfortable with the fact. Of course, the guy's in love with her, and she's safe.

That, of course, is what keeps him safe. From me.

I'm concentrating on reaching the coffee shop when I hear the opening of a door that causes a warning to tick down my spine. I pivot to see a van door slide open. Everything happens too quickly for me to grasp. Two men jump out, grab me, and yank me into the vehicle. The door slams shut, and we're instantly driving into traffic.

I blink several times, shocked by how quickly that just happened. The van floor is cold beneath my butt. Two mask-wearing men face me, while there's a driver up ahead. I quickly scoot away from them until my back hits the far wall. Gazing at them, I hold still.

The men take off the masks, and I blink. I don't recognize one, but the other one is scum-sucking Alexei Sokolov.

"What in the blazes are you doing?" I partially lean forward.

He smiles. "You're safe. Just take a deep breath."

"Safe?" I sputter, reaching for the gun at my ankle hidden beneath my jeans.

He almost casually grasps my wrists before securing my weapon. He looks at the small .22 caliber. "This is a tiny gun."

"I know what it is," I say. "I need a smaller weapon if I'm going to fit it at my calf. Rosalie is going to kill you for kidnapping me."

His expression doesn't change. The guy next to him is big and burly and looks like he could break a car in half if needed.

I lean back against the far wall again and pull my knees up. I'll be able to kick from this position if necessary, though I have serious doubts about whether I could take both of these guys, not to mention the silent driver up front. "Why are you kidnapping me?"

"I need you to do some work for me," Alexei says

evenly as we careen through traffic. He grabs my bag and rifles through it. "Good. No more weapons."

No. All I have is my trusty laptop and a couple of discs. Man, I hope he's on video killing David Fairfax on the disc Rosalie gave to me—if I can fix it. "Don't mess with my laptop or my games."

"Games?"

"They're good for eye-hand coordination," I say. The discs aren't labeled. Does he even know what's on the one from the Fairfax house?

He tosses my backpack to my feet.

I wonder if there are security cameras in the area where they kidnapped me. It had all happened so quickly. Plus, these idiots had worn masks. I guess they're not idiots now, are they? I think through my morning, and betrayal that turns to fury cuts through me. "You sent the text from Rosalie's phone."

Alexei nods. "I did."

"She's going to kill you." Glee fills me.

"Only if she finds out."

Now dread replaces the glee. "Are you going to kill me?"

He studies me for several moments, and I study him back. I have to admit, I see the appeal. His black hair is thick, and his dusky skin brings out the deep glow of his black eyes. He has Russian features, straight and strong, and his body is hard-cut muscle. The glittering panther tattoo across his neck is both beautiful and terrifying.

"I suppose that's up to you. Do you want to live?" he asks.

I'll answer that later. "How did you break through the encryption on her phone?"

He lifts one shoulder. "I saw her key in the code."

I'm going to smack her so hard next time I see her. She knows not to let anybody see a code to anything. She's trusting this man far too much. I may have to take him out. Of course, he may have the same plans for me.

"Are you going to kill me?" I ask again.

His gaze hasn't changed. Neither has his expression. "I would prefer not to do so."

The man next to him looks at him swiftly and then looks away.

"Why did you just say that?" I ask.

"Because it's the truth," Alexei says smoothly. "I want us to have a good working relationship, and that has to begin with honesty."

"Your buddy's surprised you told me that."

He nods. "I'm well aware."

We drive into the underground garage of one of Silicon Valley's high-rise buildings, only seven or eight blocks from Rosalie's law firm, and the van parks near the elevator.

"Here's what's going to happen," Alexei says. "We're going to exit the vehicle, walk nicely to the elevator, and ride up to the penthouse. The security cameras are briefly disabled. You scream, I'll stop you. You try to run, I'll stop you. You try to fight . . ." He pauses.

"You'll stop me?" I ask sarcastically.

His gaze warms, and, frankly, it's a little charming. "Yes."

I don't see as I have much choice right now, so I do exactly as he says. I can't run from all three of them, and we ride the elevator to the penthouse. Nobody sees us. Nobody hears us. We walk out into what can only be considered a ridiculously opulent entryway with real marble tiles in gold-gilded accents.

"This place is cheesy," I say.

He shrugs and opens the double door, gesturing me inside the resplendent space. "It was the only one available on such a short notice."

The place feels too far away from the ground. Escaping via a window isn't possible if I want to live. "I deeply regret that Rosalie has unfrozen your funds." I stomp inside and look around at the already furnished front room. The furniture is stark white, the accents black and gold. Some people might find it beautiful and cold. I find it cheesy and dorky.

Alexei gestures me back to the right, and we move down a long hallway. He opens a door to reveal a plush bedroom decorated in whites and yellows.

"Guest bedroom," he says, "is yours." He moves to the next room where several computers are already set up, and my interest is piqued. They're top of the line, and they're new. So he's taken me for my computer skills. Good. For a few moments, I feared that he had kidnapped me in order to manipulate or blackmail Rosalie.

I walk over and sit in a chair perfectly ergonomically set for my height and weight. Apparently, people with money can make things happen quickly. "What do you want, Alexei?"

He leans against the doorway, looking tall and powerful. "I have a list. The first thing I want to know directly from you is why Urbano Reyes wants you dead."

"I don't know who that is." A chill hollows me out from the inside. "How do you know he wants me dead?"

"Because I promised to kill you for him."

I can't breathe. Fear flexes icy fingers beneath my skin. I scrutinize the computers before facing the threat again.

"You want me to conduct work for you, and then you're going to kill me?"

"Your fate is in your own hands." He presses his lips together as if not wanting to say anything further and then sighs. "If this helps, I don't like killing innocent women, and from everything I can tell, you're about as innocent as they come."

The hottie Russian is dead wrong about that. Rosalie obviously hasn't told him that I nearly killed Thorn Beathach on purpose. That's a fact I'll keep to myself. "You don't seem like a guy who breaks your promises."

"I'm not, but your death would greatly upset Rosalie, which would upset me. Also, some things are more important than promises to the head of gangs, don't you think?"

"I truly do when it involves my life," I say quickly. Is he messing with me?

He smiles. "You're funny. I see why you and Rosalie are friends."

I rather he considers me funny than a threat. "I imagine a hit has been taken out on me by my stepmother," I say. "I'm surprised she has done so in a way that can be traced."

"The contract can't be traced." Alexei contradicts me. "Obviously, money has changed hands, so maybe you should investigate. I've given you enough computers to do so."

"Yes, you have," I say, curious at the power I have here. Not that I haven't built my own. "What do you want from me?"

"I want you to conduct a deep dive on everyone involved in my case and figure out who set me up," he says. "I also want all information that you can possibly find on Hologrid Hub, my stepmother, and my half brother. I mean absolutely everything, Ella. Then I want you to start hacking into their systems."

I throw up my hands. "I'm still trying to hack into TimeGem's systems. These things take time. Probably a lot of time."

"They'll take as long as we need."

I sit up. "You can't kidnap somebody for that duration of time."

He carelessly lifts one shoulder. He looks every inch the mafia don today in long black slacks, a white button-down shirt, and a gilded watch encrusted with amethysts.

He should be careful. I know how to infect those.

"Who's going to miss you?" he asked, his voice not unkind. "Besides Rosalie and Alana, you're not close with anybody."

"Yeah, but Rosalie and Alana count," I retort instantly. "Alana has the force of two of the most powerful families on earth behind her. Rosalie has a law firm."

His smile shows even teeth. "I'm not afraid of other families or little law firms, Ella."

Why would he be? I lower my chin and make sure I have his full attention. "Rosalie loves nine people in this entire world—her seven boarders, Alana, and me. She won't forgive you if anything happens to me."

"I'm well aware of that fact." He gestures to the computers. "I have safeguards in place that if you try to reach out for help or to any of your contacts, I will be alerted immediately, and the entire system will shut down. Your reach has been limited to the police force, anyone connected with Hologrid Hub, and Nero Tech."

I look at the consoles. "What is Nero Tech?"

"It's a company here in town, and I want to know everything about its owner, Harold Fissure."

I've heard of the guy but that's about it. "There are very few people in the world who could have created safeguards like you have in place here."

"I'm well aware. One of them set this up for me."

My fingers itch to reach for a keyboard. "Then why do you need me?"

"He's a contractor and only had so much time. Plus, he's good, but he is not as good as you," Alexei admits. "The years you've spent trying to hack into TimeGem are invaluable for hacking into Hologrid Hub, I assume. Nobody has that knowledge like you do."

It's a fact, and I'm impressed by his ability to put information into order. This guy knows what he's doing. "If I say no?"

"You're not going to say no," he says, as if the idea hasn't occurred to him. "You lack money, and I'm willing to pay you very handsomely. I'll make you a rich woman just from this job alone."

I'm tempted. The more money I have, the better my chances are in regaining control of my company. "Why didn't you just ask?"

"Because you would've said no."

He's right. No amount of money would've forced me to work with him. "What if I decline your offer right now?"

He shrugs. "You're not going anywhere until you do as I ask. This is a nice place to live, but I know you're someone who values freedom."

"I am." So, he's studied me a little bit.

He leans away from the door frame. "Also, I want you to do a deep dive on Rosalie and all of her boarders. I want to know everything about each one of those men, and I want to know everything about her."

I remove my backpack and place it next to me. "No."

One of his dark eyebrows lifts. "Excuse me?"

"No. I might consider, for a very good price, the other jobs you've offered me, but I will not spy on Rosalie for you, or any of the people she cares about."

He looks at me for several long moments, and I imagine most people would quake.

So I explain better. "I don't have many lines in life, but that's one of them."

"What if I threaten you?" he asks mildly.

"Go ahead," I answer immediately. "You can do whatever you want to me. I will not betray Rosalie."

Something passes through his expression, and it might be admiration. Or a good plan to kill me. I'm not sure.

"Very well," he says. "Get to work on Howard Fissure first. I need to know everything about him, and I don't expect that task to take you long." With that, he turns and leaves me alone with this spectacular setup.

I grin and start typing. I might as well get to work. Alexei Sokolov has just made a colossal mistake, and he doesn't even know it. I can do two jobs at once, maybe three, and one of them will be taking him down.

TWENTY-SEVEN
Rosalie

After lunch, I finish drafting two contracts for one of my local clients that works exclusively in brokering the sale of new pharmaceuticals. The business is extremely lucrative, and I'm grateful to have it on my roster. I'm enjoying my mix of transactional law and litigation. Still, it's a surprise the firm assigned me Alexei's case since I practice civil litigation and not criminal. But I do have a good track record, so perhaps it makes some sense. Finally, after a dinner of a granola bar I filch from the kitchen, I sit back in my chair and roll my neck.

I invited both Alana and Ella to have drinks tonight, but Alana is apparently out of town with Thorn on a tropical few days together, and Ella hasn't returned my voice message. When she's involved in a project, she often goes quiet for a short while, but not this long.

I call her again, and she doesn't answer.

An inkling of worry filters through me, but I reach under my desk and pull out the box of discs from Alexei's case. I've only gone through about half of them, and they're all from the Amethyst Pony and different nights where he and his buddy Garik goofed off and played their music.

I wonder idly if Alexei still plays. He seems to have lost that part of himself, and it's too bad because it's quite charming. The enjoyment when he's playing and singing is obvious, and I hope that sense of fun is not gone forever.

I wipe my hand over my eyes. I can't believe the things he said in the shower earlier. I believe him, and I don't know that that's the future I want. But I can't deny that I'm definitely falling, and falling fast.

Merlin's offer of getting me out of town also surprised the heck out of me. Fleeing is never the answer, as far as I'm concerned.

I stick in another disc and watch as Alexei and Garik perform at the former Amethyst Pony. I make notes of who I can see in the video and compare them to the people in the other videos. There are several women who are often around them, and I wonder if any of them would kill to protect Alexei. I've watched enough of the CDs that I've been able to write down names of several of his groupies.

Maybe Ella can conduct background checks for me. Now that Alexei can pay, I'll make sure that she is rewarded for that, if I can find her. I glance again at my silent phone. It's so odd that she hasn't at least called me back once.

I finish the current disc, pull out another one to insert, and hit play. A darkened bedroom comes into view. I sit back. This is new. Then I watch as Blythe Fairfax saunters into the room wearing a bright-red teddy that barely covers anything. My gut cramps. I really don't want to watch this.

Alexei walks in from what appears to be an expansive bathroom. He's wearing black silk boxers, and I lean forward. Silk? He just doesn't seem like a silk guy. He's younger, definitely by seven years, and he lacks several tattoos and scars. It's odd to see his neck bare without the prowling panther.

His smile is wicked. I reach for my notepad and my pencil just in case they say something of value. That's why I'm going to watch this. At least, that's what I tell myself. Then Alexei moves toward her like the prowling panther that isn't on his skin yet.

She feints a move toward the door, and he's on her, tossing her to the bed. He lands on her, ripping off the teddy, and then he's kissing her. Mouth, neck, breasts.

No biting.

Why the heck does that go through my head? I try to keep from throwing up as they have sex. Twice.

Watching his body move against hers, into hers, has a dark rock settle in my stomach. I shouldn't care. This happened before we even met, and it's not like we're married. He's neither gentle nor rough with her, but they both get off. Twice.

Relief takes me when it's over, and I look with trepidation at the remaining discs.

I can't believe this. I feel sick to my stomach. I call Ella, and she doesn't answer. Muttering, I shake my head. What is wrong with her? I leave her another message. "Hey, Ella. Call me back. I'm getting worried." I click off, and then I note I have a text. Relief begins to fill me as I press the buttons for text, and then my heart sinks as I see it's not from Ella, but from Alana. I click it.

ALANA: Hey, hon. Thorn squired me away for a few days in Mexico. We're having a great time. You and Ella can join if you want. Let me know, because then I'll tell Thorn.

I'm sure Thorn wants to keep Alana to himself for their little getaway.

ME: Thanks, but I'm in the middle of several cases. Have fun and don't marry him until we can all be there.

Smiling, I click off. Maybe I should try to text Ella.

I press her name and look down. Wait a minute. Her last text says that she'll meet me at Bernie's Coffee House. What? I scroll up to see a text sent from me to her, telling her to meet me. What the hell? I didn't do that.

I look at the time. It was very early that morning. When I was showering? Or when Alexei had come in? Betrayal slices through me faster than any sharpened blade. He texted Ella? Panic then grabs me by the throat. Why would he do that? No wonder she hasn't texted me back. I call him and reach his voicemail. I want to yell, but I click off.

A text instantly arrives from him.

ALEXEI: I'm in the middle of a meeting at the bar. I'll call you after.

The heck he will. I jump up and hurry out of my office. It's after six, so most of the place is closed. I'm not surprised to find Garik once again in the waiting area.

"I thought you were supposed to wait downstairs," I say, furious.

He looks up from reading a bridal magazine. My eyebrows lift. He shrugs. "It's the only one I haven't read in here. Alexei wants me closer to you than downstairs. This is where I'll be. You're lucky I'm not in your office."

I'm so angry, I can barely breathe. "I want to go to the

Amethyst right now." I stomp toward the elevator and jab the down button.

Garik reaches me. "Alexei's in the middle of a meeting."

"I am well aware of that fact." I barrel inside the elevator. "Take me to him now, or I'll go there myself."

Garik studies my heated face. "His phone is off or I'd call him. I have a feeling you're about to make a big mistake."

I growl as the doors close. "No. Alexei is the one who made the mistake."

We make it to the car, and Garik drives silently through the city.

I've never in my entire life been this furious.

Garik pulls up in front of the Amethyst bar and leaps out to open my door. "Rosalie, everyone is still inside." He nods toward lines of vehicles on both sides of the street. "Trust me and don't go in there." One of his large hands lands on my arm

I shrug him off and hustle toward the door, yanking it open. "You asshole," I nearly shriek, stalking through a suddenly quiet room of men toward Alexei, who stands near the bar.

He pauses in saying something and looks at me, his black eyes glittering.

Pain and terror rip through me. Ella is every bit as close to me as a sister. In fact, she *is* my sister. And I know he took her. I keep moving, becoming aware of the tension choking the atmosphere.

Men, at least twenty of them, are seated throughout, at tables, all dangerous and all watching me.

My stride hitches but I keep moving. Perhaps this is a bad idea.

I falter.

Alexei's arm snakes out, and he hauls me to his side, his heated arm unrelenting around my waist. "Men, this is Rosalie Mooncrest." His voice holds no warmth. No familiarity. "If you'll excuse me for a moment, I apparently have something to handle." He nods at a fifty-something man in light-gray suit near the pool tables. "Sergio, finish cataloging all of our assets."

Then he turns and squires me beyond the bar and into a small storage room holding shelves and shelves of alcohol. The door shuts firmly behind us.

I push free of him and back away until I hit the far wall. "I am so going to kill you," I hiss, trying not to cry. Has he hurt her? Would he?

He's wearing a high-end black suit with a crisp white shirt along with shiny black shoes with matching belt. "Do you like being alive, Rosalie?" he asks silkily, his hands going to unbuckle the belt.

My mouth goes dry. "Are you threatening me?"

"Answer the question." He releases the buckle and pulls his belt free.

"Um, yes. I like breathing," I gasp, my stomach flipping inside out, my gaze locked on that belt.

He folds it in two and stalks toward me. "Those men in there? The ones you just disrespected me in front of?"

Oh, fuck. I look for an exit, and the only one is right behind him. "Um, I—"

He continues as if I haven't spoken, looking larger than life. "Every one of them has probably killed at least one person, and some quite a few more than that. And you know what's keeping me alive? You alive?"

I gulp and shake my head.

"Respect with a healthy dose of fear. Of me and what I

can do. What I will do." He reaches me and gently runs the leather down the side of my face.

I flinch. "I'm sorry." My legs tremble so much, I'm afraid they'll let me fall. Then I remember why I'm here. "Ella." My head snaps up. "You took her."

"Yes."

I can't breathe. "Did you hurt her?"

"No."

I search his face but can't read him. Can't see the truth in his eyes.

"I wouldn't hurt somebody you love, Rosalie," he murmurs. "I need her expertise for now, and she's safer where I put her than she was on the streets yesterday. Trust me."

The truth rings in his tone. Relief makes me dizzy. "I want to see her."

"At the moment, your wants are irrelevant to me." He places the belt on an old beer barrel at the end of the shelves, and more relief than I can interpret runs through me. He grasps my hips and lifts me, his mouth taking mine.

Hard.

Liquid desire pours down my throat and alights every nerve on fire. The events of the day, all the emotions crash through me. The adrenaline from pissing him off, the agony of watching him on a disc with somebody else. The sheer terror of what might be happening with Ella, all bursts through me and then compresses, losing me in his kiss.

His hand tunnels roughly through my hair, and he jerks my head back and kisses me deeper, bruising my lips, and then he bites along my neck and down my throat. I gyrate against him, my brain fuzzing. He's everything.

He rips open my blouse and my bra before scraping his whiskered jaw down my torso to suck on both breasts.

Pain flashes along my skin. He bites a nipple, and I cry out. I'm frantic. I reach for his pants and rip them open, shoving them down.

He yanks up my skirt and tears away my panties. "God, I want you. This had better be okay."

"It's okay," I breathe. "I want you. All of you." It's the truth. I've never needed anybody this badly. Part of it might be relief. Relief that he hasn't hurt Ella and he isn't going to hurt me. He kisses me again and his fingers find me. I'm more than wet and ready.

He growls low and bites the tender area where my shoulder meets my neck. Erotic pain flashes to my aching nipples. Desire zings through me, right to my clit.

I gasp his name and move against him. He shoves down his boxers and presses me against the wall. With one hard thrust, he impales me. I cry out and wrap both arms around his shoulders, both legs around his hips, holding tight. This is incredible. It's everything. There's nothing but him. He starts to pound, his fingers digging into my hips and holding me in place. I start to spiral and he slows down. "Wait," I protest. "Don't stop."

He kisses me again, going deep, and tweaks one of my nipples. I moan against his skin and feel even wetter, when he kisses me again, nipping across my jaw to bite my ear lobe. My entire body shudders.

This is a craving that can't be healthy, but I don't care. He pulls out in one smooth motion and tosses me onto my stomach over the old beer barrel.

I gasp and grab the sides, surprise freezing me. Then he's right there again, holding my hips, pulling me back, and shoving deep inside me. I groan his name and turn my head to the side. He pulls out and then pushes back in.

It's amazing. It's wonderful. I urge him to go faster. The only thing that matters right now is that orgasm that's looming so close. More importantly, he asked and I gave consent. How could I not? He pulls out again and I protest, but his fingers are at my clit, plucking and playing.

Wind whistles and then I hear the sharp crack of leather flat against my ass. I hear the sound before I feel the pain. It rushes through me with heat, and I cry out, partially rising but still gyrating against his talented fingers. In the back of my shocked brain, I realize that pain and pleasure can mingle. I would've bet against that fact, and I would've lost. I shouldn't like this . . . but I do.

He hits me again. The sound is deafening. "Alexei," I whisper brokenly.

He doesn't stop. His fingers keep playing, and I ride them wildly. I'm so close to an orgasm that waves are starting, and he hits me again in rapid succession. One, two, three more times.

"Don't ever challenge me again in front of a room full of killers," he whispers, his tone low and dangerous, heating my ear.

Fair enough. The belt warms my ass in a way that can't be healthy. Pain careens through me. Then all I can feel is his fingers and the pain and the heat and the fire as it spreads through my lower half, even up to my breasts. This is insane.

He hits me again, and I take it, almost rising for it this time. What is happening? I want more. Right or wrong . . . and I'm afraid he knows it. His fingers slow.

"No," I gasp.

Three more hits in rapid succession and I cry out from each one. His fingers stop and I push back against him.

One of his arms bands around my waist and the other

holds my neck. He hammers into me fast and deep. I hold on, pain echoing across my butt through my entire pussy to right where we meet, right where I need him.

This is too much. I can't think of anything. My brain is completely gone. He hammers harder and harder, and finally I explode, shrieking his name. The orgasm lasts forever, prolonged by the heated marks on my butt. He jerks hard inside me with his own climax, and we both come down panting.

Tears slide from my eyes, and I wipe them slowly away. He leans back and my legs fall to the floor. My skirt is still up around my waist, and my bra and shirt are shredded, leaving me bare to him. Taken.

I focus on the belt he tossed back on the barrel and blink, trying to return to reality. My legs trembling, I stand and turn to face him, my knees wobbling.

He slowly tucks in his shirt, pulls up his pants and zips them.

In a daze, I turn to look at the closed door. Reality hits me harder than a wet brick. There is no way everybody out there didn't hear everything. Heat flames into my face, but I can't move.

He looks at me, tall and powerful. Devastatingly in control. "Do we have an understanding?"

I can't move. He did that on purpose.

There's even a bite mark on his neck from me. I shake my head, mortified. My body's still somehow on fire. My temper tries to make an appearance, but the humiliation is too strong. Even my glare feels submissive. "What was that? Another claiming?" I want to sound snappy, but my voice is hoarse.

He smiles and the sight is nowhere near kind. "No, baby. That was a taming."

TWENTY-EIGHT
Alexei

I adjust my shirt before walking out of the storage room, and note my men in groups with somebody taking notes. It's good to see everybody working together.

A young foot soldier named Jerry looks up at me with a shit-eating grin. "That was something," he says. "When's my turn?"

The air instantly sharpens with cold. I cock my head. "What did you say?"

His smile wavers.

"That's what I thought." I manacle him by the back of the neck and rip him from the chair. I slam his face down on the table so fast, I hear a couple of gasps, and then I do it about eight more times, watching different teeth roll out of his mouth. He tries to hit back, and I slam him so hard he goes limp. I give him a couple more good whacks for measure and then throw him onto the ground where he bleeds onto the dirty floor.

I look around at everybody watching me. "Does anybody else have anything disrespectful to say about Rosalie Mooncrest?"

A younger guy finishes chomping ice next to me. For good measure, I punch him in the face. His chair tips over and he falls flat, grabbing his nose and rolling to the side. "From now on, no chewing ice, gum, or anything crunchy. Ever and especially if Rosalie is around. Period. Got it?" I say quietly.

A couple of the men look down at the bleeding mass at my feet, but nobody says a word. "Good," I say. "Rosalie is under your protection. Anybody disrespects her and they die."

Garik clears his throat. "Disrespect includes chewing ice?"

"Yes," I growl. "Anything crunchy, and if you have a fucking cold or allergies, stay away from her. You sniff and I'll break your nose." Apparently, I'm all about lessons tonight. I walk through the throng to where Garik stands by the door. "Have them finish making the lists and then make sure they all leave," I say quietly this time.

"Rosalie?" he asks.

"You can get her from the storage room, then take her home. I need somebody on her house all night."

"I'll be there," Garik says.

I think of the men behind us. "You could take shifts with somebody."

He shakes his head. "I don't know who to trust yet."

I breathe deep. "Thank you." It's not a word I would give to anybody else in my organization.

"Of course," he says, his gaze behind me making sure no one comes at us. "What about Jerry?"

I shrug. "I don't care. See if somebody wants to take him to the hospital. If not, toss him out back." He's moaning, so at least he's not dead.

"You've got it," Garik says.

I stride out into light rain and head to my bike around the corner. It's not raining too hard, and I have work to do, so I ride rapidly through the city to the building I purchased earlier and nod at my man at the reception area before entering the elevator and riding to the penthouse. The place smells like pizza. Frowning, I walk back to the office to see Ella munching happily on a slice of pepperoni.

"What?" she asks, frowning.

"How did you get pizza?"

She waves a hand. "Oh, Geoff and George went and got pizza," she says. "You know, the guys you have guarding the elevator in the parking garage?"

"I don't recall giving anybody permission to do so."

She shrugs. "We have to eat, dude." There's pleasure on her face, and I doubt it's from the pizza. She's already addicted to this computer setup. While I'm sure her setup is impressive, she lacks the funds I now have.

"Did they both go?" I ask.

She rolls her eyes. "Of course not. One stayed here to guard your whole building. Did you buy the building?"

"I did," I say.

"Huh. Ten floors, businesses on each, penthouse on the top." She nods. "It's a good investment."

"Thank you," I say wryly. "That is my aim."

She grins and then turns back to the computer.

"Have you found anything yet?"

She looks at me over her shoulder as if affronted.

I hold up a hand. "Sorry."

She looks back. "Yeah, Howard Fissure is an asshole."

"That I already knew."

She shrugs. "Okay. So he runs Nero Tech, but honestly,

he's been partially forced out. There was a mini takeover about six months ago."

"Why is that?" I stride into the room.

"According to corporate emails, and maybe a couple of private ones I hacked, people think he's doing drugs, but . . ." She hops in her seat. "This guy's involved in *selling* drugs."

Impressive. The little hacker should be a detective. "How do you know that?"

"Money, offshore accounts, known associations," she says. "A couple of the accounts are too hard to crack, even with these resources. My gut feeling is that he's working with several organizations and not just Twenty-One Purple."

"What about his schedule?"

She taps a few keys. "The FBI has bugged his house, so I hacked into their surveillance."

"Go on."

"His routine's pretty standard. He gets up around five, jogs for three miles, gets a coffee at a stand on the corner of Fourth and Madison, goes back to his place, showers, gets ready, heads to work. He's at the office most of the day, even though the board has taken many of his duties away, and then he may do a charity function or have a date. I printed out a list of his known acquaintances." She nods over to a piece of paper on the far table.

"How does he distribute the drugs?"

"According to the FBI surveillance, he meets up with a member of Twenty-One Purple at that coffee shop once a week. It looks like happenstance, but it isn't."

I roll my neck, smelling Rosalie on me. She'll always be on me. "So the feds don't have enough to bring him down?"

"Not yet," Ella says. "They're close though."

"That's good to know."

She kicks away from my desk. "All right. Are we done?"

"Not even close," I say. "Have you conducted your deep dive on Rosalie's boarders yet?"

Her frown is mutinous. "No, and I'm not going to. I thought we established that."

"Don't you want to know who Rosalie lives with?" I ask. "To make sure she's safe?"

Ella snorts. "I've met all seven of her boarders. She's as safe as kittens. They'd all jump in front of a bullet for her." Her brows draw down. "Would you?"

"In a heartbeat." Whatever expression's on my face must satisfy her because she nods at the pizza box.

"There's more if you're hungry," she says.

"Is that an olive branch?"

Her lips purse. "I'm not sure yet. The kidnapping is definitely against you. However, the offer to pay me handsomely, I'm still weighing."

"Good to know."

Her hands dance happily across three keyboards. "You have a great setup here."

"It's top of the line," I say. The woman is amusing, and I can see why she's Rosalie's friend. "It's the best I could find."

She nods. "I could put a couple of things together to get more juice, but yeah, whoever your source is did a good job."

I glance at my watch. According to Ella, Howard Fissure is at home right now. "Tell me about Fissure's home."

"Sure." She gives me the lowdown, including the security. It's not as impressive as I would've thought. I wait until she finishes listing problems that could arise if I break in.

It occurs to me that she could be absolutely messing with me and setting me up. But she's not that stupid. In fact, she's not stupid at all. She has no idea what my men will do if I don't return. Frankly, neither do I at the moment. I can't have Garik watching both Ella and Rosalie, so I have the best men I can on this building. At the moment, Ella seems to be enjoying using my computers, so perhaps this will work out.

"How would your stepmother put a hit out on you?" I ask.

She jolts and then turns around. "I don't know. To be honest with you, I'm not quite sure how that works."

"Maybe go through her attorney?"

"It's possible."

Any payment would be in cash, and I doubt there's a way to trace the source. I may need to talk to Reyes myself to find out. The idea of returning to the prison fires anger through me. It's probably not a good idea.

My phone buzzes, and I glance down to read a text from Garik.

GARIK: Men gone, deposited Rosalie off at home. She hit me—is definitely pissed.

I hide a smile.

ME: Where did she hit you?

GARIK: Right in the gut, low and hard. She's pissed, man.

Yeah, not mad enough to leave when everybody was still there. It's a lesson I hope she's learned.

ME: Keep an eye on her place tonight.

GARIK: No problem

I slip the phone back into my pocket.

Ella glances over her shoulder. "Rosalie's going to wonder where I am."

"Rosalie knows exactly where you are," I say calmly.

Ella's eyes widen. "You told her?"

I shake my head. "She figured it out. She is not happy."

The smile Ella flashes is full of warning. "You don't know Rosalie when she's not happy. This might actually be fun." She turns back to the keyboard and starts rapidly typing.

I turn and stride out of the room and through the empty penthouse. I don't have enough men I trust to be here with her, and she can't leave anyway. My men control the elevators, and I trust my guy in the control room.

"Where are you off to?" she yells.

"Business," I say, opening the door and then shutting it. It's time to take care of Harold Fissure. Just as I reach the elevator, my phone buzzes and I lift it to my ear. "Sokolov."

"Hey, it's Percy." The guy sounds like he's yelling.

My breath heats. "I can hear you, Percy. You don't need to bellow. Is Rosie okay?"

"She's fine, but I arranged a meeting for you with Alexander Ivanov and Andre Vasiliev for tonight."

I ride the elevator down and stride toward my motorcycle, my brain automatically calculating what I know of alliances within the organization. Those two men have the largest families and the most connections out of the entire local Bratva. "Are you setting me up, Percy?"

"Of course not. I could, but I'm not," he says. "They know about your impromptu meeting today with lower-level members of the organization. They're willing to meet with you and discuss coming on board."

I straddle the bike. "Why?"

Percy coughs. "They haven't been paid in a little while."

I pause. "Are you kidding me?"

"I never joke about money, man," Percy says. "They think you'll be better at the helm so long as you stay out of prison. That's their only hesitation."

"I'm not returning to prison for any length of time. When do they want to meet?"

"Half an hour. Belle's Diner, on the outskirts of San Jose."

I glance at my watch. It's now late enough that the diner should be closed. That makes sense.

"I have to be there," Percy says. A door opens. "Hey, Garik," he says.

"Percy," Garik returns, his voice strong through the phone.

"He can't bring you," I say. "I need him on Rosalie."

Percy coughs several times. Old man cough. "Don't worry. I've got Rosalie covered all night."

"Excuse me?" I murmur.

"Yeah, I have Wally who's ex-MI6, and Kenny who's an ex-spy for the U.S. I'm pretty sure it was the U.S. Anyway, they're fully loaded, man. No one's getting to Rosalie tonight, and she said goodnight a couple hours ago."

I rub my eyes. Did she not do *one* background check on these people she let into her life? My girl needs protection around the clock. "All right, Percy, I'll meet you there."

This will be a good detour before I surveil Howard Fissure for the night. I already miss Rosalie, and that just won't do. Ignoring such thoughts, I make the drive as quick as I can and approach the block carefully, driving around several times but not seeing any cars that should alarm me. There's only one dark town car, and it's parked right out front. This could be a setup.

Garik and Percy roll to a stop, and I get off the bike and head toward them.

"You armed?" I ask Percy. I already know that Garik's wearing a small armory.

"Of course." The old man looks at me like I'm crazy.

I walk into the diner to note the two men sitting at a table in the corner. I look around, trying to sense any threat. It's pretty much all around me. Two men emerge from the kitchen, one eating a piece of bread, both armed. I recognize them as Alexander's nephews. The eldest nods to me, walks over, and locks the door. The shades are already drawn, and I note another younger soldier in the far corner. I don't recognize him.

I move forward while Garik and Percy both take point. If somebody starts shooting, they'll be able to take out at least the two men at the table with me. I sit down. They've aged. Of course, I probably have too.

"It's good to see you," Alexander says.

I nod. "Same. I hear you haven't been paid."

"No. We don't know where the money is. I think they're putting more and more into that social media company they own."

"It's not doing well?" I ask.

Andre sips on what smells like coffee. "Not as well as it should be."

Concern for the amethysts and my servers roughens my voice. "I'm trying to consolidate the organization again. Are you in? I don't have time to dick around."

Alexander nods. "Only if you can guarantee you won't be going back to prison. If you do, any agreement we make with you would end with us being dead."

"I'm not going back to prison. I was already granted a new trial, and there's a chance that won't occur. If it does, believe me, I'll take care of the matter." I was too cocky before. I should have at least bribed a couple of jurors, but now I know better. "I give you my guarantee, there's no way I'll lose another trial."

Alexander reaches across the table. "We're in then."

We shake hands, and I shake hands with Andre as well. Relief filters through my chest, but I don't show any emotion. I stand, nod at Garik, and stride toward the door.

"You can't do this," the man from the corner yells. "I won't let any of you."

He points a gun at me and fires. I dodge to the side and reach for my own weapon. Percy tries to push in front of me. Damn it. I pull my weapon just as the guy in the corner shoots again, and I nudge Percy out of the way. Pain rips along my right arm.

Then everybody fires at once, hitting the guy in the corner. He goes down with more bullets in him than I can count. I look over my shoulder.

Alexander shakes his head. "I knew we shouldn't have brought him."

"Who was he?" I ask. There's no doubt the guy's dead.

"Name is Yaroslav. He's Draboski's second cousin and just arrived in the country a month ago." Andre shoves his gun back in his holster.

I study the dead man. "Is Draboski going to be a problem?"

"I'll take care of it," Alexander says.

"Good." In fact, it's the least he can do to appease me right now.

Percy looks at my arm. "Dude, are you okay?"

"I'm fine. I may need a stitch or two." I push the old man out the door into the light falling rain. "What were you doing trying to take a bullet for me?"

"That's my job, right? Aren't you the new boss?" He wipes water off his bony forehead.

I blink. He has a point.

He knocks my good shoulder with his gnarled hand, and pain ticks through to my bullet wound on the other side. "What were you doing jumping in front of a bullet for me?" He throws my words right back at me.

I sigh heavily. "You're Rosalie's. I couldn't let you get hurt."

He takes a step back, his eyes wide. The rain slashes all around us. "She really is yours."

"That's what I've been saying," I bite out.

He blinks. "Yeah, but you love her."

I step back. "That's ridiculous. Love doesn't exist. Let's not get carried away, Percy."

His smile brightens his age-pocked face. "Oh dude, this is a good thing." He winks at Garik. "Come on, let's get back home. It's almost breakfast time. I'm starving."

TWENTY-NINE
Rosalie

After an afternoon hearing, I drink a double espresso at my desk as I try to concentrate on work. Alexei didn't return to my house last night, which is a good thing because I probably would've stabbed him to death. I still can't believe what he did to me in that booze closet at the bar yesterday.

A small part of me, one that I'm trying to quash desperately, was lonely last night. I wonder where he was—not that it's any of my business because I don't care. I remind myself of that fact as I keep typing.

Joseph Cage walks into my office. "Where are we on the Bernanki merger?"

I look up and my eyes focus. He's dressed in a nice, beige-colored suit with a salmon-colored tie today. "The documents are with the buyer. We just need signatures."

"How about the Waltisi contracts?"

"The three employment contracts? The other side's negotiating and sending over their stipulations now." I sit back and hide a wince as the welts on my ass protest. Welts from Alexei's belt.

Cage moves into my office. "What about Alexei Sokolov's murder defense?"

Just hearing his name sends shards of fire through me. "I'm filing an appeal as to the overturning without prejudice tomorrow," I say. "I spoke with the primary detective, and he seems solid to me. In addition, he's looked over all the charges against the judge and the prosecuting attorney, and while there are many, he doesn't see any that lead back to Alexei or his enemies." Of which, I feel like one right now.

"So it's possible Alexei wasn't set up."

I look over at Miles's boxes. "Yeah. I haven't gone through Miles's notes yet. That's my plan after I finish this brief."

"Miles was a good attorney." Cage leans against my desk and plays with a silver paperweight Alana once gave me.

I stiffen. "I read the trial transcripts. He did an okay job."

"Okay?" Cage asks, his eyebrows raising.

I nod. "He missed a couple of objections he should have issued, and he made a couple of silly ones, but nothing that would point to purposeful error."

Cage sighs. "We could subpoena Miles's banking records."

"I already have." I shift my weight and attempt to find a comfortable position. Every time I move, somewhere on my body aches from Alexei. Unfortunately, the sensations are arousing. I am so screwed up. "I sent it to the executor of the estate yesterday morning."

"Who is that?"

I glance at my notes. "Larry Coswell at Banks and Georges." It's a rival firm, which just meant that Miles wanted privacy. "He wasn't married, and I don't think he had any kids. He just had work, so it should be easy to acquire his records," I say. "I'm curious if there are any deposits we can trace back to a source. Of course, this was seven years ago, so we'll see if I can even get them."

"Miles was a good guy." Cage shifts his weight on my desk.

I don't like people sitting on my desk. I put my cup of coffee right where his butt is every morning.

His gaze lingers on my mouth. "I have tickets to *Wicked* this weekend. What do you say?"

"She politely declines," Alexei says smoothly as he walks into the room. Tension spirals from him to me, heating my face. I want to contradict him, but now isn't the time.

Cage pushes away from my desk. "I believe she can answer for herself."

One of Alexei's eyebrows rises. Today he looks every inch the mob boss, with a high-end suit that includes a jacket, all black, and stark-white shirt. No tie, though. "All right. Go ahead and answer."

Man, I want to throw something at him. Where's my letter opener, anyway? "Thank you, Joseph, but we've already had this talk. I'm not going to the theater with you."

Cage blushes a deep crimson. "Very well. I'll leave you to it then." He brushes by Alexei without a word.

Amusement fills Alexei's gaze.

"Don't you look happy," I say. "I turned him down because I wanted to do so, because it is stupid to date my boss, not because of you."

"Whatever helps you sleep at night, princess," he says. "Or go ahead. Go on a date with him. See how that ends up."

I cross my arms. I still want to ask him where he was last night, but I won't give him the satisfaction. "I've changed the passcode on my phone."

"I'll figure it out again," he murmurs.

What an ass. "You didn't figure it out. You watched me because I trusted you."

"You've never completely trusted me, have you?"

I don't want to play this game because he's probably right. "Where is Ella?"

"She's safe."

How can I trust him when he kidnaps my friends? "What do you want, Alexei?"

His gaze heats. My nipples spring awake along with my clit. I glance toward the door. He wouldn't. His chuckle is low and masculine. "I was busy last night and came to check on you as soon as possible."

"Check on me?" I snap. "I'm fine. Never mind that you totally humiliated me in front of a bunch of gun-toting mobsters yesterday. How soon do you think one of them will come calling?"

He cocks his head. "We weren't in front of them, and you needed a lesson. First, you're fortunate said lesson came with an orgasm. Second, don't worry about your safety. Like I said, that's my job. I made it clear to every one of them that if they even *think* of disrespecting you, I'll cut out their tongues and shove them up their asses."

"That's descriptive." I gulp and take a moment to run through my feelings. I'm still pissed. Slightly appreciative that he insisted upon respect from mobsters. The orgasm was spectacular. Yet his casual note of violence scares me. Although the feeling of safety, oddly enough, is a bit addictive. I haven't felt safe since I was a kid, and Alexei plans to protect me. Am I grateful for that? Enough to go along with his actions?

Nope, I still want to shoot him. "I have work to do. Some of that is trying to keep you out of prison, although the more I'm around you, the more I think you should wear an orange jumpsuit until you're too old to move."

"Good," he says. "Garik requires time to sleep. You are to stay here until I pick you up after work."

My mouth gapes open. "You're not here giving me orders."

He shrugs and then slightly winces. "Take it any way you want, but I will pick you up at five and then we'll go to dinner. We should talk about where you want to live."

"I'm living in my house." I push my chair back and stand. It feels better to face him on my feet even though he's a good foot taller than I am. "Why did you just wince?" Is he hurt? I don't care. Nope. Not at all. I hope he's not hurt.

"I took another bullet last night—just to my outer arm. It's okay."

I blink. He took a bullet? "Seriously?" Surely Hendrix had closed off the back door to the amethyst servers, so no way could Alexei heal himself with the energy exchange again. "Have you been to a doctor? Who shot you?" Not that I wouldn't have, given the chance after the debacle in the storage room.

"I'm fine. Didn't even need stitches. We can discuss it at dinner. Your firm has decent security, so you'll be fine if you stay here until I fetch you. Understand?"

He stares at me and I stare back. My knees tremble. He just waits.

"Why are you doing this? Acting like we're going to live together?"

He leans back against the door. "Because we are."

How is he so freaking certain? "You don't even know me. The sex is good, and you think I'm pretty, but that's not enough."

His gaze heats. "I do think you're pretty, and the sex is off the charts. But you're highly intelligent, have a great sense of humor, and own a heart that's all soft and kindness. I want it."

My chin drops. "I'm not soft and kind." I'm a freaking attorney who's a tornado in a courtroom.

His chuckle holds genuine amusement. "You're broke financially because you take care of seven old men who need you. Sure, they adore you, and that must be a good feeling, but you'll let yourself lose everything to help them. That's sweet. That's kind. That's all fucking mine now."

Just when my heart goes all soft for him, he has to throw in a badass possessive term. "You should've stopped with 'kind.'" Even so, I feel all warm and squishy inside. I need to get a grip around this man. He's just too . . . much.

"I have somewhere to be, Rosalie. Tell me you get me and that you'll stay here until I return." That amusement still dances with the hot possessiveness in his eyes. "Don't make me belt you to the chair." He sounds way too interested in the thought, and there's not a doubt in my mind that he'll do it. I can't even imagine my embarrassment when my paralegal wanders in at some point.

"Fine. I have plenty of work to do, anyway," I say. "You might want to rethink your career. Mafia bosses get shot a lot."

"I got shot protecting your Percy," he returns easily. "Usually I wouldn't have moved, but I couldn't let one of your pets get killed." With that, he winks and walks out of my office. I drop back onto my chair and quickly call Percy.

"Hi, Rosalie," Percy answers. "I'm outside. We need more fertilizer for the shadier area in the back."

I shake my head. "Were you with Alexei last night?"

Percy is silent for several heartbeats. "Darlin', these phones aren't secure. All I'll say is that I owe Alexei big time. We can discuss the rest later."

So it's true. "We will *so* discuss this when I get home," I sputter. Can I ground an eighty-year-old man? I think I can. The guy shouldn't be driving—he can barely see. "Tonight, Percy." I end the call without pleasantries. So Alexei really saved Percy for me?

My traitorous heart warms. The massive haul of kitten heels is sweet. Saving my Percy is soul-stirring. I'm falling for Alexei way too fast, and he won't let me slow down. How can I be furious and loving toward him at the same time? Life is supposed to be orderly and make sense.

It doesn't . . . but it sure as heck isn't boring, either.

My phone buzzes and I glance down at the screen. If Percy wants to make nice, he can wait all day. I don't recognize the number. "Rosalie Mooncrest."

"Hey, sister," Ella says.

THIRTY
Rosalie

Relief fills me so quickly I get lightheaded. "Ella, I've been so worried. Where are you?"

"That's the thing. I need a little help getting out of here."

Determination races through me. "Of course. Where are you?"

"Remember that building that has the little shop with the tarot cards?"

"Yeah, the high-rise?" I ask.

"Yes, I'm trapped in the penthouse," she says. "I can control the elevators but have to time it exactly."

I open the bottom drawer of my desk and pull out a nine millimeter. It's unregistered and a gift from the guys at my house because it's nearly impossible for the good guys to get a gun in California these days. "How are you calling me?"

"Through a computer."

Of course. She can do anything with a computer. "Did Alexei kidnap you?"

"Yep," she says. "He actually doesn't seem that bad, and the system is pretty ingenious, but I'm ready to get out of here. Although, I could use the money if he wants to hire me without kidnapping me."

My friend's claustrophobic, and I panic for her. "You're not in a small area, are you?"

"It's a pretty big penthouse, but like I said, I need to escape. Now."

"Okay. All right, so he has no idea you're calling?"

She snorts as if I've offended her. "No. It took me this long to hack the system, and there's a laptop here I'm bringing with me. It's top of the line."

"I wouldn't steal a laptop from Alexei."

"He kidnapped me," she bursts out.

Yeah. She should do what she wants. "Good point. All right. Take whatever you want," I say. "Are there any valuables there?" Maybe we can fence a couple of baubles. I figure a kidnapping negates any crimes in response.

"Not really. Place came pre-decorated."

That's unfortunate. But impressive that Alexei is already buying up property with his money. If the funds are frozen again, it'll take several extra and difficult steps to secure real estate holdings. "Okay, tell me what to do."

"The security he has here isn't bad, but he doesn't trust enough folks yet. That's why I have to make my move now. Once he takes full control of those people, I'll never get free."

I gulp. Will I ever get free? Do I want to be free of him? Questions to handle later. "Agree. Tell me your plan."

"Currently, he's got one guy in the control room and one guy on the main floor entrance. It's a little central area with a main hallway next to it that goes to the shops. Then there are businesses on the next five floors and residences after that."

"Okay," I say. "I don't know exactly how to help you."

"This is what you're going to do." She very carefully lays out a perfect plan.

My friend is a genius, and anticipation runs through me. It's time for Alexei to lose one in this stupid game we're playing. I grab my purse and hurry to the door. "I'll be there in a few minutes. This is going to work, right?"

"Oh, fifty-fifty chance," she says. "Just be careful and be ready."

Great.

I dash to the elevator and down to the main floor where I run outside and hail a taxi. So far so good. I get in the back and give directions to the high-rise. "I need you to park right near the tarot card store."

My driver has to be about eighteen, with earnest blue eyes and slicked-back blond hair. "Okay, but I can't park there for long."

I slip him a hundred-dollar bill.

"Whoa," he says.

"Believe me, it hurts." The bill constitutes exactly half of my emergency fund.

His tires squeal as he hits the gas pedal. "No problem." Within minutes, he reaches the tarot card store, and I open the back door. "I hope you have a good day," he says happily.

"I'm not leaving." I scoot back over.

He frowns and looks at the open door while we idle at the curb. "I don't understand."

"You will."

Seconds later, Ella barrels out of the front door, runs across the sidewalk, and leaps into the cab, slamming the car door. "Go, go, go," she says.

"Shit," the driver yells, hitting the gas. "What's happening? Where are we going? Who's chasing us?"

"Long story," Ella says.

Looking through the back window, I turn to see a burly guy in a full suit run outside, bark something into a phone, and gesture wildly at us.

"You better turn quick," I say.

"Okay," our young driver bellows, turning at a corner and nearly hitting a bread truck.

"Keep going," Ella says. "Now go left. Now go right." She gives the poor kid directions, and he follows every time, seeming to have fun. Finally she leans forward and taps his shoulder. "You can stop here."

I look around. "I don't know this area."

"I do," Ella says.

The car stops, and Ella slaps the back of the driver's seat. "Thanks, dude. She already pay you?"

"She gave me a hundred bucks," the driver says, smiling. "This is the most fun I've had in a long time."

I scoot out of the taxi and land on a clean-swept sidewalk. "If anybody asks and if they scare you, you can tell them exactly where you dropped us off, okay?"

"Like who?" He pales.

I don't answer him and shut the door.

"Come on," Ella says, hurrying around the back of the taxi. "This way."

We're near several car dealerships in a nice area of town. I follow her, twisting and turning around blocks and several businesses. "You know we're on camera?"

"Yeah, yeah, yeah," she says. "Don't worry about it."

We jog for several blocks, and I'm wishing I had worn tennis shoes and not new kitten heels, when we reach an area replete with nice bars and restaurants.

"Out back," she says.

She finally leads me to the back of a place called the Morning Diner to a small parking lot. She motions at a white Buick. It's dented, old, and small. "This is mine. There are no cameras back here."

"All right."

We get into the car, and she starts it immediately. "Duck."

I duck. I have to admit, I'm having fun.

She turns onto a main street. "You didn't bring your phone, did you?"

"You told me to leave it at the office."

"Good. You can be traced via your phone." She drives sedately onto the street, and we continue for a good fifteen minutes. "All right. You can sit up now."

Grunting, I push myself off the floor and sit. "Where are we?"

"I have a safe house a couple blocks from here."

I brush hair out of my eyes. "You have a safe house?"

"Yeah, don't you?"

I shake my head.

"Everybody needs a safe house, Rosalie." She reaches in her bag and hands over the evidence disc from Alexei's case. "I managed to decrypt part of the Fairfax evidence disc this morning. Whoever corrupted it introduced a virus right around the time of the murder, and so far, that part of the disc is fried. The virus continues through the day, but it weakens. I engaged in a multi-step remediation process by first implementing a robust heuristic-based antivirus scan. Then I reconstructed some of the corrupted sectors by employing an error-correcting code to restore data integrity."

She is totally losing me. "Do you have a video of the murder?" I hold my breath.

"Ug. You are totally not impressed with everything I did."

I am but I don't understand it all. "Ella."

"Fine. So far, I've been able to fix the end of the disc because the virus weakened as the video continued throughout the day. Mainly, I have a recording taken outside the house after the murder. You're going to want to watch it."

The hair rises on the back of my neck. "Is Alexei on here?" I don't want to see him committing a crime.

She pulls a laptop out of her backpack with one hand and plops it onto my legs. "We have a ways to go, so feel free. You need to see this."

I flip open the lid and insert the disc. The video loads with a date stamp showing the day of the murder. The outside of a palatial mansion takes form. "The Fairfax backyard is beautiful." I zero in on the small pond.

"Yeah, I know."

There are several police officers wandering around and crime techs doing something on the deck. My heart starts to quicken. "What do you have?"

"Just watch."

A young, uniformed officer moves toward the pond, and I see him take something from beneath his jacket and throw it in.

My heartbeat kicks up until I can feel the throb against my ribs. "Oh my God. That's the knife. A police officer threw it in?"

"Not quite. Look closer."

I click up to better see the officer's face. He turns, glances at the deck, and keeps going.

"Holy crap." I sit back, stunned. "That's Hendrix Sokolov."

"Yeah," she says. "Alexei's good old brother set him up."

Adrenaline floods my system. It's true. Alexei is innocent. The entire murder was a setup. "So he didn't get a fair trial."

"Looks like it. The question is, what do we do with this new information? We could sit on it and blackmail Hendrix. I mean, if we want money."

I tap my bottom lip with one finger. "We could give it to Alexei, but I'm not inclined to help him right now. I do have an idea. It's not a nice one."

"Tell me."

For answer, I reach in my pocket for my phone, only to find it empty. "I don't have my phone."

"It's okay. You can use the laptop." She reaches over and types something quickly. "Who do you want to call?"

"Alana," I say quickly.

Ella types another code with one hand before focusing back on her driving. I marvel at her when the laptop rings like a phone.

"Hello?" Alana answers.

"Alana," I say. "Hi."

The sound of the ocean filters through the background. "Hi. Are you coming to visit?"

"No, we're in the middle of something. However, how would you like to have one of the best social media posts of your life?" I ask.

"I'd like that a lot," Alana says.

I smile. "I don't know if you want to post it on Aquarius Social or Malice Media, but whichever it is, the stock's going to gain value immediately."

"Ooh," she says. "I love it. What do you have?"

"A little video of a crime scene. Give me the email

address where you are, and I'll send it your way." This is probably a bad idea, but it might also save several lives. If the truth is out there, then there's no reason for Hendrix to continue with a hit on Alexei. Maybe. Maybe not. But now the police will have to arrest Hendrix. He had the murder weapon. At the very least, he interfered with an investigation. At the most . . . maybe he killed David Fairfax to set up his brother.

Alana chuckles. "I can't wait to see the video. Thanks for this."

Ella giggles. "Alexei is going to be beyond pissed."

"Then he shouldn't have kidnapped you," I say smartly.

"Amen, sister," she agrees.

THIRTY-ONE
Alexei

I scroll through the phone in the back seat of the car as Garik drives, fury engulfing me. Alana Beaumont comes up on the Aquarius Social feed, and I watch the post again.

"Hello, friends. You are not going to believe the dish that I have," she says. "The tea is about to be spilled." She looks around and, apparently, she's somewhere tropical because the ocean rolls beautifully behind her. "I just received this video. You remember good old Alexei Sokolov and how he was just released from prison because of the corruption of the judge and prosecuting attorney? Well, apparently, the poor guy really *was* set up. Wait till you take a look at this."

A video comes up on screen of Hendrix, my half brother, tossing what appears to be a bloody knife in the pond at the Fairfax mansion. No doubt the fucking murder weapon. He's dressed as a cop and nobody notices him. As smoothly as he enters the scene, he walks right back out. Oh, we've never been close, but still, a sense of betrayal cuts through me.

I scroll to another video of Hendrix being arrested and handcuffed at Hologrid Hub. He's stoic, with his jaw set, and frankly he looks pissed. I understand. I just used every contact I now have to put a dent in his mother's attempt to bail him out, and it won't last long. Maybe a few more hours.

"We're here." Garik pulls up to the police station where the jail is located. "This place makes my skin itch."

"Me too." I open the door just as Hendrix walks out wearing a gray suit with a jacket over his arm. His shirt is unbuttoned and he's lacking his usual power tie.

Reporters dash toward him and he pushes them away. "No comment."

His gaze meeting mine, his chin lifting, he crosses toward me. I shift over and leave the door open while reporters shout questions at us both, taking pictures. Without answering, he shoves a couple out of the way, enters the car, and slams the door.

"Hello, brother," I say.

He rolls his neck and looks at Garik and then at me. "Why did you bail me out?"

"Because I made sure your mother couldn't." I study this brother I barely know. After our father died, I was sent away to live with relatives. We weren't even raised together. "The evidence is pretty damning." I want to punch him in the face.

He stares at me. He has our father's size but Lillian's looks, with his narrower features. Most women probably find him attractive. I can change that for him. "We wanted you out of the way. That's not a surprise to you." His voice is as deep as mine.

"No, it's not," I say. "Still, we do share blood."

He smooths down his expensive pants. "Half. Again, why did you bail me out?"

"To talk. I'm taking over the organization." A part of me, one I don't want to admit, really doesn't want to kill my own flesh and blood.

He rolls his head back. "I've heard."

"Are you going to fight me?"

For answer he turns his head and looks at me, reminding me of our father for the briefest of moments. "No."

I narrow my gaze. "Are you lying?"

He snorts. "No, I'm not lying. I'm not fighting you. I don't want Hologrid Hub."

I shake my head. "What game are you playing?"

He places his folded jacket neatly on his pants. "I am not as good at charging the crystals as you are. It drains me for days afterward."

I blink. "You don't get a rush? You don't gain strength?"

"No, I hate it. Cal and I together could do a decent job, but he's been killed. The fact that we haven't gone after his killer, whoever that might be, has definitely weakened the organization."

"They don't trust you," I say softly. Neither do I. He is a good liar, and I respect that.

He shakes his head. "We don't know who killed Cal, and the fact that we haven't just taken somebody out for the murder has lost us respect."

"Who do you think killed him?"

"I don't know. He was a jerk with women. It could have been anybody."

I sit back and tap my chin. "What about Thorn Beathach?"

Hendrix lifts his shoulders. "I've heard the rumors. The families arranged a marriage between Cal and Alana Beaumont, but Alana didn't want it. Cal was going to force it, but I don't know of any instance when he and Thorn crossed paths. So if Thorn did kill Cal, he did a good job covering his tracks." Hendrick shrugs, looking tired with dark circles under his eyes.

"So you truly don't know."

"Nope. Plus, I don't want to go to war with Beathach," Hendrix says quietly. "Can you imagine the disaster of the local Irish mob and the local Russian Bratva in an all-out war?"

Yeah, I actually can. I don't want that either. "There's no evidence that Thorn killed Cal."

"No," Hendrix says "My gut feeling is that he didn't, and that Cal just pissed off the wrong husband. But again, nothing."

I pinch the bridge of my nose. "Why did you get in my car?"

Hendrick smiles, all charm. "You're not exactly going to kill me after all those press people took our picture, are you? I mean, you were reckless years ago, Alexei. I assume that has changed."

"That has most certainly changed. I'm not reckless. You set me up seven years ago by throwing that knife in the Fairfax pond."

"Obviously," Hendrix says.

Garik looks with flat, dead eyes at him through the rearview mirror. "Did you kill Fairfax?"

"No." Hendrix says. "I took a knife from the kitchen, rolled it in the blood from the floor, and then tossed it into the pond." He winks, almost in slow motion. "Are you recording me?"

I want to punch my fist through his face. "I went to prison for seven fucking years."

He looks at the panther prowling across my neck. "You needed it."

I cock my head. "Excuse me?"

He shrugs. "Come on. You were in no state to run the Russian mob. You were a playboy. You were stupid. You'd be dead if you hadn't gone to prison."

Unfortunately, there may a bit of truth in that statement. That doesn't let him off the hook, however. "Now *you're* going to prison."

"We'll see. I'll find myself a good lawyer. A video from seven years ago could definitely be altered."

He's not wrong, and it's doubtful Ella will ever testify as to how she decrypted the damaged disc. Even so, I now have enough money and power that I can make sure he goes to prison. "I don't know. I think you may do a little time," I say.

He sobers. "I guess we'll find out, won't we?"

"Yes. After you're released, I'll make you and your mother a deal."

"What's that?" Hendrix looks outside at the dreary, gray day.

"I'll give you enough money to go somewhere else. Pick a country, not this one, and live. Have fun. Start your own company. I don't know and I don't care."

Hendrix nods. "I'll speak with my mother. Part of that deal is that I don't go to prison."

"No." I lose any expression of civility. He's lying and thinks he's playing me. I'm giving him the truth. "You're going to spend a couple years there. In fact, you're going to plead guilty when they charge you and reach a plea deal. I want you in for at least two years. A little payback, you know?"

His eyes narrow. "Go fuck yourself."

"Very well." We reach the palatial grounds where he and his mother live. "Drop him at the gate," I tell Garik. "He can walk the distance to the house."

"Sure thing." Garik pulls to a stop near the gate.

"Hendrix," I say. "You'll love prison. You'll make so many friends."

He gets out of the car and slams the door.

Garik looks over the seat at me. "What now?"

"Now we need to find Rosalie," I say. "I'm sure she's with Ella, and since I can't find them, at the moment neither can anybody else, so I'm not worried about her safety. Well, until I find her."

"I have everybody on it, Boss," Garik says. This is new. He's never called me boss before. "We're scouring the city."

"All right." Apparently, she didn't learn her lesson the other night. My girl is a bit stubborn—and reckless. "Get Merlin on it at Rosie's house too. He's as good as Ella, or at least he's close on a computer. He should be able to track her."

Garik snorts. "None of those men are going to help you find Rosalie."

I sigh heavily. "Tell him that she's in danger. Most likely because she is."

"I will," Garik says. "What about you, Boss?"

That's going to annoy the shit out of me. "Knock it off."

He coughs. "I figure it's good to get people thinking of you that way."

"I understand the psychology, Garik. It just sounds weird."

"Okay. I'll think of something else." He drives through town.

I shake my head. "Drop me off on the corner of Piston, will you?"

"Sure. What's your plan?"

I keep that one to myself for now. "I don't have one. I do need you to find Rosalie."

"Okay. It's getting dark. You armed?" he asks.

"I'm always armed."

He pulls to the side of the somewhat quiet street. "Why don't I come with you?"

"This is something I need to do myself. Let me out."

"Okay." He stops completely.

I exit on the corner before making my way toward Howard Fissure's apartment building as Garik drives away. Fissure's gate opens and I quickly duck behind a tree. He drives out. I call Garik back. He returns immediately and I jump in the back. "Follow that car."

"Seriously?" Garik asks. "I feel like I'm on a sitcom."

"Only if the sitcom ends in murder." We follow Fissure to a restaurant on the upper end where he strides inside and meets a platinum blonde we can watch through the window. "Who is that?" I ask.

"No idea, but she sure is pretty. A little young for him," Garik says.

My stomach growls. "I haven't eaten today."

"Do you want me to get us some food? This may take a while."

I look around at several of the restaurants in the area. "Yeah, go ahead. You choose."

"Excellent." He slides out. I have a clear view of Fissure and the blonde, and I watch them eat a four-course meal. About halfway through, Garik returns with falafels for us.

"Falafels?"

"I had a craving."

I eat mine, noting it's just as flavorless as I remember. I could go another seven years without eating one—or maybe nothing tastes good because I can't find my woman.

Where the hell is Rosalie? I work the phone, calling many of my new followers, and so far, nobody has found her. I have to admit that Ella is good. Even Merlin hasn't tracked Rosalie down. I called him, and he's begrudgingly helping us because she might be in danger. However, there's true panic in his voice when he relates that so far, he hasn't located either one of them. If he hasn't, then nobody else has. That's some reassurance.

Finally, about midnight, Howard and the blonde emerge. He gives her a long kiss and grabs her ass at the curb, and then the valet brings a Porsche for her. She gets in and drives off.

"That didn't end the way I thought it would," Garik says.

"Ditto."

Fissure waits and the valet drives up his BMW. He tips the guy and gets in, driving away. Garik pulls away from the curb, and we follow him through the city, away from his home.

"Where do you think he's going?" Garik asks.

"I don't know, but the farther it gets away from the city, the easier it'll be to take him out."

We reach a rougher part of town with several dive bars and restaurants, until Howard pulls behind a long-ago burned-out building. Garik turns around the block. We both exit the vehicle in a hurry through the rain, toward the back of the building where we see Fissure meeting with a member of Twenty-One Purple. The guy's wearing head to toe purple, so definitely not incognito.

They exchange an envelope, and the guy nods over at what looks like a snowmobile trailer. It's dented and rusted out, but there's still the outline of a snowmobile on it. The Purple member takes the envelope and hurries away. Howard makes a call on his phone and walks over to the trailer, opening a side door and looking inside.

Garik angles his head from my right. I blink. There are several kids, all dirty, all young, maybe five or six years old, huddled in the back. "Fuck," Garik says. "They're trafficking kids?"

"Apparently," I note. "Stay here."

Howard slams a door and then walks toward his BMW. I keep to the building as he lifts the phone to his ear to speak. "Yeah, I've got them. Straight from the southern border. They're in the trailer. Pick them up and make the deliveries now. And next time, Albert, this is your job, not mine. I don't give a shit if your wife is in labor." He clicks off.

I reach for the knife in my boot, and I'm on him before he can blink, flipping him around, pulling his hair back, and slicing his neck. Blood spurts over the top of his car, and he gurgles, shuddering wildly. He's dead before he hits the ground.

I wipe the knife off on the top of his jacket. It's one of my favorites, and I'm not leaving it with him. I stick it in the sheath, making a mental note to sterilize everything later. Not that I'll be a suspect in this one. There aren't any cameras here, and the authorities are going to find not only him, but his phone records about those kids.

I walk back toward Garik. "Garik, do you have a burner phone?"

"I've got two." He pulls one out of his pocket.

"Good." We move through the rain back toward the

car. "Call in an anonymous tip to the cops about those kids in the trailer, and disguise your voice."

He nods. "I'm already on it." He quickly makes the call. We dodge into the vehicle and quickly leave this desolate area.

I arrive at Rosalie's house and climb up to her suite, ditching my clothes and taking a shower. The place feels empty without her, and I'm seriously irritated. It's nearly dawn, which means wherever she is, she's not coming back. It's also Saturday, so there's no need for her to go to work. If she thinks she's going to ghost me for an entire weekend, she's lost her mind.

A knock sounds on the door, and I open it with just a towel around my hips. Seven men stand on the entryway. "Where is she?" Merlin asks.

"I don't know. I need you to find her."

Percy scrubs both hands down his face. "Do you think she's been kidnapped?"

"No. I think she's with her friend Ella, and I think she's putting herself in danger."

Wally winces. "Yeah. There's a lot of chatter, people trying to find them both after that disc showing Hendrix being arrested was released. They figure since Rosalie's your lawyer, she had something to do with it."

Heat rushes through me. "Everyone's looking?"

"Oh, yeah. Cops, your family, even the Twenty-One Purple gang."

The last one gives me pause. I must not be working fast enough for Reyes, and he's hedging his bets. He's never been stupid.

Merlin clears his throat. "Also, I monitored your known phone numbers, and you have a message on one."

I look at him. "You did what?"

He shrugs. "I'm telling you, I'm looking for Rosalie. If you did something to her, you're going to deal with all seven of us."

I don't have time to handle this right now. I left my phone at the penthouse, considering I was off committing crimes all night. "What did the message say?"

"It was from a guy named Urbano at the prison. It didn't make a lot of sense."

"What did he say?" I repeat, blood rushing faster through my veins.

Merlin tugs on his green bowtie. "He said he was just checking, that his commissary account is low, and that three out of five numbers isn't enough. He said he'll have somebody else invest his money. Do you know what that means?"

"I know what that means," I say. "Can you access my accounts?"

Now Merlin draws back, looking affronted. "Of course."

"Put some money in Urbano Reyes's commissary account at the prison." Truth be told, I had promised to do that.

"What about the three out of five investments?" Merlin asks.

I'm too tired to lie to these guys. "He means kills. And now it's four out of five finished."

"Oh." Percy frowns. "I guess you better get the fifth one done, huh?"

I shut the door in their faces, turning to reach for my clothing. Unfortunately, the fifth one is Ella Rendale.

THIRTY-TWO
Rosalie

"**R**osalie, wake up," Ella says urgently.

I roll over and blink, for a moment thinking we're back at the boarding school in Switzerland. I flip on the light. Ella's hideaway is a cute two-bedroom Craftsman in a quiet residential neighborhood. I tossed and turned for a while last night thinking about Alexei, but finally I drifted into sleep. "Wh-what?" I mumble.

"You're not going to believe this. Get out of bed." She pulls me from the bed, and I pad barefooted into the adorable kitchen where she has her laptop on a fifties-style red-and-silver table. I sit in a matching chair and yawn widely, dressed in one of her small T-shirts and my underwear. "What's going on?" I'm still half asleep.

She flips a laptop around so I can see the screen. "Hendrix Sokolov was murdered last night."

I jolt wide awake. "Are you serious? The news is reporting a murder?"

She shakes her head. "No. I hacked into the local PD system. The media doesn't have it yet."

I look at the microwave. It's six in the morning. "Where's Alexei?"

"I don't know," she says.

I stand. "You need to take me home." I brush my teeth, capture my thick hair in a ponytail, hurriedly get dressed, and soon she's driving me in the battered old white car to my place. We screech to a stop on the front curb. "Thanks."

"I'm coming in," she says, hauling her backpack with her laptop over her shoulder.

I pause. "Alexei's probably here."

"I know," she says, "but I'm not letting you go in there alone."

My heart warms. "All right." We march up the front walkway through the big front door, hearing boisterous laughter from the kitchen. I frown. She looks at me and shrugs. We walk through the formal living area, that I've left the same as my aunt had decorated it decades ago, into the now modernized kitchen.

All seven of my boarders sit around my oak table eating pancakes with Alexei and Garik. I stop short in the doorway.

"Oh, hi." Felix looks up. "We hoped you'd get home soon."

Alexei finishes chewing and sets down his fork. "Yes, we were."

While Felix sounded thrilled, there's a darkness to Alexei's tone. His gaze flicks past me toward Ella. "Miss Rendale."

She smiles. "How's it hangin', Sokolov?"

I think amusement dances in his eyes, but I'm not entirely sure.

He pushes away from the table and crosses around

toward us. I take a step back, but Ella remains in place. Keeping his gaze on her, he pulls her backpack off her shoulder.

"Hey." She tries to grab for it.

He partially turns and yanks out the laptop and disc. "These are mine."

She pushes him. "You gave that to me, and the disc is Rosalie's."

His gaze slams into mine over her head, and I want to take another step back. "I didn't give you the laptop, and when you found information on the disc to exonerate me, you fucking posted it online. That put both of you in crosshairs. Period. I won't allow you to purposefully end up in danger." He says the last directly to me.

Ella reclaims her backpack. "The disc is only partially repaired. I'm not done."

"Oh, you're done." He hands the laptop and disc to Garik before returning to his seat and clasping his fork. "It's going to cost me more, but I'll have my computer guy come back for a couple of weeks." He digs into his pancakes.

I take a deep breath to steady myself, studying the assembled men. "What are you all doing?" My stomach growls.

Ozzy, who as far as I know, worked for an electrical company his whole life, flips another pancake at the stove. He's the oldest of my boarders, at about ninety, and is also the best cook. He's long and lean like a string bean, and I worry about him eating enough. "We looked for you all night, so we thought we'd eat and try again. I told everybody you'd be back in time for breakfast, but no one listened to me."

It's a tradition with my boarders for us to have a big

breakfast together every Saturday. I find it sweet that he thought I wouldn't miss our meal.

Vehicles screech outside and everybody stills. Garik stands. "What's going on?"

I wince. I'm not quite sure how to say this, even though Alexei and Hendrix aren't close, it'll probably hurt. "Somebody murdered Hendrix Sokolov last night."

Alexei pushes away from the table, his eyes going dark. "Are you serious?"

"Yes. Ella got the news before anybody else. The media doesn't have it yet."

He cocks his head. "You didn't let your friend Alana know? She could post all about it."

All right. We kind of deserve that. We did send the footage of Hendrix planting the knife in the pond directly to her, and she posted the video all over social media.

Someone knocks sharply on the door. "Alexei Sokolov, come out now."

Today he's dressed in dark gray slacks and a white button-down shirt. "I take it I'm a suspect?"

Ella nods vigorously. "According to the warrant they were putting together, you're the last known person to be seen with him."

"Where was he killed?" Garik sputters.

"Right outside of his family home. I guess your family home, Alexei," she hurriedly bursts out.

"That's where we dropped him off," Alexei says grimly. "Time of death?"

Ella shrugs. "I have no idea. I was up working on the other destroyed file from Blythe Fairfax's home. I figure showing Hendrix planting evidence is one thing, but if we can catch him actually committing the murder, all of this will go away. Well, that was before he died." She frowned. "You didn't kill him, did you?"

"Don't answer that," I say instantly, turning into his lawyer.

Amusement dances across his face. "I didn't kill him."

It sounds like he's telling the truth, but he's also trying to consolidate power as a mob boss, so I'm not entirely sure I believe him.

More pounding echoes on the door. "Open the door. We're coming in."

"Just a moment," I call out. "All right, let's go."

He walks calmly around the table, his heat instantly engulfing me. "We have things to discuss, Peaflower."

"I'm sure we do. There are more important matters to attend to right now," I say smartly, looking down at my skirt and wrinkled blouse. I don't have time to change. "How did they know you were here?"

Alexei shrugs.

Wally brings up a computer feed over in the far corner. "I have security all around this place. If we're being watched, I didn't know it. My guess is they traced the phone records. You've been in and out of here, Alexei."

"It doesn't matter how they know." Alexei glances over his shoulder at Garik. "Take advantage of this matter, will you? You have access to the funds, and you know what I need."

"Are you sure about this?" Garik frowns. "We can go out the back if you want."

Alexei rolls up his white shirt sleeves. "No, this is what I want—it's actually the perfect opportunity." He nods at me. "All right, attorney, let's see how good you are." There's a mild undercurrent to his voice I don't like, but I don't really blame him.

"What are you two talking about?" I ask. That is some kind of bro code. What matter? What does he need? "Alexei?"

"This doesn't concern you," he says quietly.

We move toward the door, and I open it to see the full SWAT team. "He's coming out and we're going in voluntarily," I say.

"He's coming with us." Detective Battlement moves toward Alexei, who calmly turns and allows himself to be a handcuffed. "We have solid evidence."

"Oh, yeah?" I say. "Last time you had evidence, it was planted. Nobody trusts you right now."

Detective Battlement blushes. "I'm aware of that, but this needs to happen."

I look at a very calm Alexei. "Don't say anything until I get there."

The detective reads Alexei his rights and then leads him down the long sidewalk to the road with all of the SWAT team following.

I shut the door and take a deep breath.

Wally turns from the stove. "We can set up somebody else if you want."

I don't want to ask. "You have experience in that kind of thing?"

He nods. "Yeah. I was a grifter most of my life, and I have pretty good connections."

A grifter? Seriously? The man makes sure I count out his rent every month to ensure he's paid me enough. I look at Percy. "And you worked for the mob?"

He nods. Wally was with MI6. Doc's definitely a doctor. That leaves two of my boarders as mysteries. "Kenny?"

Kenny looks up from his pancakes, today dressed in a flannel shirt and overalls. The guy looks like a retired farmer. "I was a spy, and that's all I'm saying." He pours more syrup over his plate.

I can't believe it. "Yardley?" I look at him. He's the youngest, and his bald head gleams in the soft light. "You weren't with a mob or an assassin or anything like that?"

"Nope," Yardley says cheerfully. "I was a nuclear physicist."

"How does that help?" Ozzy throws up his arms.

Yardley shrugs. "I didn't say it did."

I'm getting a headache. It's roaring in from the base of my skull. "Come on, Ella. I need a ride."

"We're all going," Merlin says.

I turn to hold up a hand. "We are not all going. You stay here and stay safe. I'll bail Alexei out with his own money, and we'll figure this out."

Exiting my comfortable home, we walk down the sidewalk and get into Ella's banged-up car. She looks over at me. "What do you think the chances are that he killed Hendrix?"

I gulp. "I don't know. He's trying to consolidate power and Hendrix did set him up. If Alexei was furious enough, I can see him dumping Hendrix's body at the family home, but there's no way he would've left evidence."

She sighs. "Things just get keeping more and more complicated, don't they?"

"Yes. Not to mention how angry Alexei is with me at the moment." He hid it well, but I felt his fury as he walked past me.

"Maybe we should leave him in jail," Ella offers.

I sit back, my mind reeling. "It's not a bad idea."

We reach the police station, and I run immediately inside, my newish kitten heels clicking on the tiles. I show credentials and soon find myself in the interrogation room next to Alexei, sitting across from Detective Battlement.

Alexei looks calm and relaxed. I glance at the two-way mirror and wonder who's videotaping us. Not that it matters. I note how strong and handsome, deadly so, Alexei looks. Mirrors love him.

"Your counselor is here. Now you can talk," the detective says, his jowls moving with each consonant.

"My client has nothing to say." Even though I feel vulnerable in the same outfit I wore yesterday with my hair in a ponytail and no makeup on my face, my voice is strong.

The detective shakes his head. "That's not good enough, Alexei. We have you on video. It's all over the news actually, of your brother getting into your car last night."

"I'm aware of that," Alexei says. "We had a nice talk and I dropped him off."

Battlement makes a couple of notations. "Where?"

"At his home," Alexei drawls.

"Stop speaking," I say quietly.

He glances at me, one eyebrow rising.

I look at the detective. "All you have is Hendrix getting into his brother's car after that same brother bailed him out?"

Battlement crosses his arms. "That and the fact that your client discovered that morning that his brother quite possibly set him up for an earlier murder." He leans toward Alexei, his belly bumping the table. "You spent seven years in prison. You're telling me you don't want revenge?"

Alexei shrugs. "What I want doesn't matter. We have a company to run." He sounds smooth and believable, but the detective doesn't look convinced.

"Your prints were found on the murder weapon," Battlement says.

I blink. "What was Hendrix murdered with? Was he shot?"

"Doesn't matter," Battlement says.

Alexei snorts. "You found my prints on murder weapons before."

It's an excellent defense. I hope I don't have to use it. "This doesn't need to go any further, Detective," I say. "You don't have enough on my client to keep him."

"The hell I don't. Forget motive. Like I said, his prints are actually on the weapon."

I sit back. "I'll ask again. What weapon was used to kill Hendrix?"

The detective opens a file folder and pulls out an enlarged photograph to toss our way. I look down to see a photo of Hendrix Sokolov on his back, his eyes open in death, and blood pouring from his neck. I peer closer and then can't breathe. What in the world?

The detective smiles. "Yes, his prints weren't the only ones found on the murder weapon."

Alexei scrutinizes the photograph. "What are you talking about?"

"Yours were there as well, Counselor." Battlement taps his fingers together and steeples his hands beneath his chin. "Do you recognize the weapon?"

I stare, not believing it. I peer closer to see my letter opener from my office, the one I used just the other day to open bills I can't pay, sticking out of Hendrix Sokolov's neck.

"Is that your letter opener?" the detective asks.

I sit back. "We're not saying anything else." It looks like I need my own attorney.

Battlement tugs the picture back to put in his file folder.

"Here's my theory, Ms. Mooncrest. Alexei visited you in your office, saw the letter opener, and took it. He picked up his brother, Hendrix, took him home, and then there was some sort of scuffle that led to Hendrix's death. The deceased has bruises on his arms. I think your client's trying to set you up, Counselor. You sure you don't want to talk to me?"

I cross my arms, my brain fuzzy. This can't be happening. "I'm positive."

"Very well." The detective slaps the file folder closed. "Alexei, you've been arrested, and you're going to be held."

I leap to my feet. "You can't hold him. We're going to request bail."

The detective shrugs. "Sorry, but I can't get in front of a judge until Monday, so it looks like your boy is going to spend a little more time in custody."

I look in panic at Alexei, but he seems calm, bored even. "The man spent seven years in prison for a crime he didn't commit. Release him on his own recognizance."

"That's not my decision, and I don't have a judge available." The detective stands. "In addition, we think he's an extreme flight risk." He looks at Alexei. "Please stand. We're going to hold you at the prison and not here at the jail. We've been informed by the local PD that they don't have the resources to keep you safe in their little cell."

My stomach drops.

Alexei stands, as always in perfect control. "Don't worry about it, Peaflower. Just get my bail set on Monday."

THIRTY-THREE
Alexei

A mere few hours after being arrested, I find myself back in the prison wearing a starchy, orange jumpsuit. The door clicks shut, and I stare across the cell at Urbano Reyes.

He stands against the rear wall, his arms crossed. "This can't be a coincidence."

"It's not," I agree. "I had to pay a fortune to make this happen."

He blinks. "You killed your brother?"

"Man, gossip reaches fast, doesn't it?"

"Yeah." He eyes me warily, a big, beefy man with a whole gang behind him, but right now it's just two of us in this cell.

"I didn't kill my brother," I say, knowing that there are ears everywhere. "So if you're trying to think of a way to get out early, that ain't going to be it."

His smile lightens his eyes. "I didn't figure. You obviously want to talk."

I do. "Did you get the money?"

"Yes. Thank you for your kind gift to my commissary account," he says. "I may have a couple of favors I need from you."

"No more favors." I set my feet and roll my neck.

I was happy to get out of prison, but even so, this feels familiar, much more familiar than that penthouse I recently purchased. The only place I've felt at home since getting out has been with Rosalie.

The odd thought hits me hard, and I blow out air. I didn't want to care for her. I didn't want to have that kind of liability. But I'm not a stupid man, and it's too late to worry about it. She's in my heart, and that's where she'll stay.

Reyes crosses his arms. "Thank you for checking on my four businesses."

"You're welcome." Those kills were easy. "The fifth one has been a bit of a problem. I think you should cut your losses with the restaurant." I throw out a business type. If anyone's listening, they won't know what we're talking about, but he has to understand that I won't kill Ella.

"Oh, no. I really need that restaurant to succeed." His bushy eyebrows rise. "It's important to me."

I let my gaze harden. "I understand that. I'm sure you have a lot of money invested in it," I say. "How about I buy the place from you? I have no problem purchasing a business like that one."

He cocks his head to the side. "Normally, I would accept such an offer, but this restaurant is personal to me."

"I checked it out. My guess is that you have some high-enders who like to eat there. Say somebody like Sylveria Rendale?" Ella's stepmother is my most likely suspect.

Reyes grins. "Yes. She likes to eat there often."

Okay, so he has no problem letting me know that

Sylveria has put out a hit on Ella. "They seem like a nice family. Have you met the youngest one, Ella?"

"She's the oldest one," Reyes responds. "And no, I haven't. I don't believe they're a close family."

I hate double talk but continue anyway. "Does Mrs. Rendale eat often at your restaurant?" Just how many murder for hire contracts has this woman taken out with Twenty-One Purple?

"Off and on. She's a good client," he says. "Which is why I can't accept your offer to buy the restaurant."

So he won't let me buy Ella's contract. "Do you have a lot of competition for the restaurant in the area?"

"No," he says. "So far, I'm the only one making money on that street."

Another good fact. So far, this is the only contract out on Ella, at least that Urbano knows about. "Are you positive that you don't want to sell? I will give you more money than she can ever pay you, no matter how many times she calls for reservations."

He winces. "No, it's not just the money. It's the reputation of the place, you know?"

"I understand."

His shoulders relax as if we reached an agreement. "Good. I was hoping you could also do me a little favor."

"Really. What's that?" I ask silkily.

He stops talking in code. "My girl and daughter have disappeared."

I keep my expression blank. "Excuse me?"

"Yeah, I don't know what happened to them. You have a lot of resources. I'm hoping you can help me track them down."

"In exchange for what?" I ask.

He shrugs. "I'll owe you one."

I can see that he thinks that's a big deal. In other words, his entire gang will owe me a favor. That could come in handy sometime. Unfortunately, I'm the one who gave his woman the money to get out of town. I'm glad she took my advice. "You know I'm happy to help you. We've been pals for years," I lie.

"I appreciate it." He nods toward an old checker set that we played too many times to count. "You want to play checkers or chess?"

"Sure. Why not? We're going to be here awhile."

He cracks his neck in a sound that would drive Rosalie crazy. "They're not going to let you out until Monday?"

"No. I'm too dangerous to keep in the local jail, apparently," I mutter.

His laugh is booming. "They don't know how dangerous you are."

"That's true. You set up the game."

"Sure thing." He moves toward the board on the tiny little table attached to the wall and pulls it to the center. A drawing floats out from beneath it.

I catch the sketch of Rosalie before it lands on the floor. "What's this?"

He grins. "You. Always drawing and then destroying the paper. You forgot to destroy that one."

I stare at my woman sitting in her cute suit in the meeting room that first day. I became so caught up in her that I actually allowed the drawing to remain in one piece? Now Reyes knows about her. About my interest in her. "She can make a man forget his own name," I admit, ripping the drawing into several pieces.

Reyes snorts and starts setting pieces in place.

I check the security camera to note the light off. Yeah, that cost me plenty as well. I pull the handmade shiv out of my sleeve. Barely shifting my weight, I stab myself in the bullet wound I sustained the other day. Pain slashes down my arm. I bite back a groan and move toward him.

His gaze lifts from the game to my shoulder where blood is already flowing. "What the fuck, man?"

I raise my voice and smash into him. "No. Stop it, Urbano. It's okay. I'm not here to spy on you. Stop it. Fuck. That hurts." I bellow for the guards, yelling for help.

He frowns and tries to get me away from him. His eyes darken, first in surprise and then in fear. I'm on him then, taking the weapon and jamming it into his throat. I pull fast, and his artery spurts blood in every direction.

His hand slaps over the wound. Blood pours between his fingers. His chin lifts. Dread and an odd acceptance crosses his face.

I jam the weapon right above his hand and into his neck. He's too weak to stop me. An alarm blares, and running feet clip through the shrill squeal. I leave the shiv in his throat and back away, hands up, dropping to my knees. The door slides open, and two of the guards run inside.

"He stabbed me." I look down at my shoulder. "I'm not sure if he hit an artery."

One guard quickly cuffs me while the other drops near Urbano, but he's already dead. The room begins to waver around me. I may have stabbed myself a little deeper than I planned, and then everything goes dark.

#

I wake up in the infirmary with a bandage across my shoulder, my wrists shackled to bars on either side of the bed, and a beeping sound above my head. The scent of vanilla tugs at me, and I open my eyes to see Rosalie sitting by the side of the bed, her face pale, an attorney's badge on her lapel.

"Hi, Peaflower," I say.

She leans toward me, worry in her eyes. "What in the world happened?"

"Got in a bit of a scuffle." It had cost me an absolute fortune to pay off the guard to get that weapon, and he promised me that Reyes's prints would be on it when they investigated the death. The guy better keep to his word.

"I've already asked for the security feed, and somehow, it went down. Do you think Reyes bribed somebody?"

My shoulder feels like I stuck a hot poker in it. "Reyes had friends everywhere in this prison." It's the truth, and there's no need to tell her I bribed the security guard for not only the shiv but to take down the cameras. He has a sick dog and needs the money for surgery.

She shakes her head, her face pale. "I've already made a motion to get you out of here. It was irresponsible for you to be put here in the first place after your entire ordeal."

It actually had cost me quite a bit. "Thank you."

"I can't believe you were attacked. Don't worry. We'll create quite the lawsuit over this." Now, red highlights her sculpted cheekbones, and I quite enjoy her anger on my behalf.

"I don't want to sue, Rosalie. I just want out."

She sighs. "I can't get you out until Monday, but at least you can stay here in the infirmary until then."

I look down at the bandage covering my left shoulder. "How bad is it?"

"Twenty stitches," she says.

Interesting. I did stab myself deeper than I thought, but at least this masks the bullet wound.

She holds my hand, worry screwing up her face. "Don't say anything here. You're under drugs."

"I didn't kill Hendrix, Rosalie," I say. "I promise."

She blinks once. "It's not like you have an alibi."

I lean toward her. "I do but you're not going to like it."

She pales. "You were with another woman?"

I don't want to lie to her, but I'm going to protect her from my world as much as possible. "I'll give you the truth this time because we're still new at this, but after that, you're away from my business. Completely. It won't touch you unless it's in a way to protect you."

Her strawberry-red lips purse as she moves her ear closer to my mouth. "Where were you?"

"Killing a guy named Howard Fissure," I whisper. Her chin drops. "He was a drug dealer and a child trafficker." Although I probably would've killed him anyway, considering I made a deal with Reyes and hadn't decided to renege until it came to Ella.

Rosalie's eyes widen. "I don't want to know that." Yet she looks relieved, anyway. The idea of me with another woman would crush her. I like that. We're on the same page.

In addition, she needs to trust me. "The last thing in the world I would do is implicate you by using your letter opener to kill somebody, Rosie. You have to know that."

She slowly nods as realization dawns in her expression. "Yeah, it's from my office."

"You need to figure out who got their hands on that."

She shrugs. "It could be anybody. We have people coming in and out of the law firm all the time. If somebody wanted to set up one of us, they could have easily dodged into my office and grabbed the letter opener. I always leave it on my desk."

"Has there been anybody new around lately?"

She frowns. "In fact, there were a couple delivery guys the other day I didn't recognize, bringing stuff in throughout the offices."

"You received a package?"

"Yes," she says. "It was just a book I ordered, though. But, there's usually only one guy, and this time there were two. I didn't think anything of it."

I blink and try to focus my gaze. The drugs are mellowing me, and I don't like it. "I see. You have cameras, don't you, in your office?"

"We do in the reception area, but not anywhere else," she says. "I'll get my hands on those and see who's been in and out of the office for the last several days." She blinks. "Blythe Fairfax was there."

Does Blythe want revenge? I did reject her. "She visited you in your office?"

"Yes." An odd expression crosses Rosalie's face. "She wanted to talk about you and showed off the many amethyst rings that you bought for her."

Amusement lingers just beneath the drugs in my system. "Are you jealous?"

A very pretty pink wanders from her chest up over her face. "Of course not."

My girl's jealous. I like that. "I never bought a thing for Blythe Fairfax. Not even dinner. She lied to you about the rings." Her eyes soften, but Rosalie still looks a little panicked every time she stares at my bandage. She cares more than she wants to admit—even to herself. "I don't like that you disappeared on me for a full night," I say quietly. "Don't do it again."

Her pupils constrict. Even so, she leans forward to whisper into my ear. "Don't kidnap my friend again."

It's a fair request. She'll probably never know exactly

what I just did for her friend, and then I realize, I didn't destroy the source of the murder contract—I only took out the weapon. So, I try to think of the right way to tell her. "You need to warn your friend Ella."

"Why, are you going to kidnap her again?"

"That's as safe as she's been in quite a while," I say quietly, forcing her to place her ear near my mouth. I doubt anybody is listening, but why take the chance? "My former cellmate accepted a contract on her."

Rosalie sits back. "How do you know that?"

I don't answer.

She studies me for several long moments and then realization dawns across her angled face. "Alexei," she breathes.

I shake my head. Now is not the time to go into specifics. I whispered most of it to her, and with the loud beeping from these stupid machines, if anyone's listening, they didn't get the details. "We'll talk about it later."

Tears glimmer in her eyes. I keep forgetting how smart she is. Obviously, she's put together exactly what happened. She reaches out and slides her hand into mine, providing more comfort than she'll ever realize.

"Visiting hours are probably about over," I say. "I want Garik with you for the rest of the weekend—until I get out on bail." I won't consider the possibility that a judge might refuse bail.

Rosalie scoots forward and rests her head next to mine. "I think I'll stay here with you for a little while."

Simple words. Soft words. But they hit me harder than a freight train. She might not fully understand it yet, but she's always going to stay with me.

THIRTY-FOUR
Rosalie

On Monday morning, I find myself dressed in my best navy-blue skirt suit, arguing passionately for Alexei to be released on his own recognizance. He stands beside me in new clothing I brought him, black slacks, a salmon-colored shirt, and a black jacket.

He glances at the shirt a couple of times and then at me. I shrug. It was in with all of his other new clothing, and I thought he liked it. He seems to like the old-fashioned black and white look. But I felt like messing with him a little bit.

The prosecuting attorney, a middle-aged woman with very pretty gray and blondish hair piled up on her head, impatiently taps her pencil on the desk.

For some reason, the sound is bugging me. Once in a while a noise other than a mouth or nose sound will feel like a spur beneath my skin.

She keeps tapping. "Your Honor. With all due respect, Mr. Sokolov's prints were found on the letter opener, which was still embedded in his half brother's throat. He was the last one to see the deceased, and there's no love lost in this family. They completely abandoned the defendant when he was convicted of murder seven years ago."

Tap. Tap. Tap. Tap.

"Falsely convicted." I slam my fist on the table. I want to grab that pencil from her. "The verdict has been overturned, and we have evidentiary proof that he was set up. I submitted a copy of the video showing Hendrix Sokolov actually planting evidence at the original crime scene."

"Exactly my point, Your Honor," the prosecutor says. "We don't know where Hendrix obtained the knife used to murder David Fairfax seven years ago. Perhaps he got it from his brother. Or perhaps he killed David. Either way, Hendrix threw that knife in the pond, and Alexei went to prison for seven years. No doubt Alexei wanted revenge."

I think her name is Vicky Sloth or something like that. I wasn't really listening when she introduced herself, because my mind has been spinning all day.

She keeps tapping that damn pencil. "The defendant has an excellent motive for killing his half brother. Can you imagine spending seven years in prison for a crime because your own brother ensured the murder weapon would be found?" She looks at Alexei on my other side as she hints that he still murdered the victim. "I'd be angry, Judge."

"So would I," the judge agrees. She's an older woman with long white hair named Valerie Flanders. "But motive is irrelevant in a criminal case, as you know. Well, legally it's irrelevant, but a jury always likes to know what it is."

"He has the means and the opportunity to have killed his half brother, as well, Your Honor," the prosecuting attorney says, slapping the pencil on the table. It rolls an inch my way.

Alexei smoothly steps behind me, leans over, and grabs the prosecutor's pencil.

She jerks.

He quickly steps back into place and leans down to scribble on a notebook.

"Mr. Sokolov," the judge snaps.

He pauses and looks up. "Yes, Judge?"

She blinks. "What did you just do?"

Alexei has the grace to appear surprised. "I thought the pencils were for everybody, and we don't have one." He leans around my front to face the prosecutor. "Sorry about that. I thought you were finished with this one."

How had he known the tapping was killing me? I completely kept my cool. Does he know me that well? "Your Honor," I say, trying to keep all emotion out of my voice.

The idea that Alexei could have been killed the other day sticks with me and forces me to make several harsh realizations. The first is that somehow I've completely fallen for the guy. The second is that he's in danger all the time. And the third is that this murder charge is real. He does have an excellent motive to kill Hendrix for setting him up years ago. Or just to regain ownership and control of Hologrid Hub now. Alexei's prints are on the letter opener, of course, as are mine.

I clear my throat and try again. "For some reason, Mr. Sokolov was sent from the jail to await a bail hearing, to prison, a place he barely escaped and was immediately attacked."

The judge looks at the prosecuting attorney. "I agree with a concern there. Why in the world was Mr. Sokolov removed from the local jail and taken back to prison?"

The prosecutor visibly swallows. "We're trying to

figure that out, Your Honor, and I haven't found a good answer. Orders came from high above, but nobody quite knows what that means."

"That doesn't sound suspicious," I retort. Of course, I must be careful because Alexei engineered the entire situation. He put himself in a cell with a murderer in order to protect my friend. He risked his life to save her, someone I consider my sister. The only reason he gave me the truth is because if there's one hit out on her and it doesn't work, there'll probably be another one.

She hadn't seemed even remotely surprised when I told her the news. I can ask Alexei to keep her safe, but I still have to talk Ella into receiving help. She's a stubborn one.

The judge shakes her head. "You know, I have to agree with Miss Mooncrest. I don't know where the breakdown of procedure occurred, but Mr. Sokolov could have been killed. He is innocent until proven guilty, and yet you sent him to a prison."

The prosecuting attorney plants both hands on her desk. "I don't know what happened, Judge. I really am trying to figure it out."

Apparently, money can buy almost anything. A fact that I do not appreciate.

The judge reads through several papers. "In light of the fact that Mr. Sokolov was nearly killed due to the state's negligence, I'm more inclined to rule in his favor in this matter. Bail is set at one hundred thousand dollars." She slams down the gavel.

I look over my shoulder as Garik exits the courtroom, no doubt on his way to pay the entire amount.

A sense of calm settles in my chest. Good. Alexei can come home with me.

"One more motion, Your Honor," the prosecuting attorney says.

I glance her way, surprised.

"This is based on new information, and we haven't had a chance to notify Mr. Sokolov." The woman hands me several pieces of paper. "We have a motion to remove Ms. Mooncrest as the attorney for the accused."

"Why is that?" Judge Flanders asks as the prosecuting attorney hands her a stack of papers.

The prosecutor steps back behind her table, her spine straight and her posture about perfect. "We just filed these with the court, Your Honor. We believe Miss Mooncrest is having an affair with her client, and we need to question her regarding this case. The letter opener is owned by her, and she could put Mr. Sokolov in the same room with it, but we need her as a witness. Attorney-client privilege does not extend to illegal acts."

I stare down at the documents, which swim in front of my face.

The judge drops the stack to her desk. "Miss Mooncrest? It would be inappropriate for me to decide this on an ad hoc basis like this. Please prepare a response, and we'll have a hearing—" she shuffles through a calendar— "a week from today at nine in the morning. At that time, you may wish to employ your own counsel." She bangs the gavel down again.

The prosecuting attorney winks at me. "We're just getting started, Mooncrest." She turns and walks away from the counsel table and down the middle aisle of the courtroom.

I look at Alexei. "This is a problem."

"It doesn't have to be." He gestures me ahead of him, and he follows me out to where we meet Garik in the hall.

"I already paid the bail," he says, handing over an envelope. "Here's all your stuff."

I don't object to this uncommon procedure. Alexei should have to go through a discharge procedure and collect his own belongings, but, apparently, they're not finished throwing money around.

We walk toward the doors, and through the glass, a multitude of reporters and cameras are waiting. We'll have to go right through them to reach the parking area.

"The back exit is just as bad," Garik says grimly.

I take a deep breath and walk outside with Garik in front of me and Alexei behind me as if they're flanking me.

Alexei's shoulder is damaged, and so I should try to protect him from anybody hitting his arm.

Lillian Sokolov rushes forward, shrieking. "You killed my son. You killed my son."

She goes for Alexei, and Garik swiftly wraps an arm around her waist and swirls her away, planting her back on her feet.

"Back off, lady," he barks.

"You killed him," she screams, tears running down her face, her graying hair a disheveled tangle around her shoulders.

Alexei's jaw hardens, and he looks at all the cameras. I do the same. This is a freaking disaster. Every potential juror we'll receive in a pool will see this.

I feel pity and even sorrow for her. She's lost both of her sons. I can't imagine that kind of pain. "We'll find out who killed him, Mrs. Sokolov," I say quietly. "But it wasn't Alexei."

She hisses and leaps toward me with her fingers and nails extended. Garik once again pulls her away from me.

"You probably helped him. We all know you're screwing him," she screams.

My stomach rolls over.

She sticks her hands in her rain slicker, looking fragile and desperate. Lonely. "It was your letter opener. I bet you killed him together to get the company—to get all of the money. I'll take you both down. I promise."

With that, she turns, her light-gray raincoat swirling, and stomps back down the stairs, cameras clicking the whole way. She reaches a running black town car at the curb, opens the back door herself, and gets in. It drives quickly off.

The reporters begin shouting questions at both Alexei and me. Garik pushes people out of the way, and we get to the curb where he also has a town car waiting. He opens the back door, and I hurry inside, scooting over so Alexei can follow me.

The reporters get closer, cameras right up against the windows that, thank goodness, are tinted. Garik elbows his way through them to cross around and get into the driver's side where he starts the vehicle and guns the engine. He has to nudge them with the car to force them out of the way, but soon we're miles from the courthouse.

I drop my face into my hands. This is a disaster.

"How bad is it?" Alexei asks.

My voice is muffled but I don't care. "Legally, it's terrible. I will be taken off your case. I'll be made a material witness, and if they can prove the affair, I'll lose my law license." Too bad hiding isn't an option. I sit up. "I know what you did for my friend." We can finally speak freely.

"I'm aware," he says.

Garik looks in the review mirror. "There will be

reporters at your place, Rosalie. Maybe at the new building you bought, Alexei, if they know about it. That's where I suggest we go."

Alexei leans back and gingerly removes his jacket. I help him, wondering how bad his wound pains him now. He's pale beneath his bronzed skin.

"You need a painkiller," I say.

"I took some ibuprofen. I'll be fine. Drive to Reno, Garik."

Garik jolts. "What? You want to go to Nevada?"

"I do. Reno's about three and a half hours. Do me a favor and make it in three." Alexei tosses the jacket on the floor.

I pick it up and fold it neatly across my lap. "I'm not going to Reno. I have a job to save."

"This is how we're going to save it," he says.

"By leaving the state?" I shake my head. "Alexei, this isn't making any sense. Why do you want to go to Nevada?"

He leans his head back on the seat and shuts his eyes. "Because they don't have a wait time to obtain a marriage license there."

I turn more toward him, shock slashing through me. "Are you insane? We're not getting married."

His answer is a soft snore.

I shake his good shoulder until he opens one eye. Then he wraps his healthy arm around me and drags me into his side. "I'm sleeping for a few minutes. We can argue then." He closes his eyes again, sound asleep in less than a minute.

How does he do that? Okay. Fine. I can give him fifteen minutes, and then we're fighting about this. I am absolutely not going to Nevada to get married.

Somehow, I nod off and find myself awakening in Nevada.

Garik pulls the car up to a cute little wedding chapel. "I'll go in and make the arrangements," he says.

"Take your time." Alexei says, his voice gravelly.

I blink myself awake and look over to see him studying me, his eyes dark.

A shiver wanders through me.

THIRTY-FIVE
Rosalie

I can't believe we're in Nevada. How could I have slept the entire way? Sure, I've been tired, but this is insane. "We are not getting married." I sound breathless. Why do I sound like that?

Alexei grasps my waist and lifts me onto his lap, making sure I'm straddling him. My skirt rides up, arousal swamps me, and panic grabs me. I push against his good shoulder, careful of the wounded one.

He claps a hand over mine. "Baby, there's too much going on, and attorney-client privilege doesn't apply to a lot that's happened. You know I set up and then killed Reyes in prison, and at some point, an ambitious prosecutor is going to ask you about that. But spousal privilege would protect us both. Plus, that letter opener is a problem. If I'm charged, they're going to ask you about my visits to your office and put me there with the weapon."

"Did you take it?"

"No."

I suck in air. "Spousal privilege attaches to conversations

between spouses and not actions. If a wife sees her husband commit a crime, she can still testify."

"But she can't be compelled because of the adverse spousal testimony privilege. It's up to the spouse if they want to testify or not in that case." I lean back. He's right. "How in the world do you know that?"

His gaze drops to my mouth. "I spent seven years in prison and read a lot." Apparently so. "That's a crappy reason to get married." Yes, I've had dreams of my wedding since I was a little girl playing make believe with my friends. White dress, red flowers, tall and steady blonde man in a tuxedo smiling with tears in his eyes as I walk down the aisle. Alexei is the opposite of all of that. "I'm not getting married in a crappy little chapel in Nevada." Not the point. My brain is mush with this man. "I'm not marrying you, I mean. You can't want a marriage of convenience, either."

His hands go to my skirt, his thumbs tucking beneath the fabric as he pushes the material all the way up. "There's nothing convenient about you."

Live wires uncoil in my abdomen. "You are not going to fuck me into agreement." The words come from nowhere and shock me.

"Is that a dare?" His voice is unfairly low, gravelly, and sexy.

"No," I whisper, very much afraid I'll lose that one.

He snaps the sides of my panties and yanks them free. "Smart girl. Now be a good girl."

I shouldn't like those words. Nope. Not at all. Yet my thighs dampen. I meet his gaze, my eyes wide.

He slides a finger inside me easily. Way too easily. I'm wet for him that quickly. "Don't be frightened."

Why not? He's terrifying. This hold on me is unreal, and I like control. For *me* to have control. "I-I don't want a fast and temporary marriage."

He stills, his finger still inside me. "Temporary? There's nothing temporary about us. This is for good, Rosalie. I'm never letting you go." Another finger slides in, stretching me, and a low hum of pleasure comes from deep in his chest.

I try not to move against him and fail. Even though the windows are tinted, I look wildly around, hoping nobody sees us.

"I'll give you the wedding of your dreams once I'm back in control at work," he rumbles, releasing my hand to palm my breast through my blouse and bra. His hand is wicked hot.

I attempt to focus but my bitch of a body is moving against his fingers, not comprehending the seriousness of this moment. "It's not the wedding, Alexei," I gasp, vulnerability weakening my voice. Not entirely the wedding, anyway. "Marriage is for real."

"We're for real." He rips open my blouse and flicks the center clasp of my bra, which flings open. "Ride my fingers, Rosalie."

I swallow, already doing just that. "No."

His smile is quick. "All right." He releases the button on his pants and unzips. "Take me out. Now."

I obey before the neurons in my brain can fire reason through me, reaching for him with both hands and freeing him from the boxers. He's thick and hard, pulsing against my hands. His fingers slide out of me, and he grips both of my hips, lowering me onto him. The fullness shocks me for a moment, and I grab his shoulders, feeling the bandage beneath one. "Sorry."

"Never be sorry." His gaze dropping, he releases my hips and scratches his nails down both of my breasts on either side of my nipples.

I gasp and rock against him. "I want love," I whisper.

He jolts and then returns to torturing me, tweaking both nipples. "You can have all of me. I fully intend to have all of you." Then he kisses me, somehow taking complete control even though I'm on top of him.

An objection starts somewhere in the back of my mind but then I'm kissing him back, pressing into his hands, lifting my hips and pushing back down on him. I widen my thighs to better balance myself on my knees. Sparks fly through me, and then I'm just feeling. Everything. His body, my need, a sense of safety I'll never understand.

He might be a danger to me, but he won't let anybody else get close. He growls into my mouth and sends vibrations down through my body to my clit. Then he manacles my hips, lifting me and slamming me back down, somehow hitting a spot inside me that has me seeing stars. After one brief pause, he does so again, controlling me with his strong hands.

Hard and fast, wild and intense, he hammers into me while lifting and yanking me onto him. I throw back my head and climb to that precarious ridge, holding my breath when I fall over. The orgasm blows through me, undulating my abdomen, sparking from my pussy to my breasts and back down. He groans and jerks several times inside me.

Finally, he lets me down, still inside me, his hands gentling.

I can't breathe.

He gently leans me back and secures my bra over my tender breasts before smoothly buttoning up my blouse. Setting me aside, he secures his pants as I yank my skirt down almost to my knees. "Let's get married, Peaflower. Time is short." He opens the door and steps out, holding a hand out for me.

Mine trembles as I take his, moving into the warm June day.

Within ten minutes, I'm standing in a cheesy wedding chapel with no panties, feeling my thighs still damp from him. As if he knows it, Alexei gives me a wicked smile. My abdomen turns over. My lips are swollen from his kisses, and my head is spinning.

I can't do this. Everything inside me hurts. Why? He's using me. For sex, for my legal skills, to fit a mob-boss role. This is wrong.

The entire room smells like gardenias. Not the natural kind, but more like a chemical scent. The chapel is cozy with only two rows of vacant white benches and plain white walls with fake flowers decorating twin windowsills on either side of us.

Panic grabs me.

Garik stands behind Alexei, while some woman named Betty dressed in a flowered gown, her bright-red hair up in wild curls, stands behind me. She has to be about sixty and the red hair is a little much for her pale skin but does match her cracked lips.

A mirror is behind her. Round, smooth, and perfectly angled to catch our images. Alexei is so much bigger than I am.

The preacher opens a large burgundy colored book. He

looks to be around fifty and weighs at least 400 pounds. The button collar of his shirt is choking him, and sweat rolls down the sides of his face. "I love a good romance," he says.

Alexei takes my free hand since I hold a bouquet of fake red roses in my other hand. My knees wobble. This is not happening.

Tears gather in my eyes. Ice freezes in my throat. I yank my hand free. "No." Turning, I run down the aisle toward the door.

I don't make it.

Alexei sweeps me up.

I struggle against him. I will not be used like this. "Stop it."

He steps outside, shuts the door, and leans back against it. "What's going on?"

I gulp. "It's too much, Alexei." A tear slides down my face. "You're too much. I won't remember that this is just for practical reasons. My heart won't. It'll feel real, and I'll be alone." There aren't any words to describe the pain.

He blinks, his dark eyes inquisitive. Then he sighs, holding me against his rock-hard chest, leaning against the door. "It is real." When I start to refute that, he kisses my nose, stopping me cold. Then he leans back, keeping my gaze captured. "None of this is a coincidence."

I frown. "What?"

He looks as if he could stand here all day. "We had access to computers in prison." He shrugs, moving us both. "We weren't supposed to, but we did."

I blink out another tear. "I don't understand."

"When I gained computer privileges early, I investigated the law firm and kept an eye on everyone there. Saw you when you came on board, and from that second, all I thought about was you. I also saw you on Aquarius Social with Alana. Began watching every chance I got. Dreamed about you every night, knowing someday I'd be free. Didn't know how."

Wait—what? "But how?"

"Used my last few favors to make sure you were my lawyer when the chance finally came. Basically bribed Jaqueline Lion through a proxy." His gaze releases me and focuses on my mouth. "Strawberry-red lips, sapphire-blue eyes, raven-black hair. Obsession can be a life saver. The mere idea of you got me through the nights."

I can't breathe. "Alexei."

He kisses me, taking us both under. Then he releases me. "I sketched your face. Over and over, so many times. Hated destroying those drawings, but I couldn't let anybody know what you mean to me. You are meant to be mine. Darkness and light. Wildness and control. It's both of us."

I blink. Could it be love? Turn to love? I'm afraid I'm almost there. Maybe already there. "Stalker." I try not to cry. He's so sweet.

"Let's get married, Peaflower. You have to jump some time." He watches me, waiting. "I'll give you everything. Especially me."

It's time to jump. Either I'll land safe and sound, or I'll break something. Either way, I'm going to leap. "Okay," I whisper.

He carries me back to the altar, keeping me against his chest. "We're ready."

The preacher clears his throat. "Do you Alexei Sokolov take Rosalie Mooncrest to be your lawfully wedded wife, to love and cherish for the rest of your days?"

"I do," Alexei says, his eyes dark, his voice somber.

I'm going to actually faint, even held safely in his arms. He tightens his grip on me as if to give me some sort of comfort . . . or as a warning. I'm not sure.

"Do you Rosalie Mooncrest take Alexei Sokolov as your husband to love, honor, and obey for the rest of your years?"

I jolt at the last word. Alexei's mouth curves in a smile. I flash him a look. "I do."

"Very well. Do you have rings?" the preacher asks.

"No," I say.

"I have one." Carefully balancing me against his chest, Alexei reaches into his pocket and pulls out a stunning amethyst square with diamonds all around the stone. More diamonds decorate the twisting gold on the wide band.

I gasp. The piece is the most stunning ring I've ever seen. He slips it easily on my finger. I look at him, startled.

He winks. "With this ring I thee wed."

I stare down at all of the sparkle. "I don't have a ring for you."

"We have some on sale," Betty says happily.

Alexei grins, and it's the first time I've really seen him smile. "We'll have one made later. One with amethysts." He's really in this for the long haul. He's not kidding about forever.

"Anything else?" the preacher asks.

I look at Alexei and I want to say something, but I have no idea what.

His dark eyes sparkle. "I promise you'll want for nothing for the rest of your days. In addition, Rosalie Mooncrest, I'll keep you safe. Nobody will hurt you. I promise."

Somehow, I believe him. It's not love and flowers and

rocking chairs. "I'll do my best," I say, not knowing what else to give him.

"I give you all of me," he says. "I don't know if I'm capable of love, but if I am, you can have it."

I blink. Something's swirling through me. "I'm very capable of love," I say quietly, going on instinct and not intellect. I hope I know what I'm doing. "I promise to love you with everything I am."

The words sound natural, and I let them loose. I've known him for a short time, but in that time, he's become everything. As necessary as life. I don't know if something like this, something so hot and bright, will burn out, or if it'll continue to flame through the rest of my life. But if I'm going to make these vows, I'm going to give them my best.

"I now pronounce you man and wife," the preacher says.

Alexei lifts my chin with two knuckles and then kisses me, soft and tender in a way he hasn't been before. I murmur something, I don't know what, and the kiss deepens as if he's promising every vow imaginable. Then he releases me and I blink, startled.

"Yay," Betty yells, throwing fake flower petals up in the air above us.

I blink as one lands on my eye and Alexei gently brushes it away. He kisses me once again and then starts walking down the aisle with Garik following us. Looking over his shoulder, I turn and throw the fake bouquet at Garik as hard as I can. He catches it and looks down, his eyes widening.

I finally feel free to laugh.

Alexei kicks open the door, and we walk out into warm Reno sunshine toward the car. It hits me all of a sudden that I'm a married woman.

Alexei's phone buzzes, and still somehow managing to hold me aloft, he reaches into his pocket and lifts it to his ear. I wrap an arm around his neck to better balance myself.

"Sokolov," he says. "When? How? Thanks. Got it." He clicks off.

"What?" I ask.

He sighs. "Apparently, Blythe Fairfax was murdered last night. They found her body this morning."

Panic grabs me and then I relax. "You were in the prison infirmary last night." Thank goodness. They can't pin this on him.

A muscle along his neck flexes. "The police want to speak with you."

I frown. Why would they want to talk to me? "Okay. I guess we need to get back." None of this makes sense.

He grins, his surprising dimple flashing for the briefest of moments. "We are not a hundred percent married yet."

I blink. "What do you mean?"

"For a marriage to be validated, it has to be consummated." Then he kisses me.

THIRTY-SIX
Alexei

I sit at Rosalie's dining table first thing in the morning with a steaming cup of coffee in front of me. We immediately returned to California after exchanging our vows, and I had all night with her. There's no doubt we consummated the marriage—four times. I like that my girl is a screamer, and she deserves an exotic honeymoon. After I get my business in order.

Right now, I flank one side of her while Joseph Cage quite unfortunately flanks the other side. We face Detective Battlement and his partner, a young woman by the name of Shelly Jones. She is husky with pretty green eyes, long curly dark hair, and light-brown skin. She dutifully takes notes as Battlement questions Rosalie.

Battlement crosses his arms. "Mr. Sokolov, you're not needed here. You should leave."

"Actually, he can stay," Rosalie says. "This is an informal interview that I have agreed to, and I set the parameters, Detective."

Pride fills me. She sounds tough even though she looks rather delicate in a pink suit. This one has another pencil skirt, and I'm finding myself rather addicted to them. Her blouse is a flowery one with all sorts of different colors, and the suit jacket is buttoned even though she's sitting. Her hair is up, her eyes are clear, and if anything, she looks a little pissed off.

I, on the other hand, am feeling quite relaxed. "I'm not going anywhere, Detective."

His gaze flicks to me. He's a beefy man and could probably take several punches before he falls.

Although I'm relaxed and present, since Hendrix is dead, I need to go and consolidate power. My phone keeps vibrating silently in my pocket, and I'm spending time here that I don't have. No doubt Lillian is making a move to consolidate without Hendrix, and I won't be surprised if a couple of the higher up lieutenants decide to try for a takeover.

Most of them don't know that the power really lies in the ability to physically charge the amethyst crystals that run the servers and just think that the company is a normal Bratva-run organization. I need to disabuse them of the idea that they could prosper without me. Yet I won't leave until the detective does.

Movement sounds from the kitchen, and I have no doubt that one, if not several, of Rosalie's boarders are listening, unapologetically, at the door. Garik is covering the front of the house. There really is no privacy around here, and I find that is something I'll probably change. Oh, I'll let her keep her boarders, but there's going to have to be some sort of distance to keep them safe, if for nothing else.

Battlement reaches for an old, battered notebook that he tosses on the table and flips open. "Where were you Sunday night?"

"I was still in the infirmary," I note.

"I'm not talking to you," Battlement says. "You're not a

suspect. We know exactly where you were. You, however, are a suspect." He's facing Rosalie now. "I find it interesting that you start dating Mr. Sokolov here and then all of a sudden, both his brother and his ex-lover end up dead."

She blinks. "I find it rather inconvenient, Detective."

He stares at her, and now both of the detectives are taking notes. "Where were you Sunday night?"

"I was here at home," she says. "I stayed Saturday night in the infirmary with Mr. Sokolov, and then I came home Sunday, worked around the house, and stayed the night here before attending the hearing yesterday morning."

"Was anyone else in your bedroom?" he asks.

Irritation clacks through me. "Considering I was in the infirmary, I would have to answer no to that question."

This time, he doesn't look at me. "Again, I'm not talking to you, Sokolov. Miss Mooncrest."

"No, Detective," she says. "Nobody was in my bedroom but me."

The door opens from the kitchen, and Percy pokes his head in. "I was here. I can vouch for her."

"Me too," come a chorus of voices from behind him.

Detective Battlement rolls his eyes. "Shut the door and leave us be."

I can't help it. Amusement dances through me. Rosalie has seven alibis if she needs them. Hell, I can create more. I do wonder who killed Blythe, though.

"Have you met Blythe Fairfax?" the detective asks.

"Yes," Rosalie says. "She and Jaqueline Lion, my boss, met with me in my office last week."

His bushy eyebrows rise. "What about?"

"That's privileged," she says instantly.

His stare intensifies. "Do you represent Mrs. Fairfax?"

"That also is privileged," Rosalie says.

"This is a crime, Miss Mooncrest. First-degree murder. You might want to work with me."

Joseph Cage sits forward finally and remembers he's a lawyer, apparently. "My client is not going to violate attorney-client privilege, Detective. But I will tell you that Miss Mooncrest personally does not, and has never, represented Mrs. Fairfax."

"Then why was Mrs. Fairfax in your office?" he asks me.

Rosalie shakes her head. "Privilege."

"I concur," Joseph Cage says.

So far, the guy is useless. I don't know why he's here, although it's probably smart to have a lawyer, but Rosalie is more intelligent than Cage. Plus, he patted her on the knee when he sat down, and I almost took off his hand. Only the presence of the detective kept me from shredding him. Of course, there's always later in the day.

Cage leans forward. "How did Mrs. Fairfax die? The news media has reported her death, but that's about it."

"Blunt force trauma to the head," the detective says quietly, still staring at Rosalie. "Have you been in contact with Mrs. Fairfax other than the time she was in your office for a reason you will not discuss?"

Now he sounds sarcastic. I focus on him. I need to consolidate the organization and get our two computer experts under my command. Now that Hendrix is dead, it might be a war of power between Lillian and me. She doesn't stand a chance, however. I'll have to do a deeper dive on this detective.

He looks around. "You ever beat anybody to death, Rosalie?"

I stiffen. I preferred it when he called her Miss Mooncrest.

"No," she says. "Of course not. Now, I've told you where I was, established that I have an alibi—" she looks over her shoulder at the closed doorway— "and that's pretty much it. I do not know anything about Mrs. Fairfax's death."

Battlement shifts his muscled bulk "It's my understanding that your boy here was pretty hot and heavy with Mrs. Fairfax. In fact, there's a rumor he killed for her. You've heard the gossip, right?"

"I believe that lie was debunked when the video of his half brother planting evidence flew across the internet," she says calmly.

"Ah," Detective Battlement says. "You mean the half brother that is now dead after being stabbed with your letter opener?"

Rosalie closes her lips. Good.

Cage leans forward. "Do you have any other questions, Detective? Because this is getting tiresome. My client did not kill Blythe Fairfax. Any alleged relationship between Mr. Sokolov and Mrs. Fairfax happened seven years ago, and they haven't been in contact since."

"That's not necessarily true, is it?" The detective winks at me.

To her credit, Rosalie doesn't move, although I can feel uncertainty from her. It's interesting how in tune I am to her moods.

I sigh. "My first day out when I went to the Amethyst, Mrs. Fairfax came in."

"What did she want?" Battlement asks.

I keep my tone level. "She wanted to know if we could

rekindle our romance. Also, she asked if I killed her husband. I said no on both accounts." I put an arm around Rosalie because I'm done with not touching her. It's been too long since I have.

Battlement watches my movements. "I see. Any other times?"

"No," I say. "I haven't seen the woman since." Which is the truth.

"Hmm," he says, looking down at his notebook. "We do have her on camera at the Amethyst that day. Do you think Miss Mooncrest would kill for you?"

"I hope I never have to find out," I say honestly.

The detective stares at my arm stretched around her shoulders. "When did you two start to date?"

"My client's not answering any personal questions," Joseph Cage interjects immediately.

Battlement dismisses him with a flick of his eyes. "Get out in front of this now, Rosalie. You seem like a decent person who got caught up in a world you don't understand. Let me help you."

She tilts her head. "You want to help me, Detective? How sweet."

If she used that tone with me, I'd spank her ass. But right now, I love the sassy side of her. I don't hide my smile. The detective flips open a file folder and pulls out a photograph to place on the table. It shows Rosalie's damaged car from the other day.

"Apparently, Mrs. Fairfax beat up your vehicle, Rosalie," Battlement says. "She had several pictures taken while she damaged your car. I find it odd that you didn't notify the police about the vandalism. Perhaps you wanted to take care of matters yourself?"

"My client is not answering that question," Cage says.

Good. I don't like this at all.

Battlement pulls out another picture. This one is of a harshly beaten Blythe Fairfax, her face a bloody mess. "She kind of looks like your car."

"This is not necessary." Cage pushes it back.

"I think it is," Detective Battlement says. "This is what you did. You may have been in a rage. You may be able to plead some sort of temporary insanity. I don't know. But you do need to get out in front of this right now, Rosalie. Trust me."

Warning ticks through me, and I don't know why. The detective is holding something back.

Rosalie's eyes widen as she stares at the picture. The murder was brutal. Blythe is beaten, and blood splatters across what looks like a white dress. She's lying on a sidewalk. Broken.

I don't care about her but wouldn't wish a beating like that on any woman. The fact that somebody killed her to frame Rosie or me keeps me cold and centered. "Where did Blythe die?"

"I'm not answering your questions," the detective says. "Rosalie, let me help you."

"I didn't kill Mrs. Fairfax," Rosalie bursts out.

The detective sighs and pulls out another picture. "Do you recognize this paperweight?"

Holy fuck, I do. It's the silver one of an apple that is usually on Rosalie's desk.

Joseph Cage must recognize it as well because he slaps the table. "We're finished with this interview, Detective. Either arrest my client or leave this house."

The detective slowly tucks everything back into his file

folder and pushes away from the table, standing. His partner does as well. "I'm not ready to make an arrest. Still have a couple avenues to pursue." He looks deadly serious at Rosalie. "However, I'm going to do so very soon. I suggest you and your attorney come up with a good plan for you to voluntarily surrender at the police department."

He walks away and pauses by the doorway. "I do like you, Rosalie. I think you're smart, and I think you still have a future. Maybe not in law. But you're caught up in a world you just don't understand. Let me help you." He finally cuts a look at me. "Mr. Sokolov, I would like to interview you at your earliest convenience."

I flash him a smile that I hope reads as a warning. "Gee, that'd be fun, Detective, but the last person in the world I want to discuss with you is my wife."

THIRTY-SEVEN
Rosalie

Sitting on my bed, I rub lotion into my arms, waiting for Alexei, who's still on the phone downstairs arranging a meeting for his people for tomorrow. Ella has long disappeared, and Garik is probably wandering the yard right now looking for threats. I'm wearing a sexy black teddy that I think Alexei will like.

As I wait, my mind spins with mysteries. Who could have possibly taken both my letter opener and paperweight from my office? Unfortunately, it could be anybody from the firm or even a delivery person.

Obviously, somebody wants to set me up.

I worry about Alexei and the internal war going on at Hologrid Hub. He's already taken two bullets and a knife wound. Of course, he stabbed himself, but that doesn't mean it hurts any less. I also wish he hadn't dropped the bombshell to everybody that we're married like he had earlier today. I was confronted by seven hurt and quizzical elderly men who only brightened after I promised that we'll have a big, lavish ceremony and that they'll all be included in the formalities.

I always figured that when I marry, I'll have Alana and Ella as my bridesmaids, but now I have two bridesmaids and seven attendants? I'm not even sure what to call them. I don't think Alexei would consider them groomsmen, but I figure if they're all wearing tuxes, who cares? I know I'm getting ahead of myself planning this ceremony, but I did take vows. Yeah, that might be a comfort and a cop-out, but I want to see where this thing will go with Alexei. I've never felt like this.

My phone dings and I glance at it before answering. "Hi, Ella, what's up?" I'm glad she's checking in with me.

"Are you at your computer?" she asks, her voice low.

"I can be." I reach for my laptop on the bedside table and boot it up on my legs.

She coughs. "I just sent you an email. Open it."

Sometimes she is so dramatic. "All right." I click on my email icon, see the email, and press PLAY on a video.

An expansive kitchen with marble countertops and stainless steel appliances comes into view. I've seen this room in crime scene photographs. It's the Fairfax's kitchen from seven years ago. The camera appears to have been mounted in the corner of the ceiling. Then a man walks over to the microwave to take out a mug. He's somewhat familiar. "It's David Fairfax," I say. "You managed to decrypt the entire disc."

"I did. It's quite a virus that was introduced."

As I watch, a younger Alexei walks into the scene dressed only in boxers. David turns, yells, and throws the contents of the mug on Alexei, splashing his torso. There are fewer scars and tattoos on him, but he still looks dangerous.

Alexei almost casually opens a drawer, takes out a knife, and stabs David in the neck before ripping out his throat.

David grabs his neck, his eyes widening as blood spurts

out between his fingers. Then he falls to the ground. Alexei looks at him for several moments, blood covering his torso and his face, then he reaches down and puts the knife into a plastic bag before walking out of the kitchen.

My entire body chills until I shudder. What the hell? I would've bet my soul that Alexei was innocent. Had I just been lying to myself? "Alexei did murder David Fairfax." The blood rushes through my head so quickly, I can hear the charge in my ears.

"I'm sorry," Ella says.

Wait a second. "Alexei took your laptop and the disc." Not that it should matter right now.

"I sent myself a copy the second I uploaded the disc the first time. Obviously." She clears her throat. "I know you probably have guards there, but I can get you free somehow. We can head out of the country. Even use fake passports if you want."

I'm numb. Lost. I shared my body, and more importantly my heart, with Alexei. I trusted him. Yet again, I'm seeing casual violence. So easy for him. "I married him."

"I don't care."

Yet I do. Or I did. We most certainly consummated the marriage. Several times. He walks into the room, looking dangerous and invincible. I try to stop my trembling. "I, ah, I have to go."

"Do you need help?" she whispers.

"No. I'll call you tomorrow. Please don't do anything until we talk." I need to think.

She clicks off without answering.

Alexei unbuttons his sleeves and then his shirt, tossing the expensive material carelessly over my blue chair. His gaze is hot and his expression masked. "Who was that?"

"Ella," I say breathlessly. "She's leaving town for a while."

He sighs, his hands going to his belt. "No, she isn't. I have two men on her right now. What's wrong?"

I gulp and force a smile. "Nothing. Honest."

He pauses and cocks his head. His belt makes a swooshing sound as he pulls it free of his pants. "You're a terrible liar. I wouldn't try again."

My mouth goes dry.

"What's wrong?" He unzips his slacks, removes them, and places them over the back of the chair. In boxers, most men look vulnerable. Not Alexei. He looks stronger than ever. Deadly, even. "I suggest you start talking."

I can't. If he can discern when I'm lying, then I don't want to say anything. Telling the truth is impossible. So I remain silent.

He sits and pulls me over, planting me on his lap facing him. I realize in that second that the bandage is absent from his arm. There's no wound.

I look closer. "You already healed?"

"Yes. I'm still receiving extra help from charging the amethyst."

Fascinating. I'm again reminded that Alana has never mentioned that she can heal herself when she charges the crystals at Aquarius Social. Maybe she can't. Perhaps it's a gift only Alexei's lineage holds. "I see."

His thumb presses against my chin, and he lifts my face. "I'm not going to ask again."

I drop my gaze to his mouth. His hold tightens, and I look up in surprise.

His gaze is relentless. "If I spank you tonight, you're not getting an orgasm afterward. Nor will you enjoy one second of it."

My butt tightens in denial. I consider my options. I know he doesn't bluff, but I'm also not sure of Ella's safety if I tell the truth. As I weigh the options, he reaches for the phone he placed on the bedside table, presses a button, and draws it to his ear.

What is he doing?

"It's Alexei. Take Ella Rendale to the safe house. Yes. Right now." He clicks off.

Panic engulfs me. "Don't hurt her. Please don't hurt her."

He deliberately places the phone back on the table. "Why would I hurt Ella?"

God. He knows. "You killed David Fairfax," I blurt out.

"That little shit," he mutters. "She kept a copy of the disc?"

I nod. "Ella can't resist a puzzle. She decoded it, and if anything happens to her, the video goes straight to the police."

His eyes go flat. Hard. "Lying is a mistake. I suggest you learn to tame that part of your personality before I do."

Tears spring into my eyes. "If you hurt my friend, I'll never forgive you."

He doesn't move. "Now that's the truth."

I can't believe this. "Why did you kill David?"

"He was a bad guy, and that's the only explanation you're going to get. I do a lot of things for my business that will never be discussed with you, and that's just how life is going to be. I suggest you learn to accept this reality. Either you trust and believe in me, or you don't." His eyes are hot coal, burning deep in the earth.

The guy never said he didn't kill David. He just said that he was set up—which he was. He lives in a world I can barely fathom, and now I live there as well. "I'm not a killer," I whisper, knowing this to my soul. "I can't survive in your world."

He brushes the hair away from my face, his large hand gentle now. "There's only one killer in this marriage, Kotik. You will survive because I'll make sure of it. Your protection is my utmost goal." He kisses me gently on the nose.

"Kotik?" I ask. He called me that once before.

"Little kitty. Always spitting fire at me." There's a fondness in his tone, even though his eyes haven't lost the intense expression.

I grind a fist into my right eye before a migraine can attack me. "Why in the world did you go back that day? You killed him and left. I saw you put the knife into the bag, and then you left." So David had been killed earlier than I thought.

Alexei sighs. "It was a normal practice for me to leave and then meet Blythe for lunch, and if I had refused, it would have been suspicious. I figured I'd get there after the maid discovered the body, but she was late that day."

I can't believe this. "Did you kill him because of jealousy?" My lungs trap my breath.

"No. He was a bad guy, who messed around with other women, girls really. Some very young ones. He also beat the crap out of Blythe, and I did want to protect her. But I didn't love her and had no plans for a future with her."

I wish those words didn't mean so much to me, but they do. I've seen him kill before, but the idea still gives me pause. He's so dangerous. To the world. Not to me.

His gaze darkens. "Do you trust me?"

It's a real question. A primal one. I look into his eyes, as I sit on his warm body. Do I? I glance around my room, searching for answers.

My grandmother's mirror catches the image of the two of us, and I swear, it appears as if a force, barely discernable, surrounds us. Dark and light, male and female . . . we look right. As if we belong to each other.

I stare back at him. "Yes." It's the truth. Even if all evidence points to a different answer, I feel him inside me. Deep. As if he's a part of me. "I do trust you." Sometimes instinct is all we have, and upon admitting the truth, my body relaxes. A pit releases and a coil unfolds inside me with a sense of peace.

"Good." He runs his hands down my arms, grasping my wrists. Then he flips us around, flattening his large body over mine, my wrists now held in one of his above my head. "I like this lingerie." He rolls to the side and tears the teddy off.

"Then you shouldn't have ripped it," I say breathlessly, captured in place. I want him but not his world. Right or wrong, I like that he wants to keep me out of most of it.

He lowers his head and nuzzles my breasts, taking an obscene amount of time lavishing each one. I'm gyrating with need before he even snaps the sides of my panties.

"You have to stop doing that," I gasp, my body tingling with need. "I'm running out."

"New rule. No panties for you." He releases my wrists and wanders his body down mine, reaching my clit. "This is my favorite place." He bites my thigh and then goes at me, not taking his time, finally. Forcing me up fast, he hums in pleasure as I cry out with a violent orgasm against his mouth.

Then he's up me again, his mouth on mine, taking what he wants.

I lean down and help him yank off his boxers, and then

he's against me, throbbing and ready. He pushes inside slowly, torturing us both. I dig my nails into his biceps, marveling at the cut muscle.

The panther on his neck gleams purple eyes at me.

Then he's inside me. All of him. Full and deep. I catch sight of us in that mirror again, and we look complete somehow.

Pausing, he leans down and kisses me, making me feel surrounded by him. "Thank you for trusting me."

Emotion swamps me and I nod, one tear leaking from my eye. He licks it away and then plants his hand over my breast—right over my heart. "Always, Rosalie," he whispers, before he starts to move. Fast and wild, he pounds into me, driving me up again. I climax with a desperate shudder, once and then again. Yet he keeps hammering.

I blink, trying to keep up, getting sore.

He reaches down and flicks my clit, arcing flames through me. I cry out, holding on, shutting my eyes. I'm reaching the pinnacle again. So close. Holding my breath, I fall over, biting his chest to keep from screaming. The waves undulate through me with brutal strength, expanding when he jerks hard against me, grunting my name.

We both quiet. My mind is spinning, and my body is done. Alexei tosses the covers over us both and cuddles me close. "I wasn't kidding about the panties," he murmurs.

THIRTY-EIGHT
Rosalie

My body is deliciously sore as I work at my computer on Tuesday morning, having called into work for a sick day. Alexei hadn't given me much of a choice, so I decided to work from home. I awakened early to hear him softly strumming his guitar, which he must've brought to my house at some point, and my heart truly warmed. The song was beautiful, and I'm thrilled he's turned back to music.

He's currently attending a meeting with mob members, no doubt dangerous people, and I can't help but worry about him. Garik insisted on accompanying him, so I have two new guys watching the front door of my place.

I'm not on board with being okay with murder. The fact that he did kill David Fairfax still throws me. I love Alexei, and I married him with my eyes mostly open. I do wonder if there's a way to run his mob with rules. Law abiding ones. I'll stick with him no matter what, but I think I can do some good with his organization.

Alexei had also promised to keep Ella safe. I'm sure

he'll confiscate her computer and try to erase the video, and I hope she works with him. He won't hurt her, but I don't have any guarantee that she won't hurt him. She can't physically, but with a computer, she's a menace. I also had to tell him of her ability to infect gemstones with a virus that can transfer to a person trying to charge them.

While I love her, I love him, too. There has to be a way to get them to like and trust each other. I'm a planner, and all I need to do is come up with a good plan. I hope Ella sees that Alexei is protecting her from a contracted hit. And I hope Alexei sees that Ella reacts out of fear and sometimes loneliness.

My phone buzzes and I lift it to my ear. "Mooncrest."

"Hey, Rosalie. It's Detective Battlement."

My heart drops. "Hi, Detective."

His sigh holds weight. "I shouldn't be calling you, but we're issuing an arrest warrant for you, and I needed to give you a heads up."

"Why?" I ask.

"I like you. You remind me of my youngest sister, who's always falling for the wrong man. She gets into trouble like you do. Also, I hate putting innocents away, but you're culpable here. Please turn yourself in this morning so we don't have to hunt you down and hand-cuff you." He ends the call.

I feel sick and instantly call my attorney.

"Joseph Cage," he answers, sounding distracted.

"Hi. Detective Battlement just called, and they're going to arrest me." A headache pounds at the base of my neck. "I need to turn myself in."

"Shit. I was afraid of that." Cage sounds much more focused. "I've had our tech folks watching the feeds from the reception area of our firm to find who might've stolen your letter opener and paperweight. So far, we've had no luck."

"Thank you," I say. "I've been racking my brain and haven't thought of anything that helps. If we have a recording of any delivery people coming into the front reception area, at least we'll have an idea where to start."

"I agree."

My head is spinning. "Do you think Battlement really has enough to arrest me?"

"He thinks he does," Cage says. "He's got motive, opportunity, and your prints. It's enough to bring you in and arrest you, which will give him grounds for a search warrant for your house."

Does the detective really think I beat a woman to death? "I would've let him search my house."

"And the firm," Cage finishes.

I rub my temple. "Oh." It's rare to obtain a search warrant for a law firm because of privilege. "I'm sure they'll limit the warrant to just my office."

"I know. I'm already having your paralegal take out all sensitive files."

I wince. "Joseph, you're not supposed to do that."

"A warrant hasn't been issued yet."

Very good point. There's a reason he's the managing partner of the firm. "I guess I'll head in to the police station now." My voice trembles.

"Hey. It's going to be okay," Cage says softly. "We're the best law firm in the state, and you're innocent. Keep that in mind."

I swallow over a lump in my throat and notice that my hands are shaking. "I will."

"You don't sound good. I'll pick you up so I'm with you the entire time."

Hope filters through me. I really don't want to be alone, and I doubt I can get ahold of Alexei right now. "Are you sure? I could just meet you there."

"It doesn't sound like you should drive." The ding of an elevator button comes through the line. "I like that the detective called you. I don't know if that means that he just thinks you're in over your head or if perhaps he believes you to be innocent. Either way, he's working with us." Cage sounds both thoughtful and relieved.

Okay. This will be all right. I repeat the mantra in my head. "Thank you, Joseph."

"Of course. I'm in the car and will be there in fifteen minutes. I promise we'll get you bailed out as soon as possible. The firm will pay for any bail you need."

Relief flows through me. "Thank you."

"Of course. I know you didn't do this." He clicks off.

Standing, I take off my suit and pull on a pair of jeans, socks, sneakers, and a lightweight sweater. If I'm going to jail, I'm going to be comfortable. I then dash off a note to my boarders with instructions for the next couple of days, just in case. Finally, I hear a car pull up outside. I open my door and jog down the stairs of my outside entrance while texting Alexei with an update of what's happening. I know he's busy, but I'm sure he'll see the texts when he can.

Cage's town car waits at my curb. The two men from Alexei's organization move toward me from the front porch, and I wave a hand. "It's okay. I have to surrender myself at the police station, and then I'll be back home."

The back door of the car opens, and Joseph Cage leans

out. "Is everything all right?" He looks at the two guys. They're both built like trucks and are obviously armed.

"My bodyguards," I say.

The first one shakes his head. "You're not supposed to leave."

He's a youngish guy named Olaf, and a couple of my boarders have been sneaking him pancakes. His partner is a couple years older and looks like he could punch through a wall with his head.

"I don't have a choice. Either I go in or the police come and get me," I say.

They look at each other, obviously not wanting to mess with the police.

Olaf rests his hand on his gun. "Most of our, um, organization is in the middle of a, well, negotiation right now."

What? I read between the lines. Alexei and his few followers are meeting and hopefully not shooting with the rest of the mob? Great. "I'm going in. I'll deal with Alexei later."

"We'll follow you," Olaf says.

"Fine by me." I hurry to the car and slip into the back seat along with Joseph. I shut the door. "I can't believe I'm being arrested."

Cage is pale in the dim light of the vehicle. "It's all right. We'll use the back door, and hopefully nobody will see you. The firm doesn't want the news media to pick up on this."

"I agree," I say. "I'm really sorry about this."

He swallows loudly. "It's not your fault. Jaqueline assigned the case to you. I would've passed on the whole thing."

"You don't care about redeeming the firm's reputation?"

Cage looks down at his jeans. "Not even remotely. I did at first, but believe me, this has not been worth it."

"I know." I feel like I should apologize again, but really not much of this is my fault. I look through the back window to see the two Russian men following us in a lifted, light-beige truck. The truck's a surprise. I'm accustomed to these guys all driving around in black town cars. In fact, the truck is a nice change of pace. I always figured when it comes to the mob, they all drive black cars. It's good that they have some choice in their vehicles. I have no problem focusing my brain on whimsical thoughts or unimportant details while ignoring danger. It makes me feel more in control.

Just as that last thought runs through my mind, a large delivery truck barrels out of an alley behind us and then slams on its brakes.

"Hey," I say. "Wait a minute. It's blocking my guys." I don't know when they became my guys, but I go with it.

Joseph turns toward me. "I am really sorry about this."

Dread slides through my veins on the heels of a rush of adrenaline. "Sorry about what?"

The window partition between the front and back seat goes down and a man turns to us with a gun pointed at Cage.

I blink. "What's going on, Joseph?"

I don't recognize the man, and the weapon has one of those slider things on it. Wait a minute. It's a silencer.

Cage shakes his head. "I'm sorry. They didn't give me a choice."

"Who didn't give you a choice?" Alarm clashes through me. I leap toward the door and frantically pull on the handle. Nothing.

"It's locked," the guy in the front seat says. I can see the back of the head of a driver who's another man I don't recognize.

I gape at my friend. How is this possible? *I* called *him* with the news that I needed to go to the police station. I set this up—not him. "What did you do?"

"They didn't give me a choice and were waiting at the curb for me at the firm."

The man from the front fires with a small pop. I jolt and push myself across the seat. Blood spurts from Cage's forehead, and his eyes widen before he slumps backward.

I can't move. Every cell in my body is frozen. I slowly turn from staring at the clear hole in Joseph's head to look at the man in the front seat.

He smiles. "We no longer need him."

I gag several times and then swallow to keep from throwing up. "Who are you?"

"Nobody that matters."

I look at my dead friend. "I beg to differ."

The shooter smiles. "Throw me your purse."

I grab my purse and hold it on my lap. "No. You're not going to get it."

He fires quickly into the seat next to me, and puffs of fabric billow up through the leather. I scream and try to get away.

"The next one goes in your leg. Just your shin because we need you alive, but it's going to hurt."

Fury takes me and I throw my purse at him.

"Thank you," he says politely, turning and lowering his window. He throws my entire purse out onto the street and then rolls the window back up. "We wouldn't want anybody to trace you, would we?" The window partition between us rises.

I look at Joseph's limp body, and bile rises from my stomach again. I can't believe he's dead. "How did you know I'd call him?"

The brute up front shrugs. "My employer has bugged the phones of whoever we could in your circle. Didn't get everybody, but your lawyer was easy."

Poor Joseph. All he did was get into the wrong town car. Why did I call him? This is my fault. I pull frantically on the door handle, and nothing happens, so I move over to Cage's side and do the same, careful not to touch him. I'm definitely locked in. I pat his pockets down, searching for anything to use as a weapon. He doesn't have a phone or knife on him.

There isn't anything that will help me in this vehicle, so I roll over onto my back, putting my head on poor Joseph's thigh, and kick the window as hard as I can. The glass barely even moves. I do it several more times.

Nothing.

We soon arrive at a more residential area and keep driving until the car stops at a massive gilded gate. Armed men guard both sides of it. The gate opens, and we drive up a long driveway with trees on either side, to reach what can only be called a mansion. It appears even bigger than Alana's family home.

My door opens. The driver grabs my arm and pulls me out. I turn sideways and kick his knee.

He throws me back against the car. "Knock it off."

Pain lashes through my shoulder. I halt and stare at the three-story, white-brick monstrosity in front of me. Wide white columns stand every few feet, appearing to support the entire front of the building. The double door is black, gilded, and larger than any I've ever seen. It opens and Lillian Sokolov walks out, her shoulders straight and her hair back to being platinum blond.

"How nice of you to join me." She smiles, no longer looking older than her age.

THIRTY-NINE
Alexei

I'm just about finished with issuing the strategy for these forty men. They now have a job to do—going out on arranged meetings to bring more followers to our side.

Finally, the last one leaves, and Garik walks over to me at the bar. "I trust about half of them, but if you show strong leadership through the next year, I think you'll receive their full loyalty. It's a strong force."

I nod. "It'll help if they're treated well. I want you to double everyone's pay within the next month or so."

His eyebrows rise. "That'll get you loyalty for sure."

"I'm not sure if it'll get me loyalty, but I'll take what I can get right now." My phone buzzes, and I look down at a text from the two men guarding Rosalie. My heart stops.

"What's wrong?" Garik asks.

"They lost Rosalie."

Garik begins moving toward the door as fast as I do. "How could they have lost her? She said she was on her way with her lawyer to surrender herself at the police station."

She texted us earlier. "I don't know." I should've instantly headed her way.

Garik quickly sends a text and then pauses as his phone dings in response. "I have two sources in the police department. She's not there, and they're making plans to find and arrest her since she didn't turn herself in."

I pause. Then my phone rings and I lift it to my ear. "Sokolov."

"Hello, dear stepson, how are you?"

I briefly close my eyes and then pause again. "Lillian, what have you done?" I'm going to kill her this time. I really am.

"I have a friend of yours here with me."

"You actually have my wife," I say. "If you hurt her, you know what I'll do to you."

Silence reigns for a few moments. "Your wife? You actually wedded the lawyer? I would have bet against that."

"Is she hurt?" I ask.

There's a rustle. "No, she's perfectly fine. Here."

"Hi, Alexei," Rosalie says. "I'm sorry. It was stupid. They killed Joseph Cage."

I wince. They murdered her lawyer? I'm starting to imagine how they captured her. "In front of you?"

"Um, yeah," she says.

"Put Lillian back on." If they allowed her to see a murder, they don't plan for her to survive the day. "Lillian, I don't have enough words to describe what I'm going to do to you if you hurt her. Tell me you get me." My voice is low and gravelly. I can barely get the words out.

Lillian sighs. "I actually don't want to hurt her. She's smart and I like her, but this is going to go my way and my way only."

"What do you want?" I bark out.

I swear it sounds like she purrs. "The first thing I want is for you to go to Hologrid Hub and charge the servers."

This is unexpected. "Excuse me?"

"Hendrix is dead. I don't have the ability, and I haven't found anyone who comes close. We're losing subscribers by the second, so the first thing I need you to do is charge the crystals."

I'm stunned for a moment, which is very rare. Does she understand that it's a two-way exchange? She must not. "All right, and then what?" I walk outside toward my waiting bike with Garik on my heels.

She chuckles. "Then we'll negotiate. Obviously, we have a problem here."

"You're the one with the problem." I straddle the motorcycle.

"Not if I don't hurt your precious. I am willing to reach an agreement, but first the servers. Call me when you're done." She clicks off.

I look at Garik. "It's just you and me. We don't have anyone else I trust to go."

He looks at me, his gaze hard. "I'll go in now if you want."

I shake my head. "No. Lillian has too many men there." The second I attack, she might kill Rosalie before I can get to her.

A rock drops into my gut. I've never felt true fear before. Not like this. I told Rosalie that I'd try to find love, and apparently I have. If she dies, there's no reason for me to keep on breathing.

I twist the key, my bike roars to life, and I'm headed down the street before I completely lose my mind. There's a part of me—a small part not terrified for Rosalie and not pissed off at Lillian—that awakens in anticipation. I miss the amethyst and need the exchange of energy. Most people don't understand, and that's how we want it.

I duck my head as I open the throttle, zipping through the city around cars, over sidewalks, and through alleys toward the main center of Hologrid Hub—feeling the energy the closer I get.

Hologrid Hub uses holographic interchanges between users so they can actually engage in experiences at the same time, the same place. Someday soon, we'll create an interface where people can experience a telepathic bond. We're not there yet, but I'm determined that my company will get there first.

I ride into the lower garage of Hologrid Hub, past armed guards who don't shoot me, and park in my old spot. I sprint into the open elevator and hit the down button.

Anticipation fires lightning through my veins. I know exactly where to go, and I descend several miles down in the earth. The door smoothly opens into the power center of Hologrid Hub.

Two armed guards are waiting for me, and I ignore them as I move past them toward a black metal door. I put my hand to a keypad next to it, and it clicks open. I can't believe my palm print still works. They really did think I was going to die in prison. One of the guards tries to walk inside after me.

"Absolutely not." I slam the door in his face.

I breathe in. The place smells familiar. It's sterile and clean, and yet there's a hint of lilacs on the breeze. Computer hubs line all four walls, while a rough and rugged amethyst stands on a pedestal in the middle. The gem is a darker purple than it should be, and I can feel its exhaustion.

Why most humans have not figured out the power they could have with the exchange of energy with a crystal or a gemstone is beyond me, but it's not like we shared the news.

I move closer to the beauty and feel power arcing between us. Something inside me settles, relaxes, and opens. The amethyst sparkles and real electricity arcs in the air. I smile and reach for it with both hands.

The second I connect, a jolt rips through me, burning my feet and my ears. I laugh and then close my eyes to force every ounce of energy I have into the large, sparkling, wild gemstone.

I'm not a religious man, but if I were, I might hear angels singing. Instead, all I hear is the hum of the servers and the beeping of machines, and then I'm lost. The energy arcs from me to the gemstone and back, filling me until I lose myself in the exchange of power.

I don't know how long I'm there. Maybe half an hour, maybe an hour. Finally, my hands drop. I take a step back.

The amethyst is now a bright purple with fire dancing along its edges. Each sharp edge and valley holds its own secrets. I know if I look at my shoulder, I'll see all the wounds have healed. Yet another secret of these crystals and our power with them.

I step away again. This charge should last at least a couple of weeks. During my imprisonment, I wondered, maybe even feared, that I lost this ability. If anything, my connection is stronger than ever.

The two armed men are waiting for me as I move back into the outer room.

"Now you can take me to my wife." Hopefully Garik is in place. I could probably break both their necks with very little effort.

Lillian has absolutely no idea what she's just done.

FORTY
Rosalie

I'm holding a cup full of apple-scented herbal tea in a palatial mansion with a woman I'd like to shoot in the head. She is all class in a pretty pink dress as she drinks delicately. I'd go for her, but the two armed men on either side of the door to this rose-decorated sitting area give me pause. They can shoot me easily.

"How is your tea?" Lillian asks politely.

"I want to punch you in the face," I respond.

She laughs. "I can see what Alexei adores in you."

"Well, gosh, I was really hoping for your approval." Even so, I do eye the tea.

"Drink it," she orders.

Instinct stills my movements. The woman wants me to drink this way too badly, and I love apple anything. She would've discovered that fact by conducting a simple background check into my life. "What is your plan for me?"

"My plan? We'll wait until Alexei gets here."

Obviously. "What do you want at that point?"

She lifts a delicate shoulder. "I'm going to have to shoot

him." She giggles, sounding like she's back in junior high. "I don't normally like to do the dirty work myself."

"That's good to know," I say, adrenaline flooding my veins so quickly, my ears tingle. "I take it you're planning on killing me, too?"

"Of course," she says congenially. "I don't have much of a choice. I figure we'll have to set up something nice. I'm thinking that Alexei discovers that you killed Blythe Fairfax, and then he kills you because he actually loved her. Then I have to defend myself and shoot him. Something like that." She waves a hand in the air as if the facts are inconsequential. "We'll figure something good out. Don't you worry."

I just stare at her. "You're truly evil." I say it almost thoughtfully, but honestly, this is just too much.

She chuckles, looking beautiful in a cream-colored suit, her hair a pretty blond and her makeup perfect. She did a good job of fooling me with the gray hair and frumpy outfits. Now she appears to be in excellent shape. "That's not very nice. Now drink your tea. I made it with dried apples."

"Nope," I say, noting she hasn't tried hers, either.

"Chicken." She glances at the tray on the table in front of her. The set is beautiful, with amethysts encrusted in both the cups and the pot. I look toward the two guys at the door. Their expressions remain blank, so they obviously don't mind her planning a couple of murders.

I think through my last week and it hits me. "You were in my office."

"I truly was," she says. "I think we had a nice visit, don't you?"

I study her and try really hard not to lose my mind. I remember her dropping her purse on the desk. "You took my paperweight." I blink twice. "Did you kill Blythe Fairfax?"

"Oh no. That was a bloody mess," she says almost chidingly. "I did take the paperweight, of course, but Marty over there is the one who, you know."

"Bludgeoned Blythe to death," I say slowly, looking at Marty. He's the guy on the left who appears to be in his late twenties with a full beard and several scars across his forehead, and he doesn't blink. Not even once.

"Yes." Lillian pushes a plate of cookies toward me. "Would you like a cookie? They're a nice apple oatmeal mix I created just for you."

"You first."

She sits back. "Well, I guess you're not as dumb as I thought."

I glance at the innocuous cookies. She's trying to poison me? I'm trying really hard not to throw up on her at the moment. I scrub a hand over my eyes. "Why did you kill Blythe?"

"My initial thought was to set up Alexei," she says. "But this turned out better because now he has a reason to kill you. Don't you see? I love it when the universe gives me a helping hand. Manifestation really works."

Reality finally hits me. Wait a minute. My hand starts to shake, so I place the cup on the saucer, where it clatters noisily.

She frowns, but no wrinkles show in her forehead. It must be quite a bit of Botox.

I can't think. My mind spins. "When you stole the paperweight, you also took my letter opener."

"I did," she says cheerfully, crossing her legs.

I gag. This is unthinkable to me.

She frowns again. "If you throw up, I'm going to shoot you. Or rather," she looks over her shoulder at Marty.

"Have you shot. Maybe just in the shoulder or a kneecap or something. I should keep you alive until Alexei gets here." Madness swirls in her eyes and she smiles again. "You should really try the cookies. They're phenomenal."

I gulp and sit back in my chair. "You took my letter opener."

"I already said I did." Now she sounds exasperated, but I am not sure I have the words.

"Did you kill Hendrix?"

Her jaw tightens. "He gave me no choice."

Oh my God. I turn and start to heave.

"Stop that." She throws a cookie at me.

I rapidly breathe in several times, barely preventing myself from throwing up. She fooled me so perfectly with her sad eyes and gray hair. In fact, she looks thinner in this outfit, even. "You killed your own son?"

She pales, but only slightly. "Hendrix was caught on that video throwing the knife into the pond—trying to frame Alexei. He was arrested for planting evidence and impersonating a police officer." She sips on her tea again as if we're just talking about the weather. "He gave me no choice. Our family had enough bad press when Alexei went to prison. Of course, I did bribe the judge and both attorneys to make that happen. I mean enough is enough. You would've done the same thing."

"I most certainly would not have. Oh my God, you are freaking evil." I try to concentrate. "You knew that Alexei took out David Fairfax."

"I did know that, but he hid the murder weapon so well. It's never been found."

Fear prickles along my skin. "So the knife that Hendrix threw into the Fairfax pond seven years ago . . ."

She tugs on a bright amethyst earring. "You're rather slow right now. Hendrix dressed as a police officer, entered the house, and took a knife from the drawer. Honestly, it wasn't even the same type of knife. He dipped it in the blood on the floor and then tossed it in the pond outside."

Wait a minute. "It wasn't the same type of knife?"

"No. Nor were Alexei's prints really on it."

I can't breathe. "So you bribed the coroner and somebody at the lab?"

"Of course."

My chest actually hurts. "Hendrix worked for you at risk to himself. How could you murder him?"

"Hendrix wasn't that good at charging the crystals," she says, waving a hand. "So I didn't see any other solution."

I just look at her for several long moments. If she wasn't talking, I would think she was normal and not an evil archaic bitch. "So you took my letter opener to frame me?"

"Or Alexei," she says. "That was my original plan, but like I said, this has turned out so much better."

How can she be calm about this? Her logic is so flawed. I look at the platter of cookies and wonder if I can get to it in time to bash her in the head before Marty shoots me. "But with Hendrix dead, nobody can charge the crystals." Does she plan to abandon Hologrid Hub?

"Oh, honey, if Alexei has followed my orders today, the amethysts should be charged for a couple weeks. By then, I'll be able to charge them."

I open my mouth but nothing comes out, so I have to try again. "You don't have a connection to the crystals, remember? You can't charge the gems." Has she completely lost her mind?

"No, but I will have a good connection soon." She licks her lips like a cat who's discovered a cream-filled bowl.

I tilt my head. "Wait a minute." I remember the prenatal vitamins that she dropped onto my desk and a horrible thought runs through my mind. "You're saying that . . ."

"Yes," she says. "Alexei's father and I used in vitro for both Hendrix and Cal. I have several more viable embryos on ice with his very strong and talented DNA, and it's time to use them. I'm not getting any younger, you know."

I flatten my hands on the table. How am I going to steal the guns from both of these men without getting shot? I have to get out of here before Alexei does something stupid and tries to rescue me.

"So you're pregnant?" I ask softly. "With Alexei's half siblings?" How does this make any sense?

"Not yet," she says. "I go in tomorrow for implantation. My doctor wanted me to take the prenatal vitamins for two months first, but I'm going to tell you a secret that most people don't know. When I was pregnant both times with Sokolov babies, I was able to charge the crystals." She giggles. "You have no idea the power that goes through your entire body when you're able to do that." Her eyes light up as if she's telling me about the best experience ever.

I feel sick.

She sighs. "I'm going to have the doctor implant three this time, because we only did one each time before. So if I have three, surely one of them will be able to harness the crystal power someday. I'll just do my best while I'm pregnant."

I frown, trying to follow any sense of logic in her. "Okay. So say you give birth to triplets, but then you're not able to charge the crystals any longer while they're just babies. Have you completely lost your mind?"

She slaps at my hand playfully. "The ability actually lasts for a good five years after the pregnancy."

"It does?" I'm intrigued even though I don't want to be.

"Yes," she says. "Last time, anyway, and I was only pregnant with one child. Who knows? It might last fifteen years this time. If not, triplet five year olds can do the job." She taps her finger against her pink lips. "Or I can get pregnant again, I guess."

Everything inside me freezes. I don't think I've ever been in the presence of evil before right now.

There's a ruckus and then the doors open. Two men shove in Alexei and then they retreat before shutting the door. He looks at both of the guards and then at me.

"Are you okay?" he asks, his voice gravelly.

"Physically I am," I say. "Emotionally I'm going to be fucked up for quite a while." I might as well give him the truth.

He looks at Lillian and then stands in the middle of the room, his legs braced. Power fills the oxygen around us, along with a terrifying tension. His eyes are a darker black than I've ever seen them, but there's something different about him. His shoulders even seem wider, and wild muscles ripple beneath his clothing.

"I see you charged our servers," Lillian says, smiling.

"I did," Alexei says.

She claps her hands. "I knew you wouldn't be able to resist. I have tons of guards around this entire property, and there's nowhere for you to go now that you're here. You have no backup, and we both know it. Being a romantic myself, I thought you might want to say goodbye to each other." She pulls a nine millimeter out of a pocket on the side of her skirt.

I push away from the table and stand, throwing my napkin on my teacup. "You have a gun?" I glance at the tea and cookies. "I thought you were trying to poison me."

"I was. There seemed something poetic about that," she muses. "I figured everybody would think Alexei tried to poison you if anything was found in your system." She glances at the gun. "I've never watched anybody die from poison. Oh well. Maybe next time."

Unbelievable. "She killed Hendrix and had Blythe murdered," I blurt out in a rush.

Alexei looks like he turns to stone as he focuses fully on Lillian. "You murdered your firstborn?"

Her browse draw down slightly. "I've always done what needs to be done to save this company."

"She's going to have in vitro with three babies tomorrow," I say, wanting to get all the truth out so he understands everything. "So she can charge the servers."

For the briefest of moments, he looks vulnerable. "You killed your own son?" he repeats, and then his face hardens again.

"I'm done talking about this," she says. "Do you want to die together or separately?"

I hold up a hand. "Tell me you brought your men. I mean, the mob."

He shakes his head. "No. There's nobody coming."

Just then, twin pings echo through the window next to me, and both guards go down. Lillian shrieks and lifts her gun. Another ping echoes, and blood spurts from her head.

Glass shatters and something hits me in the temple. Darkness swirls around me, and I feel myself falling. Pain lances along my cheekbone as I hit the ground. My vision is gone. Terror slithers through me.

A ruckus echoes around me before a series of explosions rend the atmosphere. I smell fire, but I can't move or open my eyes. More gunfire cracks through the air, followed by the sound of pounding footsteps.

"Rosalie. Rosalie wake up."

I know that voice. It's dark and it's mine. Then I feel a kiss, his mouth on mine, and my eyelids flutter open. I reach up and slide a hand through his thick hair. His eyes open on mine, and he releases my mouth, leaning back.

"Rosie?"

I blink. The side of my face feels wet. I try to touch my face, and he holds my hand back.

"You've been cut, glass right in the temple."

"Here you go." Felix runs inside with a washcloth. "This is cold. We have to bring down the swelling right now."

Alexei gently places the washcloth against my head and helps me sit up.

"Doc?" I ask, looking up. "What are you doing here?"

Percy runs inside with a semi-automatic weapon over his stooped shoulder, followed by Wally and Kenny. Soon all seven of my boarders are in the room along with Garik, Alexei, and a few men who look Russian.

"What in the heck just happened?" I ask weakly.

Alexei shakes his head. "You wouldn't believe me if I told you."

Percy moves closer. "You okay? Wally and I shot through the window. We didn't mean to hurt you."

"You took out both guards?" I'm still dazed.

"Yeah. The seven of us descended on the place right about the same time as Garik and his force," Percy says. "We almost shot each other, but it worked out."

The world is not making sense.

Alexie sighs. "I didn't have time to call in the mob, but these guys were already ahead of me."

I look at Alexei, then I glance back at my seven elderly men. "What do you mean you descended on the place? How did you find me?"

Percy has the grace to blush. "We keep a tracker in your shoes."

"Excuse me?" I say, and then wince as pain lances through my head.

Wally nods. "Yeah, we always have. We've been worried about you, and boy it was a pain in the ass putting trackers in all those new kitten heels you bought." He gives Alexei a look.

Alexei looks right back.

This is a complication of which I had not expected. I grab Alexei's hand. "I love you. Thought you should know."

He leans down and kisses me again. "I love you as well, Peaflower."

EPILOGUE
Rosalie

Three weeks later

I stand outside of my pretty pink house as the sound of whirring saws and pounding hammers fills the afternoon. Alexei agreed that we'd live here and then purchased the homes on every side of us to tear down so we can build a compound of sorts. I look over to the guest house, where several of my boarders are hard at work.

They accepted the offer of the free home, but they want to create it themselves. I'm a little worried what that means, because I saw plans for tunnels that would lead from the property in case of emergencies, as well as a place for a good ammunition depot. I'm not sure they know that they're retired, but considering I'm surrounded by a good portion of the Russian mob most of the time, I choose not to worry about it.

Ella walks up from supervising the guest house, her laptop under one arm. "Hey." She and Alexei declared a peace between them, and Ella promised she destroyed the video of him murdering David Fairfax.

"Hi," I say. She's agreed to stay for a week or so. She's

always been a free spirit, and she likes to train all over the world in hacking and computers. I know she'll get that wanderlust soon. But for now, at least she's safe.

She kicks at a pebble. "I did a bit more research into David Fairfax."

I look around to make sure Alexei isn't near. "You promised to stay out of that situation."

She shrugs. "Couldn't help it. Turns out Blythe Fairfax spent a good amount of time in different emergency rooms around the state."

I blink. "Alexei said David abused her."

Ella nods and watches the men at the guesthouse. "It certainly looks like it. Plus, he had a series of girlfriends through the years, even during his marriage, who all showed signs of pretty terrible abuse. Several underage." She pats my arm. "Though I don't think killing him was right."

Neither do I. Maybe. I'm not sure. "Why didn't anybody ever press charges?"

"I think they were too scared. He threatened to kill them, from what I read between the lines."

Perhaps he had deserved it. But the good news is that I don't have to worry about it because it's in the past.

My future lopes toward me from the main house, his gaze catching on Ella and then the elderly men arguing over by the guest house. He shakes his head as if he's not quite sure how he ended up in this situation.

Ella snorts. "I'll go referee at the guest house." Giving Alexei a look, she flounces off.

He reaches me, takes my face in his hands, and kisses me deeply. I close my eyes and kiss him back. The love I have for him is hot and everlasting, and I've decided just to revel in it and not worry. He's everything.

Releasing me, he sighs.

I look toward Ella, who is rapidly retreating, then back at him. "Thank you for trusting my friend and for letting all seven of my boarders live next to us."

"You owe me. A lot."

I chuckle. "Yeah, and speaking of owing you, I think there's a lot to learn from the guys."

One of his dark eyebrows rises. "You don't say."

I nod. "They're all reformed and act like a family. We can do the same thing with the mob. You know. Build loyalty with incentives instead of fear. Like have scholarships, subsidized childcare, paternity leave . . . you know."

He looks toward the group. "I'll think about it."

So much warmth fills me that my cheeks burn. "The song I heard you playing early this morning. It was beautiful." He belongs with a guitar in his hands.

"Thanks. It's called Rosalie."

Something flutters in my abdomen. "I love you. Thought I should say the words in a nice time instead of just when bullets have been flying."

His lips twitch. "I love you, too. Have for years." He ducks his head and tosses me over his shoulder, taking long strides toward the house. "You definitely owe me. Let's go find out if you've learned to be obedient. You had better not be wearing panties."

My whole body shivers.

Because I am.

Playlist

"Snow White" — Dennis Llyod
"Sounds of Someday" — Radio Company
"Mockingbird" — Enisa
"Castle" — Halsey
"Pretense" — Talia Shay
"You're Not God" — Ryan Jesse
"Take It All Back" — Tauren Wells & Davies
"Cant Help Falling in Love" —Tommee Profitt
"Ready for War" —Tommee Profitt & Liv Ash
"Angeles" — Radio Company
"World War 3" — Ruth B.
"A Thousand Years" — Christina Perri
"Take It All Back" — Tauren Wells, We The Kingdom, & Davies
"A Storm is Coming" — Tommee Profitt & Liv Ash
"Austin" — Dasha

ACKNOWLEDGMENTS

Even the darkest fairytales are woven by more than one hand, and I'd like to thank everybody involved with getting this second Grimm Bargains book to readers. I sincerely apologize to anyone I've forgotten.

To my own very own Huntsman—Tony, who fearlessly protects my heart and pushes me to keep chasing my dreams. Your strength and unwavering support mean the world to me.

To Gabe, my brilliant civil engineer, whose logic and problem-solving skills I can always rely on, and to Karlina, my artistic visionary, who inspires me with her passion and creativity. I'm endlessly proud of both of you.

A heartfelt thank you to Caitlin Blasdell, my incredible agent, for believing in this dark and daring tale. And thanks also to everyone at Liza Dawson Associates.

Thank you to Elizabeth May, my editor at Kensington Publishing, to whom I've dedicated this book. Thank you also to everyone who works so hard at Kensington: Alexandra Nicolajsen, Steven Zacharias, Adam Zacharias, Alicia Condon, Lynn Cully, Jackie Dinas, Jane Nutter,

Lauren Jernigan, Kristin McLaughlin, Vida Engstrand, Barbara Bennett, Sarah Selim, Kait Johnson, Andi Peris, Justine Willis, Renee Rocco, Carly Sommerstein, Cassandra Farrin, and Kelsy Thompson. We've published more than forty stories together, and I really do feel like I'm part of the family.

A special thank you to the Rebels, my fierce and loyal street team. You're the heart of the story's world. A huge thank you to my social media wizards, Anissa Beatty and Kristin Ashenfelter, and to Rebels Kimberly Frost, Madison Fairbanks, Joan Lai, Heather Frost, Gabi Brockelsby, Leanna Feazel, Suzi Zuber, Karen Clementi, Asmaa Qayyum, and Jessica Mobbs.

Thanks to my incredible publicity teams, Book Brush and Writerspace, for providing the creative tools that bring my vision to life and for helping me connect with readers in meaningful and lasting ways.

Thank you to my family, friends, and loved ones who have stood by me through every late-night plot, test, and moment of doubt: Gail and Jim English, Kathy and Herbie Zanetti, Debbie and Travis Smith, Stephanie and Don West, Jessica and Jonah Namson, and Chelli and Jason Younker. Your encouragement, love, and belief in me keep me going even in the darkest of times. I'm endlessly grateful for each and every one of you.

Finally, thank you to all of the readers who've jumped into this darker world of fairytale retellings with me. I know Grimm Bargains is a bit darker than my other eighty books, and I appreciate you taking the leap. I hope you're enjoying these new adventures!